The Peacekeeper

by

Cheryl Starr Munger

The McGregors Series

The Peacekeeper

Cover Art by *Debbie Taylor*

The Wild Rose Press, Inc.
PO Box 708
Adams Basin, NY 14410-0708
Visit us at www.thewildrosepress.com

Publishing History
First Black Rose Edition, 2018
Print ISBN 978-1-5092-2146-2
Digital ISBN 978-1-5092-2147-9

The McGregors Series
Published in the United States of America

"Will you heal Elspeth, please."

He knew he begged, but felt he had no choice.

"No, Ian, I will not, but behold the beauty and fight of life." The God of light swept his arm in front of him and disappeared. He was once again in his body. The stake was gone and he jumped up to fight Athdar and Drakkor. They too were gone.

He ran to Elspeth and grabbed her hand. Everyone was released from their frozen states and Eoghan was there.

His brothers were hugging and talking, but he could only see Elspeth. He pulled the knife from her chest. "Wake up dearling, please." She didn't move. He watched in slow motion as the blood seeped from her chest and drop by drop slid slowly down her side and off the table to hit the floor, each drop a splash he could swear resounded through his body. The whole slow-motion scene surreal. The ripples from each drop flowing through him, killing him as surely as someone slowly pushing a knife in his heart and twisting. He watched her life blood leaving.

Then in a sudden moment of clarity he pressed his hand to her wound to try and stop the bleeding. He fell to his knees and lay his head to her chest and listened to her heart beat slow.

In his anguish, he raised his head and gave a grief ridden howl that bellowed from deep in his soul, echoed loudly through the cave walls, shaking all around. All his brothers stopped and gathered around concern etching their worried faces.

Silence hung in the air as he buried his face in her neck and sobbed. She lay dying, still, silent, and pale.

Dedication

To my son and daughter
who I love with all my heart.
Thanks for being my best friends.
And to my grandchildren
who keep the one piece of my heart
that makes it beat.

Acknowledgements

"*A Fond Kiss, And Then We Sever*" was originally published in 1791 by Robert Burns and is now part of the Public Domain.

Prologue

Close to the top of a mountain near Mystic Kingdom, in the opening of a large dark cave, stood the God of Dark. His long raven hair damp and stuck to his face and neck from the humid heat of the day. The cave provided no shelter from the heat. It was damp and moldy, causing the air to hang thick and heavy. No matter to him, he lived and thrived in heat. He liked this place.

The bottom of his crimson and black robe hung over the opening's edge as he leaned out and looked down. Two men slowly climbed toward him, one carrying a small bundle, the other a large bag. The God of Dark impatiently watched as they ascended.

He sighed at their slowness and raised his hands. The men were immediately transported to the cave, landing in front of him. He eyed King Rulm and Drakkor sharply.

"You brought the infant," he rumbled.

"Yes," said Drakkor. "It wasn't as hard as I thought it would be. What about when he is returned? Will his mother sense he is no longer her son?

The God of Dark hated questions, but he answered non-the-less. "Her memory of what he was like is gone. I've replaced them with new ones. She will raise him as her own until which time he is returned to us."

"Why now, after all these years. Why are you

bringing this Seamus back, and why is he so important, who is he?" asked King Rulm.

The God of Dark turned toward the king, his eyes flashing flames. "Because," he bellowed. "Merlin has been doing good, so much so that it was time the scales were balanced. It's time his brother returned. And I will be the one to bring him back. With a spell from the *Grimoire to the Dark* he will once again be given life. The God of Light says he likes balance, as far as I'm concerned, this will be balance." He turned toward the alter, the glow coming off from him bathing the cave and everything in it with an eerie red glow.

Drakkor took the sleeping baby and placed it upon the alter, removing the blanket and leaving the child naked upon the cold stone. The child awoke and began to wail. "*Sileniseo Absoliteus*!" The God of Dark raised his hand. The baby fell quiet.

"Let's get on with it," he said. "You two will perform the spell, I will put Seamus' spirit in this body as the child's spirit leaves. I cannot create a spirit. Only the One Great God can do that, but nowhere is it said, that I cannot manipulate one that already exists." He laughed.

"Won't the God of Light know what we are doing, or the very least, the One Great God?" asked King Rulm.

He turned toward the king with impatience. "He will only see the death of a child nothing more. He won't know we've placed another soul in this body. This cave is warded; the child is warded, and here I can open a thin veil from hell to pull Seamus through. This is the only place where the God of Light and the One Great God will not know what we are doing." He laughed. "It's time for me! Do you understand? I've played by their rules long enough, today that stops!" He was out of patience and small sparks shot from the glow surrounding him. "Do you have the knife that Merlin made and used to kill his brother?"

Drakkor pulled it out from the bag he carried, removed it from the sheath, and lay it next to the baby on the alter.

"The *Grimoire to the Dark*?" he asked.

Drakkor smiled as he removed the book and placed it on the alter.

"Good let's begin," he rumbled. Drakkor placed a bowel of herbs mixed with Seamus' ground bone near the child while the God of Dark drew blood from the motionless baby.

Holding the babe over the bowel he let a few drops of blood fall from the infant and they began to chant. The child didn't cry, didn't whimper, eyes closed as if asleep from the spell that he'd put him under.

"*Reenta Oppresucto*," they chanted together. "*Suprenta Elemi, Obliicum Pestempra*," and with a final flare, they shouted, "*Extermiortis Noctius*!"

The sky outside became dark and lightning flashed and arced from cloud to cloud. Inside the cave the torches flared high and static electricity shot through the air. A ball of white light rose from the child and hovered for a second before shooting through the roof.

The God of Dark grew in size, his hair flying in all directions, flames for eyes, his light bright. *"Alterempra…Alteritus…Seretus…Vengerrgio Caneus!"* Beside him hovered a dark, murky cloud. As the white light left the baby the dark cloud entered and he healed the wounds to the child.

The static electricity subsided, the snapping and popping stopped, the sun once again shown outside, the flames from the torches receded, and the baby opened his eyes.

"It is done," he rumbled. "Return the child to its mother."

Chapter 1

30 years later

The sky was dark and gloomy. No clouds, just gray, with swirling vapor wisps of fog over the loch. Ian McGregor sat atop the trunk of a lonely fallen oak, staring at the churning waves as the wind whipped his locks of black hair from its queue and across his stubbled chiseled face. Winds howled and whistled through the nearby pine branches, his ears numb from the cold early spring. He sat still and silent without feeling any of it.

Merlin was on his way, and that meant the peace he had known since his father and brother's death, was at an end. For eight hundred years he had fought for peace. Fought for the ones who were wronged. Fought for the innocence of the humans of inner earth, and for those from his own outer earth. He was tired, but when Merlin called he could never refuse the wizard, who was also like a father to him. He wouldn't refuse him now.

He was half fae, half vampire, but that is not what made his family so special. No, each of them had special and unique gifts that those of singular species did not possess. He chuckled. His family had always been unique.

At one time vampires couldn't walk in the sun,

now they all could. Thanks to the spirit witch Circe it was now possible. When she approached the vampires offering her gift so long ago, a kinship was born. Her offer didn't come without payment. They were charged with protecting the witches that resided on inner earth in return for her working her magic.

Witches and vampires then became as thick as blood. It was a win, win situation for both sides. He shook his head at the complexity of her spell. How she mixed vampire blood with sunshine was beyond him. But then how could he question her abilities, when he, himself could tell a lie coming from a man's mouth and know the truth at the same time. He learned long ago not to question others intangible gifts.

Each of his brothers and sisters, had their own. Together they were formidable. Also, thanks to Circe, they now only drank blood to stay young and healthy. Needing to only consume it every few days. They ate food like humans and they could enjoy the intricate flavors and textures of a variety of meals.

Ian gathered himself from his musings and stood, a strong gust grabbing his long coat, whipping it back. He turned toward his home and headed up the hill to meet Merlin.

Ian walked steadily up from the loch toward the castle. He was late. He could feel cold dread slip icily through his bones. "What does the old man have on his mind now?" Whatever it was it would not only involve him but his brothers as well.

Another mission he was sure of it. He knew that the long period of peace was too good to be true. His family was an old family, he himself eight-hundred years. His parents twice as old. His mother fae and his father vampire, like his father before him, born that way, he and his siblings as well. His father and twin brother dead. Both killed during their last mission.

He picked up his pace, quickly climbed the stairs onto the portico, and walked through the heavy double doors, just in time to see Merlin sit down at the long table with a tankard. He was alone. His mother must not have seen him arrive or she would have been sitting with him, laughing and talking.

"Merlin, you ol' fool, now what brings you here?" he asked, slapping him on his back, as he passed him by, on his way to the side board.

"Well grab a seat, Ian, my boy. 'Tis good to see you."

"You too, Merlin," said Ian grabbing a tankard off the sideboard. He poured mead until it foamed over the top and sat down across from Merlin waiting for him to answer.

Merlin sighed, pulled his hand through his long white hair then down over his beard, looked at Ian across the table in the McGregor castle.

"Ian, Drakkor is poisoning the fae and vampire alike. His army is growing. He's creating masses of beings there's no precedent for. Flagitious creatures. You being half-fae and half-vampire, the oldest of all your brothers, with all the powers of both species, are why you are my first. But you are also my friend, my confidant, and my surrogate son."

"Ahhh, Drakkor the dark demon, my least favorite arse. Please Merlin, you ken what you are aboot. Doona bait me, get tae the point." Ian drained his cup of mead and slammed his cup to the twenty-foot, highly polished table, silver eyes blazing.

"If your mother saw that she'd have your hide." Merlin laughed and became straight-faced and serious again. "Ian McGregor there will come a time when you will die in pure heart, you will become ethereal, you will understand all that has been taught you, you will gain your freedom from your past. You will understand."

"Ole man enough with your riddles. You've promised this gift of ethereal, and I still doona understand it. Either shut your geggie, or tell me what this is really aboot?"

Merlin frowned. "If any other man spoke to me in such a way he'd be a toad by now. Fine. I have amassed a group, combining a triad of species who will be working together. This army which I have named *The Myriad Army* consists of the Ocrul, the Crimson Keepers, and…you are not going to like this…the Crixior. I want you to lead them. I *need* you to lead them in this unknown deadly battle against these new creatures.

"My baws tae you! For one I work alone or with my brothers, two you can forget it! I'd maybe work with the Ocrul, or the Crimson Keepers, but you have me damned if I'll step foot in the same room with even one Crixior. Let alone a bunch of them damn demons. Or yet tae lead the damn bastards. They killed my father and my brother; you canna ask me tae do such a thing! I doona care what anybody says. Not even for the so called "good Crixior." A demon, is a demon, and as far as I'm concerned, they're all bad!"

"Not all. These few demons have proven themselves worthy beyond measure in our fight against evil. There are some, by some fluke, that have light in them. They have been pardoned by The Plelin Courts, the Ayriris light angels. In fact, by Junius himself, and allowed to fight against the faction of demons called the…"

"Yes, I ken," interrupted Ian, "the Asurads. The bad arse demons. Still I doona want tae work with any Crixior. Good or bad. Besides you retired me. Now you want me tae lead fae, vampires, and demons all rolled into one? That's a war in itself. The Ocrul fae, doona enjoy working with Crimson Keeper vampires. Crimson Keeper vampires, doona enjoy working with Ocrul fae, and you want tae throw demons in the mix? You're plum crazy Merlin, they'll all be dead by nightfall, the first day, and you want me tae lead them? You're oot of your head!"

"Yes, Ian, I do. Drakkor's armies are growing. He's kidnapping fae and vampires, and somehow turning them into Asurads, or Kearals, as I call the new demon, and they don't lose their fae or vampire powers when they are turned."

"That's nae possible, if they are turned Asurad they lose their fae and vampire powers. They just become Asurad, malevolent, all powers are gone, except the new ones they get as demon. Och my Goddesses! Their combined powers would make them almost impossible tae stop. Kearals? How can that be? Besides one has free will, they canna become demon unless they agree. Most fae and vampire wouldn't do so."

"Wrong and wrong. Drakkor is somehow taking them or tricking them. They do lose something, however, when turned."

"What?"

"Their good hearts. They become completely evil.

Without their knowledge or say so these men are losing their souls." Merlin frowned and took a long, slow drink of mead.

"What?! Och! What have the angels tae say about it? Are the Ayriris Light Angels of the Plelin Courts involved and does the Akuphis Dark Angel's Court ken?"

"The Ayriris know, the Akuphis are not talking about anything. But the Ayriris have no answers and are as confused as I am. Last I could find out was that Drakkor was collecting kings from various parts of the world. He was last seen in the valley of Mystic Mountain. Before you meet with your new group for training, I need you to leave this magical parallel earth plain, through the Lulara veil, to the human inner earth, and look for Drakkor there.

"Don't interact yet. I know your history together, and your hatred for him killing your father and your twin. If you didn't know him so well, and I didn't need you so badly, I probably wouldn't be putting you in this position, but you're my best. I need you, the fae need you, the vampire's need you, your mother, eight brothers, and four sisters need you."

"Did I hear brothers?" Angus spoke up stomping into the gallery.

"That'd be me as weel!" yelled Cameron.

"He's not going on a mission without us!" said Conall.

"Who's going on a mission?" asked Moira. She swept in, lavender gown floating about her feet. "You retired my son, remember Merlin?"

Merlin stood, and instantly the huge three-story gallery felt small and confined. With a grumble, Merlin put up his hands, then tilted his head. "Greetings, Angus, Cameron, Conall, Dougal, Taryn, Finn, Connor, Lauren. Boys! So, good to see all of you again! And Moira, beautiful Moira, mother to my army."

His mother smiled and leaned to kiss Merlin affectionately on his cheek. Leaning back her smile died. "Merlin, you retired my son and his brothers when Lachlan and Eoghan were killed in your last battle, by that black hearted leader of the Asurads, Drakkor, Remember? What brings you here?"

"Can't I visit my extended family and share the love?" He winked with a wide grin.

"That would truly be wonderful if it were so, but I think that's not the case," said Moira. She smiled, the love she had for Merlin showing brightly on her face.

Turning from him she called for her maid. "Bradana, please bring mead for all now, and make sure cook adds the cream covered with the fennel seeds and sugar, and plums stewed in rose water to our feast this evening, along with stuffed capon. Add two more pheasant and sturgeon cooked in parsley and vinegar as weel. Those are your favorite dishes, right Merlin?"

"Ah you haven't lost your touch my lady, or your memory I see." Merlin gave a short bow and a grin broadened his old wrinkled face, placing a small kiss on her hand.

"Right away my lady," replied the maid, hurrying toward the kitchens.

"Now Merlin, we shall sit, and you will tell us why you're here, and this mission that my boys will be sent on. How have you been? You've been away quite a while."

"I was down for a bit but am fine now."

"Och my, I thought wizards never get tired? What happened?"

"You know me I forget to eat. That is, unless, I am at the McGregor Keep." Merlin winked and grinned. Turning serious once again, Merlin looked about nervously. "Where are the sisters, Brenna, Fiona, Catriona, and Akira?"

"Not tae worry, they are in the solarium sewing new gowns, since the fabric merchant stopped two days past they have sequestered themselves there. We will be lucky tae see them before next week."

In the few hours they had before dinner, they talked about how they were going to deal with the Drakkor situation. In between arguments from the boys, which was a daily occurrence, and one Ian's mother would never let come to the dinner table, Ian let his brothers go at it. After all they were hot-headed McGregors, they needed their outlet.

However, Merlin saw it differently. "Stop! Now! This is serious."

The place became dead silent. "I have amassed a new group called "*The Myraid Army*." They consist of the Ocrul, Crimson Keepers, and Crixior. Ian here is going to be their leader."

The boys all started shouting at once. "Not the damn Crixior! No way tae lead the black bastards! Bastard killed my father and…"

"Stop!" said Merlin, "and listen! Ian, we need stealth." Merlin continued, "If you're found, I don't want them to know about your brother's. I need surveillance and I need you to find out as much as you can. Even though I can see in their world, Drakkor is somehow blocking me from their planning and how he's changing the Ocrul and Crimson Keepers, what the kings have to do with it, all things we need to know. We need to get a handle on it, before these people with their eclectic ideas, interfere with the ecliptic nature of things on a grandiose negative scale. Get me?"

"Weel that got my attention," said Taryn, the ever logical one. "What the bullocks did you jest say? What the hell does that mean?"

"Sorry living in the future, past, and present all the time, sometimes, somethings, can get mixed up. Needless to say, we're in some mighty big trouble," mumbled Merlin. "Ian find out what you can about the king's, why Drakkor wants them, but stay back, don't let him discover you, if you can. I'll watch what I can, work with the angels, and see what we can figure out.

"I can open a portal at any time if you need it, and I can send your brothers, but for now let's just get information. Then we'll plan for attack and do it right. After we get information, Ian will work with the Myraid Army. Oh, and King Arthur needs protection. I won't have him in on this at all.

"It seems Drakkor is after kings, and it's only a matter of time before he goes after Arthur and his army. If Arthur even thinks there's a problem, he'll head long into it, swords a blazing. We can't have him captured. He has the largest army, he's my king as well as yours, he must be protected at all cost. That is why I'm sending Connor, Finn, Angus, and Taryn to watch over him."

"Why them?" asked Cameron. "The rest of us just supposed tae sit on our fingers and wait it all oot? Bullocks!"

"Angus is the meanest son off a..." Merlin looked

at Moira and didn't finish. She smiled. "He's an ambitious fighter, smart and deadly. Taryn is level headed and logical, easily breaks up fights. Connor is a strategist, he could place and lead a dozen armies. And Finn, King Arthur loves Finn, he makes him laugh. Everyone needs some happiness in the middle of trouble."

"Hey," said Finn. "I'm an excellent soldier why I've—"

Merlin cut him off. "Yes, you are an excellent soldier. I remember the battle at Bundaberg and Chriss Hall, and I can go on about your skills, but you make King Arthur laugh. Make sure you do so, fight if you have to, but bring that boy his laughs."

"*Again!*" said Cameron, "What exactly is our position in this?"

"You, Conall, Dougal, and Lauren with me. You'll be working with the angels. Cameron, you remember everything you have ever read. I have grimoires I want you to look at and see if there is anything that is in them that could help us in our fight against the Kearals. I would like to try and save the fae and vampire that are being changed if we can, as many as we can. Any spell to reverse what is being done will be helpful. Conall, you see what's there, that's not there, even spirits. Dougal, a mage and my master in magic…self-explanatory. Lauren, you have premonitions, and dreams of future events. Very helpful."

Angus cleared his throat. "Soldiers tae King Arthur, gifted tae you. I see."

"Shite," said Merlin. "Sorry Moira, lost myself again." She tilted her head. "You're all gifted!" Merlin finished. "Different powers to each brother."

"Shall dinner be served now. my lady?" interrupted Bradana.

"Please now would be a fine time. Och, Bradana please have someone deliver meals tae the girls in the solarium. They're busy sewing, and I think they'd like tae stay there. Thank you."

Bradana bowed and skittered away.

Conversation changed drastically during dinner. No talk of missions, no arguing. Moira smiled at her boys and Merlin, but Ian noticed the faraway look that came in to her eyes and it made him feel uneasy. He knew that when one of their kind mated that if one died the other was quick to follow.

He didn't understand it, but the way his mother explained it to him, once they found their mate their souls wove together, bound together tight. If one should die, it was inevitable the other was right behind. The longer they fought against it the more their mind would deteriorate.

He was proud of his mother and knew the sacrifice she made, forcing herself to remain alive for the love of her children. Somehow, she kept her mind. He didn't know how, but figured it was pure stubbornness on her part, and her love for her family. She continued to take the blood that kept her young. But he was seeing the affects that staying alive was having on her.

He knew how difficult it was on her. Perhaps when or if he ever found his true mate, he would truly understand, but it had been eight hundred years, he wasn't sure he ever would. Of late his mother had drifted in and out of another world and he had seen it get progressively worse since his father and brother had been killed. He only hoped she wouldn't take the route that many took when they lost their mate. Perhaps he was selfish in that, he didn't want to lose her too. Angus's loud voice brought him abruptly back to the conversation at hand.

"Och, tae hear Finn tell the story you'd think he caught Nessie the Lochness! It was a turtle, not an ancient monster the size of the loch, and it bumped the boat, didn't almost turn it over." Angus shoved more worogild in his mouth laughing, then choking.

"Serves you right!" said Finn. He slapped his back and handed him his mead. "You weren't there, you doona ken what happened."

"Och," said Taryn, "you were tuppin' the blacksmiths daughter at the cottage. Remember? Cute lil' thing too."

"Taryn!" reprimanded Moira.

"Sorry Mither."

He was quiet listening to his brothers. This was home with the banter and the laughter, but he once again glanced toward Moira as she leaned back and became distant again, until Merlin mentioned Lachlan's name. Her eyes cleared, and she leaned forward to catch what was being said. Yes, he was definitely getting worried about her.

"And he shot another arrow into that worogild for the third time before it went down," continued Merlin. "Biggest damn, sorry Moira, biggest worogild to have ever been caught, and many hunted that giant one. If memory serves me, that's him hanging on that wall over there." He pointed toward the wall with his knife, sweet potatoes dripping off.

Connor laughed, and said, "Hey remember the herd of worogilds that came crashing through at the Battle of

Drummond Bay?"

"Those men who were hidin' ready tae attack us?" Dougal laughed with a mouthful. "They were runnin' oot and aboot like they'd been caught with their pants down. Easy victory that was."

Talk and laughter remained throughout the meal and dessert. Finally, things quieted down and their thoughts were brought back to the mission. Ian glanced around the table, they were all looking at Merlin, waiting for him to speak.

"I guess I've explained our situation as best as I can," said Merlin.

He saw Merlin look at each of them in turn, pride in his eyes. It was good they'd had time to heal over Lachlan and Eoghan's death, he thought. He knew Merlin was going to bring them all out of retirement, and he sighed.

"It's time," said Merlin. "I've said my piece, so all prepare, and I'll ready the portal."

Ian watched as Merlin grabbed his mother's hand and bent to kiss it. She smiled and it warmed his heart. Merlin seemed to always have that effect on his mother, he thought. He'd have to make sure Merlin spent more time at McGregor Keep.

"Moira, my dear," said Merlin. He smiled at her, "you've outdone yourself. Dinner was excellent and company suburb. It would have been nice to see the girls, but under the circumstances, thank you for sending up their dinner and not mentioning I'm here. I'll see them soon, I'm sure."

Merlin leaned in and whispered. "If you hadn't been married to Lachlan, still married to Lachlan, always be married to Lachlan, soul mates for eternity,

I'd marry you myself."

"Shush." She blushed. "You're like the brother I never had."

Merlin smiled, eyes twinkling. "Never the less, my lady, oh, I'll have some soldiers watch over you and your lovely daughters while your sons are away. You will always be well guarded. Now I must take my leave."

"Thank you, Merlin. Protect my boys, and you, take care of yourself. We are family you ken," she said, and Merlin smiled.

Chapter 2

Elspeth McLellan lifted her face to the sun and smiled. Walks in the garden courtyard, of the inner-city castle walls always uplifted her, and she enjoyed every second she could steal away to be here. She enjoyed life here, albeit she'd only arrived a short year ago, returning only after her brother Athdar found her at the convent she was taken to and raised after her parents died. She had lived here prior to her mother's death and her father's alleged abandonment, but that fateful year she'd been whisked away to the convent.

Memories flooded her mind. She looked around deep in thought. The monastery was okay to grow up in, but her freedom in Mystic Kingdom made her ecstatic. Home, and she did feel at home, so familiar yet so foreign. She had never wanted for anything but her mother. She had her father's red hair and coloring, but inherited her mother's temperament and good heart. She also wore her mother's soft features, beautiful smile, and sparkling eyes. She missed her so.

She sighed, and frowned at the thought of her death, bringing back the unwanted feelings of losing her at seven winters. The echo of giggles and her mother's bright face as she swung her around in circles, brought the ache in her heart back. She never saw her laughing-eyed father after that. Many said he fought in the king's army relentlessly, and ultimately died of a broken heart. She never forgave him for leaving, she wanted to, maybe even understood it, but the hole in her heart remained.

Her thoughts turned to being taken to Northern England to be raised in the monastery. There she healed the sick and injured. Mother Thomas Adley, an odd name which no one discussed, took her under her wing and raised her like a mother hen. She was her mentor, her teacher, her guardian, and her friend. She remembered her with a smile and sadness, as she'd died two winters past of old age.

The place was never the same afterward, it was a place of emptiness and sadness, once again Elspeth felt the loneliness of losing someone she loved, so she was glad her brother, Athdar McLellan, discovered her on a reprieve from their arduous journey.

It was the first time she'd seen him since she'd arrived at the monastery. When she was first taken to the convent to be raised, the king took her older brother to live with him. When he found her, he'd talked her in to going back home to the place her life began. Elspeth shook herself, would she never get those last moments of her mother and the sudden change in her life from her mind? She sighed and continued her walk toward the woods. She ventured to her favorite path amongst the giant oaks of the park.

Coming to the bridge, she sat on a white stone bench, and watched as the crystal water of the lazy river flowed beneath it. Small ribbons of sunlight hit upon the water, and it sparkled like jewels upon a crown. Colorful fish flitted in and out of the bolts of sunshine and made her laugh. She loved it here.

She liked being alone, in this spot, with her

thoughts to herself. She was busy as a healer, being able to find this time of relaxation, was priceless. It wasn't that she didn't enjoy being the healer for the kingdom because she most certainly did. People loved her and she them. The children were such a joy to her.

She thought back to when she found out she was born a healer. At six winters, their family hunting dog came back from a hunting trip with serious injuries. How she loved Wiley. Caelan, her father carried the limp animal upon his lap into the court yard, shouting for Athdar to take him to a healer.

Without thinking, Elspeth ran to him as her brother took the pup in his arms. She grabbed onto Wiley with tears flowing down her cheeks. Her hands became warm and a green glow surrounded her. The light and warmth from her hands entered her whimpering friend. He yelped, and her brother feeling a jolt of the healing heat, dropped the dog, but she grabbed on and wouldn't let go. Finally, Wiley wiggled, and she freed him. He was completely healed.

She smiled thinking about his short brown haired, lanky body, and when he shook his tail, his whole behind wiggled. The people in the courtyard had been rendered speechless. That was when she was told that healers were born with the gift and were extremely rare. She was told by the kingdom's elderly healer that only the pure of heart could use the gift.

One could learn the healing herbs for illness and sores, but a magical healer had to be born with the gift, it could not be learned. Since then she studied as much about healers as she could. Chanting in the old Gods language brought more energy from the Gods to add to her powers. She spoke the ancient language well, praying to them while healing.

The severity of the injury determined the amount of energy needed to heal the wound or illness. Sometimes she felt drained to the point of fainting, having given all she had to give. She couldn't bring someone back from the dead, but close to it. She enjoyed who and what she was, taking care of the sick, the injured, anyone who needed her gifts. She was very busy in her kingdom, and she loved the people.

A muffled sound brought her out of her thoughts. Again, a cry came and a plea. Elspeth got to her feet and followed the sound. She was going to call out when she heard an angry man's voice.

"You whore!" she heard, and a slap. The woman cried out. "Please don't!"

She heard another slap. Elspeth's heart raced, and she ran toward the clearing, in the direction of the sounds. When she rounded the trees, she stopped, shocked and immobile, she stood frozen to the spot.

There was her king, King Rulm, assaulting a poor bloody faced young woman with wild tresses of raven hair soaked wet with blood. Her eye was swollen shut and blood pouring from her nose. Her jaw crooked and obviously broken. "Fight me whore, I like it when you fight!" The girl whimpered and grew lax, her eyes shining over. She was in shock.

Without thinking Elspeth screamed, "Stop!" and ran toward them. The king raised his head and turned toward her. The evil she saw in his black eyes turned her stomach, and she took a step back in fear.

"Stop," she said again, though this time her voice was quieter, smaller somehow. The king moved away from the young woman. "You'll pay for that Elspeth," he spat through gritted teeth. "You think your brother will save you?" He laughed. "You are wrong, and you are next."

Elspeth shook her head and backed away. She looked at the girl who now lay dead. The king started for Elspeth, his anger apparent, breaking her fear she began to run. "No!" she screamed.

The king's laughter rang in her ears. "Your brother won't save you!" he shouted. "Who do you think ruts beside me in battle!" King Rulm roared again in laughter, and she ran faster.

Where could she go? The gates would be locked, the king would find her, and she'd be dead. Her brother, Athdar? She felt sick. She came to the river. *"The cliffs!"*

If she could get to the cliffs she could climb. King Rulm would think her trapped there. It was forbidden to climb the cliffs because of the dragons, she had climbed there when she was little. It had been years. Could she do it again? The dragons should be out hunting and she could hide in an empty cave. She would have time to think about what to do next.

The dragons, albeit a danger to people, because of the proximity of the cliffs, also protected the kingdom from intruders. No one ventured too near their caves.

Even though dragons would delight in a human meal, they hunted the fields and ate the animals that fed on the crops, mostly worogilds, six-legged animals with a soft thick coat. People not only used their meat, but their hides as well.

Their co-existence with the dragons was beneficial for both sides. Since the dragons refrained from attacking humans despite their desire for human flesh, the kingdom appeased them by offering up those who were convicted of horrible crimes.

The offering was something of a blood sport for those who enjoyed such things. Spectators would gather and wait for the bell that called the dragons to be rung. It was something that she, as a healer, could not understand. Archers stood ready just in case the dragons descended upon the crowd. It was the closest to the dragons most would ever dare to venture.

She was afraid, but she would take her chances, after all she was dead if King Rulm found her, and she feared what he would do to her before he killed her. She thought about his wife the queen. Did she know? She was tall, beautiful, striking, strict, but she never seemed evil, nor did she mistreat her people. She must not know what her husband did behind her back.

Before she knew it, she reached the familiar cliffs. Where was the hunting party? No time to think about that now, she had to climb. With shaky hands, she ripped her emerald skirts to her knees, tied the strips around her waist, and began her ascent. She found the places she used to know as the best footholds and skittered upward.

When she hit the halfway mark, she paused to think about where to go next. She intensified her climb when she noticed the sky and the coming dusk. She had almost made it when the sky turned red. The dragons would soon be leaving their caves to hunt. She looked for a way to hide from the dragons and spotted a shrub growing out of the side of the cliff. There beside it a ledge. She would wait there.

Climbing onto the ledge behind the bush, she leaned back and sighed. She caught her breath and closed her eyes for a second. When she opened them, she looked down to the valley below. It was so small, the river a winding ribbon, falls roared in her ears, and she looked down at her hands wrapped around her knees.

Her fingernails were broken and bloody, her knees raw and bleeding, her shoes were tattered, a toe peaked out muddy and caked in blood, but she didn't feel it. Her fear had her in a hypersensitivity mode beyond anything she could feel physically.

Before she could think too much about what state she was in, she heard the first roar of the dragons. Almost like a call to all. Then the flurry of wings and the giant, colorful animals flew from the caves. She watched one in particular weave its way from behind the falls. Smart, she thought, very good hiding.

That was where she'd go. She watched in amazement and awe as they rose up in the air in a flurry of giant wings and colorful bodies and disappeared toward the fields. She realized she had a healthy love for the large beasts.

She stood, and with the last bit of light, made the last of the climb. With her body close to the wall, she sidestepped behind the waterfall being careful to feel for the opening. When she came to it she crawled inside and dropped. Just inside to the right was a small fall that came through the roof and landed in a pool that eventually flowed along the crack, back outside, where it joined the mother waterfall.

A place to bathe, she thought, as her eyes dropped shut, and she lay against the wall. She fought sleep, as she had to leave before the dragons got back, but for the first time since escaping the king, she felt safe and exhausted. She couldn't keep her eyes open.

A dragon roared somewhere outside, and she woke with a start. Memories hit her like a rock, she knew the dragons were on their way back. She jumped up, and her breaths became fast and short. She hugged the wall in fear and it dawned on her. She was dead now, after all she did to get here, she was sure as dead. With wild eyes, she looked from left to right. What to do now?

She heard a louder dragon scream followed by a lower pitched one. Together the screams came fast and furious. They were fighting! Fighting! She moved to the edge of the opening and through a slit in the water she could see two dragons fighting in the moonlight. Then as soon as the fight started, it stopped.

She moved back and leaned on the wall once again. Moments later she heard scraping, and she looked to the opening, her fear replaced with awe. A head the size of a huge boulder looked through the opening. Florescent green and shimmery yellow scales adorned the majestic head.

Bright greenish-yellow almond shaped eyes turned toward her and narrowed. Short ribbed spikes adorned either side of her head, in rows moved back to the neck, and reminded her of a woman's hair braided tight to her head in two rows. The dragon opened its mouth to blow fire at her, to incinerate her. She screamed, *"No!"* internally as she'd lost her tongue.

The dragon came closer to her and reared back. The thing was as big as a two-story dwelling. She shook and put her hands over her eyes waiting for the flames. Then she felt the floor rumble, and an oomph came from the dragon. She slid her fingers apart and peaked through. The dragon lay on her side, blood flowing profusely from a wound in its stomach. "Oh, my," she exclaimed, and without thinking ran toward the dragon.

"*Stop*," said the dragon. Did she really hear that? She took another step and again heard "*stop*." This time she knew it came from the dragon. She stared at the injured dragon, and her desire to heal increased. "*Wait*," thought the dragon. "*You understand me?*"

"Sort of, I think. You thought something very strongly or I imagined it."

The dragon closed her eyes, then opened them again. "*Impossible*," she thought. *"Do you carry the dragon mark?"*

"Mark? What mark?"

"No one has communicated with a dragon in over a thousand years, except wizards. Are you a wizard?"

Wizard? She shook her head, maybe she was imagining things. She shook her head to clear it. "I'm a healer."

"*Maybe why*." The dragon sighed. *"I'm dying, good is your spirit, your color I can see. Take care of them."*

"Take care of who? The other dragons? Who did this to you?"

"Father theirs, comes at time they hatch, eats male offspring. Not all dragon father's do, and not all kingdoms are like that, but he doesn't allow males to live, only females. He's killed all males who have tried to move inside our kingdom. He's killed all male children who survive. He's the only undefeated male amongst us living." The female dragon sighed in pain. *"Gone is my time. Take care of them."*

"Who?" asked Elspeth again. She walked to the

dragon. It opened its eyes and looked toward the back of the cave. It opened its mouth, and she jumped back. The dragon took a deep breath and blew fire. Her gaze went to the back of the cave, and there on a large nest encrusted with more gems than she had ever seen, sat what appeared to be two dragon eggs, almost as large as the dragon's head. "N...Nnnnooo. I don't know anything about dragons."

The moonlight came through the hole in the ceiling and draped over the dragon's belly and brought her mind back to healing. This time before the dragon could open its eyes, and lift its head, she ran and placed her hands just above the wound. She leaned her head back and began to chant in the ancient language.

Immediately light encircled her, illuminating the cave. The dragon opened one eye but was too weak to do anything else. She looked at Elspeth in fear. The light flowed from her hands and encircled the wound. The bleeding slowed and the wound closed. Just when she thought she wouldn't have enough energy to heal such a large creature, she heard the dragon's thoughts. "*My children.*"

She intensified her chanting. The light and warmth increased. Elspeth glanced at the dragon as it moved its head and opened both her eyes. Amazement and something else, something endearing came from the wondering look, and then Elspeth heard her. "*Saphira,*" thought the dragon. "*Name mine, Saphira.*"

Elspeth caught the name and whispered "Saphira." Then she collapsed on the floor and her light went out.

Chapter 3

Elspeth woke to warmth and a crackling fire. Something digging in her cheek made her open her eyes and her hand moved to push it aside. Focusing on her surroundings she realized she was laying in the nest of gems holding the dragon eggs.

Everything came back like a bad dream and she lurched. Fear grabbed hold and she scrambled toward the edge of the oversized nest. Looking around she saw no huge dragon about and thought her luck had come back. Maybe she'd live after all, maybe she could leave now.

As she slowly stood up, aches in her muscles, cuts and bruises, gave way to excruciating pain and weakness, a moan tumbled forth, and she thought she'd be sick. She sat back down. Weariness washed over her, but it did not diminish the awe she felt. Looking around she saw the glitter of the woven nest of emeralds, rubies, sapphires, gold, silver and so much more.

"Why there's more treasure here than many kingdoms all put together." She glanced at the small fire under the hole in the roof and watched as lazy smoke filtered up and out. "Do dragons need fire to stay warm? How ironic." She giggled. She heard the flap of large wings and looked toward the opening. With the folding of her wings, the dragon she had healed, descended upon the opening, blocking all light in the cave's doorway. And of all things, large branches full of berries were clutched in her long claws. Very long claws.

"*Hungry thought you may be*," said the dragon. Her thought was tinged with amusement."

She sat dumbfounded. "Hu…hun…hungry? Uh…ok, hungry."

Saphira laughed, as much as a dragon could laugh. "*My life you saved, my babies a chance they have, I protect you always.*"

"No need surely. Healing is what I do." She lifted her chin, with pride, grinned at the large dragon, and suddenly felt a kinship with the huge beast. Her fear somewhat alleviated she stood and walked toward the colorful dragon.

Saphira bent her head down so they were eye level. The dragon half closed her eyes and rubbed her face against Elspeth's shoulder in affection. She laughed and stroked the side of Saphira's face. Then Saphira stretched her neck, flung her head back, and blew fire directly at where she stood. Not a yellow flame this time, but one of blue.

She stumbled back in horror sure death was imminent. But she stood unharmed. Confused she looked down. Just above her heart there was a hole in her blouse and a perfect replica of Saphira burned into her chest. *It didn't hurt.*

Saphira laughed again. "*Now you carry the dragon mark. I know you had a hard time putting in order what I was trying to say to you. It was hard for you to understand me fully, but now that you carry the mark you will understand me completely. You will be able to communicate with dragons. All dragons. I think because you are a healer you could pick up my thoughts. Though I know not how or why you did. No human has had the mark in over a thousand years.*" She bent to move the jewels around in her nest. She stood and looked toward her eggs, made a cooing sound, and with her nose nudged the eggs closer together. Standing full height, she once again turned to Elspeth.

"*You have to save a dragon's life to carry the mark. Not an easy thing to do, since normally we do not get along with humans. We sometimes eat them, but only to keep them afraid of us. If we didn't they'd hunt us. We only eat the unfavorable humans. We do not prey on the innocent.*"

Elspeth looked at the dragon in awe, yet somehow unafraid. She watched as the light and shadows played off her colorful scales, saw the sharp intelligence, and changing emotions in her eyes, and wondered how anyone could ever kill such a majestic creature.

"*But now, no dragon shall ever hurt you,*" Saphira continued. "*All dragons will help you. You and I are forever connected, mind to mind. My children will also share that gift with you. You need only think of me to come to you or call I'll be there. I belong to you, and you me,*" she explained. Leaning down, she nudged her shoulder with her nose, then looked straight into her eyes.

"*If you need a lot of dragons call upon the force of us. Your mark will glow and be a beacon for them. They too will aid you, if you need them. We will hear your call from great distances. Now eat.*" Saphira nudged the berry branches closer to Elspeth's feet.

"Saphira? I do not understand. Why would I be

honored enough to receive such a mark? I'm nothing more than a plain peasant girl, from the monastery no less. I have no other gifts other than my healing. I'm really very simple. I'm not a soldier of great strength, nor do I hold a world of people in my hands. I'm just a woman and a weak one at that. There is no greatness to me that seems worthy of such a thing. For such a great thing, why me?"

Saphira laughed. *"Strength comes in many shapes and sizes, Elspeth. It took courage for you to climb the cliffs into the den of the most feared of creatures. When I lay on the floor dying, you could have saved yourself, but instead knowing none of this, or what I would do to you, you stayed and healed me without a thought to your safety. Such a brave thing. You have an inner strength that is great, a heart of purity, which is rare, and a kindness and knowledge of the life around you.*

"You as a healer, respect all living things. That in itself is a rarity. No, Elspeth you know not the amazing qualities you have. Even though I have no true answer as to how this all came to be, I know there is a reason. In all of life there are reasons, and you shall find out soon enough. We both will. Now you must eat to build your strength for whatever it is that is coming."

She glanced down at the dried blood on her hands, and the dirt on her dress. She wasn't hungry, but she did wish she could have a bath. Forgetting the dragon could read her mind Saphira answered. *"Eat first, I will then take you to the river to bathe."* Waddling to the corner of the cave Saphira picked up something and came back and dropped it at Elspeth's feet. A hunk of old meat, smelly old meat. She grimaced. "Uh, the berries will be enough, thanks."

"Oh," Saphira said. *"I forgot you cook meat. Why you burn good meat I don't know, but here…"* Saphira reared back and blew fire, scorching the dead piece of meat, so it looked like black leather.

She laughed. "Really Saphira berries are all I'd like to break my fast." She smiled at the dragon. She sat and ate her fill of the best tasting berries she'd ever eaten. "Where did these come from? I've never had anything so wonderful."

"They grow on the top of Mystic Mountain where no man can go. It's the only place they grow. We feed small quantities to our young. They have healing properties and encourage strong growth."

Elspeth frowned, even though she did feel much better, invigorated. "But that mountain is cursed. No man can go near without fear of dying. Men and women alike, are turned to stone statues."

"For humans yes, but the mountain is not cursed, it is blessed. Especially for dragons. Eat now, and we will see to your bath. I will leave you to bathe. I must keep close watch on my eggs. They are soon to hatch. When you are finished call me, and I will return to get you."

"Oh then, you shouldn't take me, I wouldn't want you to miss that. It's okay really."

"Nonsense, it takes time for them to crack through. It takes only seconds to get you there and back. That way you can take time to enjoy your bath. I insist. I can never repay you for what you've done for me. Let me enjoy being, how do you say it? Friend, family? Let me be your family."

She couldn't explain the love that enveloped them both, but she knew her life would never be the same from that moment on.

Chapter 4

Ian McGregor looked up from the river where he'd washed the dust from his face, to listen to the most beautiful singing voice he'd ever heard. He walked along the edge and through the bushes toward the floating melody. When he separated the branches, he gazed upon a creamy white back, and the longest, most brilliant red hair he'd ever seen. Over the woman's shoulders and down her back were curls of bright, fire red hair that softly cascaded to her hips.

He stood and stared, his mouth agape. She lifted her hair from her back and tied it in a knot on the top of her head, dipped to her neck, swam around, stood again, and began to wade toward the edge. Och Goddesses, please turn around. He silently prayed. Her shoulders glistening with droplets of water, her arms above her, her narrow waist, and then her round buttock came dripping from the depths.

His mouth went dry, and he licked his lips, then she turned. Her emerald eyes glanced in his direction. Full creamy breasts invaded his senses, he became as hard as a rock, and he jerked in anticipation. My God, was he but a randy lad and a voyeur? He disgusted himself. Letting the branch snap back he turned to leave, but he stepped on a twig and it snapped.

"Who's there?" came a nervous but lilting voice.

He quickly turned back and looked again through

the branches. He stood still, holding his breath. He couldn't leave and he didn't want to stay. He was afraid to move for fear she would see him, and he didn't want her to find him like this.

The woman immediately put her arms about her breasts, and she dove back in the water. She looked about frantically. "Who's there, I asked?"

He stood silent and still not wanting to give himself away. Then he heard horses and men shouting. "We've found her!" Three soldiers jumped from their horses, armor gleaming in the bright sun. More soldiers came from the thick forest around the trees. Seven men in all surrounded her. She stood shaking in the water. Her emerald eyes darted back and forth looking for a way out.

"Och shite," he said as he looked at the men. Good thing his sword was still at his side, and he hadn't climbed in the river yet himself. He knew what he was going to do before he did it. Bullocks, he thought. Scrambled thoughts of his mission sailed through his mind. He was here on order from Merlin. Voices brought him back to the present.

He tore his transfixed gaze from the beauty in the lake to the commander standing nearby.

"You are wanted in the Holy court for treason, Elspeth McLellan. I'm here by order of the king to bring you in alive!" The commander sneered. "And I will, after I'm done with you." His black eyes glared in a way that made the woman cringe and Ian noticed the disgusted look cross her face. Ian wanted him dead for his words alone. He tensed with anger, almost giving himself away.

"It's a lie!" she screamed "I caught the king

35

assaulting and killing a lady! He wants me dead because of it!"

"*Silence!*"

He could see her lips quiver. Treason? That was a serious charge. Death for that, but did he believe this beauty? Yes, he did. With his gift, he knew she was telling the truth. Who was this king?

"Och, shite," he said again. He was going to save her. He gave the MacGregor war cry and jumped through the bushes at lightning speed. Before anyone knew what happened, he swung his sword. The soldier went down with his first swing. One jumped in and tore open his arm before he turned and took the next soldiers head clean from his shoulders. He fought two at a time and dropped them both with little effort. The commander and the last two tried to surround him.

He laughed. "You think you have the baws for this wee game of yours?" He danced about. "You are folly tae me, you lame brain wallopers, you willna live throughout the day. Bring what you got, and I'll be flitting with you, but you willna live much longer."

He laughed and threw his sword back and forth between his hands. Strong legs and large thighs spread wide, muscles bunched and relaxed up and down his arms, muscles twitched at his shoulders, and his chest pumped one side at a time. He might have laughed at these men outright, but he was a no-nonsense guy.

His eyes sharp, his tongue sharper. The men looked at the commander with trepidation and fear. Elspeth stared at him, and he laughed again. "Weel, my merry maids, what have you? Cat got your tongue or is it your baws? Maybe you are wee girls and your baws are caught in your skirts! Ha!"

He got his results. The commander yelled and lunged, and the two men flanked him on either side. He threw his sword to his left hand and without looking at the one who was just to his left, coming up behind him, took the man's head clean from his shoulders. Without losing momentum, he tossed his sword, and it flew from there up in the air. He put his right hand behind his back and caught it, slashing through the side of the other. He accomplished this without ever taking his eyes from the commander.

Ducking low and missing losing his head from the commander's blade, he twirled and pivoted, bringing up his blade through the commander's neck and piercing to the back of his skull. The last man fell. He turned to look at the one they called Elspeth McLellan. She stood in the water with a shocked look on her face.

"Wha…wha…how'd you do that?" She spit out. Ian watched as she stared at him. He pulled his hand through his black hair, pulling the locks that caught on the shadowed beard adorning his strong square jaw. He wiped blood from a wound across his bicep, and he almost smiled. Her perusal traveled from first his face and slowly down his chest, and across his sculpted stomach, then stopped on his green and black kilt.

He immediately felt naked in front of her. His chest was bare, his tartan lying beside the river. But he still had his kilt on, and it was there her eyes stopped. Feeling the heat of her gaze only made him grow and the front of his tartan began to bulge. She must have realized she was staring, for her face immediately turned scarlet. She quickly looked away, then she shuddered, and he knew it wasn't from the cold. "Oh, my," she said, making him smile.

"Close your mouth dearling and get dressed. We need tae leave here afore more come." The instant he looked in Elspeth's eyes a flash of what his parents had been telling him his whole life went through his head and stopped him dead.

He stared into her eyes and recognized her as his mate. An unseen force so strong drew them together with an explosion of instant understanding. Fleeting, instantaneous images flited through him. Elspeth as his wife in another life, Elspeth growing large with his children, Elspeth and him growing old together, dying young together, having children, not having children, over many lives.

Lives spent together over and over. He knew this woman like the back of his hand, and he knew without a doubt the love they shared was unquestionable. He felt it now, like the force of gale winds on an ocean tide.

He heard the voice of his mother. "You are like two sparks joining together in a flame. It's in our family, you will see, you will ken. Your souls will ken each other, even if your heads aren't ready to accept it, sometimes a McGregor may ignore it for a while, especially a stubborn one. The souls doona lie, and eventually your heart will tell your head, it's unavoidable. You will ken. She will ken.

"Your souls join like the finest weaving of a spider web, and the love will blossom. If you've kenned her before, you will remember her now. Us McGregors can be stubborn and at times we do not recognize this at first, but eventually we do, and will. We can throw up that stubborn wall, but the kind of love we McGregors have, will break down that wall until it crumbles to dust and blows in the wind, dissipating like an invisible ghost."

Those words had always confused him, and he always thought them nothing more than the rambling of his mother so in love with his father. Until in just a flash of a second, he not only understood but felt her words. He'd lived with this woman in other lives. He somehow knew she saw and felt it too. "It happens to all the McGregors." His mother had said. He had had many women and never believed it would happen, until now. He was staring at his mate and the love traveled through him and bloomed.

For that one second, time stood still, but years and lives of information and feelings settled in his gut, changing everything he thought he understood about his life. He could see the wonder in her eyes. It felt like time stood still and days, months, years, memories had traveled through his soul, and it was just him and her, the only ones alive on the planet.

Then the entire thing dissipated like a cloud on a windy day, and just left them with the knowledge that they were mates. All images gone, forgotten, but the purpose of it and the residual effects lingered in them, leaving wonder and awe. It left them feeling as if they had known each other their entire lives, so familiar to each other. Her look reached inside his chest and grabbed his heart, he was lost to her and he knew it would be forever. He gulped. Shaking his head, he said, "Are you feeling weel?" he asked, concerned, not sure what to say.

She shook her head yes about five times, blushed, and turned to walk out of the water. He didn't know if her nervousness was from the soldiers and the fight, or what she had just felt for him. He hoped it was for him.

The moment was broken, and neither knew what to say or do. Reality cloaked them once again, and the world around them came back in focus. Was everything they just shared a dream? "God's," she said. "I only wanted a bath!" She dressed quickly in her torn skirts and blouse and turned toward the open valley. "Are you coming? There are sure to be more and you're no longer safe."

He laughed. "Aye, I'm coming," and he took up behind her.

She lifted her arms and shouted "*Saphira!*" Moments later the sun clouded over and Ian heard the flap of wings and a loud roar. He looked up at the largest dragon he'd ever seen. He had never been this close to a dragon before and his mouth gaped in wonder. "Close your mouth," she said smiling. "She's our ride out of here."

He didn't fear much, after all he was a man of war, but he did have a lifelong fear of dragons. It was simple, don't get close to a dragon and live, get close and die. When he was a child, nightmares would plague him of monster dragons burning and eating him. It did not help that his younger brothers played on this and instilled more fears whenever they could and laugh about it. As everyone got older no one dared to mention dragons around him.

"A horse I'd ride," he replied. "A donkey I'd ride. Maybe even a worogild, but I'm not riding on that, and weel now you should ken it!"

Elspeth laughed, and it sounded as beautiful as her singing. He smiled, deep dimples showing in his cheeks. He followed her out toward the dragon, as she was tucking her wings beneath her. The dragon leaned her head down and Elspeth rubbed the side of her face, planting a kiss to her forehead. "Yes," answered Elspeth, "they found me."

"You can talk tae the beast?" exclaimed Ian. They both turned to look at him.

"She's not a beast! She's my friend! Now come, I've explained you saved my life and you're coming with me, unless you want an army after you as weeeel," she drawled then smiled.

"You're making fun of my speech, you are." He scowled, then walked toward them. "A dragon," he mumbled.

Elspeth laughed again as she stepped on the wing that gently brought her to the back of the dragon's neck. "You are next." She laughed again. "I'm sorry," she said. "You're just so cute when you scowl."

"Puppies are cute, ducklings are cute, baby horses are cute," he mumbled. "I'm a mon!" He said. "I'm *nae* cute!"

She laughed again. "No, I suppose not. Now get up here."

With a bow, he snarled, "yes, my lady!" He climbed on the wing and Saphira brought him up behind Elspeth. "This weel be taking the death of me yet. Ian McGregor dead from falling off a big scaly lizard bird with fire from her mouth. Scales cleavin' my baws from beneath me kilt tae sink tae the fish in a grand loch where they throw up green scales and my eyeballs.

"My toenails black from fire, and hair straight tae its ends as if struck from a stormy lightning. My lips will be gone for sure and my teeth sticken oot my nose.

41

My ears will be ripped off my head from giant turtles, and my brains sucked oot through the holes by the Lochness, who probably breathes fire as weel. I'll sorely be laughed at, at me funeral."

"What in the devil you mumbling about? Grab the spike in front of you," Elspeth explained, "and hold tight!"

Just then the giant wings began to fan out, up and down, and the wind from them blew his hair across his face. "Bloody hell, this is the biggest bunch of blarney. Riding the devil himself. Wait 'til my brothers hear aboot this." He groaned. "I'll just never tell them." He closed his eyes then they were airborne, and it was quite smooth. He relaxed somewhat, then wondered where exactly they were going. It didn't take him long to figure out. They were headed to a cliff, smack dab toward a waterfall.

In an instant, they went through the falls and landed inside a cave. In the quiet he heard scratching. "What is that?" he asked.

"The babies," Elspeth said simply. She said to Saphira. "The babies! Oh, isn't it wonderful! Go ahead, we'll be here." Saphira moved toward the back of the cave after picking up some meat from a pile near the entrance.

"Come," said Elspeth, "I know a place we can go and give them time to be together. Follow me," she said, and took his hand. They went to the cliff face where he followed Elspeth onto a ledge.

It was a short distance and perfect for them both to sit comfortably. After a minute of silence, and their shared enjoyment of the view of the valley below, Ian turned to her and looked into her bright emerald eyes.

He felt a warmth pass between them and he thought of her beauty standing naked in the river. The knowledge of knowing her rushed again through his blood. He felt as if she were, and had been, his for eternity.

His thoughts gave him a randy hard on, heat shot through his veins, he was so hard in fact he couldn't ever remember feeling this strongly before. Clearing his throat, he said. "Is this where I kiss the damsel in distress?"

"Damsel in distress? I just saved your hide!" she laughed.

"After saving yours!" Before she could respond he leaned over and gently touched his lips to hers. Even though he knew her by soul, this felt like a first kiss, and the excitement overwhelmed him. A bolt of heat shot through him and he felt her shudder as if she felt it too.

Her face became flush, the light shining off her hair where it flowed like liquid copper glistened. Ian had never seen such raw and innocent beauty and it humbled him. He could smell her unique perfume of arousal and his manhood jerked beneath his kilt. His mouth went instantly dry and he trembled slightly. Trying to be a gentleman, he pulled back and put his forehead to hers. "Want tae try that again?"

"I uh…you were…mayb…we should just."

She suddenly went silent.

"What?" asked Ian noticing the glazed look on Elspeth face.

"The babies are here. Come on she wants us to see them." Elspeth grabbed his hand.

"Els' you really can talk tae the dragon, can't

you?" Amazement lit his face.

Elspeth turned to him, opened the hole in her blouse, and showed him her dragon mark. "Tell you about it later. Come let's see the babies!"

Little *squawks* and *squeals* reached their ears as Ian, hand in hand with Elspeth, entered the cave. Saphira was feeding strips of meat into their little mouths. "Aren't they adorable!" said Elspeth.

Ian noticed all the jewels. "You could buy Mystic Mountain with all this."

Elspeth frowned and gave Ian a stern look. "The babies!"

They were kind of cute in a reptilian way. "*Squawk!*" One pecked Ian's arm and they all laughed. Ian reached over and touched the lil one's head. "*Squawk!*"

"*A boy and a girl!*" said the proud mamma. "*Kalon, my son. Sorrilth, my daughter.*"

"What did she say?" Recognizing Elspeth's look when she communicated with the dragon.

"Oh, Ian we have to protect Saphira and her babies! She's named them. Sorrilth her daughter, Kalon her son." Then she explained to him what happened. "He'll kill her son and probably her and Sorrilth too. We have to stop him."

He thought about his mission. "I...ah...I'm supposed tae...there's things I have tae..." Seeing the terrified look on Elspeth's face he said. "It can wait. Aye, I'll help you."

Elspeth threw her arms around him and kissed him hard on the lips.

"Wow, anythin' else I can do for you? Kill a man? Empty the ocean? What can I have if I save the world?"

He wiggled his eyebrows and grinned like a cat who ate a pet bird. Elspeth slugged his shoulder and laughed.

Saphira stepped toward them and she had a worried dragon look on her face. At least that's what Ian thought a worried dragon look would look like. "What's she sayin'?"

"Shush," said Elspeth. Ian watched in wonder as the dragon stared at Elspeth. "She says, Darlath, bringer of death as he's called, will come tonight to kill them all. He is the father. He's mated with all the females of their hoard whether they have wanted to or not."

A groan came from Saphira. When they turned to look, a tear bigger than his fist dropped from her eye and splattered to the floor. In that instant, without explanation, the fear left him, and he fell in love with dragons. Clearing his throat, he said, "I weel champion you dear lady of dragons. I will not fail you."

Elspeth turned and relayed the message to Saphira. Saphira turned, lowered her head in submission, and placed her face directly on Ian's chest. Two more monstrous tears fell from her eyes and landed on Ian's feet.

To keep from tearing up himself, said the only thing he could think of. "You wet my feet!"

They laughed and Saphira snorted. "Was that a dragon's laugh?" he asked Elspeth.

"She picked up what you said from my mind when I understood it." The dragon snorted again, and they all laughed. Until it got serious again.

Chapter 5

Dusk was coming, with Sorrilth and Kalon fed and sleeping, Saphira paced the cave snorting puffs of smoke and grunting. Tears came from the big dragon.

"She's afraid," said Elspeth.

Ian couldn't handle a woman crying much less a dragon. He never knew what to say. He tried to think of something to get her mind off her troubles, "Now Saphira if you continue tae do that you'll drown us. How can I champion you, if we're dead?"

This didn't fool Saphira, and they both turned to look at him and he shrugged. Elspeth giggled. "Saphira said vampires can't drown." That was enough to lighten the fear a bit, he thought. "I didn't know vampires existed," she said. "I thought it was a myth, can you...?"

"There's no time now, Elspeth, I will answer all your questions later, right now we have more pressing matters. We will stay strong and I have Dragon Slayer my sword." Ian touched his sword. "No dragon is gonna kill you, or your bairns, I promise."

Elspeth related to Saphira what Ian had said. Saphira nodded her head and blinked away the tears.

"That's the spirit," said Elspeth. "We will win." Then came the first dragon roar of the night. Feeding time. Darlath was on his way.

He prepared them for battle. "Stay in here. Doona

go oot Saphira. Stand by the dragon bairns, and you doona get in the middle. Elspeth, beside Saphira, doona interfere, I doona want you fried. Positions."

"Och." Smiled Elspeth. He caught her intense study of his body as he gave his orders, stopping him midsentence. He noticed the intense blush that rose on her cheeks and he smiled as she quickly looked away clearing her throat. For a minute, he felt almost naked again, but before he could think any more about it, a roar blasted outside the entrance.

He pulled his sword, spread his legs, and put the blade above his shoulder. As soon as the huge black head came through the opening Ian struck. The dragon shook his head and the strike didn't even cut his face, but it did enrage him. He roared.

The cave shook, and the large dragon entered. The beast reared back and he struck it again and again. The dragon simply looked bored. He reached out a claw, grabbed him and threw him to the wall where he promptly slid down to the floor. The dragon was getting closer to the babies. Saphira blew fire toward Darlath and he blew back.

"It's getting damn hot in here!" he shouted. Running toward the black dragon, he managed to stab Darlath in the side, but not enough to be serious. Pulling the blade free, the dragon howled and turned toward him. He smiled his predatory smile. "Goddesses, the look in your eyes makes a pissed off Lochness look like an angel. Come and get me you overgrown, deformed, bawless lizard. I bet your Mither kicked you from the nest just because you're an ugly son a bitch. Ha! I bet you spit tar and smelly dead stuff. No wonder the ladies hate you. What's the matter you black bastard!? Sceeered?" he drawled, then grinned.

Darlath stretched and stood taller, flung back his head to blow fire, and Ian shouted. "Elspeth, how the hell do you kill a dragon?"

Elspeth looked at Saphira then back to him. "Up through the stomach where it's soft. Through the heart!"

He flung himself toward the dark one's middle when the dragon let his fire fly. Large blasts of fire, then smoke spewed out, and he stood still, realizing he was in the line of fire, then suddenly he dropped, and everything went black.

Elspeth screamed. "You killed him, you beast, and she started for Ian, then Darlath reared back again. This time for her. But before he could blow fire again, a roar louder than anyone or anything had heard before shattered the moment in the cave, and everyone but Ian looked toward the door.

Within moments a massive white dragon entered blowing fire at Darlath. Even though the white dragon was much larger than Darlath, the black attacked.

"*Ator*?" squeaked Saphira. The fight became intense, roars resounding off the cave walls. It went on and on. She couldn't get to Ian. Tears streaked her face, she wanted to save him. He couldn't be dead. No, she wouldn't believe it.

She'd just found this wondrous man, and she desperately wanted to explore the unexplainable feelings she had for him. She didn't understand it herself, but she felt something she never knew existed, and it overwhelmed her. She wanted him, in all ways, she wanted him. The thought of him dead squeezed her heart and dread flowed through her veins like hot, thick, oil. She almost wanted to die herself. She shook her head and thought about Saphira and the babies.

As she looked back at the black dragon fighting the white, she prayed if the white was good, he'd win. But luck wasn't with them. Darlath gripped his teeth around the white's neck and blood gushed. He pulled the white toward the back of the cave stumbling over Ian. She felt shock when she saw his eyes open and focus on Darlath's stomach above him.

She felt him draw what energy he had left in him as he struck his sword home and pushed up in Darlath's heart. The dragon tumbled sideways dead and the white pulled back and fell on top of the black beast. Ian fell back, and his eyes closed, looking truly dead and beyond help.

She immediately ran to him. She leaned over his charred body looking for any sign of life. None. No breath, no heartbeat. "He's dead," she screamed. "No, No, No!" Then she saw the white dragon was bleeding badly. She pulled herself up and put herself in healer mode. She'd deal with grief later.

She knelt over the dragon's bleeding neck and put her hands above him. She leaned back, and with all she had, she chanted to her Gods. Bright white light surrounded her and immediately streamed from her hands soaking in through his wounds. The sounds of the babies crying out, soothing noises from Saphira, the sound of the waterfall, all died away as she focused her thoughts on the dragon.

She had never concentrated this hard on a healing. She wanted him healed and she wanted to go back to Ian. The strength from her chants gave her more energy than she'd ever felt before. Soon she felt he was healed.

When she opened her eyes, the massive dragon moved slightly, she moved from his neck and he stood to his full height. Elspeth had never seen anything more magnificent. He bowed to her and turned toward Saphira.

At first, she was afraid for Saphira until she saw her face and felt something else, something sweet. *"Ator,"* said Saphira. *"I thought you dead."* Ator walked to Saphira and they entangled their necks, rubbing back and forth. Later, she thought as she ran to Ian. When she knelt beside him she sobbed. She touched his forehead tenderly.

When she moved her hand, the charred skin fell away, and to her surprise healthy pink skin lay underneath. She leaned in to feel for breathing. Shallow, but there. She felt for a pulse, slow and erratic.

"He's *alive!*" She bent her head back and chanted vigorously. White light hit Ian in the chest like a bolt of lightning and before she'd even had a chance to focus, he mumbled then grabbed her arms.

"Elspeth," he whispered lovingly. She opened her tear stained eyes, wiped at her face, and hit him in the shoulder.

"I thought you were dead! I don't know anything about vampires, you scared me to death."

"Vampires canna die. Weel they can, but not from fire. Werewolf bite could kill me, a forged blade made of the blood of fae and vampire could kill me, a wooden stake soaked in holy water can kill me, lightning perhaps, chopping my head off, but nae fire. It would have taken three or four days tae heal, but you? You are amazing. It doesn't mean it didn't hurt like hell, it most certainly did. My whole body burned and I thought…"

"Oh, shut up," she said interrupting him with a smile.

He shuddered. His steal blue eyes heated and he kissed her. She flung her arms around him and hugged him close.

"Wait," he said. He stood up and shook the ashes from his body and walked to the stream of water coming from the ceiling. After washing away all the debris he stood naked before her, his desire apparent. She looked at him, all of him, longingly. He grinned. She saw lust and longing in his gaze and felt her blood heat. He had an overwhelming effect on her, one she knew she couldn't or wouldn't ever deny. Suddenly they were the only two there. They ran to each other and embraced. Her tears came again, and they kissed softly at first, then harder, urgently, fervently.

Then reality hit. Two dragons stood in front of them. Two very amused dragons who were waiting for them to realize they were not alone. Ian cleared his throat and she felt him take control of his desire. He broke away and took Elspeth's hand in his. "Yes?" he asked the dragons, tilting his chin up.

First Ator looked at Elspeth. *"I would have lived, thank you for healing me, but the one who truly saved my life, was he."* She knew what he thought because she had the mark, and she had a pretty good idea what was coming next.

"What? What did the big white bloke…" Ator stood taller and leaned back his head. "Och nae you doona! I willna be fried again. That's the thanks I…"

Without giving Ian any time to finish his comment, Ator opened his mouth immediately letting loose a stream of blue flame, hitting Ian's chest, just above his heart. An exact replica of the magnificent white dragon appeared on his chest, complete with rainbow reflections. Ian grabbed his chest and looked down. "It doesn't hurt!"

"That's what she said." Saphira looked at Elspeth with a dragon smile.

"I understand you!" said Ian.

"You will understand us all now," said Ator. *"There's much to discuss and I didn't have time for interpretation, so I had to act quickly."*

"Thanks for that," mumbled Ian.

"You're welcome. Merlin sent me."

"I thought you dead," said Saphira.

"I know as your caretaker I let you down, but Merlin came to me with some great importance." Ator cleared his throat.

Ator looked first at Saphira. *"I was to care for you Saphira. You were mine and I left."*

"I thought you loved me. We were to be mated at my maturity. I loved you so much Ator. So very much."

Elspeth stood with Ian, clutching his hand as they looked back and forth between the dragons.

"Saphira," continued Ator, *"my love for you has never waned. I will always love you, only you. My thoughts have always been with you."*

"Can dragons love?" Ian leaned over and whispered the question to Elspeth.

The two dragons stared at Ian. Ator spoke. *"Dragons can love more fully and deeply than most humans. They mate for life, and rear their young together, they know happiness and sadness. Some are like Darlath, power hungry, bullies, evil. Like some humans. May I continue?"* He stared at Ian.

"Doona let me stop you. You're doing a good job of…"

"Ian!" the three said in unison. Ian smiled and twisted his fingers over his lips as if he locked them tight.

"As I was saying, Merlin came to me. I had to watch over a family, a very important family. They work hard to keep peace in this world and theirs, a parallel world, their earth called outer earth is magical, here in inner earth more human. So, he moved me to outer earth where a lot of mystical things happen. It was my duty as the leader of dragon world, as king of the dragons, to make sure peace could prevail. I would only go if Merlin promised to keep you safe. He did, so he moved me to The Shadowed Cliff above…"

"Grafyq Fjord," mumbled Ian, finishing Ator's sentence. "The cliff above my castle. The Fjord on our grounds. You were watching my family."

"Let me tell you, your sister Akira is such a handful, is she not? She talks almost as much as you." Ator grinned, a dragon grin. *"And I never saw so much fist fighting between brothers."*

"I only talk a lot when I am in battle. It's a strategy I use tae make my opponents flounder. Strategy, my dear dragon, 'tis all."

Saphira sniffled and a tear dropped. Ator turned toward her quickly. *"Saphira there are stories of what I've done, had to do, but believe me when I say I love you. Merlin says now it's time. We never have to part again. You and your babies, which are now mine as well, will live in the Shadowed Cliff together, forever. Yes, I claim them as mine, if I had been here they would be. But right now, they need our help. Much must be*

53

done. Ian must stop Drakkor, and Elspeth's king may be involved as well as her brother. They need our protection.

"Tomorrow, males from my hoard will be coming here to choose mates. All good dragons. There are so many in my hoard that some wanted to start new here. Merlin knew the situation, but he needed for Ian and Elspeth to save us. As unfortunate as it was for you to endure Darlath, when it came time, they did what they needed to do, to save us. So, that we can save them. The rule of the mark. You know it as well as I. There was no other way. Forgive me."

"The mark," said Ian. "That old bastard goat, why didn't he tell me? Why dinna I ken a dragon lived in *my* cliffs?"

"You were deathly afraid of dragons, Ian," answered Ator.

"What?" giggled Elspeth. "Now I understand the ride."

"Not now Elspeth." Ian stated flatly. "What now?" Ian looked at Ator.

"Right now, I see to my family. I can fly you to where you want to go for a few days. We will meet in three moons again to discuss things." Ator looked lovingly at Saphira.

"Uh, not necessary. I could just mist Elspeth someplace, but I can only do that here on inner earth or outer earth if we were there, but I canna mist through veils. My cottage on the loch in outer earth is where I want to go, where we'll go. I need a portal for that. MERLIN!"

A blue ring appeared and Merlin stepped through. "At your service, Ian. I knew you'd call."

"You rat bastard. You've some damn explainin' tae do."

"Toad, Ian. Don't forget." Merlin laughed. "Ator explained enough to you. Now you want the cottage at the loch. You have three days, deserve three days, but afterward back to business. I've supplied the cottage with food, peat, and wood. Your family doesn't know you're coming, yet." Merlin laughed. "Not until you want them to. I've cloaked it. But you will want them to meet Elspeth. Am I wrong?"

"Shut up Merlin, and let's go, sometimes your ability tae live in the future scares me."

"You two go on ahead I have some explaining to do to the lovely Saphira. Perhaps she will even forgive an old rat bastard like me. Isn't that what you called me Ian?"

"Excuse me, Merlin, you just make me so damn mad withholding things from me."

"Some things have to be for your protection. Besides the future can always change. I usually only see one path, the right one, when there are many paths to the future. You'll understand in…"

"Due time." Ian finished. "Yeah, I ken. Come Elspeth I want tae show you a most beautiful place. My home."

She took his hand and they entered the portal.

Chapter 6

Standing on a soft mound of grass, under the cloudless sky, Elspeth stared at the sparkling loch in front of her. Trees reached their arms out across the water, leaves shining like two shades of bright green satin with the mild winds twisting them, fluttering back and forth in the bright sunlight. The air smelled of crisp clean sunshine and a hint of loch, as a gentle breeze rolled up over the grassy knoll. She'd never seen anything so beautiful.

Beyond was a massive white stone castle on a hill with cliffs off to the right, the sunlight casting gentle shadows across the front from giant oaks cocooning the castle in a blanket of soft imprints, like fingers holding a goblet, softly brushing up and down the sides. The air smelled clean and sweet, of springtime. It was like a beautiful painting. Beside her was a large two-story stone cottage with a portico along the front facing the loch. "Ian, this is your home?"

Still holding her hand, Ian watched her reaction proudly with a smile on his face. "Yes, dearling, and later I'll take you on a tour. Right now, I'd like tae give you a tour of the cottage." He wiggled his eyebrows in a way that made her giggle.

Then she looked down at the torn, bloody, and burnt dress she'd been wearing for days. Even with the bath she had, she felt dirty in her clothes and she was covered in ash that came off Ian. She thoughtfully fumbled her fingers through her tangled hair and looked at him with a grimace. "I…I'm…"

"Bonnie!" whispered Ian. "Come, kenning Merlin he's thought of everything. He's quite magical you ken, and thoughtful at times. I'm sure there's a bath waitin'. Shall we find it, hmm?" Ian smiled and led her through the portico and inside the cottage.

The great room had shafts of light from high windows making a pathway down and evanesce across a long highly polished table and across the massive rock walls.

Large colorful woven tapestries of horses, forests, hunting dogs and gardens, hung freely draped down each wall. The dark wood and a fire in the giant stone fireplace brought the feeling of warm and cozy to an otherwise very large space.

"Is everything here so big? The rooms are big, the cottage big, the loch big, *you're* big!"

Elspeth was a bit nervous and she sensed him pick up on it. "You think this is big wait 'til you see the castle. Come Elspeth, let's find a bath and get cleaned up. You'll feel better once you do." They went up a beautiful winding staircase and at the top a long hall overlooked the first floor.

"This is the room I use when I want some peace just on the right. Eight brothers, weel there were nine, and four sisters," he continued, "and a mon needs his privacy sometimes."

He opened his door and they walked through. The walls had cross swords, a shield which she assumed were his colors of green and black, like the colors of his kilt and tartan, with a dragon on it of all things, a large stone fireplace with a small crackling fire inside, a large 4 poster bed that could sleep four, thick plush furs about the bed, and upon the bed about six beautiful different colored gowns, and a pale blue and a light green night dress both of sheer silk.

Elspeth couldn't help but go touch the beautiful fabrics. Her smile was contagious, and she turned toward where Ian happily stood watching her.

"They, they're the most beautiful gowns I've ever seen. For me?" she squeaked with watery eyes glancing at him. Ian nodded. In all her life, no one ever gave her these kinds of things. She put her hand through one of the silk night dresses and realized she could see her hand perfectly through the material. Her face flushed at what that meant.

"You willna be wearing 'em…much." He grinned.

She looked about, and steam rose from a tub in front of the fireplace. "That's the biggest tub I've ever seen, why it's big enough for…"

"Two people," finished Ian. "Weel three but with me in it and a small woman, two." He looked at her longingly. "You join me, dear Elspeth?" he asked, walking toward her.

She shook her head yes quickly and repeatedly, as she always did when nervous. "Oh, Ian." She closed the space and wrapped her arms around him. "I don't know why, and I can't explain it, but I'd share anything, everything with you. It's as if I've been with you forever, and I've just been waiting for you to come home." She kissed him.

Softly and tenderly at first, then hunger hit them. He crushed his mouth to hers and she felt him go instantly hard.

She saw the look in his eyes, noticed his firm warm body against hers, and felt the length and girth of him grow where he was pressed up tight against her. Her mouth went dry, her blood heated, and she could feel him tremble as he held her close. She lost all sense in her mind when heat traveled throughout her body and landed in her mid-section. These feelings were unlike anything she had ever felt, warm, exciting, inviting, she wanted more.

As his hands brushed aside her hair and he gently kissed her neck, she felt branded in the best of ways. She wanted that brand engulfing her body, her whole body. She shuddered as he blew his warm breath down her neck, and stopped at the dimple in her collar bone, and gently twirled his tongue there. She wasn't sure what to do, so she stood enjoying his ministrations. She couldn't think, didn't want to think, just feel. She could hear his heart pounding. Or was it hers? She didn't know.

He ran his hands up along the back of her neck and through her hair bringing her tighter to his lips. With his other hand, he brushed her waist, reaching to gently knead her butt cheek and pull her against his erection. He was showing her what she was doing to him. He ground himself on her side and moaned.

She felt him breathe deeply and knew he was taking in her scent. He again gently kissed her neck along her throbbing jugular where he licked then nipped. She groaned. She felt his teeth scrape against her neck and she shuddered.

He moved again to her mouth demanding urgent kisses from her, and she could do nothing more than oblige. Her warm breath traded with his, their tongues dancing and swirling, if she didn't stop she may faint, or die, but boy would she go a happy and fulfilled woman. And that is precisely what he made her feel like, a woman. She had never felt so wanted, almost demanded, and it thrilled her to no end.

She took her hands and softly explored his chest and around his shoulders sending a shiver through him. She enjoyed his hard-sculpted muscles, that bulged with every motion. She enjoyed his male scent, it sent her senses reeling. When he nipped her neck, her fingers curled, nails digging and pulling. It made him groan against her neck which sent a shudder through her. He ground his erection, rubbing against her, faster and harder. She knew her impatience drove him crazy as she pulled at his tunic. They tore at each other's clothing not knowing how anything came off and Ian broke their kiss and backed away.

"Let me eyes feast on your beauty, Els. From the first time, I saw you, I thought you an angel. Brought tae me from heaven. I wanted you so bad. If you kenned how hard you made me at just a glance at you at the river, you may have run screamin'. But I'd never seen anythin' as bonnie as you. In all the worlds, or my hundred's years of life, it's you I want, only you."

She let him caress her with his eyes, and he slowly looked at her, his gaze gently traveling up and down her naked body. She blushed under his intent gaze, it was hard for her to stand still in front of him, she felt bashful. She watched as he glanced at her, his silver eyes blazing a burning trail down her stomach and hips. Then his eyes stopped at the bright red v of silky curls.

She blushed even more if that were possible and met his gaze. Eagerness ravaged her, she wanted to touch and kiss him. But she wanted to feast her eyes on all he was, like he had done with her, he was so magnificent. Large broad, sun kissed, olive shoulders, long wavy midnight hair tied back, tight muscular chest, his bulging arms that drew attention at the river, then she looked farther down and blurted, "You're huge! That will never fit!"

Ian laughed. "It'll fit perfectly dearling. We were made for each other. You'll see. Come let's bathe, take it slow."

Elspeth sunk down in the warm water and sighed. Silky heat blanketed her tired muscles. Ian entered behind her and sat her on his lap. She couldn't help but notice the very hardness to him as he repositioned himself. He poured sweet smelling oils in the tub and began to wash her back. "Ummm," she murmured and closed her eyes. He washed her long tresses of red hair, massaging her scalp. He lingered on her breasts dropping the cloth and using his hands to massage her breasts, tweaking her nipples and plucking, causing her to moan.

He slid his hands along her thighs and a groan escaped. He rubbed her curls around, sliding between her moist swollen lips, but never touching her sweet spot. In nature's way, she wiggled for him to touch her. She moaned and leaned back against him.

Arching up her hips she came out of the water. But he didn't stop there he massaged her buttocks and returned to her curls. He pushed her long hair to the side. He licked along the pulse of her throat and she felt his teeth brush against her again.

"Stand for me Els, turn tae me and stand."

She whimpered, moaned, and wanted to do

anything to relieve the tightness in her. She wanted, no needed him, and she wanted him now. She stood facing him.

She let him explore and enjoyed it as he spread her legs apart massaging her thighs, then softly slid his fingers gently up and down from her breasts and over her belly. He brushed at intervals across the hidden bud at the apex of her opening, and then back around her hips, she gasped.

He spread her legs farther and leaned in toward her bright red curls. "What are you doing Ian?" Where he was going was unheard of. "The church…wouldn't…"

"Gods would," he replied with a grin. "Let me taste the most delicious flavor a mon could ever ask for." With that he licked her curls, he smothered his face in her blanket and moaned. She could feel his hands tremble as he softly brushed them over her belly then down to her back side where he gently grabbed her.

He squeezed and kneaded her buttock and pulled her close to his face. His moans vibrated against her skin and she tingled all over. Leaning her head back and giving him more access, she lost all thought of propriety and just felt. And oh, how she loved the feeling.

"Ask me, Els. Ask what you want I weel give it tae you."

"Y…yo…you. Oh, Goddesses Ian. Please make me… just, please I need…you."

She smiled as he laughed, and then he smothered her with his mouth and tortured her with his tongue. He laved around her hardened button, stroking and gently sucking until she felt herself starting to quiver.

Her moans and desperation had her pulling his hair,

tangling her fingers in his long dark locks. He chuckled and grabbed on her nub with his lips, sucking gently until the muscles in her thighs did a dance of their own. She didn't know if her legs would hold her. He must have felt it because he grabbed her thighs and hung on.

The tension in her belly wrapped tight and she thrashed her head back and forth groaning and finally something snapped and soaring to an unimaginable place, she saw stars. Spasms overtook her, she screamed his name, and when she didn't think she could take anymore, she floated back toward earth. When she opened her eyes, and looked at him, he had a grin from ear to ear.

"You love me now, doona you sweetling?"

She laughed. "Let me wash you now, and I'll show you, just how much I do!"

Ian laughed. "Come tae me then, me bonnie lass!" Standing in front of him she leaned over, and started with his hair and scalp, making sure to bend before his face where her swollen breasts brushed against his lips.

He was so hard he was ready to explode. He was trying to give her slow, but all he wanted was to drive deep and have his way. Instead he planted his hands on the edge of the tub, knuckles white, and held on waiting for what would come next. He smiled at the thought of his innocent fire haired beauty.

She leaned over him, brushing her breasts against his face and mouth. It was more than he could take. He had held himself in check this entire time, when she drove him nuts with her smell, touch, tenderness, and moans. He knew then without question she was his.

The words "life mate" ran strongly through his body and mind. The mating ritual for vampire included exchanging blood. His incisors dropped again. What the hell was the matter with him. This was the third time in one day he'd lost control of his incisors. He'd never had the desire to share blood with anyone in such a manner.

He had to have blood every three days or so to remain young, and it was never uncomfortable for anyone, but the sharing of blood, becoming mated was entirely different. Rutting was fun, but it was just that...a good romp. With Elspeth, he wanted more. He wanted to exchange blood, to hear her thoughts daily and for her to hear his, to be connected.

His mind wandered for a second. Perhaps she'd make the change for him, and they'd have a family and live hundreds of years together. He inhaled the scent beside her ear. He'd wait and talk to her later about how the mating ritual tied them for life. He didn't want to scare her. Right now, he wanted to love her, drive her wild, watch her face, and taste her.

The scent of her arousal was driving him insane. She brushed her breasts against his face once again. Ian growled at the sight of the beautiful scene in front of him, and just when he was going to grab her she quickly straightened, turning to him she held up the dripping cloth with a grin on her face.

"Enough woman! A mon can take only so much!" She laughed. He jumped up splashing water over the sides of the tub and grabbed her. Without drying off he strode to the bed, both of them dripping wet, and tossed her atop the furs. He knocked the gowns to the floor and jumped on top of her. He kissed her hard, stroked her in a frenzy, kneaded and plucked her breasts, and couldn't get enough of her.

Ian looked in Elspeth's eyes. He warmed at her

half-lidded expression and seeing the trust there humbled him. He knew she was an innocent, he didn't know if she'd ever been kissed. He wanted to be gentle with her, slow, sensual, and give her first time all the attention it needed. This allowed him to slow down and savor, where a second ago he trembled at the thought of burying deep inside her warm flesh.

She stared into his eyes and he saw a bit of fear, a bit of longing, and most of all love. He could feel it. They both could. It enveloped them both, and inside he felt something warm unfurl deep within his soul.

He felt protective. He wanted to bottle her up in his love and make sure nothing ever harmed her. He felt tenderness melt through him, and he leaned in and gently kissed her, long, tender, tasting her. She gave back and their dance together ensued. He left her mouth and kissed gently down her neck, he trembled like he never had before, uncontrollably, his hot breath garnering a little mew.

He licked down between her breasts then turned and took a nipple in his mouth. He gently sucked and flicked his tongue over the hardened nub, then turning his attention to the other one. He felt himself harden to the point of being painful. He didn't mind, she was worth the wait, he wanted to savor her, and Gods he was certainly doing that.

Never had any other woman affected him so, and he had many over his eight hundred years, no one compared to her, not her beauty, nor her soul. He couldn't believe he'd found her, that she was here, and he was holding her, touching her, tasting her, loving her. He shuddered at this intense realization and buried his face in her silky-smooth stomach and rubbed his lips back and forth savoring the texture of her skin, the intoxicating smell that was her, he felt he was about to burst.

With trembling hands, he moved lower until he once again knelt between her thighs. He looked at her face bent back, flush with lust, her eyes closed, and her lips parted, her breath coming fast. He bent and took her in his mouth and she groaned. He brought her to a fever pitch then stopped and looked at her as he moved atop her. "Look at me Elspeth," he whispered.

In a moment of stillness, he looked in her eyes with his forehead to hers. "It'll only hurt you the first time, and I'll be careful. It canna be helped sweetling. I'm sorry."

"I know Ian, I just want you. Please...I can't wait any longer."

Holding her gaze, he entered her slowly. He trembled with anticipation, trying hard to hang onto some sort of control. When he reached her barrier, she moaned, and he entered swiftly, tearing past it. He stopped buried deep inside, he squeezed his eyes tightly shut.

She was so soft, so tight, her wet heat engulfed him, and he almost spilled his seed. He stilled himself clenching his teeth waiting for the throbbing to quit, hoping to take control of himself before everything ended then and there. My Goddesses where was his control.

She cried out at the instant intrusion and he passionately kissed her. He held her tightly, stilled. He waited until she started to relax, kissing her slowly, patiently. His tongue tasted her lips, and on her sigh, he entered her mouth. A moan escaped her.

Brushing her smooth skin with his hands, he waited for her to go at her own pace. When she began to move her hips, he pulled back and entered smoothly, setting a slow pace.

Gently he entered and withdrew. He knew when she completely forgot the pain as she increased the thrusts joining him halfway up to his downward ones. "More," she said. "Please Ian, I want more."

He laved her nipples, licked up the length of her neck, then kissed her hard.

She groaned and returned his kisses with a fervor of her own. She kneaded his shoulders and stroked his chest. She kissed him. She licked and nipped her breathing punctuated by little mew sounds. She increased her aggressiveness and thrusts and he readily complied.

He looked at her face, her head bent back, eyes tightly shut. "Look at me Els, open your eyes and see what you do tae me. Look at what we are together." She opened her eyes and melted in the depth of his blue gaze. He leaned up, buried deep and pushed deeper.

"Look at us locked as one." She gazed from his face and down his chest to where they were joined. He pulled almost all the way out and entered deeply again, burying himself. On his knees, he picked up her hips, and buried himself once again. She groaned. She looked back in his eyes.

"Please, Ian more." He increased the pace, and she wiggled around him, grinding and thrusting. "Harder, more!" She pleaded with her gaze and started to close her eyes again.

"Nae, doona," he said softly. "Watch and feel us." With eyes half open she gazed again at him. He let go of her hips, leaning closer he massaged her breasts. He licked the tight nibs. He leaned back and grit his teeth to try and hold his control, waiting for her. Sweat beaded his neck and ran down his back.

He knew when she was close, he could feel her muscles tighten, hear her gasps, she arched under him and then she let go screaming his name. She shattered in his arms, quaking, their eyes locked together.

At the first ripple he lost himself. With the roar of her name they came together with an intensity Ian had never experienced before. Gasping for breath he held her tightly and turned them on their side, entangled in each other's arms and legs, remaining inside her still hard.

He brushed the hair back from her flushed face. Eyelids lazy, half-closed, her emerald eyes stared into his as if his soul was caressed by hers. He didn't have any words but didn't need them. He felt something pass between them binding them tightly together.

He smiled, and she snuggled in closer her face warm against his neck. He pulled the fur over them and they fell in a deep sleep as the sun sank over the mountain and left the room draped in ribbons of moon light.

On and off all night they'd awake and make love. Sometimes fast and furious, other times slow and long. When late morning came, and the sunlight filtered over their faces, they awoke to make love again.

When finished, Ian leaned up on his elbows and said, "You're beautiful Elspeth McLellan. Let's eat and you can tell me something aboot yourself. I'd like to ken everything aboot you."

"Weel, I lost my parents at seven winters. I grew

up in a monastery and I'm a healer. I love caring for people, animals, and now dragons. I have a deep respect for all living things, including many flowers and plants that aid in healing. My brother found me a year ago and brought me back to where I first lived." Thinking of Athdar made her instantly sad.

Ian picked up her sudden discomfort. "What is it Els? What has you troubled?"

"Something the king said about my brother. He said he rutted beside him in battle, insinuating that Athdar was as cruel as he, in abusing women. I've never been close to my brother because he's a lot older than I am, but I wonder at his cruelty. Something about Athdar makes me nervous, almost afraid, always has. Isn't that a strange way to feel about one's brother?"

"Weel how aboot, together, we figure things oot?"

That brought a smile to Elspeth's face. "Tell me something about you, Ian."

"Weel, you already ken I am vampire, weel half vampire, the other half fae. I ken you doona understand what it means tae be a vampire or fae as you are from inner earth. I ken there are tales aboot us, and some knowledge of our existence, but not many ken of us. I ken you must have questions that I'd be happy tae answer."

"What does that mean exactly? Do you have special powers like I do as a healer? I've heard of fae and vampire only in stories. I thought they were myths. Do you have to drink human blood to live?"

"Els, let me begin with this," he said, sitting up pulling his hands through his tousled hair. "I'm not from your earth, although I help protect the mortal realm. I'm from here. That's why we had tae use

Merlin's portal." He looked at her confused expression, as she sat up facing him. Och weel, he thought, she may as well know.

"There is a parallel world, two earths, we call our's outer earth. You live in inner earth. In between is the Lulara Veil. The only way to travel through the veils is through a portal. You are all mostly human. Here, where I'm from we are many different species, fae, vampire, werewolf, demons, trolls, among others.

"Basically, people like you but with certain powers and abilities. When inner earth is threatened, there are certain ones of us who travel there tae, weel, help even things oot. We protect the humans. We do it discreetly of course. I drink blood every few days, but not tae live on. I eat food like you, but the blood is what keeps me young, from growing old. I am eight hundred years old. I'm sorry Els, I can stop," he said noticing her grimace.

"No," she said crossing her legs. "What you said just took me by surprise. Go on please, it won't change how I feel about you."

Feeling comforted, he continued. "I doona have tae drink human blood, animal blood works, not as weel, but even if we partake of human blood we doona kill for it, and it is quite nice for the donor who gives it. Our incisors impart a chemical that leaves the donor with a euphoric feeling. They enjoy it, and everyone is happy. I wipe their memory then, so they doona remember.

"I can turn tae mist and transport to anywhere I've been afore, except through the veils, or if I were tae transport you with me, we could go tae anyplace you've been on inner earth, even if I haven't. Our connection allows for me tae do that. I couldn't with just anyone, but I ken you can tell we have a special connection.

"I canna transport between worlds, or through veils, for that we need a portal. The fae part of me can call on the forces of nature, rain, snow, bodies of water, wind, heat, these things, and I've had tae in battle. Sometimes I can call on animals tae come. Mostly small animals. They like me. I can conjure up fireballs as a weapon and throw them. I usually like my sword, Dragon Slayer, though." He grinned. Warmly placing his hand on her shoulder, he gently turned her and brought her on to his lap. He sighed then continued.

"My brothers and me have special powers, unique tae us," he said putting his chin to the top of her head and staring off in space. "I can tell a good mon from bad. Even if they lie tae me, it comes tae me in truth. I hear the truth while others only hear the lies. I'll tell you later about my brother's gifts, because I have tae tell you aboot us.

"If you'd have me I'd like you tae be me wife. Being my wife means the mating ritual. We'd share blood, not much, just enough tae bond. Its verra enjoyable to share and most mated like tae do it every time they make love. Increases the pleasure.

"You'd also be able tae hear my thoughts, and me yours. Not always though, there's like a door we could shut if we have private thoughts we'd like tae keep tae ourselves. Let's say, for example, I was in battle and I dinna want you to ken what was happening, I could shut you out. You can see where that would be a good thing. But if you ever needed me you could reach out to me and I'd always hear you. After we mate and our first bite you'd carry my mark on your neck and me yours. It's like a brand that shows we're mated. We will also carry a type of mated smell that warns other vampires to stay away." He paused, as if waiting for her to stop him. When nothing came he continued.

"We'd have many children and the gift tae you is living a verra, verra long time. We'd live *together* for a verra, verra long time. Would you want that Elspeth? Would you consider being my wife? We'd have tae have a wedding my mither would skin me if we dinna. We can go through our mating ritual at any time. You will go through changes to become like me. It can be painful, but the results you ken. What do you say?"

"Ian, as strange as this is, and for as quickly as my feelings for you have escalated, whatever or whoever you are is what I love. I can't explain why I loved you the second I laid eyes on you, but when I looked in your eyes I felt as if I'd known you all my life."

"It's the way of the McGregors. We wait, sometimes a long time, until we meet our mates, and it only takes the first look tae ken, and I ken when I first saw you back at the river, that I felt the same way aboot you."

"I too feel, I want to be with you and only you. Yes, I will be your wife. Yes, I will make the change, no matter the pain. The pleasure of being with you outweighs any pain I can imagine. Yes, I'd like a family with you, more than anything." With tears in her eyes she kissed him, and they made love again.

With the sun reaching noon, he lay atop Elspeth, watching her closely. "Hungry Els? I'm starving. We have a cold closet off the kitchen, shall we go see what Merlin left us? Then when we've had our fill we can bathe in the loch. It's a little cool but verra nice and invigorating. You will not have tae get dressed. Merlin cloaked us with plenty of space, that is if you doona want tae get dressed that is. I canna wait for mither tae meet you. She will love you, I ken. Come..." and he grabbed her hand anxious to share his joys with her. He'd never wanted to bring a woman here before, but her, she belonged here, and it made him happy.

Chapter 7

King Arthur stood with his two closest knights at arms. He was angry at the news they brought him, and he shouted. "I want you to find Elspeth McLellan now! If you know she's in Mystic kingdom, get her, and bring her to me at once. You say she's wanted for treason, well then, they may have already hung her. Strike that! I'm coming too. In fact, make ready we will go now. I want her taken alive. Now! Before some heads role!"

"Who's, heads are rolling?" asked Finn striding in. "Anyone I can behead for you?"

"No killing withoot me!" said Angus just behind Finn.

"Your majesty," said one of three guards rushing in. "We couldn't stop them!"

"Weel, you ken us Arthur. Canna stand a party withoot being invited." Connor grinned.

"Who we killin?" asked Taryn

King Arthur looked from his guards to the men. "McGregors!" A joyful look of surprise replacing anger. "Did Merlin send you? Oh bullocks, what now?" He motioned for the nervous guards to leave.

Angus looked at Arthur and wondered at his ability to go from angry to happy in the matter of seconds. He had a bad feeling in the pit of his stomach. Arthur had the innate ability to find trouble and he had a sneaking suspicion this trip wasn't going to be any different. Now the question is, can we keep the king alive? They would have to, they always had to. He loved Arthur as they all did. He smiled, suddenly very glad to see him.

"I wanted tae go fishing." Smiled Finn. "And since your loch has the best fishing, we came here. Thought you'd need a break from kingly duties, and besides you have the best ale! I feel like getting in my cups and telling stories and bedding some of the prettiest wenches alive. You canna have them all you ken. Besides they need a break from all their bruisin' from falling at your feet. My ma says it's always nice tae share, you ken!"

Arthur laughed. "You know Guinevere has my heart. She's at her aunts now waiting for her cousin's baby to be born. She'll be gone for days yet. But boys! You can't tell me you're here to fish. I know better than that."

"What were you talking aboot Mystic Kingdom for, king?" Angus asked.

"I'm looking for a woman who is in a lot of trouble. Her name is Elspeth McLellan. Know her? She is to be brought to me at once."

Angus frowned, here it is, he thought. Gads he wants tae head right where Drakkor was spotted, and where Ian is at right this moment. The one place we were supposed tae keep him from going, he wants tae go. Without thinking he blurted. "You canna go, Arthur. I mean we just got here. Canna it wait? Why do you want this lady so bad anyway?"

"None of your business, nor anyone else's!" Anger crept back in Arthur's voice. "I want her found, now! My men and I are leaving today to find her and bring her back."

Taryn looked at Arthur with a furrowed brow. "Listen, Arthur, this woman angers you it's obvious, but we just got here. Canna we rest tonight, drink some ale together, catch up, and if in the mornin' you feel the same, we'll all go together."

Angus gave Taryn an angry look. Taryn raised an eyebrow as if to say, "let me handle it."

Connor said, "Great idea! Let's enjoy ourselves tonight and sleep on it. I doona ken why one little lady has you so upset as tae set yourself off tae go after her though. What did she do?"

Arthur scowled. "As I've said, no one's business. I found out she was at a monastery in England, and after sending men there, they return to tell me she's at Mystic kingdom and wanted for treason. I have my reasons I want her brought directly to me, and I won't be questioned about it again."

Connor held his hands up in surrender. "Fine." He smiled. "If you have someone show us tae some rooms where we can freshen up after our long journey, we can do that, then be at your disposal. We have a lot tae catch up on, and later some wenches tae make us smile."

After cleaning up, Angus and the rest of the McGregors went down to meet with Arthur only to find him gone on an errand. Angus was sure this fiasco was going to turn in to something they were going to have to fight their way out of. It was always this way, whenever Merlin or King Arthur were involved. If it wasn't a party, it was a mess Merlin would put them and one they would have to keep Arthur out of. What did this woman do anyway? He wondered over it as they headed to the great hall for some mead and talk of their own.

Angus glanced at Connor clearing about a half cup of mead, and no servant in sight, waiting for the question he was afraid Connor was about to ask. His blond-haired brother cleared his throat, blue eyes sharp. "Why do you think Arthur wants tae go tae Mystic Mountain? Is it really because of a lady?"

He wiped mead from his short dark beard leaving a scowl on his face, hearing the question he knew Connor was going to ask. "He canna go and we have tae figure a way tae keep him aboot here. Nae, he's not tae go."

"Maybe we can plan a hunting trip. Arthur loves tae hunt. Maybe then he'll just send a couple men tae look for the lady." Finn smiled.

Taryn frowned. "Always a party planner, Finn. I do think it's a lady he's after. I doona think he kens about Drakkor…yet. You ken his scouts are smart. He'll find oot sooner or later. You also ken when he makes up his mind aboot somethin' he doesn't change it. We can try for huntin,' but he willna agree tae it."

"Do you always have tae be so blatantly skeptical? There must be something we can do." He was getting perturbed. "I could break his leg," he mumbled, "he'd have tae stay here then."

Taryn leaned back with raised eyebrows, "Logical, Angus, not skeptical, and you can't break a king's legs. Even you ken that. You ken Arthur as weel as any of us. We may have tae end up goin' with him just tae protect him."

"Starting the party without me, boys?" Arthur's boots *clipped* against the stone floors. He entered removing his riding gloves with two Knights flanking him. "We've been having trouble with insects on two crops and I thought I'd see to it myself."

"Sounds like we need tae stay here," Connor said. "We can help you figure oot the problem, Arthur. Send some men tae look for the woman, and we'll see tae the problems here."

A young dark-haired serving wench came in carrying food and more mead. Two more followed with more food and placed settings in front of the men. Arthur sat down in his intricately carved chair and leaned back at the head of the table, a scowl on his face, anger creases about his eyes.

He looked over at Finn and noticed him staring at the dragon heads curled around the arms of the chair. Finn always did like the finer things life had to offer. He looked at the place through Finn's eyes.

The whole room was bright, tapestries pulled back from long narrow windows to let in an abundance of light. It shown off the gold gilding surrounding the room. Marble statues of God's and Goddesses looked almost alive, placed strategically around the grand hall. Large plants lived beside the statues. Bringing the outside in.

Arthur frowned. "No, we leave first thing in the morning. Before anyone else deals with her, I will. You can stay here and enjoy yourselves, or you can go with me. It's your choice. I have matters settled and we leave at daylight."

The McGregor men glanced at each other. "Looks like we leave at daylight," Grumbled Taryn.

"And no party tonight, Finn!" He scowled at Finn. "We need tae have our heads aboot us. I will not have anyone falling off their horses in the morning," he stated, glaring, brow furrowed and frowning.

"Who died and made you leader, Angus?"

"Angus is right," replied Connor, giving Finn the look of *grow up*. "We have tae be on our best."

"Well," said Arthur. "We'll have a party when we get back. I'll have Jameson plan it. Now tell me what you boys have been up to. Have you heard from Merlin? How's Moira and your sisters? Where's Lauren, Dougal, Conall, Ian, and Cameron? Why didn't they come?"

He and the rest of his brothers laughed and everyone started talking at once. Of course, leaving out everything about Merlin and making excuses for the other brothers. The men played off each other's stories and finally Arthur had all his questions answered. Dusk turned to night and it was time for sleep. He had a bad feeling about going to Mystic Kingdom to look for this woman. Merlin had told him specifically to keep him away. Did Arthur have a direct line to trouble that always pulled him in? He was beginning to think so. It was going to be a long journey and he wasn't looking forward to it. Not at all.

Chapter 8

Lauren groaned, tossing back and forth, sweat drenching him in his dark dream. He was standing in the corner of Merlin's bedroom. Merlin was in bed asleep, before him stood a dark figure holding an open book. The figure chanted, his words indiscernible. Full moon light came through the open window and blanketed Merlin.

Merlin grimaced in his sleep. The man reached out his arm and with his thumb made a cross on Merlin's forehead with what looked like blood. He stood silently pleading for the man to lean over so he could see his face.

The figure leaned back and chanted some more, but he still could not understand the words. The man shut the book and laid it on the bed beside Merlin. He could see the title *Grimoire to the Dark*. He knew it important to remember that.

Then from the cross on Merlin's head, came a thin wavy stream of a greenish transparent light. The man leaned over, opened his mouth, and sucked in the greenish vapor. It took less than a second.

He gasped at the sight. The man quickly looked to where he stood. He was tall, sandy colored hair, eyes of ice, Lauren didn't recognize him. Instantly the man wiped the mark from Merlin's head, grabbed the book, opened a portal and jumped through. He woke up.

He jumped from the bed and woke his brothers shouting. "Merlin, we have tae get tae Merlin." The men jumped up in a frenzy from their cots in the library. "What! Where? Who?" They all shouted.

"Hurry! I'll tell you, after we get Merlin."

They raced through the library and to the small room Merlin stayed in. There was no moonlight, the tapestry covered the window keeping out the chilly spring weather. He settled down. "It hasna happened yet. Good. How long do we have? Merlin wake! We must talk now."

Merlin rubbed his eyes. "Can't an old man get any sleep? Can't this wait until morning?" Throwing his legs over the side of the bed he tugged down the edge of his night shirt. White hair sticking out, he looked at the boys and said. "You know at a decent hour when most men talk."

"Nae, I had a dream. We need tae talk now!"

Merlin grunted. "To the library then. I'll call for drink and we'll see what this is about."

After everyone had a strong brew in front of them, torches lit with plenty of light, sitting at the long library table, they all looked at him, waiting to hear what he had to say.

"I'm telling you Merlin, he sucked a green light oot of you. He had a book he chanted from. It was titled *Grimoire to the Dark.* He put blood on your head in the shape of a cross, sucked in this greenish light that came from your head oot the center of the cross, it scared me, and I made a noise, then he saw me. He wiped your head, grabbed the book, and believe it or not he opened a portal and jumped through."

Merlin's face drastically paled. "Only I can open a

81

portal. I mean there's stationary portals, but to create one, that is something only a wizard can do. Unless a mage did it, but they have a spell they conjure. Did this person say anything before opening the portal?"

"Nae, just waved his arm and it appeared."

"Then it's a wizard, it has to be. But I'm the only wizard left. My brother was the only other wizard I know of, but I killed him long, long ago."

"You never mentioned a brother, Merlin," said Conall.

"He was the essence of evil. Did you say *Grimoire to the Dark?*" Merlin asked as he got to his feet not really needing an answer. "Seamus, my brother, the worst wizard ever born, must have been returned. If this is the case, we are in a lot of trouble. I think I understand now. It's not just the inner earth that Drakkor is after. It is Drakkor and Seamus together, Seamus is after outer earth. If that happens all good would be destroyed and that means *everything* good."

"What was Seamus doing tae you while in bed?"

"I'm not sure, but I know where we can find some answers. You see the book you speak about belonged to my brother. Since his death no one has seen it. No one knows where it is. But…" he said as he walked away from them toward a wall. "…We do have help."

Chanting and holding out his hands toward the rock wall, they watched, as his words got stronger the rocks appeared to dissipate, and then disappear altogether. In a small dark cavern of the rock wall, Merlin inserted his hands and withdrew a large thick book. Old, brown covered leather with simple words on the front, "*Grimoire to the Light.*" Once the book left its hiding place, Merlin repeated the incantation in reverse, the opening closed, and the wall became solid.

He walked over and handed the book to Cameron. "This is my book. Seamus was guardian of the *Grimoire to the Dark,* and I, *Grimoire to the Light.* We are the guardians of these books. Books we were entrusted with but not use. Mine was given to me to take care of by Junius of the Plelins, the Ayriris Light Angels Court. Seamus was given his by Kahn of the Akuphis from the Dark Angel's Court. Together these books can create or destroy worlds.

"After the Armathian War almost destroyed both earths, the factions of light and dark made peace, and split what was once one grimoire, apart making them two, with the intention they never again be used together. We were warned that if they were, we'd face execution, and as the last two living wizards, extinction. These grimoires will not work alone, one feeds on the other. However, there could be a problem." Merlin frowned scratching his bearded chin.

"I know much of what *Grimoire to the Light* contains, not every incantation, or spell, but quite a bit. I would have to assume Seamus knows *Grimoire to the Dark* in the same way. But we would have to have access to both to understand the whole."

Lauren cleared his throat. "Shouldn't these courts be warned?"

"Not yet, we don't know enough, or even what the grimoires have to do with it. I really don't want them coming down on me when I don't know anything for sure yet. See what you can find out in those books, Cameron. Discuss it with Lauren, see if it mentions anything about what you saw. If what you saw is what I think. My brother was ingesting my ether, part of my soul.

"And with it my memories and knowledge, if he succeeds, we're doomed. Through my memories, he could garner important information from this book, but not only that. He's been gone a long time. The knowledge of all he's missed will go to him the instant he ingests my ether. If he's working with Drakkor they have a plan. He won't look like the Seamus I knew and probably goes by a different name.

"Someone had to find the magic, find his body and bones, and do an extensive spell to have him reborn. It calls for blood sacrifice. And not just any blood. The spell requires a newborn baby's body. And it takes a God to be involved, a Dark God. If that is the case, we are looking at trouble with a capital T. If I remember the spell right, at the exact moment of death, blood is poured from the body, the soul of the baby is released, allowing the other spirit to enter, then the God brings the body back to life.

"The baby would then have been raised as his parents' own, with them never knowing it is really Seamus inhabiting their son. Horrible, dark spell. One that should never be used." Merlin frowned.

"I believe that Drakkor is responsible for the spell and is the one who helped bring him back. It takes three to speak the incantation. I don't know who the third person would have been. If they have plans together, I need to find out exactly what they are. We need to get busy. If I appear sick, you'll know it's happened to me. I won't have any memory of it. Tell me again everything you saw Lauren, maybe we can figure the time frame."

"Weel. I noticed it was fairly warm. You had the

tapestries pulled back from the windows. There was a full bright moon letting light through."

"Hmm," mumbled Merlin. "Full moon was two nights past. It will take twenty-eight moons to be full again. Late spring now, in the time until the next full moon, it could be that warm. I would say that is the time we have to stop him. Tell me exactly how he looked, maybe I know him."

After Lauren described him in detail, Merlin said, "Hmm he seems familiar to me. I have a hunch, but I must speak to someone first, then see Ian. Conall you will move inside my room with me. I'll have a bed brought in. If Seamus comes, he'll be cloaked and no one else will see him, but you should be able to see him with your powers of seeing what's not there. If we can't stop him before that, maybe you can.

"Cameron read all you can of the grimoire then discuss it with Lauren. Help me figure this out. Dougal my master mage, if something happens and I can't counteract his magic, I will need you to be ready to do it for me. Know the spells well and get anything you need for them ready. Lauren anything you see in dreams or otherwise, no matter how insignificant, tell me and the others right away.

"The angels are coming to meet with me today. We will tell them what we've talked about. Maybe they will have some ideas. I wish the God of Light and the God of Dark would come to our aid, but as with all Gods they won't interfere with free will. It's just their way. Oh well… It's almost light and I need to go." With a swirl of his arm, Merlin was dressed in his long garments, he threw open a portal, and disappeared.

Chapter 9

After they spent the second day together, enjoying the loch and each other, they spent the night entangled in each other's arms, sleeping deep until morning. Now it was time for Elspeth to meet part of Ian's family. She was chewing on her lip looking at the gowns before her. "I can't decide!" She turned toward Ian who was standing watching her with a smile on his face. "Which should I wear, Ian? They are all so beautiful."

"It would please me if you wore nothin'."

"Ian! Please this is not funny. I want your mother and sisters to like me."

"They'd still like you if you wore nothin'. Might think you a bit touched, but they'd still like you."

"Eweeee! Okay!" She closed her eyes and turned around in a circle, reached down and pulled up a pale, yellow dress. Opening her eyes, she said, "Okay, I'll wear the blue!" She dropped the yellow and picked up a gown with a dark blue velvet bodice and a v that pointed to her waist, light blue silk long sleeves that came to a matching v over her hands, and full skirt of light blue silk with a dark blue underskirt.

"I'll never understand a woman's way of thinkin'." Laughed Ian, then he grew quiet, looking thoughtful. "You get dressed and I'll be right back."

"Where, are you going?"

"Hush now. You'll see. I'll be right back." He

hurried from the room.

When he returned, he stood in the doorway and stared.

"Well don't just stand there, please help me with my hair. It's tangled and messy I can't do anyth…what is in your hands Ian?"

He pulled his hands from behind his back and in them were handfuls of gentian flowers. Little blue flowers to match the dress. "I thought you may like these for your hair. Here I'll help." He pulled the ribbon from her waist and cut off a piece long enough to circle around her head. "Sit and give me your brush."

"How would you know about a lady's hair?" She smiled.

"I have four sisters, remember?" He picked up the brush and brushed her long tresses. He put the band around her head and tucked most of the flowers under the ribbon. Her hair flowed free, shiny, and silky down her back. When he finished he handed her the looking glass.

She held the glass up looking left to right. "You're so thoughtful, Ian. It's perfect! How do I look?" She stood and twirled.

"Perfect and bonnie. My mither will love you! Let's go, shall we?" He reached for her hand and pulled her to her feet. They headed toward the castle.

"Mither!" Ian hollered. They entered through the twelve-foot glossy waxed cedar doors, banded in iron, swinging inward.

She looked up to see a woman who must be Ian's mother and four beautiful young women come running in. "What's the matter, Ian? Is everything…" The woman stopped and stared. She felt the weight of her gaze. "Why Ian, who is this lovely lady?" Ian's mother smiled and floated toward them to take her hand. She blushed and smiled at the beautiful dark-haired woman.

"Elspeth McLellan, lady." And she curtsied.

"Please," said Moira. "Call me Moira, we don't stand on privilege here. We're all friends." Moira looked at Ian. "Weel do you have anything tae say?" All his sisters came up and stood around them.

"Mither." From her he pointed to each sister. "These are my sisters, Brenna, Fiona, Catriona, and Akira. The last two we call Cat and Kira when they are likable." The two younger girls groaned at their nicknames but smiled happily. "This is Elspeth McLellan. She's agreed tae be my wife!" He stood proud, smiling, and put his arm around her waist and pulled her tightly to him. Chaos erupted as they all started talking excitedly.

She turned to watch Moira gaze at her eldest son. With tears in her eyes his mother said. "Ian McGregor, you remind me of your Da. You really love her, I can tell."

Turning toward her, she took both her hands. "Welcome tae the family, I could use another daughter. I think we shall get along fabulously."

"Thank you, Moira. I was anxious to meet you all."

"Och Elspeth, would you do us sisters the honors of making your weddin' dress? We have new material brought tae us from the Orient. We'd love for you tae see and pick some oot! This is the first weddin' in our family. Oooh, it'll be such fun. We can wear our new gowns!"

"Kira." Ian gave Akira the look of a stern reprimand.

"I'd love it, Akira." She smiled. "I've always wanted sisters!" The giggling girls grabbed her and headed to the stairs when a scream came from the kitchen area.

"Lady Moira, come quick!" screamed Bradana. "Sorcha has cut herself badly. She was cuttin' cabbage and the knife slipped…"

She turned quickly. "Let me!" she said running after Bradana.

Moira started to refuse when Ian said. "Let her, Mither she's a healer."

Everyone followed them to the kitchens. Lying on the floor in a pool of blood was a young girl with her arm torn open, blood gushing from a cut. They stilled as she knelt and placed her hands above the wound, leaned back and began chanting. The healing light surrounded her, left her hands, and entered the wound.

She heard them gasp in surprise as the wound began to knit. The only other sound in the room was her chanting. When she finished, she opened her eyes and she saw everyone staring at her, in complete silence.

Then Sorcha mumbled, opened her eyes, and Bradana ran to her daughter. She looked at Elspeth. "Thank you so much, my lady. You saved my daughter." Then she cried and held Sorcha close.

They were walking back to the great hall, the girls all asking questions about her healing ability. She laughed and started to answer, when a portal opened, and Merlin stepped through.

"Good, you're here Ian, Elspeth. You need to come with me now."

Moira stepped up, "What in the world now? Merlin!"

"Moira it's of the essence they come with me. I'll explain later. Please Ian. Now. Elspeth?" She looked at the girls then Moira. Moira tilted her head, "Go ahead we ken how Merlin is. Please come back as soon as you can." Moira smiled then added, "We have a weddin' tae plan."

She smiled, curtsied, and took Ian's hand and they entered the portal after Merlin.

****

"My, she's bonnie!" sighed Fiona.

"Did you see what she can do?" asked Akira.

"Kind of quick for marriage, do you think mither?" asked Catriona.

Moira laughed. "Your father and I kenned the moment we met each other that we were meant tae be together. We loved each other at first sight. Ian's waited hundreds of years tae meet his mate. In a way that's long enough, dinna you think?"

Akira frowned. "What did Merlin want, mither? We dinna get a chance tae show Elspeth the material."

"I doona ken daughter, but she'll be back. Whatever you haven't sewed, save the rest for when she comes back. Go fold it up and make it nice for when she sees it. Kenning all of you it's probably strung oot everywhere."

"Aye," Akira said. "She's right. Let's go." They all agreed and went running up the stairs, in fits of giggles and laughter.

Moira stood thinking about Merlin with a worried look on her face. She looked upward. "Lachlan please bring everyone home safe." She turned to go see how Bradana and Sorcha were doing.

Chapter 10

Elspeth and Ian entered Merlin's large library from the portal. Ian's brothers stopped what they were doing, turned, and stared at Elspeth.

"I wish everyone in my family would quit starin' at my future wife," stated Ian with a frown.

"Where'd you find such a bonnie woman, Ian?" asked Lauren. "And what did you do to her tae convince her tae marry the likes a you?"

Conall smiled big. "Let her spend some time with me and she'll change her mind."

Ian grumbled. "Elspeth, my brothers, Conall," Conall nodded. "Lauren." He did the same. "Dougal, and Cameron. This is Elspeth McLellan...my future *wife!"* He declared ostentatiously.

Merlin cleared his throat, then waited as they all turned to him. "I need to discuss with all of you what I believe to be. Thanks for coming Ian and Elspeth. I have some bad news Elspeth. Please sit you two."

"What are you yappin' aboot Merlin? Exactly what's goin' on?" Ian had a frown, but he led Elspeth to a seat and sat himself.

Merlin didn't enjoy telling them what he knew, but he explained everything he and Ian's brothers had discovered. After bringing Ian and Elspeth up to speed, he turned to Elspeth. "I've talked to the Ayriris Angels of the Plelin angel's court and I've found out what happened after your brother was born. Your brother is not yours, but mine. I'm afraid the only true thing that is left of your brother is his body. His soul is gone. Your brother is actually Seamus and he was brought back to life as a baby. He stole your brother's body."

"But that's not possible, my mother was pregnant, she gave birth to Athdar," she said. He's alive I can feel it. I don't know why, I just do," she said, hysterically not making any sense.

Merlin smiled sadly. "Yes, she was pregnant but Seamus' spirit or essence if you will, replaced your brother's. The child you remember as *your* brother Athdar, has always been Seamus, *my* evil brother."

Gods, Merlin hated doing this to her. She wasn't seeing reason. "Your brother's body was the only thing left after Seamus' spirit entered his body. I'm sorry, but when he took over your brother's body his soul was released. You never actually knew your real brother."

He didn't have the heart to tell her they could have imprisoned her brother's soul, he really didn't know where the poor soul was, and neither did the Ayriris angels, only the One Great God would know. He couldn't bring himself to tell her the torture her brother must have endured for the ritual to be completed.

"I'm sorry, I'm afraid…"

"Doona you even say it, Merlin. I willna have Elspeth think the worst." Ian grabbed her hand and gave it a gentle squeeze. "We'll find oot, you have my word."

"I can't help thinking the worst, Ian. Drakkor seems very bad, and now I also understand why the king laughed when he said Athdar was just like him. But in my heart, I know my brother is still alive somehow. I can feel him. We have to help his soul, Ian.

"But Athdar? I always thought something wasn't right. I don't know him well. I wasn't raised with him, but I never felt comfortable around him." She began to cry again.

Ian immediately put his arm around her and hugged her close. "Doona cry, sweetling, I'm here. I promise you, we will find oot the truth. Damn it Merlin! Won't we!" he said, looking angrily at Merlin.

He cringed, but he wasn't responsible for it, he was just the bearer of bad tidings. Ian and his brothers looked at Elspeth with pity. He felt very sorry for her loss, but not pity. Perhaps she could feel her brother's spirit somewhere. He would find out where his soul went. If he could. At the very least he was damn sure going to try. "We'll figure it out, Elspeth. I'll do my best to find out for you.

"Right now, we have more pressing matters. First, if Seamus, who I'll call Athdar from now on, gets the chance to take my ether it can kill me. Unless he takes just a fraction, which could give him just enough insight about the book. This is probably what he wants. There are two ethers in each of us, light and dark. The dark ether heavy and oily, the light, well light."

"Aye," interrupted Cameron. "From what I've read there is one drug for light ether, another for dark. The two can be mixed and used together tae kill or suck oot the soul, but I think Athdar and Drakkor are the ones responsible and are looking at men who are more evil than good," he said tapping his fingers to the grimoire subconsciously.

"Because, when they use the drug tae remove the light ether, only evil remains. When we are born, we have equal amounts of light and dark, as we grow and take on traits developing who we are, the side we choose grows with it. If a mon lives a good life, his light ether grows, overpowering the dark. The same is true for the dark. What we end up with is either a good mon with a good soul, or a bad mon with a darker soul, or somewhere in between. However, never is either one depleted. People can and do change, so does their balance of ether."

"So. You're saying he's draining good ether from fae and Vampire, tae turn them demon and they keep their powers? How are they changing soldiers into demons?" Ian asked. "Are they draining their ether?"

"Theoretically that is how they are keeping powers of fae and vampire," continued Cameron. "With only evil left they would be strong leaders in an evil army. No lightness tae balance them oot. We think the kings are taken and changed, then they change their malevolent soldiers into evil demons.

"To change the evil soldiers takes only blood, of course they have tae agree tae give up their souls. Not much trouble there. With good soldiers, perhaps an ether drain, depending on light and dark balance. If a mon is almost purely good, a complete ether drain could kill him, as there isn't much evil ether left to sustain him.

"With the fae and vampires same story, but they'd never agree, they would put up a fight against it. Ether leaching, if I'm correct, on them as weel. Although it would be much harder tae do. If Seamus and Drakkor are planning such a huge move as tae take over both worlds, they would need the fae, vampire, and demon soldiers. The fae and vampire willna make an army, but leading demons makes sense," said Cameron. He leaned back in his chair and pulled his light blond hair back off his face.

"The kings are bein' targeted for their soldiers. This covers great distances and many tae turn. Drakkor and Athdar canna do all the changin' themselves it would take a tremendous amount of time, so we believe the turned kings, fae, and vampires are doin' it," explained Cameron.

"How do we stop this madness, Merlin?" asked Ian.

"First," Dougal answered instead. "We stop Athdar from killing Merlin, and from gainin' his knowledge. We have aboot twenty-five days tae prepare. I'm workin' on some magic spells now. Cameron is still readin'. The angels are oot working on answers, Conall has his eyes open looking for anythin' unnatural, and we're waiting on Lauren's dreams and visions."

"What I need from you, Ian," explained Merlin, "is for you to get in Mystic castle and find out what you can. Athdar is there for a reason."

"How am I tae do that? Walk right up. Hi, I'm Ian McGregor and I want you tae tell me every evil thin' you're plannin' on doin'?"

"I have an idea," spoke Elspeth for the first time, in a small voice. "I'm wanted for treason so says King Rulm, even though I caught him assaulting and killing a young woman." She looked around at everyone looking at her. "I didn't commit treason!"

"I know," said Merlin. "Please continue, no one believes you of treason. I assure you." Mumbles of agreement crossed over the table.

"Well, they don't know who Ian is. He could make

up a name and take me to turn me in. They will throw me in the dungeon until a trial is had. It's the law. He should have just killed me in secret. Saying I committed treason was a mistake on his part. Now that that is out, they will bring me in alive. But I fear the real reasons the king wants me alive...I saw his face, it was pure evil, and the look in his eyes told me he wanted me in the way he had used that poor woman."

"That will ne'er happen to you, Elspeth! I willna allow it!" said Ian.

"Ian, if I turn myself in it will give you time to see what you can find. By the time my trial comes, you can call on Merlin and he can get us out through a portal."

"Nae, nae absolutely not! Tae dangerous. We'll find another way!" he said slamming his fist to the table.

"Ian it's risky but a good plan," said Merlin. "We'll have to work out some details, but I think it will work."

"Aye, it's true that Athdar and King Rulm doona ken me, but what if Drakkor is there."

"I think it's a chance we have to take," replied Merlin. "If he is, stay out of his way, but I doubt the three of them are together. There is too much they are doing. I doubt Drakkor will be there."

"It's settled then." Smiled Elspeth. "I need to do this. I need answers. Let's smooth the wrinkles and figure this plan out."

"Did I say I love this woman?" asked Merlin.

"Watch your tongue ole man 'fore I cut it oot!" Ian stood up and slapped his hands on the table. "I doona like your plan a bit! But *if* I find it fairly safe, I'll think aboot it. *Think*, mind you, key word. That's all."

"Well then, let's talk this through and see what we

can come up with," said Merlin.

After a heated discussion, with some various ways to do things, they ended up sticking to Elspeth's plan. "Come," said Merlin. "Ator and Saphira are waiting for you. I need to check on the boys with Arthur. Go on through yourselves and give my best to the new parents. I'll drop you some clothes later along with some food fit for people." He laughed, lifting his arms, flipping his wrists, and opening a portal.

Before they could leave another large portal opened at the end of the library. Ian stepped back from the portal as everyone turned to look at the large circle of rainbow light. From the colorful opening, stepped Kahn of the Akuphis Court, the Dark Angel's court, and Junius of the Plelin Court, the Light Angels court, the Ayriris angels. The room quickly turned silent as they all stared in astonishment.

Merlin's face twisted with concern. He'd seen the other angels earlier and knew that this surprise visit from these two did not bode well. He glanced at the grimoire lying on the table. Shite, they were in trouble now.

Merlin could feel Elspeth tremble beside him. The newcomers were a sight. One dressed in flowing robes of white, rainbow highlights woven in straight white hair that fell to his knees. His eyes, a pure silver that almost matched the white of his hair and robes.

The second his opposite. Black robes trimmed in scarlet, with raven hair falling to his shoulders, his eyes an endless black that shimmered red when he moved.

Clearing his throat, Merlin greeted them. His voice calm despite his surprise. "Welcome, Junius and Kahn, to what do I owe this honor?"

"This is not a social call," answered Kahn.

"We've heard about circumstances concerning the Ocrul and Crimson Keepers. We understand some nefarious magic has been changing them into a new breed, a new type of monster. We were concerned about the grimoires." He glanced at the *Grimoire to the Light* on the table.

"I see the one you are responsible for, is seeing the light of day, and has been removed from its hiding place. What do you have to say about this Merlin? Why are the McGregors in the presence of the book and who is this lady? You are aware that no one is to know of its existence?"

"Please sit with us and I'll explain everything I know."

After being seated, he closely watched the angel's reactions as he told them what he knew. They nodded and groaned, clearly agreeing with Merlin that there was great cause for concern. When finished, Junius spoke up.

"We were afraid something like this was happening, but we needed to hear the details from you. We are taking necessary precautions to aid in stopping this insanity before it gets out of control. I need to briefly speak with Kahn alone. If you would leave us for a moment. I will call for you when we've finished. The hall will be fine for you to wait." Junius waved his hand toward the door dismissing them without a look in their direction.

Merlin closed the door behind him. "I'm sorry, I may have just signed your death warrants. This isn't good." He started pacing and pulling on his long locks of beard.

"Hey," said Dougal, "We are all doing the best we can tae take care if this. You were only trying tae take care of it without involving those Nyaff bampots!"

Merlin stopped his pacing and broke out in a grin. "I wouldn't let them hear you calling them irritating idiots if I were you." He laughed. "You're right, we are doing what we can, and I'll be damned if I let them keep you out of this. We need all of you McGregors and Elspeth." Merlin straightened up, seeming determined.

A booming voice came vibrating out through the hallway wiping the grin from Merlin's face. "You may return!" They became quiet and one by one filed back in.

Motioning for them to be seated, it was Junius who spoke first, standing. "We have decided, Merlin, that your ideas have merit. Under the circumstances, we will allow you to follow through with your plan, provided no one else becomes involved. I will reiterate that no other shall know or come in contact with this grimoire other than yourself, Cameron, or Dougal.

"We understand Dougal's need to understand the magic being used, and the need to be prepared with counteracting measures to thwart any kind of unforeseen dark magic. Cameron's precise memory of what he reads will come in handy and saves time from anyone else having to look it up. He may be called on for a quick spell against an action no one thought of before. All is as it should be, however there will be a change. Kahn?"

"Yes," Replied Kahn standing. "You will move everything here at Arvendon Hold to Pendragon Citadel in the Wesladus Veil immediately. Merlin, you will take Ian and Elspeth there when we are through. The place will have to accept both of you in order for this to work."

Merlin stood. "But, it is a place of luxury, for those Ayriris light angels who need peace and tranquility. It is not a place to bring the Myraid Army to train or get ready for war. Why not somewhere in between the inner and outer earth in the Lulara Veil?"

Junius sighed. "First, because we have moved from that location. It was time for a change. Secondly, no one would think to look for you there and most don't know of its existence, and it is heavily protected. Thirdly, it's large enough for you to headquarter your new Myraid Army. It has plenty of room for training, comfortable for everyone, and the views and oceans are very therapeutic. The Ocruls, the Crimson Keepers, the Crixiors, McGregors, you Merlin, and Elspeth, all of you working together on this very dangerous undertaking need such a place.

"Most fae, vampires, and good demons have trouble simply being around each other let alone working together. It is the perfect setting to encourage everyone to get along. There are long houses laid out in several rows, enough to house all the Myraid Army comfortably.

"The castle will accommodate the rest of you and the library is large enough to house all your books, Merlin. There's a large lab for magic, and a greenhouse with herbs for many spells. It's a dream for any mage, even for the wizard himself. You will find it meets every need. Of course, when things are at rest the McGregors may return home often, and I'm sure you won't all be going at once. It will work. You *will* make it work."

Merlin brushed his hand down over his face in contemplation. "It's really more than I could ever ask for. Thank you." He bowed his head.

Ian appeared to be overwhelmed. "How is everathin' tae be moved?"

Merlin smiled with a wave of his arm around the room. "Magic my dear boy. I can have everything moved and put in its place within a day."

"So be it," replied Kahn. "Ian, Merlin, and Elspeth will go now. Moving done on the morrow. Have everyone settled in the day after that. Then Ian and Elspeth will return to their plan of getting inside the castle. They may talk over their plans with the dragons today after you visit Wesladus and set up some help from them should they need it.

"The dragons will be a good addition to the Myraid Army. Ian, see to it that Ator assembles a group of his smartest and strongest. They will also need to move to the Wesladus Veil in the Veater cliffs above Pendragon Citadel.

"We have a warded stationary portal set up to allow travel between the two places. You will use one of the already stationary portals from outer earth to inner earth. The less we do, the less there is for our enemies to figure out. The rest of you continue what you are doing. I think that is all. Are there any questions?"

As the people around the table shook their heads, Junius said, "then this meeting is at a close. I will say this. This new group, the Myraid Army, and all of you will be watched by us closely. At any given time, we feel the need to shut you down we will. Call it a trial period if you will. There will be no room for mistakes. Good luck and may the Gods be with you," and with that Junius and Kahn walked to the back of the library, opened a portal, and walked through leaving everyone silent, alone with their own thoughts.

Chapter 11

Ian and Elspeth followed Merlin through the portal into Wesladus, the outer veil. As they stepped through, Ian glanced around with astonishment. The clouds hung heavy and bright, gulls swung out over a glistening ocean screeching as they dove to the crystal waters. He took a step in the whitest of sands, everything so crisp and bright it almost blinded him. A warm breeze engulfed him and the sweet smell of ocean water soothed his nerves.

An instant peace washed over him and he noticed by the look on Merlin's and Elspeth's faces they were feeling the same. He looked up and down the beach. There were cliff areas and gently rolling hills that led down to the ocean. Forests of trees, open valleys, and nothing but wild nature surrounded them. He frowned, there in lie a problem. "Are you sure we are supposed tae be here, Merlin?"

"This is the portal Kahn showed me. It is supposed to bring us directly to the castle and the long halls. I don't see any of that, let alone training yards and all the other things you'd think was supposed to be here. Perhaps we should walk the beach and see if we are missing something."

He looked around. "I think we should go up. Maybe if we go to the top, toward the cliffs, we could see the castle."

A shadow suddenly passed over them, blocking out the sun. They all stopped to look up. He saw the most beautiful golden eagle soaring overhead. It radiated light, and he couldn't tell if it was coming from the bird or the reflection of the sun. The place felt magical.

As they watched, it circled, then landed on the beach next to them. It began to change shape. It grew to the most beautiful woman Ian had ever seen. She stood before them in golden robes and her hair as bright as the sun.

"You may think me a woman Ian, but I am an angel. I am the angel to the One Great God. I am the one the Ayriris Angels of the Plelin Courts answer to. I alone stand beside the One Great God. I am here to welcome you to the castle, to give you a tour, and to tell you that this place holds many secrets. There are some things you will learn in due time, when the place wants you to know. You and your army will be safe here."

"But I see no castle. There is nothing but wilderness."

The angel laughed. "That is why I am here. No one sees what is truly here without first being welcomed and accepted. Some things aren't as they seem," she said stepping up to Ian. His first impulse was to step back, but he remained still.

She raised her hands to the heavens and in a clear beautiful voice, sang words Ian had never heard before. Then she placed her golden hands upon his head and sang out some more. As she did, the place around them began to change.

A huge, sprawling, glowing castle rose above them on the top of the cliff. It started as a purple cloud that dissipated and before their eyes became a white marble castle with arches and meandering additions. Gardens appeared and dotted the hillsides toward the cliffs. Behind the castle were the long houses that Kahn had described. He looked at Merlin and Elspeth and knew they were seeing the same.

"How can this be?" asked Ian. "What's there, wasn't."

"There are layers to everything," answered the angel. "It is why this place is so well protected. You, Merlin, and Elspeth have been accepted. Your purpose here true and good. Your army shall be accepted and they will all see what is truly here. This place will be good for your men. For fears here are abated, a sense of wellbeing will surround you. It will take time for full transformation.

"I don't envy your beginnings with your men, but you will soon see changes taking place. The castle holds secrets, when you need to know those secrets they will be revealed. Who you choose to let in will be accepted, choose carefully, Ian McGregor. These lands are now yours to guard. You protect your men; the castle will protect you. Now I shall show you around."

As they walked through the gardens, the angel led them up to the main portico that was the main entrance to the castle, Ian felt a sense of peace fall upon him and hoped the others felt it as well. It was like entering another world.

Elspeth let out a sigh as if she'd just tasted the nectar of the Gods. They entered a very long portico with many open archways. Between each archway stood life size marble statues of different gods and goddesses. On each side of the largest arch the statues reached twelve feet tall. A god on one side and a goddess on the other. The archway itself spanned twelve feet and Ian looked to see how it was built that it could hold such heaviness. The marble in the walls fit so tight he could barely make out the cracks between the slabs. "This place had to have been built by gods," he exclaimed, speaking his thoughts out loud.

The angel again laughed. "This place was designed by the oldest and wisest masons that ever lived. With them and the magic of the universe this place was born."

"I feel a peace here that is otherworldly," said Elspeth in awe.

He turned to look around once more. "Yes, me as weel. It's as though my troubles are melting away. I'm afraid if it is that way for everyone, my men willna want tae fight and training will falter. Without the needed focus and motivation, they could get themselves killed stepping back into the worlds in which we live."

"Oh, goodness no," said the angel. "This place has the knowledge of all things, and that includes each of you individually. Call it a work in progress of the fight between good and evil. It's about balance. Knowing when to fight, and when not. Call it having more clarity. They will do exactly as they should do, they will practice with more clarity, they shall fight better than ever.

"This place doesn't change who you are, it offers you peace when you need it, lessons when you need them, and sometimes it doesn't give anything at all. However, you will see in time as your men come to understand certain truths about things, they too will change. They will become good soldiers here."

They walked the grounds, visited the training yard,

and she explained about all the buildings and places. Ian kept thinking about the safety, and finally asked. "Aboot the protection," he questioned. "I understand this place is magical, but anythin' can be destroyed, there's always a way in."

Once again, the angel laughed. "The magic of the universe is great; all knowledge lies within it. The greatest of wizards from near and far called upon magic in the building of this place. Some as great as Merlin here. It knows the heart and soul of each who travel here. It has its ways of protecting against evil. Trust me."

"You mean there are wizards other than myself?" asked Merlin. "I thought I was the only one left."

"My dear Merlin, you have been an excellent wizard to a very, very small portion of one universe. There are universes within universes, and universes outside of yours. There are more universes than you can count, in fact they are endless."

"Endless?" mumbled Merlin deep in thought. "I knew I couldn't be the only one. Why wasn't I asked to join in on the building of the castle?"

"The wizards were your father's father's fathers. Many came together for the making of you my dearest Merlin. I shan't explain things that I have no authority over, but you come from the best of the best of wizards. This place was built before you were even a thought. Was the answer sufficient? If so, we must be getting along, as Ian and Elspeth need yet meet with the dragons."

"Do you ken everything?" asked Ian. "And the name Pendragon. King Arthur's name. Are the two related?"

The angel's laughter was like a bubbling brook or the most melodic melody. He could listen forever.

"In answer to your first question. I know a great deal," said the angel. "But only the One Great God knows all. To the second, King Arthur's forefather took the name Pendragon from this very place. It saved his life once, he was so enthralled he took on the name in its honor. Come, I'll show you the rest of the castle, now that you've visited everything else outside and have familiarized yourself with everything there, we will finish here on the inside, so you can be on your way."

When they walked back up to the portico where they first started, they went through the doors entering the great room, Ian thought he'd have to catch Elspeth from fainting, as it was, he steadied her. It was enormous, with huge tall windows looking out over the ocean adorning one wall, elegant intricately woven tapestries pulled to the sides. There was glass in the windows, Ian had seen glass before and it was rare, but never anything like this. Sunlight streaming through cut edges made tiny rainbows dance in the sunlight.

He stood and leaned against one of the six columns holding the massive great room up and stared, some of the windows were pushed open and he could smell the sea. There were rows of highly polished long tables of a dark wood he'd never seen before. The fireplace was so big you could fit twelve people standing upright with head space to spare.

To the left was a large archway that opened in to a luxurious sitting room with a smaller fireplace giving the room a sense of hominess and comfort along with several elegant, yet comfortable chairs covered in bright materials. Ian saw the smile on Elspeth's face and knew she was deeply impressed.

He felt she would indeed love it here. He would too, if not for the battles he knew were sure to come with having such great comforts.

They traveled through a great many rooms of the castle, in each Elspeth oohed and awed, but when they got to the master suits where their bedroom was, she gasped out loud. It was glorious. In one corner, flanked by windows on each side, sat a large rectangle tub made of marble. It held steaming aqua water.

"Is someone going to take a bath," asked Elspeth?

The angel smiled at her question. "High in the cliffs just behind the castle rests a hot mineral lake, from there trenches bring the water to the castle, it moves through the walls and in each of the bed chambers there is such a tub. The water stays at a wonderful warmth all the time. It flows in and out continuously from small holes at the bottom. The hot mineral spring lake is constantly fed so the water flows freely without worry of using too much. There are such things as these tubs in the kitchens as well for cleaning, only smaller and higher for easier use."

"This is amazing," said Elspeth as she rubbed her hand down the coat of arms standing beside the fireplace.

"This is your room. Off to the side is a nice sized solarium through those double doors, if you would care to look."

Elspeth opened one of the doors and gasped. Ian saw that there was one long bench built in the bottom of each of the window frames, seven windows in all, and around in the circle were four, very comfortable looking chairs. The windows started at thigh-level and rose upward to the ceiling. Someone could curl up against the window on the comfortable looking cushions or sit with comfort there enjoying the view of the ocean. The wall that held the doorway also had two small marble fireplaces, one on each side of the double doors. Ian thought it would give the feeling of sitting high in the clouds. The view itself was spectacular.

"I have never seen, let alone been in a bedroom that had its own sitting room before," said Elspeth. "This room is the most beautiful room I have ever seen. I am sure to love this room most of all," she said in awe.

"There are more bed chambers if you care to see. Or you can look as you move in, you've seen the important areas. I'm sure it will take days to familiarize yourself with everything. The large staff has the day off, so I could show you around, when you return, the entire staff will be on hand, along with the stable men and all others."

"This is quite fine…um. We never got your name. What is it?" asked Ian.

"Oh goodness," said the angel, "how inappropriate of me. Ariel. My name is Ariel."

"Well, Ariel you have been quite generous with your time, and we are largely impressed. Thank you for showing us around. I think we will take our leave now, and finish here as we move in."

"As you wish, I will see you to your portal. Good luck, Ian McGregor. To you and Merlin as well," she said to Elspeth as they turned and walked out.

Chapter 12

.

"*Squawk, squawk.*" Sorrilth and Kalon strained their colorful necks upward toward the meat Saphira held out.

"Cute lil lizards, aren't they?" asked Ian scratching the green one's head.

"*That's Kalon, Ian, and he's a dragon, not a lizard,*" Ator corrected. Turning he looked at Elspeth and Ian. "*So, what you are telling me is we are moving to the Wesladus Veil and you want me to assemble my dragons to move as well?*"

"Yes, we need all of you in this fight against these new monsters. Damn bunch of *Kearal* if you ask me. I'm goin' tae have a hard-enough time gettin' Ocrul, Crimson Keepers, and Crixior tae work together, let alone fightin' against these *Kearal* bastards. Pick your best dragons Ator, the more the better, but nae any lackeys."

"*My dragons have just chosen new mates. They will move with them. I will not leave Saphira behind again.*" He rubbed his neck down Saphira's in affection. "*I can persuade some from your cliffs. There are some that have stayed behind to protect the females and your family.*"

"Nae, leave them. They are needed there. The ones here will do. How many do you think you have?"

"*Fifty to fifty-five. They are my strongest and make*

up 100 in strength and cunning. I will assemble them today and inform them of the move. You can go with me Ian. Saphira I will leave you now, will you be okay while I'm gone?"

"Please Ator, go." She snorted a little laugh. *"You are driving me crazy. You have left my side only when hunting. We have more meat and berries than we need. Please, go and help Ian. I will visit with Elspeth. It will give us both a break."* She rubbed up and down his neck and he wrapped his neck around hers.

"That must be a dragon hug," he whispered to Elspeth.

Ator turned. *"It's a might better than what you were thinking about the day you were fried."*

Elspeth laughed. His face turned red. Elspeth laughed harder. As did the dragons.

"Uhhh…"

"Cat got your tongue?"

"Hush Els…" he frowned. Then Ian grabbed her around the waist and hugged her close. "I'll be back soon," he whispered.

"Well I'm off," said Ator as he strode toward the cave entrance. *"Come, Ian."*

He hesitated, not sure if he wanted to take another dragon ride. If I fall it will only be broken bones, he thought. I'll heal. Bullocks, he followed Ator to the opening. Ator extended his massive wing for Ian to climb on.

"You're much bigger than Saphira. Will I fit up there? Because, if not, I can wait here."

Ator snorted. *"Get used to it. I'm sure it won't be the only time you will need to ride."*

Ian climbed aboard and Ator walked to the ledge

just left from behind the waterfall. He spread his wings and dove from the cliff. Ian screamed. "You did that aperpouse, you large hunk a meat!"

Ator snorted and spread out his wings to a great span, and began to raise and lower them, the wind around Ian growing with each long stroke through the air. He rose toward the sky and out over the valley. In a large clearing, he landed smoothly. After letting Ian down, Ator raised his head and roared, then roared again.

As he watched, dragons of every color came flying from the face of the cliffs. One by one they landed in front of Ator. The sight of so many large and glorious dragons in one place, left him feeling awestruck.

Ator stood taller and rose above them all, clearly the largest dragon there. Although Ator didn't speak out loud his voice boomed non-the-less.

"I know I have asked you all to move here with me and you followed. I am here to ask yet more from you. Creatures, new creatures are being created every day. The Kearal, as Ian has called them, are mighty, and pure evil. Now both the outer and inner earth and every creature that inhabits it is in danger.

"We have watched over Ian and his family for years for a reason. He stands with me today and I stand here only because he saved my life."

He heard many voices in his head as the dragons all mumbled in shock. He stayed silent and waited on Ator to continue.

"Yes, he is marked. It's been thousands of years since we've had a marked one. There are two. Ian's mate saved mine, Saphira from Darlath who was well known to you. We will all protect Ian and his. The

113

pressing matters we face now are the new creatures that are upon us.

"We have been asked by the Plelin, Akuphis, and by Merlin himself for an army of dragons to fight and live with a newly formed group called the Myraid Army. This army will be led by Ian and his brothers. It's not only they who need us, under these drastic circumstances and for our own wellbeing, we need them. Together we will defeat this new threat."

A green shimmery dragon moved to the front. *"Where are we moving to?"*

"Good question, Falkor. You have always been my best. Step forward." Falkor moved out front. *"We are going to the Wesladus Veil and moving inside the Veater Cliffs above Pendragon castle."*

Falkor stood still for a moment. *"Isn't Wesladus the outer Veil, outside inner and outer earth?"*

"Yes, it's the safest place for us to train and prepare for battle. You may bring your mates. Who will go with me? For all who wish to stay may do so but remember we are all in danger. Those who do not wish to go may now leave."

He and Ator stood quietly. No one left. *"Good,"* said Ator." *Falkor stand beside me."* Ator waited until Falkor was beside him before continuing. *"Falkor is my chosen. You will take orders from him as you would me. If by chance I die, he will lead, until such time as my son is old enough to take over. Any questions?"*

"When do we leave?" asked a red dragon.

"We leave tomorrow, Kemoth. Spend the rest of the day with your mates and prepare for tomorrow. Thank you all for your support and for being my long-time friends. You may go."

In a flurry of color, the dragons lifted toward the sky. Wind from their wings blew hair across his face. Pushing his hands back through his hair he turned to Ator. "What majestic creatures!"

"Aren't they though." Ator's chest puffed up and he turned. *"Ready?"*

Ator leaned down and he climbed aboard, no longer afraid of dragons, or flying. He felt good. He smiled thinking about Elspeth, and what may or may not lay ahead for them, hoping for quick results so he could settle happily with her.

Chapter 13

Arthur's group entered Grimwood forest. Angus listened intently for any noise that seemed out of place. He was rather uneasy, and since he was in charge of this expedition, it lay on his shoulders to see to King Arthur's safety. He had always been the one to back up Ian, even when Eogahan was alive. Eoghan was a good man, but not the fighter or leader that he and Ian turned out to be. If ever there was a question, Ian sought out Angus for help instead of his twin.

So, it was an unsaid truth, that if anything were to happen to Ian, Angus would take his place. Always to be in charge when Ian wasn't there, he once again listened for any trouble. It was a rather dark lush forest with small rays of light filtering through. It was still cold and small thinning patches of snow gave way to last year's coat of leaves. Where the sun hit, frost glittered.

The horses pranced and crunched through snow and twigs, snorting cloudy mists. They were tired and so were the men. Here they would camp. Angus rode up beside Arthur. "We've made good time Arthur, but we still have another day's journey tae Mystic Mountain. Do you still wish tae continue on?" Angus was hoping for some answers, but so far Arthur was tight lipped. "Arthur how long have we been friends? Why are you lookin' for this lady? Is she the only reason you're makin' this trip?"

"Angus, we've been friends for as long as I can remember. It's extremely important that I find this woman. Please as a friend, don't ask me why. I won't tell you or anyone else. Just trust me that it is imperative that I do. I will just say that I know she is in a lot of trouble."

"All right Arthur, you ken best, and we will help you the best we can. You ken that."

With that Angus rode ahead to his brothers. "Connor, will you scout for a place to camp. With luck, we can camp early and maybe hunt a worogild for dinner. We have some rations, but something hot sounds good for the cold bones. It will lift the spirits of the men."

"Sure, I'll split off now. Finn! With me! We're tae find us a good place tae camp. You look east, I'll go west."

****

Connor kicked the sides of his horse and took off. It wasn't long and he came to a small clearing with a creek running through it. He jumped off his stallion and tied the reins to a tree. He went to the creek and bent down, cupping his hands, he splashed the cold water over his face then drank deep.

Glancing up he searched the edge of the forest to make sure it was safe. While contemplating the campsite, he was tapped on the shoulder. Without thinking he pulled his sword out as he jumped to his feet. He almost took the man's head off, but stopped just in time. "Merlin, you lavvy heid! I almost carved a smile in your neck! Doona you ever do that again! I could've killed you! I dinna see your portal or hear you.

117

What are you doin' here?"

"Checking on you boys and Arthur. Why are you here? You are close to Mystic Kingdom. What are you and your brothers thinking letting him come here? Where's Angus?"

"Weel we have a problem, and you ken how stubborn Arthur can be. He's got a stick up his arse over some lady he's really angry at, and he willna tell us why. We've tried tae talk him out of lookin' for this Elspeth McLellan who's wanted for treason, but he insists on takin' the law in his own hands. So, we figure we'll help catch her and get back to his castle as quickly as possible. At least he can concentrate on her punishment and stay outta trouble focused on that."

Merlin stroked his beard the entire time Connor was talking. "No, Connor, now there's a problem. You see Elspeth McLellan is innocent. She is also a healer who happened to catch King Rulm assaulting and killing a young lady. He wants her dead because of it. We need her. She's an integral part of our forces against this evil we face. She's the only healer we have. She is also going to be the wife of your brother Ian."

"*What!* What did you just say?" He ran his hands back through his blond hair, then down over his face. "Merlin, being a traitor isn't the only reason King Arthur wants her, maybe not even the main one. He's verra preoccupied with whatever she's done tae anger him, and he's nae tellin' anyone what that is. He's adamant aboot getting her. We tried keeping him at the palace, but he is not bein' swayed. Tell me Merlin, what the hell is goin' on?"

With a furrowed brow and frown Merlin filled him in on what had happened. When he finished, he sat on a log staring at the creek. Connor sat down beside him. For a moment, they were silent, and the bubbling creek was the only sound.

After a bit, he broke out laughing. Merlin turned to him with a scowl. "What the hell is so damn funny?"

Between snorts and trying to catch his breath he got out. "Ian…" hahaha, Ian and a friggin' dragon?" With more uncontrollable laughter he doubled over. "Wait 'til the rest of the boys hear the story."

Merlin grinned. "Now stop. We have more important things to consider, so you better pull it together. Seriously Connor. You *must* keep Arthur away from Mystic Kingdom for at least a few days. Ian and Elspeth are going to get inside the castle to find out what they can about Drakkor. Ian needs time to find out as much as he can. Somehow, we have to keep Arthur from Elspeth. They must stay separated. Let's go see Arthur and I'll talk to him."

****

Angus was talking with Arthur when Connor returned with Merlin in tow. Arthur was frustrated and it showed clearly on his face. When he saw Merlin, his expression changed to joy. "Merlin so good to see you. You, old goat! To what do we owe the pleasure?"

"I've come for a visit."

Arthur laughed. "Checking up on me is more like it. If you're here trouble follows. So, let's make camp and you can tell me what that trouble is. Fair?"

"Toads," Merlin mumbled, frowning. "Between you and Ian I'm going to end up turning you both in to toads. Old goat my ass."

"That's old too, old man."

Merlin broke out in laughter. Arthur jumped down

from his horse and hugged him. "Welcome, Merlin. I haven't feasted my eyes on you in ages, and you haven't changed a bit. Looks like life's been good to you. How fair you?"

"Good, good. Connor found a good place to lay camp. Why don't we do that and we can talk. Sounds li…" Suddenly a ball of fire flew past Merlin's ear and stopped him dead in the middle of his sentence. "Damn! Kearals! The new and improved demons! Angus, you're the one in charge! I've got Arthur."

Suddenly they were surrounded. Kearals stood with hands full of fire balls. One stepped forward. "We want the king and his men and they'll live. Fight and you all die."

He looked at Merlin. Merlin tilted his head. Angus understood and gave the McGregor war cry and hoped Merlin could keep Arthur safe. No longer noticing where Merlin was going with Arthur, Angus jumped in the fray swinging his sword.

His brothers followed giving their own war cry and Arthur's soldiers quickly joined in the battle. The horses scattered in fear. With fae power, he threw up his arms and called upon the rain. Icy sheets pounded down around them, making seeing almost non-existent. The Kearals balls of fire fizzled out before they hit. He stopped the rain, then the brothers charged the Kearals. There was a group of three and Finn brought forth lightning upon them. They burst to flame and then turned to dust.

Connor yelled, "Angus behind you!"

Angus sliced off one Kearals head, pivoted and sliced off the two behind him without breaking stride. One of the Kearals called on the earth and the ground beneath rumbled. Dust spewed in geysers making it hard to see. Taryn brought forth gale winds blowing dust and dirt away. All the while the McGregors fought on.

Arthur's soldiers did their best, but Arthur had brought only a small convoy. They were falling fast.

Angus, Connor, Taryn, and Finn were eating through the Kearals quickly. Suddenly there were only three Keral left standing. Seeing that they were alone without support the Keral showed their fear by fleeing.

He looked around for Arthur and Merlin and did not see them. He was not surprised. Arthur's twelve soldiers were dead. He did not know how many Kearal there were, because dust piles where blown or washed away. He knew some escaped. Not good. They stood in silence. Everyone was cut up and bleeding from battle, but their wounds were already healing.

He took a deep breath and then spoke. "They were our brothers. The Ocrul, Crimson Keepers…fae and vampire. This madness has to be stopped!" He turned and looked at his brothers breathing heavily, bloodied, their swords tilted toward the ground, slumped shoulders. They all felt it, their brethren, dead. Arthur's soldiers all dead. Angus looked up. "*Merlin!*" A portal opened and out stepped Merlin.

With a glance around, Merlin said, "Come. We're going to Pendragon, Arthur's there."

He followed his brothers through the portal.

Chapter 14

The sky was clear blue. The giant Veater Cliffs were busy with dragons flying in and out, brilliant shimmering colors flashing against the bright sun. The ocean roared against the rocky shores. Warm winds gusting. The day was perfect, the scenery perfect, down in the Wesladus Veil, on Pendragon grounds, not so perfect.

Ian and his brothers, Connor, Finn, Taryn, and Angus were doing their best to squelch arguments between the Ocrul, Crimson Keepers, and Crixior. Finally, Merlin's voice booms across the land and echoes off the cliffs. "Enough! Whatever arguments you have against each other stops now!

"There is a much bigger problem we face than your attitudes against each other. If you do not work together all lives are lost. Let me be clear! You will listen to Ian and his brothers, you will train and work together as one. You will act as men, and as soldiers. You were each chosen as the strongest, smartest, and having the highest morals of your species.

"Show us we weren't wrong. This posturing will stop now. We will fight this war and win. Now I am going to introduce you to your leader. This is Ian McGregor." Merlin held up his arm. "Ian, you may take over. He walked up to the towering podium.

"Thank you, Merlin." He stepped up on the high

platform overlooking the combined group of fae, vampire, and demons. "We will split into groups. In each of these groups, twelve people, four of each species. Each group of twelve will train together, work together, remain together throughout the time as we are a collective army in the fight against evil. You will be known from this day forth as *The Myriad Army*. Remember this title, make it proud, and fight for what is right!"

He looked over those gathered on the field. "We are here to save our brothers, and that is what we will do. Fae and vampire are bein' changed into demons against their will. Human soldiers are bein' changed by the multitudes. Some agreein' and some not. You will welcome the Crixiors as they ken demons and have their powers. They are willin' tae fight against their own in the name of justice and good.

"Thank them, they aren't your enemy. Each group will have a name, decided on by its members. No arguments, just do it, and welcome each other to this common cause. My brothers will train you.

"McGregor's up here." His brothers pushed through the crowd of mumbling soldiers. "I will introduce your commanders who will be training you." He introduced each of his brothers by name.

"They will be your commanders, and you will follow their orders without question. If there are no questions, pick your group." There was a lot of talking and men slowly made the collective groups.

"My brothers will return now and pick their group of twelve and you will introduce yourselves to them. Then pick a name for your group and see me for registration in Pendragon hall. That will be all." Ian walked off the platform and left the noise behind to enter the massive marble castle.

* * * *

Arthur and Merlin sat in the solarium of Pendragon Castle talking. Merlin explained everything to him, including the truth about Elspeth McLellan. When finished, he asked Arthur. "What is it you want of Elspeth McLellan, Arthur? And you *will* tell me."

"I will tell you, but you are the only one to know. I mean it Merlin, not a word to anyone."

"First let me know what it is, then I will say if it is meant to be kept secret."

"Fine," said Arthur. He told his story to Merlin and finished with, "see why I don't wish anyone to know?"

Merlin sat stroking his beard in contemplation. "I will keep your secret, but I have an idea. You must promise to not look for Elspeth until this issue with the Kearals is resolved." Merlin grinned. "I have the perfect solution to your Elspeth problem." And he told Arthur his plan.

Arthur sat dumbfounded but agreed with Merlin and his condition.

Merlin wasn't finished with Arthur though. He looked at his friend knowing he wasn't going to like what he had to say. "Arthur, I want you to stay in the Wesladus Veil, here in Pendragon castle, until this is over. All kings are in danger and no one can afford to have you captured. I cannot risk losing you."

"Absolutely not! I have my kingdom to protect. My soldiers, my wife, and my friends. What about them? No Merlin I will not stay here and hide."

"I was afraid you'd say that, so I have a plan B. I will cloak your kingdom. It will take a lot of my power,

124

but I can do it. Just make sure you keep all your people within the boundaries I set. If it is to work they must stay inside. I could shroud the area too, where they couldn't walk through the barrier, but that won't work. You'd have to explain it and mortals just wouldn't understand.

"Besides there's a law governing inner earth against knowledge of outer earth's existence and its magic. It would play havoc on the mortal mind. We have enough upset with what Athdar is doing now against the mortal realm. No, just make sure you keep your kingdom confined. Tell them of a deadly illness spreading. That should do it."

"Good idea, Merlin. That I shall do. Now please, I want to return home."

"I shall take you, and make sure you're cloaked. We will discuss how wide the boundaries need to be. Let us go." Merlin waved his arm and a portal opened.

****

Ian sat at the highly polished long table and greeted Angus with the first man in line. "Angus what is the name of your squadron?"

"We are the *Axuard Squadron.*" He wrote it down. "First man, name and species please." He had four groups of three columns for the species. He had only to write their title above the three columns and write in the person's name in the species column. When finished, Connor's group of twelve lined up.

Connor said, "We are called *The Xiann Squadron.*"

"Species and name, please," he said, going through the next twelve.

Then Finn walked up. "We are *The Sanguine Squadron.*" The line of twelve went through.

Last in line, Taryn, assembled his group and said. "We are *The Qruhr Squadron.*" His twelve went through giving name and species. All in all, everyone seemed to be getting along, even if the species weren't fully interacting yet. Time, he thought, and a good workout.

He stood and climbed on top of the table. "Let me have your attention!" The room grew quiet. "You will not split up with only your kind to the long houses. You will also find these long houses tae be different than what you are used tae, instead of being totally open it has a main hall but separate rooms for each of you. There is at one end of each long house, a bath house which you will each be expected to use daily."

Moans went about the room, and he raised his hand. "This is for your good as well the rest of us, if you get my drift." That brought about laughter. "The Axuard Squad will take the lower long house, The Xiann Squad the one above, The Sanguine Squad tae the east, and The Qruhr Squad the one above that.

"There willna be any segregation amongst you. Your commander will each take the larger chamber nearest the bath house, until which time he chooses one of you as leader tae the other eleven. If you want this position and larger more comfortable lodging, you'll have tae work for it.

"Each commander will watch your training closely and choose accordingly. Once the leader is chosen, the commanders will return tae Pendragon, and as leader you will then answer tae your commander. If anyone has, at that time, complaints, go tae the leader. If he canna resolve an issue he will report tae his commander. There will be no separation of species in this army.

"You are now all brothers! Protect each other and become friends. Each row house is on the hill, up the side of the cliff. There's equal views of the ocean so no one long house is different from another. Pick your rooms and meet in the training yard in one hour to begin training. Dismissed."

The day was hectic. Even though everything had been moved to Pendragon the day before and settled rather easily, today was tough. He didn't know how many fights were broken up, but there were many. Finally, at training the McGregors managed to wear out the different species with a rigorous workout.

After dinner, they practically crawled to their rooms. There was no more arguing, in fact everyone was quiet. He was tired and he did not do any of the training.

He was finding out how the magic of the castle walls worked. It wasn't apparent at all times but when he needed it the most, it was then peace washed over him, seeping in through his tired muscles, renewing his strength. He just made sure everything went smooth and things were in order, in the castle and the long houses.

He could only imagine how tired his brothers were. He sat at the long table with mead, waiting for them to report to him before retiring for the night. Cameron, Conall, Dougal, and Lauren, after spending the day working in the library and lab, were exhausted and already abed. He was just waiting for the rest.

Earlier when they were all together, and Merlin filled everyone in on current happenings, the brothers had broken out in laughter over the dragon story and reminisced about the many times he had been afraid of dragons. Times he had forgot about or wished he had. They laughed so long and hard it took Merlin a half hour to calm them down so he could finish.

He knew that would happen. Best they got it over with, he thought. He frowned. He thought of Elspeth and missed her. She had spent the day with Saphira helping with the dragon bairns. Merlin should be here with her any minute. This would be their only night before their trip to Mystic Kingdom. Truth be told, he was very worried about their plan. He could not shake his feeling of dread.

"Ian why so down?" asked Connor as he came trudging slowly across the room. Taryn, Angus, and Finn following him.

"Nothing boys. Just tired, been a long day. You? Come sit, have some mead." The men grabbed cups off the side board and poured themselves some mead and sat on the long benches. "Tell me how your first day went."

Finn was the first to speak up. "After the arguments ceased and they put energy in their training, it turned oot good. For me anyway. They listened weel, already good fighters, and they have initiative. I have a good bunch of soldiers. I like them as men. I think this will work."

"I agree with Finn for the most part," said Connor. "Some of my men took training a little too seriously. I thought someone was going tae get seriously hurt. But, they fought like soldiers and did a damn good job. Took everything I threw at them, they did."

"I was tough on my crew," replied Angus. "I hit 'em hard. They took it though. A strong bunch, I've got. I dinna let up either. I figure if I could keep going, so could they. I showed them some moves they didn't ken and they picked it right up."

"I did the same," said Taryn. "I dinna give them any chance to argue. They sure left dinner tired. Wait 'til I get them up at sunrise." Taryn snickered.

"Sounds good. I figure aboot seven moons, and then give them a day of rest and relaxation. Hopefully they doona start their own war."

Connor looked at him. "What had you looking so forlorn when we first came in?"

"I'm worried aboot Elspeth. She's supposed tae stay here with us as healer, after we return from Mystic Kingdom. I doona like that plan, and I doona want her here while all these men are arguing."

He shook his head, "we may have tae go tae Mystic Kingdom tomorrow, but I just doona like it. It doesn't set right with me, but for trainin' I'm thinking of sending her tae home. She can get tae know mither and our sisters a bit and plan the weddin' with them like they all want. There's just too much tension here even with the unusual feeling of peace. Just until things get settled. You ken?"

"I think that's a splendid idea Ian," Merlin said as he came down the grand staircase with Elspeth on his arm. "If you two do well through the trouble of getting in and out of Mystic Castle, I think she should spend some time with your mother and sisters. When we are ready to go to war well, that's a different story. We'll have people who can tend to superficial wounds, but we will need her as healer. Also…"

"No one asked me what I wanted," interrupted Elspeth. But I do like the plan. It would be wonderf…"

129

She looked at everyone staring at her and went quiet. Ian realized she had yet to meet his other brothers.

It was very quiet. Then Finn broke the silence. "I think I'm in love." He gave a dramatic sigh, and he swooned putting the back of his hand to his forehead. It was so dramatic everyone laughed. Connor choked on his mead. Angus snorted. But Ian just looked at Finn with a frown.

"She seems tae have that effect on every man," stated Ian.

"But the only one I care about having that effect on is you, Ian McGregor." Elspeth walked over and leaned down wrapping her arms around Ian's shoulders and kissing the top of his head. "I missed you today."

"Aye, and I you. I want you tae meet the other half of my brothers." They all stood at once and benches on both sides fell over. Elspeth laughed. He frowned and stood. His brothers all came forward. With his hand, he gestured to each one. "The one who is in love with you is Finn." Finn bowed low taking Elspeth's hand and gently kissing it. "My utmost pleasure, my lady." Finn grinned and wiggled his red eyebrows, blue eyes twinkling mischievously.

"Stop it Finn, ere I gouge your eyes oot! This is Connor."

"My lady," Connor said with a bow and a kiss to her hand, prim and proper.

Ian continued. "This is Taryn." He bowed.

"And this is Angus, the grouchy one," finished Ian with a laugh. Angus bowed.

"This is Elspeth McLellan. My future wife. Doona get any ideas, she already said aye tae me."

Elspeth blushed profusely. "So, nice to meet all the

handsome McGregor men. My there's a lot of you."

"Would that be a lot of handsome men, or just a lot of men, or who's handsome? Just curious." Grinned Finn. "You never ken."

He snarled. "Awa'n bile your heid, Finn, 'fore you pick your carcass off the floor. I'll wrap that face of yours 'round that pole if you doona shut your yap. That's my bride your speaking tae!"

Elspeth put her hand on Ian's shoulder, laughing. "Awe Ian, he's cute." Finn frowned. He remembered what he said to Elspeth when she called him cute, broke out in laughter.

"Cute! Finn, your cute!" Ian roared.

"Shut up, Ian," said Finn. Then everyone laughed.

Merlin stood there pulling his beard. "Let's sit and go over your plan once more for tomorrow, Ian and Elspeth. Then we'll all get some sleep."

After a couple hours went by, they were done discussing things. Everyone said good night and he, Merlin, and Elspeth climbed the stairs, while the rest of the McGregors left for their chambers in the long houses.

Chapter 15

Ian stopped Elspeth at the door. Without saying anything he picked her up, and she squealed. He pushed the door open with his foot and carried her into their magnificent opulent room. He put her down and they both looked around. Huge tapestries covered a row of large windows overlooking the ocean. Knights on horses with mountains and forests covered the tapestries.

Gold gilding molded over carved cornices surrounded the high ceilings, framing it in. A marble fireplace held a crackling fire making the huge room cozy. Gold statues adorned corners. On each side of the fireplace were two full length set of armors complete from helm down to sabatons. It was so complete and complex you could almost see the fingers in the gauntlets. Complete with plate metal and scale for around the neck.

Exotic wood wardrobes, larger than Ian had ever seen, butt up against two sections of one wall. A long finely carved cabinet of the same wood, low and long, in between. A small square marble tub in the middle with the steaming aqua water flowing in from two small holes. Neatly folded linens sat next to it, and on the other side, a large oval looking glass on a stand.

"Beautiful," whispered Elspeth.

She looked at the huge carved, red velvet canopied

bed. Ian could tell from her amazement she'd never seen anything like it. "Is this a palace?" She asked.

"Weel, this is a place the Ayriris angels from the Plelin courts came for rest and relaxation. As you see they have access tae many beautiful things, being angels and all. They have since moved onto bigger and better things, I imagine."

Putting his arms around Elspeth he whispered in her ear. "Shouldn't we take advantage of this beautiful room whilst we have the chance?" He turned her and looked in her bright green eyes. "I'm nae sure what will happen tom…"

"Shush," said Elspeth putting a finger to his lips. She reached up and kissed him. "No talk of tomorrow. Let's just be together. Make me forget the world. Just for tonight, please Ian."

"Say nae more, my fire haired princess." He pressed his lips tenderly to her forehead, and she sighed. He met her lips and softly kissed her. He brushed his hands up and down her arms, and she shuddered. He instantly became hard.

His blood ran hot, how he wanted her. He wanted to make love slowly and tenderly, touching and tasting her everywhere. She drove him crazy with desire and his hands trembled. He was going to do this slowly and take his time.

He smoothly brushed his fingertips down the side of her neck. Still kissing her he took one hand and slipped her dress from her shoulder. He tenderly kissed her neck along her shoulder and licked his way back up. She shuddered. She in turn put her hands on his buttocks and pulled him tight up against her where his arousal pressed against her side.

She moaned and it nearly drove him wild. He broke away and slowly pushed her other sleeve down onto her arm and plucked the front of her gown from her breasts. Full mounds greeted his eyes. Her light nipples puckered tight from his gaze.

Her corset pushed the heavy breasts up toward his face enticing him, and he kissed them, then licked the puckered points. He pulled the ribbons free from her corset slowly, going down one row at a time, widening it as he went and laving at the new silky skin as it appeared. It was a front laced corset so he enjoyed removing it slowly.

She trembled at his touch and she put her hands under his shirt moving up and down from his waist to his chest, loving the feel of his tight muscles. She kneaded his chest and drew her nails down over his stomach. All the while their tongues danced back and forth in heated torment.

The feel and taste of his mouth was intoxicating. She grew hot and warmth pooled in her abdomen, slick wetness gushed from her pulsing insides and ran onto her thighs. He pushed her dress down past her hips where it hit the floor. He tore at the last bit of her corset and he threw it aside. Picking her up he placed her on the bed all the while gazing into her eyes. She moaned. "Please Ian remove those clothes at once. I want to feel your skin on mine. I want you inside, please. Now."

He chuckled, "Not yet, sweetling. I will be tasting you first. She leaned back and spread her legs wide giving him full view of her glistening thighs. His gaze turned toward the heat of her. He ripped his shirt off, shucking his boots and when he pulled down his pants, he was raging hard and throbbing when he finally bounced free. He gently placed himself between her legs and leaned down.

With his hands under her hips he pulled her up to his mouth. With one long stroke of his tongue he licked over her nub nestled amongst the tiny red curls. She cried out and lifted her hips. His tongue probed the inside of her, in and out.

He chuckled and the vibration drove her wild. "Please Ian." She moaned. His tongue darted in and out of his mouth barely stroking her, driving her insane. She clawed at his shoulders then pulling his hair. Thrashing her head back and forth she again pleaded with him. She was wound tight and she wanted more, wanted him inside.

Finally, he sucked fully onto her, nibbled and then licked. She pressed her thighs tight to his head to hold him there. She trembled and when he started sucking she screamed his name and came apart. It was a vicious orgasm and she thought she was going to pass out when softly she came floating back, she opened her eyes.

Sitting up, she threw Ian onto his back. "Your turn," she said with a twinkle of devilment in her bright green eyes. She straddled him, but instead of climbing on top of him she leaned down and licked his pebbled nipples. He groaned and she knew she was doing something he liked. If she liked what he did, she figured he'd like what she was going to do. She wanted to drive him as mad as he drove her.

She loved the taste of him and she stroked his chest with her tongue working her way down. She brushed her breasts against his hard erection and it jerked beneath her. She sat back and looked at him. She grabbed around the middle of it and he groaned.

Leaning over she took her tongue and tasted the tip where a bead of moisture clung. The salty taste aroused her.

When she dove down all the way around him her hot wet mouth was almost his undoing. She stroked him up and down with her mouth. Finally, he had to stop her. He wasn't going to last like this and he wanted inside. "Enough Els, I canna take any more." She sat back and looked at him with a grin.

"Don't move," she said, and climbed on top of him. She slowly guided him inside of her and they both moaned. Finding her rhythm, she began to increase her thrusts. Throwing back her head, Ian watched her, her wild red tresses bouncing around her shoulders and over her breasts. He reached up and placed her hair behind her, enjoying looking at her flushed face and bouncing breasts.

He'd never seen anything more beautiful. Her wild red hair in disarray, her parted lips, and little mews drove him wild. He grabbed her hips and he began to thrust up harder. She met his passion with her own.

Before they would end it right there, he flipped Elspeth to her back. "Look at me Els." She gazed into his eyes. "I doona ken what the future holds, so tonight I'd like tae make you truly mine. Do you want tae mate? If not, we can wait. It's just…"

"I thought you'd never ask. Of course, Ian, I want nothing more."

He kissed her gently and started moving again. The little reprieve cooled them somewhat, but in seconds they were straining toward each other. She was so hot and wet he didn't know if he could wait.

She moaned and thrashed her head back and forth,

eyes wide. Then she felt it coming. When she bit her lip and her inner muscles tightened, he knew she was ready. Grabbing tight on her hips he thrust up hard and she screamed his name.

On her first contraction, he lost control, at the same time he bit her and drank heavy of her blood. Letting go and shouting her name, he buried himself and came with her. The orgasm lengthening and stronger than he ever felt before.

"Now bite me and drink my blood." She instantly bit him taking them through another tumultuous orgasm. Instinct took over and she drank, completing the ritual. His thoughts rushed through her head, and he shared his feelings. Her thoughts rushed him and he felt her love for him. Together they truly united and became one. A tear melted from her eye.

Their closeness was on a level neither understood, but knew it was something that could never be broken. It was always this good with her, but this was special. He could not get enough. He collapsed on top of her tucking his face against her neck. "I love you," she whispered to him.

He pushed the hair from her face. "I love you, too," he whispered back.

Suddenly she cramped, then cramped again. She moaned then screamed out. Ian held her and brushed her hair back. He knew her body was making the necessary changes. She would become vampire. Fae had a different ritual, one that was not painful.

He would share that on their wedding night. That was a ritual, blissfully shared, and entwining their souls. She couldn't become fae, you could only be born one, but the mating ritual would bind them together in the way of the fae. She broke out in a sweat and whispered his name.

"I'm here sweetling, I willna let you go."

****

For an hour, she cramped, her bones were on fire, her skin prickled, she felt like she had the flu a hundred-fold. Then it died to an ache, then to a warmth. Her hearing was acute and she could hear tiny insects, her teeth lengthened, and she wanted blood. Ian leaned over her, exposing his neck.

"Here Els, you'll need blood. I'll feed you on and off all night, and by morning, you'll be changed." He pulled the covers over them and tucked her up against his side. "Rest while you can, you'll wake hungry a few times, but the worst is over."

Chapter 16

The next morning, Ian looked at Ator in the cave behind the waterfall. A few of the dragons had returned to their original caves in case he or Elspeth needed their help. They were going to walk to the castle, a half day's journey. They had to go through the canyon of Mystic mountain, where men went and never came out. He shuddered at the thought.

But they could not take the chance that any scouting soldiers would spot them riding a dragon. It was the only way. "You ken," he said, "you can change your mind and we can stop this nonsense now. I doona like this plan one bit. I doona want tae lose you, Els."

"We're here beside you Ian," said Ator. *"At your first call, we'll be there, if you need us."*

Elspeth smiled and straightened. "You won't lose me Ian. We can do this. I need answers as much as you do. After all my brother, well…whoever he is, I need to know. Maybe I can find out exactly what happened with my brother. I know he's gone, but there are still so many questions. Just maybe Merlin is wrong, maybe they didn't use my brother just replaced him. I need to know, Ian. The whole thing doesn't feel right to me. I need these answers, and don't ask me why, but there is something not right with this story. I can feel it in my bones."

He frowned at the thought. Knowing Drakkor as he

did, he knew the bairn would not have lived, but he could not tell her that. He wished there was a way to avoid having her find out the truth, but he knew her better, so he didn't say anything.

She would not rest until she found out, and hopefully he'd be there to hold her when she did. He pushed his hand back through his hair, then down his face. So much to think about, so many dangers. He just hoped this insidious plan worked.

"Weel, we best get started," he said. "Ator will you take us to the edge of the valley? We'll start from there and go past Mystic Mountain. I think we're good to that point. No one will see us. Past that, though, there may be soldiers or scouts either looking for Elspeth or kings. Arthur was damn lucky, but some of the bastards got away. They'll ken aboot him. Damn Kearals, damn Drakkor."

Ator strode to the opening. *"I'll take you to the base of Mystic mountain. Come."* He turned his large head toward Ian, blue eyes serious. *"It will work, Ian. Have faith in Merlin, in Elspeth, in us. We won't let harm come to either of you even if we have to burn down Mystic Castle and all in it."*

"Thanks, Ator, you are a true friend. I'm ready." He climbed aboard Ator. The female mates to the dragons were safely tucked away in their new homes in the Wesladus Veil. He wished Elspeth was there, tucked away in Pendragon Castle, in their new bedchamber, with him by her side. He thought about last night. It was the most beautiful night of his life. He wanted many more. He shook his head. "Come Els. We best be gettin' on with it."

She stepped up on Ator's wing and climbed in

front of him. He knew her thoughts mirrored his. They were quiet.

Ator soared high and Ian enjoyed the ride and view. He thought Ator did it on purpose. He let go of the spike and wrapped his arms around Elspeth. "I love you," he whispered in her ear inhaling her sent of Jasmine and woman. She cupped his arms with hers and leaned against him. They were high enough they would not be seen. Then Ator flew up and circled a couple of times then over the top of Mystic Mountain and toward the valley below. Landing toward the back where no one would see them.

"Thank you Ator," he said as he climbed down. He took Elspeth's hand and helped her off. He didn't let go of it as they watched Ator take flight and disappear over the mountain top. They started walking. As they walked a narrow path between boulders and cliff edges of Mystic Mountain, he studied his surroundings.

The trees were getting their spring leaves, they twinkled from the breeze in the bright sunlight. Some deciduous trees were covered in spring blooms of white and some held large red blooms, some just had colorful leaves, and there were a lot of conifers. For being a cursed mountain, it was beautiful.

There were all kinds of trees. Birch, Alder, English Oak, Ash, Hazel, and Rowan to name a few. He noticed the Rowan had red berries from the year before, and there were spring flowers growing along the sides. He noticed Bluebell, Bramble, Dog rose, Foxglove, and the deadly Nightshade, blooming along the mountain side. Bright yellow, blue, and red flowers dotted here and there.

Higher up, the pines were thick, thinning the higher

up he looked until his eyes reached the snow caps. Lodgepole Pine, Sitka Spruce, Douglas-fir, and Western Hemlock were among the ones he noticed. How could such a beautiful mountain turn man to stone?

Soon they came to an area where men and women stood frozen in time. Granite, they were all turned to granite. He looked in amazement at the different statues. As he looked higher he noticed something odd and he stopped.

"Els, what are those statues of?" He looked at what appeared strategically placed creatures of granite. They weren't huge, but rounded, with pointed ears and long spiked tails. They had elf like faces. He pointed toward one. "Do you ken what that is? It's a statue of a creature I've never seen afore and I've been around for eight hundred years."

"They are said to be the guardians of Mystic Mountain. The myth says when a person touches the mountain they come alive and turn them to stone. It takes but one touch from the creatures and any living thing becomes stone. No one is excluded. They are called garg...gar...gargoyles. That's it gargoyles. But it's a myth that has been handed down through generations.

"Maybe they once lived and were turned to stone as the others were. Some say they were placed there as a warning. There are many stories. You know how myths go. They are probably here for some unknown reason. Someone probably made the statues to scare people away. I think they're kind of cute myself. It would be fun to see what one would look like if it were actually alive."

"I think they're ugly little statues. Whoever thought to make one had a vivid imagination." He chuckled. "Damn ugly if you ask me. I wouldn't want tae meet one of those little devils, they probably stink, and eat little bairns."

"Ian!" said Elspeth with a giggle slapping his arm. "You have such an imagination. If they were alive they would probably be friendly, cute little creatures."

"Bah! Cute my arse! Stone devils are more like it." He laughed. "Let's get out of here as quickly as possible. It's too eerily quiet and I think their eyes are following us."

"Don't be ridiculous, Ian." Laughed Elspeth. "Statues can't see."

He swung Elspeth around and kissed her. "You are so bonnie when you laugh. I could stay right here forever and listen tae you. Will you sing for me, Elspeth, as we walk? I love your voice. It's so quiet here. It's like everything is dead. You notice that? Listen…no sounds. No birds, lil critters, insects. It's nae natural."

Elspeth stopped and they listened. "You're right it's like everything knows this mountain is cursed.

"Yes, I'll sing. What would you like to hear?"

"Do you ken any old Scottish ballads?"

"Yes, my da was Scottish and he loved tae sing." Elspeth laughed remembering her da and heritage.

"You speak my tongue! Elspeth. What, or should I say who, changed your speech?"

"Mother Thomas used to smack my mouth if I spoke my Da's tongue. Said it wasn't proper for a young English lady. I soon learned, and it's a habit I now have. Do you ken the song *Ae Fond Kiss?* It was one of me Da's favorites." Elspeth broke out in an old Scottish love song.

Ae fond kiss, and then we sever!
Ae fareweel, and then forever!
Deep in heart—wrung tears I'll pledge thee,
Warring sighs and groans I'll wage thee.
Who shall say that Fortune grieves him,
While the star of hope, she leaves him?
Me, nae cheerfu twinkle lights me,
Dark despair around be nights me.

~*~

I'll ne'er blame my partial fancy:
Naething could resist my Nancy!
But to see her was to love her
Love but her and love for ever.
Had we never lov'd so kindly.
Had we never lov'd so blindly,
Never met—or never parted
We had ne'er been broken hearted.

~*~

Fare—thee—weel, though first and fairest!
Fare—the—weel, though best and dearest!
Thine be Ilka, joy and treasure.
Peace, Enjoyment, Love, and Pleasure!
Ae fond kiss, and then we sever!
Ae fareweel, alas, forever!
Deep in heart—wrung tears I'll pledge thee.
Warring sighs and groans I'll wage thee…

Near the end of the song they had stopped walking, and as the last of the note died away in the canyon, he turned away to keep from tearing up. To hear a Scottish ballad sung in such a beautiful voice in the canyon, and by his beloved, Ian felt like he died and went to heaven.

"I love you, Els."

"I love you too." She took his hand and they continued walking in silence.

Time slipped away and before they knew it they were at the river. They could see the castle up ahead. It was early afternoon, and the sun still shone brightly. "Weel, we're almost there. You ready Els?" he asked as he pulled a rope from the pocket of his tartan.

She nodded and held out her hands. "As ready as I'll ever be."

He tied her hands together loosely, leaving a long end which he held onto. Just like they had planned. She was after all his prisoner. He still did not like it, but time to act his part. He dressed in red and black colors so he wasn't wearing McGregor colors.

He was using the name Heralth MacPherson, a name Merlin made up. There were MacPherson's about but they were so far away Merlin didn't think anyone would know. They crossed the bridge and came to the castle gates.

"Who goes there?" a booming voice shouted from the parapet.

"Heralth MacPherson! I bring you a prisoner! Elspeth McLellan the traitor to the king you're looking for!"

"Open the gates!"

****

Elspeth was nervous. The memory of the look in King Rulm's eyes still haunted her. She had to stay strong and face him. Two guards approached to escort them to the castle. One guard shouted for another to alert the king. They were led down the path that Elspeth had used every day. Somehow the joy she'd felt before shattered.

People stopped to stare. She glanced at people she knew, some she'd healed. Most glanced away when she looked at them. She couldn't blame them. How would she feel if the tables were turned and she was watching a believed traitor being led to their death?

She wanted to cry, but instead held her head high and hoped no one would notice her shaking. They were being led up the stone stairs to the castle and when she reached the doors she thought about bolting.

Ian picked it up and whispered. "A little late for that. Stay strong. I'm with you. I willna let anythin' happen tae you."

She tilted her head as if to say okay. She swallowed hard and put her hands to her stomach to help relieve the knot in it. They were led through the double doors where King Rulm sat on the throne. Athdar was standing beside him, a look of contempt on his face.

King Rulm sat on his throne upon the dais, speaking to Athdar. He quit speaking and looked up when they entered. Surprise and a look of triumph passed over his face when he saw her. He motioned for the guards to bring them forward. The court was packed with people and the guards had to weave in and out to get to the front.

"What have we here? Elspeth McLellan, and who might you be?" he asked Ian with an evil stare.

"My name is Heralth MacPherson, and I am here with a prisoner whom you've been looking for."

"Clear the courts!" He obviously wanted this meeting private. He leaned to his two trusted guards on either side of his throne. "You two shall stay. Everyone else, out!" While they waited for the room to clear, he glared at Elspeth.

She started to sweat and her hands were shaky. She didn't have to play a part, she was literally downright terrified. She knew Ian felt her fear, but he couldn't do anything for her.

After everyone was gone, he looked at Ian. "Why have you brought her here, Heralth?"

"My family is sick. I was hoping tae reap a small token for my efforts of capturing and bringing her here tae you."

"Brann," the king said to his guard, "bring me the box. Mr. MacPherson deserves a reward for this traitor's capture." The guard left. "Where did you find her, Mr. MacPherson?"

"I was travelin' tae market here, King Rulm. Some soldiers met me on the way and told me tae look out for her. I saw her near the dragon cliffs. I immediately knew it was she you were lookin' for from their description."

The guard, Brann, returned with a black box and handed it to the king.

"Well, you deserve a reward for her capture," he said opening the box. He handed two gold pieces to Brann and motioned for him to give them to Ian. "You may receive your reward with my thanks, and you can be on your way."

"King Rulm, if I may."

"What is it, MacPherson?" The king was becoming annoyed.

"I've been traveling for weeks. Might I spend the night and be on me way in the mornin'?"

The King sat back. "That is a fair request. So be it.

147

Brann will show you to a room where you can get a bath and he'll have some food sent to you. After you break your fast in the morning, you'll depart."

"May I ask one more question of your highness before I leave?"

"Yes, yes make it quick. I'm very busy."

"When will the trial be for the young lady? Will she be hanged if found guilty?"

"Why should you care MacPherson? Is she somebody to you?" The king sat up straight with a snarl on his face.

"Nae, not at all. I think a person found tae be a traitor should suffer, 'tis all."

The king grinned. "Oh, she'll suffer. The trial will be the day after tomorrow. If she's found guilty, which I'm sure she will. Her death will be painful."

"Two days? I thought it customary for a period of at least a week before trial."

"My court, my rules."

She shuddered. The king had the exact same look he had the day he killed that poor girl. Suddenly she found her courage. She didn't know where it came from, whether it was the injustice of his killing the lady, or to find out the possibility her brother might still be alive, she didn't know. "You killed that girl. Did you also kill my brother?"

The room became dead silent. "Ah, I see you've found out some truths."

Athdar stood with a murderous look on his face.

The king paused as if choosing his words carefully. "I saw a man kill your brother as a babe. He was dealt with. Athdar, this fine and good soldier, was just a babe at the time and needed a home. Your mother and father took him in. He is your brother."

Ian leaned toward her. He whispered. "He tells the truth, Els, he watched someone kill your brother. I'm thinking that Drakkor was the one. I'm sorry."

The king frowned. "What did you just say to the prisoner?" He didn't miss anything.

Ian blurted, "I said it served her right and I called her a traitor." She felt him cringe.

King Rulm's patience was at an end. "Brann see Mr. MacPherson to a room. Guards!" he shouted. They quickly came through the door. "Take Elspeth McLellan to the dungeons at once. Trial for her treason is in two days. Court is in order again, let the people back in."

Athdar stood with a smile on his face.

She was grabbed by two guards, each holding tightly to an arm. She glanced back at King Rulm and saw the look in his eyes. The ice-cold terror she felt at seeing how he looked told her he was going to have his way with her and that was not good. Not at all.

Chapter 17

Ian did not waste time resting in the room he was given. It wasn't the greatest of the rooms by castle standards. It was a small windowless and unadorned room. Something he would expect a man of his supposed stature would get. He did not care.

He ate quickly to keep up his strength and did not lounge in the small tub of hot water that had been brought for bathing.

It was late afternoon and he was worried about Elspeth. He hoped she was okay in the dungeon, but what did he expect, he knew this would happen. He was unsure what King Rulm might try to do.

But Merlin was watching and listening, if she should call his name for help, he'd be there with an open portal. He did not want to give himself away this early in the game, but Ian knew Merlin, safety of his people first.

He waited for the tub to be picked up, and when it was, he went out to explore and see what he could find. He was on the first floor near the kitchens and he wanted to avoid the throne room. He knew the third floor was probably the King's sleeping quarters.

He figured Athdar was on that floor as well. If he was practicing magic and the castle was anything like the castle in Wesladus Veil, they probably did their dirty work on the fourth floor or the tower.

He would cloak himself to get there without being noticed, but he didn't want to waste time taking a tour. So, the fourth floor is where he'd start. Cloaked he headed for the gathering hall where the stairway was. He looked up and counted five stories above him.

The fifth's hall opening overlooking the great hall was much smaller than the other floors. There were towers that were higher, but he thought they'd be no use for what he was looking for. He started his climb.

Each floor he passed had a long hall overlooking the great hall where the tables sat for feasting and meeting. Two sets of three twelve-foot tables took up the room. On a dais sat a table overlooking those below. That's where the king and queen ate along with those they deemed important. It was probably where Athdar and Drakkor sat.

The thought of Drakkor turned his stomach and made him angry. Bullocks they all made him angry. With a grunt, he increased his pace up the stairs. He passed the second hall, two more floors to go.

When he reached the third floor he noticed the hall was empty. Maybe he should check this floor after all. He would stay up against the wall near the doors. Even though he was cloaked, he was still nervous. He guessed the middle door would be the King's bedroom.

The next room would be his lady's room. He silently and slowly opened the king's door. When he looked through his mouth dropped open. Gold everywhere. Statues, gilding, even two full length suits of armor enrobed in gold stood beside the marble fireplace. The king sure loved his treasures. A large marble tub was built in against the windows with three steps up but held no water like the rooms at Wesladus.

He felt sorry for the ones who had to carry the water to that tub. It could bathe five people at once, he figured. He didn't want to think about what might go on in such a large tub, especially knowing what he knew about the King. The tapestries had a lot of gold threading woven through the pictures. He thought he'd get a headache from the reflection if the sun was shining through.

Red velvet adorned the canopy bed with embroidered gold edging. There was so much, he wondered how the people of the kingdom fared. There were probably a lot of hungry people. He never had much use for such opulence. Even his brother Finn who liked fine things would be appalled. He quickly shut the door.

Curiosity got the better of him and he peeked in the Queens chambers. He wondered if she was like her husband. He was quite surprised by what he found. Everything was nice but done pleasantly in blues and greens. There were paintings of horsemen and hunting dogs, two of the same of a beautiful woman, and there was one of a young gentleman with black hair and blue eyes.

There was a collection of dolls which he found amusing. He shook his head and silently shut the door. He passed two maids in the hallway entering the king's chambers. It was close, but they did not even look his way. So far so good.

He retraced his steps and headed back up the stairs. As he was going up two guards were coming down. He would not get past the two big men side by side. He turned around and ran down the steps. One of the men stopped. "Did you hear that?" he asked the guard next to him.

"No what? Are you hearing things again?" He laughed. "I think you're still in your cups from last night. We're on duty Jax, don't let the king see you."

"I thought I heard shuffling feet." He shook his head and laughed. "You're right. I better stay clear of King Rulm if I want to keep my head."

Ian stood holding his breath waiting for the guards to pass. It was probably their watch and they were checking floors. He waited to see where they'd go, when he saw them heading downstairs, he went up to the fourth floor.

He checked every door on the fourth floor but could find nothing other than storage rooms and more bedrooms. He stood at the stairs wondering where to go next. Scratching his head, he looked up the remaining stairs. These were obviously unused and much narrower. At the top, they veered off and going to the right they wound around and up. The tower he thought.

Magic wouldn't happen there as there was not enough room. He'd check the doors on the fifth floor. He looked through two doors and found storage. One had the linens for the castle, old tapestries, and miscellaneous things gathering dust. The other room, a very large room had furniture stored in it.

He was very confused now, there was no space large enough to conduct magic. There was only one door left, very narrow and small he almost let it go, but he figured he'd better check it. When he went to open it, it was locked.

Fortunately, it had a key hole he could mist through, but he'd have to uncloak himself. Not a good idea, but something he'd have to risk. He looked around and saw no one. He turned to mist and traveled through the keyhole.

When he returned to himself he was astounded. There were no windows in the small room, but it was light as day. There were shelves on the three walls, and on each shelf, were small, tall bottles. Inside each was ethereal smoke that glowed brightly with a greenish tint.

The substance in each swirled as he looked at them. There were hundreds of them. He moved to study them more closely. Each bottle had a label. He picked one and held it in front of his face. The eerie glow made his blood run cold.

When he looked at the label he almost dropped the bottle. It read *Aiden Baird* and underneath was the notation *fae*. He was afraid of what he'd found. Looking all around he felt he must be looking at fae, vampire, king's, and soldier's ethers.

He went from shelf to shelf reading names and species. He took the bottle with Aiden's name and tucked it in his boot. He knew Merlin would want to see it.

Just as he tucked it away he heard footsteps and the agitated voices of two men. He couldn't understand them, but they were getting closer. When he heard the key in the lock he hurriedly cloaked himself and backed against the wall closest to the door hoping to escape through the door after they entered.

He held his breath. Athdar and King Rulm entered with a torch. Ian hurriedly went out. Athdar put the torch in the holder on the wall and moved to close the door.

"Did you feel that?" he asked the king.

"Somethings not right! I felt waves in the air!" He ran into the hall and threw up his hands toward the stairs.

He froze mid step. King Rulm came running out. Athdar walked toward the stairs speaking an incantation. He felt his cloaking disappear. He could do nothing. He remained in position, one leg up, the other bent ready to take the next step. The only thing he could move were his eyes.

Athdar walked closer to him, "Mr. Heralth MacPherson. What are you doing up here?" There was an evil gleam in his eye and Ian felt anger pour off him. He made it as far as the stairway, Athdar stepped away from him, and walked back down the hallway to the door they just came out of, he stepped up to the door to the room holding the ether bottles and shut and locked it. He slipped the key in his pocket, then returned to the hall.

"What are we going to do now?" King Rulm asked nervously.

"Do shut up Aifric." Athdar went to the balcony. "*Guards!*" He shouted, and immediately three came running up the steps. Before they reached the top of the stairs Athdar released his hold on Ian.

"Seize this man! He was caught thieving from the king! Search him! You'll find gold he stole." Two guards held a struggling Ian down, while the other searched his tartan. He'd forgotten the two pieces of gold the king gave him. Damn why did he ask for a reward? It was still in the pocket of his tartan.

The guard found them and held them up. "Thief!" he yelled, "he has stolen from the king! What should we do with him?"

"Have him tied out for the dragons, blow the horns

155

and announce it! He will not live to see tomorrow. Hurry it's almost dusk!" King Rulm had found his voice and took control.

****

After they left, dragging the struggling Ian, King Rulm turned to Athdar. "What do we do now? What if he speaks of what he saw?"

Athdar stood at the banister overlooking the great hall where they were still struggling to control Ian. His knuckles were white from his tight grip upon the railing. He turned to look at Rulm. "I'd be more concerned about who that man actually is."

"What do you mean?"

"That man is not Heralth MacPherson and he's not a simpleton. Come let's watch as the dragons tear him to pieces and eat him." Athdar laughed. "A pleasure it will be. What a fitting end to a rather boring day." Athdar roared.

Chapter 18

The guards drug Ian by the arms. He fought them with everything he had. He was losing his head, the only thing he could think about was Elspeth. How was he going to rescue her now? He knew this damn idea was a bad one. He could not yell for Merlin, because Athdar was here.

He did not know what would happen to her tonight, but he felt King Rulm would live up to what Elspeth knew him to be. He was near panic. He could not call the elements while in the castle, it would bring down the walls.

Athdar's spell had weakened him and he could not turn to mist or teleport. Even if he could, he could only go as far as the dragon cliffs, anywhere else and he'd be too far from Elspeth. He needed to stay as close as possible.

Whatever spell Athdar used had basically turned him human. Perhaps he could pull together enough energy to call on the elements once they cleared the castle walls. He did not want Ator to come. He was afraid the guards would harm him when he failed to devour him. He didn't know what to do. He'd never felt this way in his life, this useless, this hopeless. Bullocks he knew this scheme wouldn't work. What the hell was he going to do?

He roared out and renewed his fight against the

guards, even in his weakened state he was a source to be reckoned with. All he could think about was Elspeth. It took four guards to tie him down. The chains were heavy, with four iron rings attached to a barbed bar driven in the ground. No matter how hard he tried he couldn't budge one. He looked at the cloudless sky It was already turning red and shouted, "Ator!"

The men at each corner of the arena blew horns signaling the dragons. People were already packed in the stands shouting. "Dragons! Dragons! Dragons!"

Ian thought of the mighty Ator and his friends. He wondered who would come. Then he heard the first dragon roar and the sky filled with dragons. Ator out front. He landed near Ian as the other dragons circled, waiting for Ator's instructions.

The crowd stood and roared. "Eat him! Eat him!" Then they stomped their feet. The roar of the crowd was immense and the noise was more than he could handle. His mind was in a jumble from the spell, his head ached, and the noise was like knife blades to his skull. Until he looked at Ator, his friend, then peace washed over him. He felt safe.

He closed his eyes then opened them again. Ator stood tall, huge, proud, and roared. He roared at the injustice of his friend. The red sky gave him a shimmery glint of red and rainbows. There would never again be another dragon as grand as Ator, and he, Ian, alone wore his mark. They were united. The sounds of the crowd died away. Ian thought to Ator, *"Elspeth! Ator, she's in the dungeon."*

"We'll save her Ian. Don't worry. I have a plan. Right now, let's give this crowd and their evil king a show. Okay?"

Ian smiled. "It's your stage Ator. Show 'em what you're made of."

Ator roared and blew fire high toward the sky. He flew up and low around the crowd roaring and giving them a sense of his gigantic size. Some screamed, some clapped, some froze. Ator flew back to him, gliding in for a landing.

The other dragons still circling. They took turns roaring and blowing fire. Finally, the crowd screamed, "Kill him! Kill him! Kill him!" Ator went to the first chain and clipped it in two with his mouth. The crowd wasn't catching it yet. When Ator bit the second chain in two and had both legs released the crowd became quiet. They watched as Ator broke the third chain.

The king and Athdar stood up. They didn't know what was happening, but they didn't like it. "Archers!" yelled the king. "Make ready!"

The archers made ready their bows and mounted arrows, waiting for the king's orders to shoot the dragons. He was instantly terrified for his friend, but laughter came from Ator. *"Don't fear for us, Ian. This will be handled quickly with no harm to us. Watch and learn the true courage that makes a dragon."*

Before the king could give his command, the dragons descended en masse. The crowd was silent but fascinated. They were waiting to see what happened next. The dragons circled low just above the crowd. Before the archers could even react, the dragons in line roared and blew fire directly upon them. Every archer turned to ash. The king screamed. "Seize him!" But no one moved, their fascination and fear of the dragons keeping everyone spell bound.

Ator broke the last chain. He looked at Ian. *"Stand*

up."

Ator called to his dragons. One by one they landed in a half circle around Ian and Ator. Ator said to Ian. *"Yell loudly to me and all dragons to bow down."*

"What?" he asked Ator with his mind. *"I'm not goi..."*

"Do as I say!"

"Oh, mighty dragons, I say this to you now. Bow down before me!"

Ator was the first. He laid his head at Ian's feet. Then all the dragons put their heads to the ground.

"Ken this that I am your leader! I will…"

"Shut up Ian and get on my back!" Ator held out his wing and Ian climbed aboard. Deafening noise went through the crowd. "Hurrah! Did you see that?" On and on, the crowd went wild as he climbed to Ator's neck.

The king shouted, "Stop them! Damn it. I said stop them!" No one moved.

Ator beat his wings, extra for good measure and showmanship. Then he took off. Flying low over the crowd so they could see him riding on his back. After a few passes, he flew higher, taking to the sky as every dragon followed, different colors gleaming in the red setting sun. They left the crowd roaring in excitement. No one had ever seen anything like it and probably never would again.

Once Ator got Ian to the cave and off his back, he looked at Ian. *"I'm your leader? Really? You were supposed to only say bow down. Who said anything about leader?"*

He shrugged. "It was for the show, you ken." He grinned. "Thanks, Ator. Och Goddesses! Elspeth! She's in the dungeon. If that evil bastard lays one finger on her." He started pacing and running his fingers through his hair. "I canna call on Merlin, Athdar is there. I doona ken what kind of power he has. If I can just get tae the dungeon. That's it! Athdar probably willna be in the dungeon. MERLIN!"

A portal opened and Merlin came through. "Elspeth is okay for now. What the hell happened Ian?"

"Your plan, Merlin. That damn plan is what happened!"

"Tell me everything. I'm afraid I was watching Elspeth, not you. So, tell me."

He told him the story up to when he entered the room with the eerie bottles, then he said, "Och Aye, I almost forgot." He leaned over and pulled the small bottle from his boot. "I found this room full of these. There's hundreds of them." He handed the bottle to Merlin.

"That's what I was afraid of Ian. The room is warded, it must be. There's empty places in that castle where I cannot penetrate. This is ether. It must belong to an Aiden Baird. We have to stop this." Merlin opened the bottle. The mist flew out of the bottle in a stream and left the cave in a bright flash.

"Where's it going, Merlin."

"Back to who it belongs. If I'm right that fae will sort of wake up and wonder what he's doing. His good will weigh with his bad. He'll have memories of everything, but now he'll think about what he's doing before he does it.

"If I'm correct he'll now have a choice about his soul. He may be changed back in to what he was before they drained his ether. At least that is what I'm hoping. Finish your story Ian, so we can figure out what to do about Elspeth. Then we need to get those bottles."

"Doona you think he's moved those bottles by now, Merlin? If you can move your entire dwelling in a day, how long would it take Athdar tae move a small room full of bottles? I've failed my mission Merlin. I've never failed my mission afore. I've failed Elspeth. God's Merlin, I have tae get there and save her."

"You didn't fail, son. You found those bottles. Now we know and have a pretty good idea how many we're up against. We haven't lost Elspeth. I'll go immediately and bring her back through the portal.

"Go Merlin, we'll wait here. Please be quick. I have tae see her."

"I know Ian. I'll return promptly." Merlin opened a portal in Elspeth's cell and hopped through.

Chapter 19

Elspeth paced her cell. Luckily, she wasn't chained to the wall. But she was terrified. King Rulm had come to tell her what had befallen Heralth MacPherson. Ian, her Ian. She was worried about him. She pulled on her hair and paced. Before the king left, he said he wouldn't put her in chains, because he didn't want her body marred.

Then he'd laughed and said he wanted to do the marring himself. She didn't care anymore, she just wanted Ian. Her heart was breaking and with everything else that happened, she broke down in sobs. She sat on the floor and put her dirty hands on her face and cried.

She cried for her brother, she cried for her parents, she cried for herself, but mostly she cried for Ian. He was right, her idea was a bad one. She failed and it was all her fault. "Stupid, stupid, plan!" she shouted.

She didn't see Merlin's portal, or him stepping through, she was too busy feeling the pain of it all. Merlin tapped her shoulder lightly, afraid she'd scream, as it was, she jumped. "Merlin, you scared me!"

"Well, well, well!" clapped Athdar. "Isn't that touching." King Rulm and Drakkor appeared, Athdar stood outside the cell bars.

"Come! Hurry!" Merlin said. "The portal! Let's go!"

Athdar laughed, his evil eyes gleaming. "You

aren't going anywhere brother." He began an incantation. Before Merlin could get her through the portal, it disappeared.

Athdar threw up his hands, and a lightning bolt struck Merlin. Chains appeared on Merlin's arms and legs. He collapsed, his eyes rolled back, unconscious.

"What did you do to him!" she screamed, running and kneeling she took the old man's head in her lap. She screamed. "I hate you! I hate you all!"

"Hate is a very big emotion Elspeth." Grinned Athdar. "Guards seize the old man! Leave the woman!" He turned to the king. "Anything to say?"

"I'll be back later, Elspeth. Alone." They all laughed.

Elspeth sat in the corner trying to keep from going into shock. They picked up Merlin and disappeared through a portal. She had no idea where they went. She'd never tried to heal herself before, but if nothing else she needed the warmth.

She wrapped her arms around herself. She whispered a simple prayer to the gods. "Please, I need help." In a few minutes, the green glow enveloped her, and she felt the surge and warmth associated with the god's help. In a matter of moments, she felt renewed, and with determination, she stood and wiped her eyes.

Chapter 20

Athdar grabbed a chair, drug Merlin to it, and tied him down. He turned to Drakkor and King Rulm. "He'll be out for a while, when he comes to I'll be able to drain some of his ether. I don't want to kill him yet, but I do want to learn more about *The Grimoire to the Light,* I need to find it."

"I want to go back to Elspeth," said King Rulm. "We have unfinished business."

"We are trying to build an army here. Is that all you can think about. What about that Scottish bastard? Don't you think we should find out why he was in the ether room?"

"Did you say Scottish? Did he have long black hair? Green and black kilt? Eyes like silver?" asked Drakkor.

"Red and black kilt. Why, do you know him?" Athdar asked. "I knew Merlin had something to do with this. I'm glad I was watching the woman. Ha! I knew it."

"I think the man is Ian McGregor or one of his brothers, wearing another's colors. They work with Merlin, and they are a pain in my ass. I killed his father and twin, about a year ago. I can't believe he escaped and on a dragon. How is that even possible?"

"There's a myth about dragons that I never believed. I may have to rethink that. Right now, my concern is Merlin. Aifric I'll return you to the castle to have your fun with Elspeth. I don't think it wise to keep her as a live play thing if you know what I mean. Have fun, then end it."

"But, I've waited years for her."

"Then have a lot of fun! When you're done, end it! Drakkor keep an eye on Merlin, I'll be back." He opened the portal and he and the king walked through.

Chapter 21

It had been at least an hour and Ian couldn't quit pacing. Stopping he turned to Ator. "Somethings wrong, Ator. Merlin should have been right back. They have him. I ken it."

Ator stood with his friend. *"I'm afraid you're right,"* replied Ator. *"I've been thinking about what to do. I have an idea. It hasn't been done in thousands of years, but I can call on the Mountain Keepers. We watch over them and they the mountain. We benefit from the berries, that which they protect.*

"We don't misuse in the taking of the berries, therefore they grow in abundance. We feed a few to our young, for health and strength. For humans, if they consume the berries regularly, they remain young. If they could access them freely, it wouldn't be long and they'd be all gone. Mystic Mountain is the only place they grow. So, now you know the secret, one of many the mountain holds.

"I will call on the gargoyles to help you. I can fly you near the castle and drop you with them. They will fly beside me. They can make sure you make it to Elspeth and to safety. Call me when you get Elspeth. I'll be nearby. I can fly you both out. Merlin too, if he's there. But if they have him, you won't find him.

"There's a portal at the top of Mystic Mountain. You can go straight to the Wesladus Veil. I could call

my dragons, but too many innocents would be killed with fire, and no guarantee of entrance to the castle. The gargoyles can turn anyone or anything into granite. You can bust open granite bars."

"You tellin' me them little Devils are real?"

Ator laughed. *"You will love Tepu. He's the gargoyle's king, but don't let his cheery attitude fool you, he can be the meanest thing alive. I will get him and bring him here. We can tell him the story and he can get his gargoyles to help. He loves an excuse to ride a dragon. I'll return shortly."*

He didn't know what to say. He was still wrapping his head around the idea of the granite devils, truly alive. He watched Ator leave and he sat on the floor. In all his hundreds of years, he could still be surprised. His thoughts were in granite, devils, Merlin, and Elspeth.

Before he knew it, Ator appeared with two little live devils. After letting them down they turned toward Ian. "You!" said the taller of the two gargoyles. "You called us devils! I won't help you!" The gargoyle squinted his eyes and crossed his arms.

"I didn't ken what you were and you got pointy tails. No harm meant by what I said."

"You called them devils?" asked Ator. *"You never call a gargoyle a devil. They are far from it."*

"I'm sorry," he said, meaning it. "I need help for my lady, Elspeth."

"The singer?" asked the smaller gargoyle, and he swooned.

The first one said, "She has a beautiful voice. We would save her. Besides she likes us."

"You were lookin' at us! I knew it!"

"We see everything!" said the larger one. "We

come alive at night mostly. Unless someone breeches the mountain. Luckily for you, you both stayed on the path."

Ator cleared his dragon throat. *"Ian this is Tepu."* He nodded at the larger gargoyle. *"This is his friend, Hermaditt."* He pointed to the shorter one.

Their fat little bellies hung out, pointed tails swishing back and forth, funny little hair tufts, one black, one red, grizzly smiles on their faces, with narrow elfin eyes. He wanted to laugh, but held it in. "Nice tae meet you," he said, and went to shake their hands. "If I shake your hand will I turn tae stone?"

"Only if we want you to," Tepu answered.

He hesitantly shook their hands. He told them the story in short form, quickly. "Can you help my woman?"

Tepu stood with a frown. "We can get you in there and out. We aren't big enough to fly you, Ator will do that."

"Please," he begged. "We need tae go now. You have no idea what the king will do or has done…if he touches her…I'll kill him with my bare hands!"

"I think Hermaditt and myself will be enough help. You know how to get to the dungeons?" Tepu asked Ian.

Ian nodded. "Let's go."

Ator wasted no time in his flight to the castle. Before he knew it, they were there. He flew past the gates and landed at the front doors. As Ian was stepping down, Tepu and Hermaditt landed softly beside them. Two guards immediately appeared, Tepu took one and Hermaditt the other. Frozen in mid yell, the first guard was instantly turned to granite.

Other than the guards walking on the top of the walls, the courtyard was basically empty, but two other guards ran. Hermaditt instantly turned the second guard to granite. They quickly entered the castle where two more guards appeared after hearing the commotion. They too were instantly turned to stone.

They entered an empty kitchen, and went directly to the back, where the staircase to the dungeon was. When he opened the door to the stairs, he heard the angry voice of the king screaming at Elspeth.

"Fight me whore!" followed by a *slap*. From what Elspeth had told him, Ian knew this was how the king had treated the other woman. He heard Elspeth cry out, instant dread ran through his veins and he ran faster, he feared what her cries meant.

His heart stopped. He took the stairs two at a time giving the McGregor war cry. The two gargoyles had to fly down the stairway to keep up with him. They overtook him before he reached the bars. He looked at Elspeth pinned beneath the king, her skirts torn and pulled up. She tilted her face sideways and looked at him, her eye already swelling shut. When she saw him, she smiled.

He lost it.

The gargoyles turned the bars to granite. "Your turn," Tepu said. The king looked astonished, his shock freezing him in place. Ian took his sword, and with his anger behind it, hit the cell doors. They shattered to dust. The king found his footing and stood up. He reached for his sword, but it wasn't there. Ian's anger increased when he thought about what the king had intended for Elspeth.

He stalked past the dust piles of what was left of

the cell doors and bars. He threw his sword down and picked the king up by his neck. He saw red. He smashed the king's face with his fist. The king was large and strong and struck back.

He lost his grip, the king stumbled back, and moved to take up a fighting stance. "Good," Ian said. "I'm goin' tae beat you tae a bloody pulp, tear you from limb to limb, feed it down your gullet, and when I'm done, you'll beg me tae kill you." He loved a good fight and he wanted one now.

He played with the king but made sure that when he threw a punch it hurt but did not kill him. He was damn sure he was going to make him pay before he killed him and kill him he would. He thunder-punched Rulm in swift movements alternating his fists as he wore the king down.

He was turning black and blue. Blood flew from his broken nose, his face pulverized. He tried to scream for guards, but his mouth was a bloody mess and he could only whimper.

When he saw Rulm beginning to pass out, he grabbed his head and forced him to meet his eyes. "Look at me if you can." His eyes were swollen, but through narrow slits, he looked at Ian. "Remember this face. You will rue the day you touched my woman." His voice low and menacing. His anger and hatred, steady and clear. "You see this face? Because it's the last one you'll ever see," and Ian's fangs descended.

Rulm reared back and shook in terror. He bit down, but instead of drinking the tainted blood he ripped his throat out. Before he fell, Tepu ran in and touched the king and turned him to granite. Then Hermaditt came from behind holding Ian's sword. Copying Ian's war cry, in a higher pitched voice because of his size, Hermaditt swung the sword and castrated the statue.

"There!" stated Hermaditt. "All is finished." He dropped the sword and brushed his hands back and forth. He went straight to Elspeth, who was sobbing.

"Did he? Did the bastard…? Els?" he asked picking her up and cradling her in his arms.

She shook her head no. She gulped air. "He just ripped my dress and he…he…he hit me. He just hit me, but if you hadn't come when you did…" She sobbed and put her face in Ian's neck.

With some relief, he held her tight. "I've got you, love. I will not let you go." He gently held her in his arms and kissed her head. "I got you."

He picked up Elspeth and cradled her in his arms to carry her out past what remained of the king, the gargoyles following behind. Hermaditt stomped on what was left of the king's appendage as he passed.

He thought the little guy might have issues.

They went up the steps and out the front door where guards descended on them. Ator flew down and blew fire across them, causing most guards to turn and flee in terror. Pandemonium broke out but he didn't have time for it. He looked over at Tepu and Hermaditt. Hermaditt was busy turning any remaining guards to stone, Tepu looked up and motioned them forward, "we've got this, you and Elspeth make your escape!"

He nodded and quickly carried Elspeth to Ator, who just finished blowing fire at another guard heading in their direction.

Ator put his wing down. *"Hurry Ian, get her aboard!"* Quickly and as carefully as he could, he climbed aboard, resting the battered and sobbing

Elspeth in his lap. She quickly buried her face in his chest, shaking. He knew she was in shock. He hugged her close to him, and once they were good and settled he noticed Hermaditt, Tepu and Ator had cleared the courtyard.

There was no sign of Athdar, or Merlin. They obviously had taken him through a portal to a destination he couldn't hazard to guess. He hated that thought, but right now Elspeth was his worry. He also knew Merlin would want him to take care of her first.

Tepu and Hermaditt came gliding up. Hermaditt again brushing his hands back and forth. Aye, the little guy had issues. *"Is she hurt?"* asked Ator concerned.

"Yes! She's hurt. Nae she wasn't violated. I need tae get her tae Wesladus."

Tepu spoke up. "You can use the portal atop Mystic Mountain."

"Good, please take us there Ator. Thank you for your help Tepu and Hermaditt. I wish it were under better circumstances."

"When the lady is well, please, have her come and sing for us." Tepu bowed. Then the two gargoyles flew off toward the mountain.

Ator turned toward the mountain. *"I will go with you to Wesladus,"* he replied, the seriousness of the moment sunk in and they both were quiet during the trip back.

Elspeth was still weeping when they reached the castle doors. Her eye was completely swollen shut, but tears managed to drop from its corner. Ian felt helpless, but he wouldn't let her go. Ator bid good night and gave his love to Elspeth.

He touched her head with his nose and she half-smiled. She seemed aware, but partly in shock. He felt her shudder again. If he hadn't saved her when he did and Rulm would have...

When he got to the great Hall, his brothers were there waiting. They all stood quietly. Finally, Connor said, "Is she..."

He answered before Connor could finish. "She'll live, but he hurt her badly." He saw them glance at her torn dress, and her breast, exposed and bloody. He tried in vain to cover her. "Nae, she wasn't violated, but any later and... I need tae get her in bed."

Angus cleared his throat, and asked, "Merlin?"

"Drakkor and Athdar have him. Cameron get tae the grimoire, work with Dougal on a locator spell, look for anything and everything. It's Merlin's brother, so we ken he's powerful and it will be hard tae find him. Do it anyway. Lauren, try tae connect with the angels in your dreams. Let them ken they have him and that we doona ken where he is. I ken it's not a for sure thing to reach them but try. We need to find out where they took Merlin."

He looked from Elspeth to his brothers sadly. "Now...I need to take Elspeth upstairs, just do all you can to find Merlin." He sighed then. With a look of derision, he stated. "I killed the king." Then turned and started climbing the stairs, then paused and looked back at them. "Please send up food and warm water." His brothers nodded but said nothing more. He went to their room, kicked open the door, and gently laid Elspeth on the bed.

A sleepy maid came right away with warm water. "I'll be right back with food. Is the miss..."

Ian stopped himself from snapping at the innocent

girl. "She will be fine, just see tae the food."

"Right away, my lord," she said and left quickly.

He brushed Elspeth's forehead and knelt to kiss her cheek. She flinched and he stopped. "Och, Els. I love you so."

She managed a small smile. "I love you too. Thank you."

"Och, dearling, I should have been there earlier. I'm so sorry."

"No, I'm sorry," she whispered. "Stupid plan."

He chuckled. He wouldn't tell her he agreed. "Shush. Let me bathe you and change your clothes, then I'll hold you while you sleep."

She smiled. "I'd like that. So tired…" She fell asleep.

Good, he thought. A soft *knock* sounded on the door. Even though there was one candle lit, and a small fire in the fireplace, the maid brought more candles, along with a tray of food and mead.

While he was carefully removing torn garments and looking at the fresh scratches over her body, he became angry again. "I wish I could kill the bastard again," he said aloud.

"My Lord?" The maid asked as she lit the candles.

"Please just light the candles and go. Thank you for everything. Now please…just go."

"Yes, my lord." She turned and hurried out.

He finished removing what was left of Elspeth's dress. Then he put the warm water by the bed. He noticed the smell of the lavender and saw leaves floating in the water. He took his time and gently bathed her body. When he got to her face, he again seethed in anger, looking at her swollen eye, and bloodied cheek. He wished he could have changed her earlier. She turned instantly but wouldn't become full vampire for at least a month while her body made the necessary changes. She was going to heal like a human and that bothered him.

There was dirt all over her face and hands. Some blood and skin under her nails. He was so mad during the fight he didn't notice that she'd fought back. Good for you, he thought. His woman was a fighter.

He dabbed around her eye, removing the dirt, and finished with her neck and face. He moved the dark water to the stand where he couldn't see all the dirt and blood floating in it and went to her wardrobe. In it were the few gowns Merlin gave her, and the two night-dresses. It made him sad to think she'd never had much. After the mating ritual, he had learned her past and how she had never had anything of value.

She had only the uniforms the nuns gave her and they were plain, scratchy, and ill-fitting. Upon her return to Mystic Kingdom, Athdar gave her a few old dresses that didn't fit either. They were too tight on her bust and hips, and too long. He knew by the look in her eyes when she saw these what it meant to have something nice, something given to her as a gift.

He remembered the tears in her eyes when she saw them. Merlin had guessed her size perfectly. These dresses were the first gift she had ever received in her life. It broke his heart to know how she had done without. She should have had these things growing up. She should have had these things as a woman. He was going to make sure she was surrounded by beautiful things. He made a mental note to be sure she would always have the finest of everything.

He hadn't done anything with all the gold he'd made. What better way to spend it than on his mate? He wanted her happy…and laughing…and singing…and children. Suddenly he was tired. He was tired of this life. But then he shrugged, and thought, someone must do it, and then his thoughts turned to Merlin.

He was always fighting evil, making it better for those who couldn't fight. Merlin devoted his entire life to good. He'd lived longer than Ian and now he was an old wizard. He wasn't sure how long wizards lived, but he was afraid for him.

Merlin was like a second father to him, always had been. He'd get him back…somehow. Right now, he picked the nightgown Elspeth had admired and returned to her side and easily slipped it on her. When he was done, he put the food and water aside.

He wasn't hungry, and she was asleep. He stoked the fire then removed his clothes, crawled in beside her, covered them both up, and held her tight. He watched her sleep, afraid to take his eyes off her.

Chapter 22

The tapestries were tied back, windows open, and the breeze off the ocean brought in the slight, clean fresh smell of the water. It wafted over them. The sunlight shown like spun gold across Elspeth's bright copper hair. Ian put his fingers in the softness and leaned in to inhale a mixture of lavender and her own intoxicating scent. He would never get enough of this.

The sounds of the waves crashing on the shore soothed him and he closed his eyes. He still hadn't fallen asleep. He was still holding Elspeth when she moaned and turned toward him. He pulled the covers up tighter against her.

Elspeth moaned again and took a quick breath. "mmmm," she murmured and sighed. "I smell the ocean and my favorite McGregor." She snuggled tighter then opened her non-injured eye. He could tell the events of the night before slammed back at her in force, when he felt her shudder. "You saved me, Ian, you protected me," she said. "No one's ever done that afore. Thank you."

"No, Els, I should've been there earlier. It should've never happened."

"It could've been worse," she said. She shuddered again. "Anyway, it's over. I'm okay. Shouldn't have I healed by now, being a vampire?"

"You are newly formed my dearling, I'm afraid

you will heal like a human. It will be about a month before you have full vampire abilities."

"Well then, in a few days, I'll be healed. I'm okay, and I'm alive thanks to you. We have tae find Merlin. They took him through a portal. I doona ken where."

"*We* doona have tae do anythin.' *We* are stayin' together until you're healed, then you are goin' tae Mither's until this is over. I willna lose you, Elspeth. I came close tae losin' you. I willna have it."

She smiled, "I love you, you stubborn arse, but I can help. I'm needed here for my healin.' I would love tae see your Mither, and I will spend time with her, but when the war starts, I will be here."

He chuckled. "You speak the language weel, Els."

"It was my first language, Ian. I like using it again. It's easy tae me. It comes from bein' around you. You reminded me of who I am." She leaned and kissed him. Just as he put his arms around her a *knock* interrupted him.

"What is it!" he frowned as he pulled back from Elspeth.

"It's me Finn. There's a fire in the third long house. Fight between a Crixior, a Crimson Keeper, and an Ocrul. The Sanguine Squadron, mine. I stopped it once, but they didn't listen. I'm sorry, but I need you for this."

"Damn, this is all I need."

"Go," said Elspeth. "They need you. I'm okay really. I really want to take a walk on the beach anyway."

"Alone?"

"Isn't this why we're in Wesladus? Aren't we safe?"

"I just doona want you alone." He pushed his hair back off his face and groaned.

"Ian!" shouted Finn. "I have to get back. Meet you there."

"Coming!" He jumped up and threw his clothes on, grabbed his sword, pulled on his boots, then kissed Elspeth. "Els, I'll try and meet you on the beach."

When he got to the long house there was banging, smashing, a lightning bolt came through the window, wind swirled, breaking glass, it was a damn hurricane in there. Ian stormed through the door, they all stopped and looked at him. Finn smiled. "Hi Ian."

"The last thing I need today is a bunch of numpty men actin' like they ain't got any damn baws. You four against the wall." They all started talking at once. Ian let his fangs drop then pulled his sword. "The next one tae speak loses his head. Against the damn wall! Finn what happened?"

"The fae and vampire pulled a trick on the demon. They put nightshade in his drink."

"That damn stuff makes any species sick. What the hell were you thinkin'?" he asked, continuing without waiting for an answer. "So, the demon attacked?"

"Not then, the fae and vampire attacked the demon, and when he didn't respond, they attacked his demon friend, that's when he finally reacted."

"Wait a minute. First give me your names. Demon one, who dinnae attack until your friend got hit, step forward."

The tall, dark, long haired demon stood forward. "My name is Lysanthir, my lord, my *demon* friends call me Lys."

"Demon friend two?" Ian stood straighter, tilted his

head, and crossed his arms.

"Bane, my lord."

"Fae?"

"Waythe, my lord."

"Vampire."

"Vander, my lord."

"Why did you two bumbling wallopers put nightshade in Lysanthir's drink? How old are you, two? Answer me Vander."

With a red face, he mumbled. "We didn't mean anything by it. It was just a joke."

"This war we're aboot tae fight is nae joke. But, for the joke you played, you two will not get dinner, but you will have your mead. With nightshade. After a lovely night of nightshade, you two will be the first in the training yard, at daybreak. Lysanthir?"

"Yes, my lord."

"Are you a good soldier? I mean tae say are you good in battle?"

"Sir, I can hold my own. Yes."

"Then right now we are goin' tae the training yard. You will fight Waythe and Vander and you all can use your powers, giving it everythin' you've got."

"Sir," said Lysanthir, "that would be like me fighting you."

"Weren't you fighting them anyway?"

"Well…yes. Yes, sir, to the training yard."

Waythe and Vander walked out with grins on their faces.

Ian and Finn stood at the edge, waiting and watching. Finn leaned over and whispered. "Weren't you a little hard on Lysanthir?"

"I have my reasons. Shut up and watch."

Vander shot fire balls at Lysanthir, while at the same time Waythe called on the earth. The ground rolled beneath the target. Lysanthir deflected them all, one by one, by just raising his hand up and out. They fizzled out in midair. He returned fireballs back just as fast. Waythe called water and rain to put out the blazes. Then he called wind to dry up the water.

Lysanthir disappeared upon attack and appeared a short distance away, avoiding flying objects. The two men drew swords and charged the demon. Lysanthir drew his sword blocked, parried, and struck at Waythe. When he knocked Waythe down he went after Vander. Vander was good but Lysanthir was better.

He blocked over and over then knocked him to the ground. Waythe and Vander, got up angry, and charged full force, but Lysanthir just appeared to be playing with them. This went on until Lysanthir appeared to tire of it. He glanced around and three rocks lifted into the air.

Twirling his finger in circles, the rocks began to rotate. The men stopped and dropped their swords mesmerized by the flying rocks. While they were distracted, Lysanthir shot fire bolts at them. They deflected.

Lysanthir started walking toward them bringing the rocks down to rotate around their heads. Since they were standing next to each other it was a rather small circle. But the rocks were going very fast past their faces. Unsure what to do they tried to follow the rocks movements.

In a split-second Lysanthir disappeared and reappeared behind the men. The rocks stopped in midair, one in front of their faces and two behind them.

The men continued to stare at the hovering rock. Lysanthir grabbed the two rocks from the air and hit each man in the head from behind. They both went down, out cold.

Ian laughed. "He's a thinker that one." He walked to the two laying on the ground and called rain. The cold water brought both men around. "Get up you two egg heads." They stood rubbing their heads and mumbling. "I ever catch you pulling another prank, no matter how small or trivial, you're out of here. We have a war tae fight, and I will not have a couple of ninny goats for soldiers. Do I make myself clear?"

"Yes, sir," they both replied. They looked a bit confused at what had transpired.

"Lysanthir you showed restraint from attacking these nimble wits when they drugged you, you showed restraint when they attacked you, when one of yours was in danger, you fought back, and you proved yourself a worthy fighter."

He chuckled again and put his hand on Lysanthir's shoulder and continued as they were walking toward Finn. "Now I willna say that at first, I wasn't a little angry at demons, I was.

"Me father and brother were killed by Asurad demons. But watching you all in training, I've learned you aren't all alike. It's taking some getting used to and I've had to rethink things, but I'm coming to understand the difference between the two demon factions. There are good demon's and you're one of them. I can see it and sense it. So, I was wrong. We ken there's animosity amongst you all, and I want these men to ken, you are all fighting on the same side. But that isn't why I am picking you, nae. It's because you are a good mon and a soldier. I am in need of a first. So, you're with me. Finn, find you a new demon, Lysanthir is moving into the lower floor of the castle.

"Get your things. I'll see you there and show you your room. Day break you're helping tae train idiots like these two. You two!" he shouted, "go clean up the hall you destroyed, then go tae your chambers, nae the soldiers eating hall, stay there until dinner time, and Finn will make sure you get your nightshade. Make sure the mess you instigated is cleaned up by then. Everyone dismissed. I'm going tae the beach and find Els. See you at the castle, Lysanthir. Finn, take control of your men," he said, with an exasperated look.

****

He stood off to the side, just behind Elspeth, watching her silently. He looked at her lovingly. He'd changed and put on his tartan, and kilt of green and black. He figured he'd spend the rest of the day with her. She was beautiful, bent over humming. She was sifting through shells, putting them in the edge of her white day gown that she was using as a pocket.

It dipped deep and he figured she'd found a lot of shells. She was humming the same Scottish ballad she'd sang the other day. Ian decided then, that it was his favorite song. Her hair glistened bright red and the ends brushed the edge of the water as the waves splashed in, then receded out.

He watched as the strands followed the lazy waves in and out, and without thinking or stopping, she unconsciously pulled them back to her. She was a lovely sight to behold.

He wanted to run his hands through her long locks and down her body. Just looking at her made him hard.

He wanted her, but only if she was ready for him. He didn't want to rush her after what she'd experienced.

He started walking toward her. "Hi, my bonnie wee lass! You collectin' the bottom of the ocean?"

"Nae, Ian," she said as she turned toward him with a smile. "If I did that, where would the ocean go?" She grinned.

He took hold of her shoulders gently and raised her up facing him. "You are so bonnie I could get lost for days, just lookin' at you." He looked at her face, her eye, turned her cheek slightly, so he could see it in the bright of day. "Does it hurt ever so much?" he asked.

"Only if I touch it or look away tae fast." She smiled again, and he noticed a crack in her lip broken open from a cut he had missed the day before. He was once again angry and had to quell his emotions. He watched as she unconsciously flicked out her tongue to gather the drop of blood that seeped out. He quickly reached out and with his thumb gently wiped the blood away. She stepped back.

"It doesn't hurt Ian, you have a look like you'd like tae kill someone, doona scowl my brave savior, it is over, and these marks will be gone in a few days. We need tae find Merlin. He's old and Athdar will hurt him. He and Drakkor. The kingdom, Ian what will happen there?"

He sighed, putting from his thoughts of killing King Rulm all over again out of his mind. "I have already decided to send Angus to take care of the queen and whatever else needs to be handled. Even though we are depending on Lauren's dreams and visions, I'm putting him in charge of training the Axuard Squad. The rest are working tirelessly over Merlin's whereabouts, Drakkor, Athdar, and the coming war."

"I see…" she said. "Weel partially." And she laughed at her own attempt at joking. He looked in her eyes as she reached up and pushed his hair from his face. Concern marred her otherwise calm exterior. He stood silent and still as she reached up to kiss him, then release his mouth to touch him softly on his neck with her lips. She let go of her dress and all the shells fell in a pile at her feet.

He held back, waiting on her as she reached up and put her arms around his shoulders. Standing on her tip-toes, she kissed him ever so tenderly. Using her tongue, she parted his lips and he groaned.

"You ken what's tae happen now," he said removing his tartan and laying it on the beach. He glanced around, looking for prying eyes, and noticed they were in a secluded cove with cliffs reaching up behind them. If someone should swim, they'd be a mile down the beach where the cliffs end. Solitude. He turned to her and lifted her day dress off and smiled when he saw that she had nothing underneath it. "Bonnie," he whispered. "Come tae me, my bonnie lady."

She stepped up to him and he tightly wrapped his arms around her and they kissed. She was certainly the instigator today, because suddenly she ripped at his kilt. He laughed. He removed his kilt, hose, and shoes, and stood gloriously hard in front of her.

He knelt on the tartan he'd removed just moments ago. His eyes never leaving hers. She melted in his arms. God's, he wanted her. So much, he trembled, and then noticed she did as well.

Mistaking the tremble for fear, he said, "We can

wait if you need, Els. You need tae heal and aren't ready for this."

"If you make me wait one more minute, I'll scream at you, then ne'er speak to you again."

He laughed. Seeing his mistake, he replied. "Far be it from me tae not give my lady what she wants." He pulled her to him.

She shoved him to his back and straddled him. She leaned down and pulled the tie from his hair and fanned it out. He closed his eyes and felt her run her fingers through his long locks. Her tentative touch doing things to his insides. Her breasts brushed his face and he opened his mouth, his tongue laving her nipples.

He felt a shudder run through her as she leaned down and kissed him. He was hard tucked up against her buttocks and his shaft jerked against her. When he grabbed her to turn her she stopped his attempt to take control. He let her. He felt she needed to take back something she may have lost at the king's hands. It would be hard on his control, but he'd give her this.

"I want you Ian, I wish to touch and explore you," she said, as she brushed her hands up and down his chest. Where her hands went her lips and tongue followed. He let her explore. Her hair fell in waves and traveled after her tongue.

He thought he'd go mad but laid there letting her explore. She laved the tight little nubs of his nipples. Swirling her tongue around them then nipping. He drew in a quick breath of air as he felt he had surely lost the ability to breathe. He lay still for her even though he wanted more than anything to throw her down and bury himself deep inside her, reclaim her, make her his all over again.

She backed up straddling his thighs and continued her tongue bath to his navel. Then she surprised him. She licked the length of him then plunged her mouth down around him. He almost lost it. Then when she wrapped her hand around him, the touch was enough to send him in a frenzy. She lapped at the bead of moisture that he knew was there, then she wrapped him in the heat of her mouth. Without notice she drew him to the back of her throat. He groaned loudly. That did it, he could take no more. "Els..." She sucked him in deep and used her hand to follow her mouth, repeating the strokes.

"Stop Els...please. I won't last." He leaned up and grabbed her wrists to stop her. "Lay down, and he grabbed her shoulders and pulled her off him. Once down she lifted her knees and spread herself wide. Ian kneeled in between her legs and placed his hands under her bottom. He sucked her button and laved his tongue over and around it. She moaned.

"Please Ian...I want you inside me, now."

He laughed and said, "Not yet my bonnie woman. I'm not done." He placed his finger inside her. She was so hot and wet.

She thrashed her head back and forth and just when he knew she was to explode he sat up and plunged in. He almost lost his seed right then but held still for a moment. Then he pulled out and buried deep again.

Elspeth looked at him, "Faster, harder, now!" He immediately thrust harder and her hips came up to meet him. She wrapped her long legs around him and held on for dear life.

The last thrust she exploded and with one more stroke, he joined her, biting her at the same time, with a gulp of her blood it engulfed them in another exploding orgasm. It continued until he pulled his teeth from her neck.

They screamed out and rode the blissful rollercoaster together. He leaned down and kissed her softly before turning to his side. They held each other until they reached earth. He looked at her. "Would you like a swim."

"I'd love tae swim." She giggled. "Come on." Jumping up she grabbed his hand to pull him up. He jumped up laughing and chased her into the waves where they laughed, splashed, and swam.

They made love once again after swimming, then lay there, him on his back toward the sun, and she on her side, her head on his shoulder. They lay in silence, enjoying the breeze and the sound of the waves.

They stayed that way until the tide started coming in, and he said. "It must be time tae eat Els. We should go." She murmured something about never wanting to leave. She was half asleep. He nudged her slightly. "Come sweetling, time tae go."

Chapter 23

The next morning came late for Ian, but he'd made it to break his fast in time. Halfway through the meal he looked up and saw Lauren descending the steps. Then everyone looked up from the tables in the great room as Lauren walked down the stairs. He noticed he looked like hell and knew immediately he'd had a rough night, most likely more dreams of Merlin. "You look like a damn bull pulled you through the gates of hell," he said with a mouthful of biscuits and jam.

"I have a lot tae tell you. Been a busy night." Lauren rounded the corner and had to take a seat down from his usual place. He saw him look down the line of brothers at the stranger sitting in his usual spot. "Who's that?"

"He's my first, Lysanthir," he replied. "Anything you got tae say, you can do so in front of him."

"Pleased tae meet you, Lysanthir. Weel, I dreamt all night aboot Merlin, then aboot King Arthur. It went back and forth all night."

"Were you able to contact the angels?"

"Nae, I tried at first, but my dreams went immediately to Merlin, then were busy all night. I didn't think I'd be able to contact them anyway. My dreams usually just receive. I have on occasion reached out, but it doesn't seem to work that way."

The cook interrupted. "Breakfast?" She asked

Lauren from a doorway.

"Please," he replied.

"Be right there."

"Anyway, as I was saying. I was walking a long narrow hall, all made of wood. It was dark even with a lit torch. Dark wood, polished floors, walls, and ceiling. Each side of the hall had doors. Rows of them. At the end of the hall I could go left, right, or straight up some stairs. I went left. I came tae a high gathering room.

"It made me think monastery, because it had an alter with crosses on the wall. I walked to the alter, and before it, laying on the floor, was a dead priest. I left and went back to the hall. At the right was another hallway with more doors. I heard a moan and it sounded like it was coming from the upstairs."

The maid returned putting a trencher of food in front of Lauren. "Thank you," he said grabbing a piece of bread, swathing it through thick gravy.

"I went up the stairs and came tae a door where I heard the moaning. I could not open it, it was locked. So, I floated through. It was a huge room. Dark like the rest of the place, eerie it was. There was Merlin tied tae a wooden chair. His hair flying in all directions. Beat up he was, and lookin' older than usual. He was alone, but he looked up and saw me. He tried tae speak, so I went closer.

"The dream you had about my room," he told me. "It wasn't future, it was past. Athdar had some of my ether before your dream. He's barely keeping me alive. He comes every day and drains my ether leaving just enough to keep me alive. It gives him power. He said he'd kill me in front of Ian and Elspeth before he killed them. Take some of my hair. Do it, before you leave.

Locator sp…sp…spell. Hurry though, he wants King Arthur, and he's using my knowledge to find him…must save…"

"Then he passed out. I have never had a dream about the past afore, so this was news tae me, and I'll be damned if I didn't wake up with a handful of Merlin's hair. Doona ask me how that happened, because I couldn't answer that, probably Merlin. Anyway, I dinna ken where he was, so I went to the window to look out. The place was in the clouds. I went downstairs and ran past the priest and ootside. It was surrounded by clouds. I ran a distance and if I hadn't been watchin', I'd have run off a cliff. It's up in the clouds somewhere. I just doona ken where."

"Did you notice anythin' else?" he asked, putting down his knife.

"Yes, verra sad, but not important. I looked through a few doors and found dead boys. I couldn't look through anymore, after the first couple doors."

Everyone was quiet.

"After that my dream changed tae King Arthur. There's Kearals and Asurads heading to Arthur's now. Not an army, but a league of soldiers. Half Asurads and half Kearals. If it were a legion of them, we wouldn't make it.

"I doona think Drakkor and Athdar have that many yet. There's still time tae beat them, but we have no time for training. These men have tae go Ian. Arthur's in danger. Trained or not they have tae go. They ken either how to get through the barrier Merlin placed or he's so weak he can't hold it. Arthur, his men, the kingdom, all sitting ducks, and these people doona care if it's men, women, or children they kill. I'm tellin' you, they're ruthless."

He cleared his throat and sat back. "Weel, Angus is going to Mystic Kingdom tae take care of the kingdom and queen. You have tae take his place with the army. That leaves Dougal, and Cameron here tae find out aboot Merlin. I'm taking Elspeth to Mither's as soon as we're done eating. I ken you probably doona like it, but I will pull no quarter aboot it," he said, turning toward her. She didn't respond, instead sat quiet in thought, staring down at her plate, so he continued.

"Lauren, you ready Angus' Squadron. Connor, Finn, and Taryn the same with yours. I'm going with you, and all squadrons are goin' ready or not. Conall I ken you are working with Dougal and Cameron, but I want you with us as weel. You may see somethin' we doona ken aboot. Dougal and Cameron will have tae find Merlin. We canna take the chance with King Arthur being captured. We leave in the morning. Training as usual.

"Lys, with the men. Watch each Squadron in training, give your best advice, and hope tae hell they take it. Make note of the strongest and smartest. We'll split them up evenly." He turned once again to Elspeth. "Els, I need you tae not argue with me on this. I need tae ken your safe." He stood and held out his hand for hers. "I canna take you with us. It's too far, I ken you wanted to be here for the war, but this is a simple battle for King Arthur and it is far away, so doona argue. Please." He looked at her pleadingly. He couldn't take her, not now, not after what happened with King Rulm, it was still too damn raw.

She took his hand, a quiet understanding showing on her face, their united souls saying more than his words, and said, "I ken I said I wanted to be here for the fight, and I want tae be, but if you feel it is a simple battle, and all will be weel, I'll go tae your Mither's, but Ian, anything else I have tae be here for. On this I will not argue with you, so let me be clear on future battles. I doona care how far they are, I am nae going to cower from my duty as a healer, and if you have need of me on this one, I expect you tae get me right away. You have tae promise that. With that being said, I shall enjoy your Mither and sisters, I look forward to it. Let me pack and I'll be ready."

She was back rather quickly, he was surprised, but then again, she didn't have much. Mental note; talk to mither.

Angus entered and was ready to go with them. He nodded to Angus. "Let me call Ator and we'll be on our way."

He called for the dragon, he was big enough to take three through the veils. He could drop them to outer earth at the McGregor Keep, where he could stay with Elspeth while Ator continued to inner earth to drop Angus at Mystic Kingdom.

He'd have to use the Mystic Mountain portal. Then Ator would return, pick him up and take him back to Wesladus so he would be ready to leave in the morning with his men. That would give him some time to spend with Elspeth and his family.

He grinned and wondered what Angus would look like granitized. The only portal he knew straight to inner earth was Mystic Mountain and the gargoyles. There was the stationary portal to Wesladus, but it only went to outer earth.

He wished he could take his men via this portal,

but the gargoyles had only given permission for him to use it. He knew they wouldn't let any more men through. It was pressing it just taking Angus, and he sure didn't want to alienate his new friends in any way.

They didn't have any other way to create a portal. He missed Merlin. Suddenly he felt very sad for him, thinking about his pain. He hoped with all he had, that the old wizard would make it.

He took Els bag and grabbed her hand and led her outside. He looked at her. "Els, I would rather be with you right now. I had planned on spending several days with you, at least 'til you were healed. Until Lauren's dream…"

"Shush," she said. "I love you, Ian, I understand. You need tae be with your men. I wouldn't want it any other way. I also ken why you doona want me at this battle. I really do understand. To tell you the truth I'm not yet over my fears of what happened. I'm not sure I would be much help."

She touched her injured eye. "Thank you for not mentioning why you doona want me tae go and for kenning why it would be hard for me tae right now. I want tae go tae your Mither's. I think I need her right now. Besides, I'm verra fond of her and your sisters. They want to make my wedding dress. I want them tae. You'll be back, you have tae. You're tae marry me." She teared up.

"Nae, stop Els. You ken I'll make it back. Nothing can keep me from you. I love you. I'll always love you."

"I doona ken what's wrong with me. I never cry and I've done so much of it lately." She hurriedly wiped at her face.

195

He kissed her gently and wondered what his Mither would say about her eye. He'd have to tell her the story. "You've been through a lot sweetling. No need tae think anything of it. I mean that. I wouldn't have let you go even if you had insisted, you ken that doona you?"

"Yes, I ken. Thank you."

"Och, Bullocks Els, if anythin' were tae happen tae you…"

"Shush," she said and leaned up to kiss him.

"Ah, here's Ator. Angus!" he shouted, "Ready?"

Ator flew straight, no sightseeing, and dropped them at the front door. Moira and the girls came running out screaming "Ian's on a dragon! He's so big! He's beautiful!" Moira smiled, "Aye, I can see that."

He noticed Ator loved the attention. He carefully lowered his wing to let him down, then turned to the young ladies. He nuzzled each, which garnered a pat, a pet, a few kisses, and a lot of squeals. Moira asked if Angus was coming down. He answered in the negative and said Ian would fill her in. Finally, he stopped the girls. "Angus has tae leave. I'll explain."

"Do you want tae explain Elspeth's eye," Moira asked sternly. "I ken you dinna do it. So how did that happen?"

"I'll explain all when we…"

"Ian, Elspeth!" Akira came running up leaving the other girls to watch Ator fly away. "How did you get tae be friends with a dragon? Think I can ride sometime? Elspeth, what happened tae your eye? Ian, did you hit her?" She put her hands on her hips, tilted her head, and drew in a deep breath.

Elspeth laughed, "Nae your brother would never

hit me. He saved me though. I'd be dead if he hadn't."

The other girls came running, screaming for Elspeth. They stopped dead in their tracks. "What happened tae your eye?" They all asked at once.

Akira answered. "Ian didn't hit her! He saved her." Fiona took one arm and Catriona took the other. They led her through the front doors. "You must tell us what happened," Akira said right behind them. "You can see the fabrics now, Och, you canna get married with your eye swollen like that!"

"*Akira!*" he shouted.

She flinched. "I mean I hope your eye is better in time for the weddin'. Mither thinks summer will be nice. What do you think? That way everyone can travel here and it's so beautiful by the loch then. A wedding. Do you think I'll ever get married?"

Elspeth laughed, "Why of course you will. You all will, you're all so beautiful."

"I willna," said Catriona. "I wish to be a warrior like my brothers."

"Oh, Catriona there are many ways we women are warriors. The biggest challenge is taking care of the men." Elspeth laughed, and so did the girls. Holding on to Elspeth, they led her up the stairs to the solarium.

"I have a mark mither." He pulled down his shirt so she could see the dragon above his heart, as they walked inside. "I saved his life, and with the mark we can talk tae each other. I understand all the dragons and they me. But they doona use their mouth, it's crazy, they speak through thought."

"That's wonderfully exciting Ian. The girls are thrilled. I doona ken if I want them riding a dragon though. I see that's nae the only mark you have," she said, smiling. "You and Elspeth. I'm happy for you. You've been busy saving a lot of lives lately. Your da would be so proud. You must tell me everythin'. I'll get the mead, you sit."

He sat as his mother poured mead into his tankard. "Mither, I almost lost Elspeth. The king from Mystic Mountain was ready tae violently take her, any later and…"

"Did you kill him?"

"I most certainly did and I'd kill him again if I could."

"Good. Now tell me everythin'."

So, he did. When he finished, he said, "Mither, Elspeth hasn't much. I have gold stashed in my box, in my bedchamber. Please take her tae market and buy her dresses and some fancy jewelry.

"She likes nice things, and she's never had them. She has only a few gowns Merlin gave her, and only two nightdresses. I want her tae have whatever she wants. I love her, mither. I want her tae be happy.

"Will you do that? I would, but I doona ken how long this war will be. I doona ken if we'll ever get Merlin back, or if we can save King Arthur. Please take care of Els for me? I'll talk tae her aboot it so she willna worry and will buy some nice things."

"I will son. I love her like a daughter. I will take her tae market. The girls have been beggin' me tae anyway."

"Weel, time for Ator. I'd like tae see Els afore I leave. Speaking of which…"

Down came the giggling girls with Elspeth laughing the loudest. He watched her as she came down. His mother touched his shoulder, "She's bonnie,

198

Ian."

"Oh, Aye, she certainly is…" He got up to meet her, and he took her in his arms and kissed her. She blushed, and the girls giggled. "Come let's walk down tae the loch," he said as he put his arm around her and led her out through the doors.

They stopped at the edge of the water, silently looking out over the loch. "Els, I want you tae ken I love you. I'm goin' tae miss you terribly. I promise as soon as we're done with Arthur, I'll be back tae pick you up.

"I also want you tae ken something. I've worked many years and have amassed a fortune. I'm tellin' you, because I asked mither tae take you tae market. I would do so myself, but weel you ken what we're facing right now. Anyway, I told her tae make sure you get whatever you want."

"Ian, I have all I want. You."

"Please Els, buy some dresses, a lot of dresses, and make them fancy with some jewels, and some fine nightdresses like Merlin got you." He wiggled his eyebrows. "I want tae see you in fine things. You're bonnie, and such a bonnie lady, should wear bonnie things. I'd like tae see you in them. If nae for you, then me. Match everythin, up. I want tae see what you pick. Please Els have fun, and don't worry aboot the cost. I have more than enough."

"Aye, I will. I shall have fun and think of you every minute." He knew she was trying hard to be brave but knew the instant she lost the battle. "Oh, bullocks," she said, and broke out sobbing. "I see Ator coming. I doona want tae let you go," she said, teary eyed. She reached up and kissed him, and she sobbed through their kiss. He grabbed ahold of her and crushed his lips to hers. "I love you Els…" he whispered. "Doona worry, I'll be back."

"I love you, Ian McGregor." She sobbed back, out of breath.

"Els," he said, pausing. "I have something for you." He reached inside the pocket of his tartan and withdrew something. He could feel a rare boyish blush spread across his face, he couldn't help it. He'd never told anyone about what he had carried with him since he was a boy. He held out his hand.

She looked at him surprised and wiped her eyes. He opened his hand, in it lie a very small, crude, carved horse. "I made this as a boy. I kind of think of it as my magical stallion. He would always take me safely through battle and bring me oot alive…"

"Ian it's beautiful, but I can't take that, it's good luck for you," she said sobbing more.

"Hush, sweetling and dry those tears. I want you tae have it. If it meant nothing tae me, what kind of gift would it be tae you?" he said as he sighed. "I've ne'er shown this tae anyone, you are the first. When I was young I pretended I was as good a wizard as Merlin. I thought if I could make this magical stallion he would see to it I would always be safe.

"I pulled plants from the ground and I have no idea what they were. I crushed them in a bowl and said some non-sense over them, then thought I had made the most magical thing ever, then I burned the leaves or plants, held the horse in the smoke, mumbled some more nonsense, and thought I created the perfect magic token."

He stroked her face. "I have carried the darn thing

for near eight hundred years, now I want you tae have it. Think of me when you get lonely and ken I will be back. Ken, I love you, Els, please," he said as he put it in her hand and closed her fingers over it.

Tears streamed down her face. "I do…do…doona ken what tae say Ian. You mean more tae me than anything or anyone I have ever ken. This means more tae me than any gift I could ever get. But, I canna lose you. I just canna. Please…" she looked at him pleadingly. She paused, then quietly relented. "I swear, Ian, be quick with this battle, come back as soon as you can, whole. I need you. I mean it."

"I ken you do, Els. I'll be back. I promise. Now Ator is waiting, I must go. Remember I love you."

"I love you, too, Ian. With all my heart," and she desperately kissed him again. He finally let go of her and her eyes never left him as he climbed aboard Ator, and they took off. He watched her stand there while her silent tears rolled down her cheeks, and thought he had never seen anything lovelier, he watched until he couldn't see her any longer. He sighed then, he already missed her.

****

When Ian got back to Wesladus the place was in chaos. People rushing everywhere. Lysanthir was directing and his brothers were shouting at their groups.

He walked toward the castle to have a few words with Dougal, Conall, and Cameron. He found them on the fourth floor in the wizard's lab.

Dougal was casting a locator spell. A map was laying on the table and he dangled a pendulum over it. Tied to it was some hair. Must be Merlin's. He watched as the object turned around in circles.

"Will that find Merlin?"

"Truth? I think they have him cloaked. Unless I can find a spell to break it, I willna be able tae find Merlin. I've tried several times. Back tae the book, I guess. You ready for tomorrow?"

"Aye, as ready as I'll ever be. Weel I must pack. See you at dinner?"

"We'll be there," answered Conall.

Dinner was busy. Cameron talked about the book. "I think I may have found something aboot cloaking. We're going to try it tomorrow. We'll try a cloak, then try breaking it, if it works, I may be able to break the one on Merlin. It will take his hair and some blood. It's supposed to be from Athdar's bloodline, since he made the cloaking spell, but I may be able to try something else. The only blood relative I ken was reborn… That's it! Athdar is reborn. Why dinna I think of that? Och! I'm so stupid!"

"What the hell is your geggie goin' on aboot? Are you nuts now?" Ian pushed worogild into his mouth.

"No," he said, obviously disappointed. "I was wrong. Never mind. Athdar wasn't born. I'll figure it oot."

He shook his head at his brother, sighed, and turned to Lysanthir. "Lysanthir you got the list of men I asked you for?"

"Yes, right here."

"I'll take it up with me and divide these men equal with the squadrons. We'll go over maneuvers in the mornin'. Connor have you some strategies figured out?"

"Aye, I do. I'm still flattening out some wrinkles. I'll finish tonight and we'll go over them in the mornin'."

"If we're done I'm headin' up, I got some things tae do. You should all turn in early. Who kens after tonight, how much rest anyone will get. See you at sun rise."

Chapter 24

Ian stood at the head of the long table in the great room. The morning meal had been cleared away, and he, his brothers, and his first, stood over a map. "If they come from south of the castle we can meet them here at the woods," he said, and put his finger on the large map.

Connor looked at where he pointed. "If we place one team here—" he pointed to a spot farther south, "cross the river here, we can have that team blindside them. We can have another waiting at the cliffs, here—" he said, pointing to another spot. "Then the other two can ambush from both sides out of the forest, forcing them toward the cliffs where they will be cornered. That way they will be surrounded. We can call the dragons and hopefully together we can stop it before it gets started."

Lysanthir spoke up. "But if they veer off and come from this direction," he said, pointing to another spot, "coming in the back way toward the castle, we will miss them and they have free rein to attack. It leaves this opening vulnerable."

"Yes," said Connor. "But this is the only route that is feasible for them to take. I agree, though, they could veer off there. Good point. Weel, we'll have to split all the teams up and put one group here to make sure they take the first intended path, we have to get them to the cliffs. Split the one group equally on both sides of the road in the forest, the one team cross the river, and the other at the cliffs to block them in, while putting a team where Lysanthir mentioned."

He looked up. "Now we ken that Drakkor and Athdar have their sights on kings and their armies. We ken Merlin has been taken and in all likelihood the protection Merlin put around his kingdom is gone, leaving King Arthur vulnerable. He probably doesn't ken. King Arthur has the largest, and he's the most important king, we knew it would only be a matter of time afore they tried to capture him.

"They must have made enough and think they are sending enough to do the job. We canna have him captured. We all agree on that. We have tae have a fool proof plan. What you're saying makes sense. Good job Connor and Lysanthir. I'm glad you are my first, Lysanthir. You are proving worthy."

He motioned toward a piece of parchment next to the map. "I went over your list and split the men up with four in each group. Since so many came from Angus' Axuard Squad, we'll have tae pull some of the men from other squads. We kenned we'd have tae regroup them eventually anyway. We'll just have tae just do it faster than we'd like. Make sure all squads are equal."

He looked at his brother. "Lauren, with Angus away at Mystic Kingdom, you have the Axuard Squad tae lead. Put them here at the river.

"Connor, I want you and the Xiann squad at the cliffs. Finn, you and the Sanguine squad take the woods since that's where we attack

"I'll be with you." Ian looked at Finn. He was a

good soldier, but maybe not a strong enough leader. After the incident at the longhouse, he'd worried about him.

Ian continued, "Taryn, you will take the Qruhr Squad and wait at the point where they can veer off. Stay quiet though. If they continue on the direct path move ahead of them and meet Finn and I at the woods, if they are faster getting there, just meet up with us.

"If by chance they do veer, attack at that point to force them back tae the road. If you need help, I'll have Ator have a dragon ready to get Finn and I tae help. There will also be a dragon hidden with each group.

"Ator and the rest of the dragons will be in the cliffs waiting for the fight. *Remember,* these new demon's, have incredible power. We're facing demon/fae and demon/vamp. I'm unsure what these combined powers can do but keep watch. We aren't goin' after something we are used tae fighting.

"Conall, since I've pulled you from the upstairs, I need you tae go to King Arthur's. Mist tae the Wattingham portal east of here and take it tae inner earth, it's an hour travel for you, but will be a day's ride from Wattingham Fort for the troops. The Kearal started from mystic mountain, we should have an extra day tae prepare after we get there."

He took a deep breath. "You can mist, but the rest of us will garner a change of horses at Wattingham Fort. The dragons will take Mystic Mountain portal, it's their safest and most unobtrusive way tae travel. They will fly ahead of us and wait and settle in the cliffs. I talked tae Ator last night, I'll mention the new plan this morning.

"Conall, explain the situation tae Arthur and have

him ready for battle. Get his people tae safety as much as you can. The castle would be good. Have them evacuate the inner city and make sure they get them inside the castle.

"From where Lauren showed us the Kearals are, we have approximately a day and a half ahead of the Kearals and a day there tae get situated if we leave this morning with very few stops. The journey will be arduous, and we need tae let the men know the seriousness of this mission.

"Athdar isn't sending all his men, he's smart, but we can put a dent in his army. I ken the men will hate killin' their own kind. If we could get the ether and open those jars these Kearals would get their souls back and be like afore. But you have tae let these men ken…they aren't dealing with their kind, they are dealing with hybrid killers, and they have tae be stopped. You each gather your squadrons then explain everythin'. I will talk tae them all afore we leave this morning.

"Conall you can leave now for King Arthur's. You will be there within the hour from Wattingham Fort. Dismissed. Finn stay for a moment we need tae speak."

When all were gone, he cleared his throat. "I ken you are havin' trouble leading these men, not everyone was born tae do this job, it's hard, you have tae be firm and resolved in your decisions and sometimes quick thinking."

He smiled at his brother and then turned serious again. "You are the baby of us boys, but you aren't dumb, in fact your kind heart gets you in trouble sometimes. If you feel uncomfortable going it's okay, I'll go in your stead. But if you want tae do this, you have tae have a clear head and when you say something tae your men, mean it, and back it up with force. You're a damn good soldier, when you fight you doona think twice. You fight like a hungry lion. Lead like a hungry lion. Now the choice is yours, but once made, it canna be changed."

Finn looked at his brother, first anguish flashed his face then surprise. "Ian you're a hundred percent right. I can do this. I'm not in this to make friends. Leaders are leaders, sometimes friends happen, sometimes not. A job, an important job needs done. I'll be damned if I quit now. I'm a McGregor, we doona shirk our responsibilities. Thank you, Ian, you just opened my eyes. I was looking at everything wrong. But, I'll be damned if I quit now. I'm in, I'll lead. And Ian thanks for not mentioning the other day, with the men, you ken."

He laughed and put his hand on Finn's shoulder. "Let me tell you how I overcame my first time as a leader. You aren't going tae believe my story." He shared the story as they walked out to the training yard, both laughing all the way.

It was chaos in the yards and Ian watched Lysanthir closely. He admired his forthrightness in organizing men. He had a detailed list and he was directing each man to stand in a particular squadron. There were four groups and he watched as men changed places quickly.

Then he called the four best from each squadron forward. "You men that were chosen by Lysanthir are the best in your teams. I expect you tae watch oot for the men in your squad. Each of you, take on two men within your squad and stick together. Now your commanders will take their new squadrons from here. Lauren is taking the Axuard Squad as Angus is called away. Connor for the Xiann Squad. Finn, you have your Sanguine Squad, and Taryn you have the Qruhr Squad. Take over."

He was impressed with Lysanthir. Usually his intuition was right, maybe it had to do with knowing when someone lied or told the truth, he didn't know, but Lysanthir was proving to be a great first.

He heard Finn shouting at his squad and walked closer to listen. "These Kearals aren't what you think. They aren't your comrades, brothers, or friends. They lost everything good aboot them. Doona think twice aboot killin' them, because they willna think twice aboot killin' you."

Ian smiled. Finn would work out after all. He watched the rest of his brothers giving their speeches to the squads, then watched as Lysanthir walked up beside him, stood and paused. Ian flashed him a wide smile. "You did a good job Lys, quick and efficient too. I'm glad I chose you," said Ian.

"Thanks, sir."

"Call me Ian. Tell me, Lys, do you think we can take on these new demons? I mean you are demon, you ken your powers, and you ken aboot fae and vampire powers. If you were like yourself, and say mix in Waythe and Vander, think we could beat them?"

Lysanthir snorted, "absolutely with those two…but no, I know what you mean. The combined powers of demon and fae or vampire, it'd be hard, but yes, I think we have a good chance of beating them. Especially with the help of the dragons. You want me with you on this? You didn't mention where you wanted me."

209

"Lysanthir, you are my first, you are tae be at my side at all times unless told otherwise. I like you Lys, you have great potential, you are smart, a born leader, but most of all I trust you.

"You see I have this gift of kenning people, when they lie I hear the truth. I have feelings aboot people and I somehow ken who they are and what they're like. When I said you were a good mon the other day, I meant it. You are in this tae stop evil.

"You could have done a dozen different things, but instead you offered yourself up for a position on a squadron with ones you knew would be against you from the start. I'm impressed with you, Lys."

"Thanks, Ian, it means a lot to me. You weren't the only one to lose a loved one by the hands of Asurad demons. I lost my wife and unborn child by their hands. I hate them as much as you."

"I dinna ken, Lys. I'm verra sorry tae hear that. It must be painful. I almost lost Els. I went crazy when I saw Rulm atop her and her courtin' a swollen bloody eye. I wanted tae bring him back tae life, just so I could kill him again. Did you get the bastard?"

"Not yet, that's part of the reason I'm here. I hope to see him and kill him with my bare hands."

"That's what I did. Beat him to a pulp and before he could pass out I dropped my fangs. I had the most pleasure ripping oot his neck at the end. When this is over, and if you doona find him. I'll help you locate him. I suppose you ken his name."

"I'd never forget it or him. He had me frozen watching him kill my wife. I'll never forget her face as she said good-bye to me. I will never forget his pure look of evil or his laughter and smile. He enjoyed it Ian.

The bastard enjoyed it. Zoflauc, is his name, I hope to annihilate him and his name along with it."

"We'll get him, you have my word. Come let's go to Pendragon castle and get food for the journey. Dried meat and hard bread, dried fruits, bare minimum but we'll survive. The cooks been puttin' it together all mornin'." They walked in silence to the castle. After collecting the food, they went out to call Ator. He was there in seconds.

"Ator change in plans. Lys found a bit of a problem in our plan, I need you to have another dragon watching at a small path about a mile from the forest for back up. One of the teams will be watching from the forest so they can keep them from veering off the road. They will only attack if they leave the main path. So, have your dragon stay as far back as he can and watch for any trouble, if the team attacks there, I need your dragon's help.

"If things go as planned, my men will then move forward to the forest and he can return to the cliffs. If there's trouble he needs to come and get us, so we can help."

"No problem Ian. We are ready to leave, at your word."

"You can leave now, and thanks, Ator, for all you've done in helping us."

"I wouldn't be here if it weren't for you. Saphira wouldn't be here without Elspeth. How is she?"

"At Mither's until this is over. She's healing. She's a fighter. I'm proud of her." He smiled thinking about their time at the beach.

"I'll ready my dragons," said Ator, bringing him back to the present. *"Then we'll be off. Good luck Ian.*

See you there." Ator dipped his head in a nod toward Lysanthir, backed up and spread his wings and took off in flight.

He gave a short support speech and reiterated what their commanders had said earlier. His brothers were good so he didn't have to say much. He wished everyone luck then dismissed them.

The trip to the stationary portal that would take them to Wattingham Fort was hectic. The men talked a lot. Ian figured after a while they would slow down, but they didn't. They were talking and laughing the whole way there.

Once they reached the fort, a change of horses was gathered, saddled, and packed. Food had been split up between squadrons and the carriers were packing it on the new mounts. Surprisingly the job was finished quickly. All mounted, they started their trek to King Arthurs.

****

Conall was fast as well. He appeared directly in the throne room stepping through Merlin's stationary portal. Arthur was surprised to see him appearing in the middle of court with all looking on. He knew whatever was happening Conall didn't have time for secrecy. The place went instantly quiet.

"Conall to what do I owe this visit," he asked, interrupting a man stating his complaint.

"Please, King Arthur, clear the courts. I have important news that canna wait."

Knowing the McGregors as he did he quickly ordered the court cleared. Once all were gone, but the two knights by his side, Conall began to speak.

"Arthur, it is imperative that the kingdom be

evacuated and the people brought inside the castle. A league of Kearals and Asurads are on their way here. They will kill men, women, and children tae get you and your army. They are two tae three days away. Ian and the squadrons are on their way. There's things you doona understand."

"Merlin explained everything. All about Athdar, or Seamus, whoever he really is, and Drakkor and everything they've done and are planning. That's why we are cloaked. We don't need protection."

"Athdar has Merlin. He's in bad shape and you are no longer cloaked."

He felt himself pale. He pulled his hand over his face. "Oh, my Gods…" He sat down, still trying to process the sudden news.

"You're right I have to evacuate. How can you and l fight the Asurads and Kearals? There's not much that can stop them if Merlin is right. Even with demons working in your squadrons there isn't enough single power."

"We do have a secret weapon…hordes of dragons are on the way to help."

"Help? They'd likely eat us!"

"Nae, Ian saved the life of the dragon king. He wears the mark and they communicate. Ator, the dragon, has his dragons flying in now to settle in Haersley Cliffs. They are waiting on Ian and his orders. We stand a good chance with their help."

He put his fingers to his lips. "I must ready my army. With all of you, us, and the dragons we could win this."

Conall held up his hand to get his attention. "Lauren's dream showed Athdar didn't send all the

Kearals, just half of his army, but the league is about half Kearals and half Asurads. Athdar has maybe a few hundred altogether.

"We can fight Asurads easily, but we willna ken who is what. I mean we can get an idea, because fae, vampire, and demons smell different from each other, but I'm not sure what the Kearals will smell like. We have tae hurry."

He turned to his knights. "You! Call my general have him see me now. You! Send my men out too evacuate the city and return to me. I want all men, women, and children in the castle at once and take help with you. Let it be known that no one is to be left behind. Even if you must carry them here. Now go."

Chapter 25

Ian walked his horse briskly, bringing up the rear of the troops. The air was chilly, but the sun shone brightly. The dirt road was dusty from lack of rain, but the green hillsides and valleys they passed were dotted with blue, red, and yellow spring flowers.

The trees were budding with small leaves a flutter, showing that spring was here. The birds were busy singing and building nests, and some critters were chattering in the nearby woods. The old trees stood proud and tall interspersed along their ride.

He thought how Elspeth would love it. He would bring her down this road one day if he lived long enough. He enjoyed what he could of the ride, but his thoughts kept straying from the battle to Elspeth.

He turned his mind back to the present, they could maybe make the campsite on the King's land before nightfall. They needed tomorrow to get ready. He hoped Conall made it and they were now evacuating the people who lived in the kingdom. He had faith in Conall and the rest of his brothers.

He prayed their plan worked and the dragons would provide the force they needed. Hopefully they would do the trick. Lysanthir slowed his horse and pulled up next to Ian. The squadrons had quieted down but talking between them remained.

They seemed to understand the severity of the

situation. He looked at his men and knew some wouldn't survive. It was just the nature of battle. He hoped they got more of the Kearals and Asurads than they did of them.

Demons can't burn alive, but fire from the dragons could make them wish they were dead. Lightning can kill. Lightning had killed some kearals when they tried to get Arthur the first time. But one sure way to kill demons was by removing their head. Or a blood sword, which Ian always carried. All his men carried them. They were forged by mages with a spell and blood from demon, fae, and vampire. Merlin had made sure that the swords were forged and ready when he first told Ian of the plans for the Army.

He thought he should have asked the werewolves for support, but it wasn't their war, his kind weren't involved, so he didn't. However, a werewolf bite would kill a vampire, demon, or fae. A bite would kill him. He thought maybe he should have gone to the wolf king, Larc, of the Bhak tribe of the Ogourax weres.

The largest tribe of Ogourax, and the largest of the werewolves. Turned, they were as large as a pony, double set of teeth, meaner than hell when they wanted to be, and the only thing lethal to all species.

They mostly stayed alone, lived in the woods and forests, hunting at night. No one messed with the werewolves, no one. Mixing with other species was forbidden to them. So, he didn't go to them for help. They wouldn't fight their war anyway. He was almost positive.

He'd had dealings with Larc before with Merlin. When Merlin introduced him to Larc he was very cordial. All the species would do anything for Merlin.

He had a funny feeling he should have asked for that help. Too late now.

"The men have calmed down." He nodded to Lysanthir. "I think it's finally settling in the dangers that they face."

"They'll get quieter as we get closer. Each man is thinking about fighting and possibly dying. It's hard to do battle, it's harder to fight a war. If one has never been in a war, they don't understand it. They glamorize it. But men that live through it, lose a piece of themselves every time they take a life. They are basically going in to kill their own. It will be hard on them."

"Och, I wish when I found the ether that I had ken all I had tae do was remove the caps. I could have at least saved a few. I dinna have time tae really do anythin' afore they captured me." He laughed. "You should've seen the crowds when Ator and the dragons bowed down afore me. And when I flew over the crowd on his back, they cheered. Baws, if it was nae a sight tae see. I think Ator is a ham at heart."

"I wish I could've been there to see it. I really would have enjoyed that spectacle. That will probably never happen again."

"Ator told me there hasn't been one tae carry the mark in over a thousand years. Now there is two of us."

"Do you know who the other is?"

"Yes, Elspeth, she saved Ator's mate Saphira's life and her bairns. So, my Elspeth carries the dragon above her heart as weel. It is a complete replica of Saphira, just as mine is of Ator."

"May I see it? I find it fascinating."

"Sure." He pulled his tartan off his shoulder baring

the mark.

"It looks so real, like the sun is shining off his scales like tiny rainbows. It's incredible, how did you get it?"

He laughed. "I thought he was goin' tae fry me. He leaned back like they do tae blow fire, and aye, he blew fire all right, but the flames were blue. It seared my chest, but didn't hurt, and the result is this. You can only get it if you save a dragon's life."

"Perhaps we may be saving some at the battle, but more likely they will be saving us. I'd like to have my very own dragon and fly on one."

"I can arrange you a flight for sure, but I'm stuck on savin' one for you. You'll have tae do that yourself."

"Well with that, I'm going to ride ahead and check the men. If you need me shout. I'll be up ahead a bit. I think I should keep up with the front while your back here. Nothing will probably happen, but with this crazy bunch you never know."

"Agreed." When he left, his thoughts went once again to Elspeth. He couldn't keep her out of his mind. He tried to think about the men and battle, but the next thing he knew his thoughts were of his fire haired beauty. Sometimes with clothes on and sometimes with them off. Mostly with them off. He kicked his horse and caught up with the men.

"We'll camp and eat here," he said a few hours later. There's a creek over beyond those trees for those who wish to freshen up. Tie the horses tae the trees and bring down several packs of food. We'll build a fire and camp. We'll be up and leaving at day break. Enjoy yourselves now, tomorrow will be hectic. You're released for the night." He went upstream to bathe. He couldn't help thinking of Elspeth in the river the first time he saw her, or in the tub bent over pretending to look for that damn cloth, or their swim in the ocean.

"Och, I have it bad for this woman," he said shaking his head and chuckling. He heard other men swimming and talking down river. Good to enjoy themselves now, he thought, then shuddered at what they were going to face tomorrow or the next day.

When he joined the rest of the men the fire was already blazing and rows of men surrounded it. Cheerfully sharing battle stories. They'd eaten and it was dark. Clouds covered the sky bringing the possibility of rain. The ground needed it, but Ian didn't.

He lay looking up at the black sky overhead hoping it wasn't a bad omen for the near future. He put his arms behind his head and sighed. He wasn't tired and didn't think he would get much sleep. He closed his eyes, at least he could rest, his mind filled with the image of finding Elspeth with the king. The memory of her sad smile broke his heart.

He wanted desperately to protect her, to be there for her. He wanted a family, a large one like he came from. In his eight hundred years, he'd wanted that, but never found the right woman, until now. He couldn't quit thinking of her, although he knew without a doubt when the battle commenced he'd be there in body and mind.

He had a switch he could push and become all business. He was sharp and on his toes, always fighting a good fight. He was an excellent warrior, but he wasn't conceited, he knew his limitations and the fact he could be killed.

But he figured since he was fighting for good, for

the people he protected, that the gods…the universe…protected him. It was those thoughts that got him though the worst times.

Now he just wanted to be with Elspeth. He missed her. Her laughing, humming, singing, and simply being made his heart sing. This must be what it felt like to be in love because he sure was feeling it. He was sure he wouldn't sleep this night. His mind wandered over many intimate moments with Elspeth. It was during one of these thoughts he somehow fell asleep, he wasn't sure which thought it was, when he did, but he did, and deeply.

Morning came and everyone was up at dawn, it was windy and chilly. It hadn't rained but that didn't mean it wouldn't. The sky was heavy with dark clouds and it was gloomy. The men were all quiet. The only sound was that of packing up camp and readying the horses. They had about a quarter to a half day's journey yet. Lysanthir came up to him while he was saddling his horse.

"Looks like we are in for a downpour. The men aren't looking forward to this trip. Their energy level is low."

"They will be all right once we get goin'. They have a lot on their minds. Best tae let them think aboot what's ahead and how they are goin' tae deal with it individually. It willna hurt for them tae do a little soul searching this late in the game. I do it myself before battle. Lysanthir are you ready for this?"

"As ready as I'll ever be, I expect. I'm packed and ready to go and so are the men. So, at your ready we'll be on our way."

"Mount up men!" he shouted, "we still have some

ridin' tae do. Let's head oot!"

About two thirds of the way to their destination for the day, the skies opened and drenched the men, it was a veritable deluge. It was windy and the rain icy. Even the horses were sluggish as they traipsed through the mud. The only sounds were the sucking noises their hoofs made every time they came up from the road. Lys was right, the energy level was low.

After another hour of travel, they reached the point of where the Kearals and Asurads might veer off. Ian halted everyone. "Taryn divide your men up, three in each group, hide around the trees and watch for the dark demons to approach. Do not be seen unless they leave this road. We will continue tae our destinations."

"I've sent the messages tae Ator via thought that we're here and tae send a dragon. Watch for him. Remember if they continue the road you need tae come tae Finn and me. If you continue tae the road near the river split your men in half and each group tae each side of the road inside the forest. We'll begin our attack there. Then we'll move them from the forest toward the river, where Lauren's squad will also attack, heading them toward the cliffs, where Connor and the dragons await.

"I need a volunteer tae go tae the castle and let Conall and King Arthur ken we are here. Tell him tae join us at the cliffs with his army. I doona want him earlier than that for fear of his capture. Who wants tae go?" A tall fae with blonde hair and blue eyes came forward. "Your name?"

"Marth, sir."

"Weel Marth, follow this road. You'll see the castle. Go there, tell them I sent you. You need tae see

King Arthur and Conall. Tell the King we are here. Tell him tae hold their army until they see the dragons fly from the cliffs. Make sure Conall kens tae wait for the dragons. Kenning King Arthur, he'd leave right away. It's imperative he hold back until they see the dragons. You got that?"

"Yes sir. I will be quick."

"After you get there you can ride with King Arthur's army. Doona double back, you could get yourself killed. Understand?"

"Yes sir. I'll be on my way."

"Good luck soldier." Marth tilted his head, and after kneeing his horse, he took off in a run.

"Let's continue on," he said. Pretty soon they came to the forest. "Finn and I stay here. Lauren, you ken where the river is. Go ahead and find your spot." He looked up and saw Ator. The dragon flew to the woods taking his place in a clearing. He waited there for the other groups to get settled. Good, he thought, the watch dragons are showing up. "Connor get your men tae the cliffs. Good luck men." Then he whispered, "We're goin' tae need it."

He and Finn divided the men in to two groups. Each group finding hiding spots in the woods that lined both sides of the road. They settled in despite their nerves. Despite waiting the rest of the day there was no sign of anyone.

He had thought this might happen. It would probably be tomorrow before they encountered anyone. There would be no fire tonight, food yes, fire no. Ian was glad it had stopped raining. The breeze picked up and his clothing dried.

His men felt better. It was going to be a long night.

He and Finn would take turns on the watch. Ian first. He sat against a tree where he could see a sliver of road, but no one could see him.

Just before the sun was to come up, Finn woke him. Riders could be heard in the distance. They went to the edge of the forest and watched. They couldn't tell who it was until the group split up. He heard an owl cry. When it repeated two more times he knew it was Taryn. He turned to Finn. "Wake the men, the Kearals and Asurads must be on the road." He went to Taryn. "Split your men, either side of the road and make ready. How far are they?"

"About twenty minutes," answered Taryn, "barely enough time." He looked at his men. "Take your places. Half tae one side and half tae the other. Let's move!" Thirty minutes later the soldiers came trotting toward the ambush. "Hold it…hold it… Now!" He gave the McGregor war cry followed by Finn and Taryn. The two squadrons mimicked their cries and came out from both sides of the road.

At first the Kearals and Asurads were surprised, but quickly pulled together. Horses reared and some riders were dumped to the ground. He wasted no time, before they could collect themselves, he severed four heads.

Suddenly the ground beneath them moved. He wasn't sure which side was causing it, but it was spooking everyone's horses. The movement quickly stopped before horses were lost. The demons threw fire balls. Luckily it had rained and the forest didn't go up in flames.

The demons nearest him pulled swords and charged. He was doing a lot of damage. He hoped his men were too. "Press on!" He shouted, meaning to push them toward the river. Together, his men surrounded the Kearals and Asurads and managed to drive them in the desired direction.

But he was losing men. Kearals were ripping out throats. The Asurad's fireballs were taking out others. Suddenly the earth cracked open releasing a horde of deadly insects. They hovered over his men. "Ator!"

The dragon rose over the tops of the trees and blew a straight line of fire over the insects, while attempting to destroy the enemy demons.

Ator used his fire to push them back toward the river. Ian glanced at the demon army. They needed them on the ground so they had better control of forcing them in the direction they wanted them to go. He made the earth roll and the horses spooked, rearing, whinnying and prancing. This time it had the affect he wanted. Almost all were unseated. The horses fled heading toward the forest.

Swords clashed around him and he smelled the scent of blood. The fae demons brought wind so harsh they had to fight to even walk. He put up his hand and shouted, stopping the wind.

Lysanthir was fighting alongside him and doing a good amount of damage. They were heading in the right direction, but not fast enough. "Push harder!" he yelled, and the men fought harder. Soon they were close to the river and Lauren gave the war cry, as he and his men moved in to join the fight.

They were pushing the enemy faster now, but their own men were dropping. Vampires could heal, but it could take time depending on their wounds. Fae didn't have that luxury. They were stabbed and could die from their wounds. All they had were their power to conjure elements.

The kearal leader shouted something he didn't understand. Suddenly there was a ring of fire around them and the demons quickly approached. He called rain to put out the fire. "Onward!" Somehow the men got a second wind and attacked full force. Ator flew around in circles overhead roaring his frustration at not being able to help for fear of harming those he was charged with protecting.

Finally, they had the enemy backed toward the cliffs. Realizing their mistake, the Asurads and Kearals changed tactics and tried to flee. As soon as they hit the clearing in front of the cliffs the dragons flew out. Suddenly bows and arrows appeared in the Kearals hands. "Och…my Gods, they are going to kill the dragons. Ator tell your dragons to retreat. Now!"

A resounding, *"No!"* Roared through his mind.

The dragons caught a group of Kearals together and one by one took turns blowing fire on them. They were down and crispy but not dead. His men were dropping yet the Kearals and Asurads didn't seem to tire. He was even tiring. A few dragons dropped.

Suddenly King Arthur and his army appeared. Coming in fresh, they had the energy to gain ground and take heads. The king's archers slowed down the enemy archers and bought the dragons some time. It seemed the tables were turning in their favor.

Then the skies flashed brightly, and lightning rained down on his and Arthur's men. He turned from the fight to use his powers to stop the lightning. He saw more arrows take flight and hit Ator. The dragon lost control and landed some distance away. His heart was in his throat and screamed, "Nae!" His anger gave him an increased sense of energy and he attacked with fervor.

He was severing heads left and right parrying along the way. Still he was afraid for the dragons and his falling men. "What the hell do you doaty dobbers take? Something that never tires you oot? Pansy waisted sissies!" He tried to bait them, but they didn't respond. "Bloody hell," he mumbled. They were like zombies and just kept coming. Some were missing arms and others were covered in embedded arrows.

If things weren't so serious Ian would laugh at the sight. The dragons were trying to individually blow fire at the dark demons, picking them off one by one.

He had to do something. He paused his fighting to call upon animals to come help him. He was concentrating so strongly he blocked out the sounds of the battle. Suddenly he felt someone or something grab both sides of his head from behind.

Instantly his mind was transported to a dark space. It was if his eyes were open but he could only see blackness. Then he heard the rumbling voice.

"You are terrible Ian McGregor. You have failed your men. They are dying all around you and it is your fault."

"My fault," he mumbled.

"You must let your life go because of your failure. You aren't fit to live. If you are mated you no longer care. You will die and let her go to suffer the consequences you created," said the melodic voice taking over his mind.

"I must die," stated Ian, stoically.

"You will not try to heal. You will not take blood.

You will shun your men and work to turn them away from us. You must do this to save future men. Tell me what you must do."

"I must turn my men away to save them. I must die," he said.

"Good," said the voice. "In that you will become the hero." He was suddenly free and confused, not able to stop the Kearal from slashing his side. Ian's head felt like fireworks had gone off in it. He grabbed it, not feeling the deep puncture wound to his side, and he fell to his knees. His thoughts cleared to the point he knew he was calling all animals. He had to hang on to bring them to help. What was wrong with him? He fought to think clearly.

He was passing out, but just before he closed his eyes he heard the growls. The werewolves! He felt pain in his side and grabbed it as he slowly pulled himself upright. He couldn't believe his eyes. Hundreds of Ogourax came snarling into the mix. Biting Asurads and Kearals alike, killing them immediately. In twenty minutes, it was over. He looked around in a daze. The weres transformed back to men. Larc stood in front of him.

"You should have called us sooner. In fact, you should have come to me a long time ago. Merlin visited with me and explained what was happening. I knew it was only a matter of time before they came for Arthur. Why didn't you seek me out and include me in your army? I have men who would gladly join your army."

He shook his head, trying to get rid of the fog. "Larc, it wasn't your fight. Didn't think you'd want tae joi…" Ian felt himself slipping and everything went black. Larc grabbed him before he fell. King Arthur came running up as well as Lauren, Connor, Finn and Taryn. They all had cuts and burns but were already healing. He opened his eyes remembering Ator. "Ator…hit…find him…please." He felt things beginning to go dark again. He needed blood and soon.

King Arthur started shouting orders. He was still mounted as were most of his men. "Get Ian to the castle, put him in the room next to mine. General Alexander get your men to take care of the fallen dragons. Get a few of the healers from the castle to help them. Find the injured and bring them to the castle. I think the Kearals and Asurads are all dead thanks to Larc and his pack. Larc join me at the castle with your men. Lauren, you, your brothers, and men to the castle. My army will search for wounded and bring them in."

"King, the fight started at the woods, there's Kearals and Asurads maybe still alive, the river too," explained Lauren.

"Alexander have your men search the woods and river for survivors. Larc can you send some of your men to kill any remaining Kearals and Asurads?"

Larc turned to his men. "Berric see to the men, have them clear the woods and river of those dark demons. Take wolf form and sniff out any hidden danger. Make sure the dark ones are dead. Then meet us at the castle."

King Arthur had Ian laid over a horse he led himself. His brothers following close behind. Soldiers were pulling the wounded on the horses with them and leaving the dead demons to turn to ash.

Larc rode up beside the King. "I heard Ian's call. He should have come to me earlier, to hell it isn't my problem. Those things are trying to take both earths thanks to Merlin's brother. And that damn Drakkor always has hands dripping in evil. He's a damn sore in my side. I know Ian will eventually heal, I just don't know how long it will take. Do you think we got them all?"

"The ones that came, probably, but Athdar and Drakkor only sent half of the Kearals, with equal Asurads. Asurads are plentiful, those we've dealt with before, but these Kearals. They have no conscience, they have incredible power and stamina.

"We need you and your pack, Larc. Ian needs you on his team, in his army. He lost quite a few men today. Good men. And I know him, he's going to beat himself up over it. I watched him and his men fight, they're good, damn good, but I fear they can't beat these new creatures."

Chapter 26

Bradana showed Elspeth where Ian's room was and she walked through his door happy. The fire in the fireplace had died down, but there was enough light peeking in around the tapestry covered windows to see things. She added a few more logs to the fire before retiring. She looked around the room. Different sized swords in rows adorned one wall and on each side of the rows were two crossed swords and a shield. The room felt very comfortable, and being in the place Ian grew up, made her feel like he was somehow with her.

Tapestries with a lot of green and black hung at the windows. Each different, depicting knights, hunting dogs, horses, and dragons.

A huge chest sat under one window. It was made of dark wood with iron bands around it. She walked over and lifted the lid. Kneeling down she brought up a few of the things laying on top. A rough carving of a dog reminded her of the small horse he gave her, and she smiled.

He liked working in wood. Her knight so fierce, enjoyed working with his hands. She realized the man she loved was a complex man with many layers. She replaced the carving and closed the lid and looked around. Another shield with a green dragon adorned one wall with candles on either side. An unlit torch was affixed to each wall. Fresh large lemongrass mats covered the floor and filled the room with a clean scent.

It was definitely a man's room. She finished looking around, yawned then climbed into his bed. She fell asleep with him on her mind.

The next morning, she awoke with thoughts of Ian still running through her mind, as if she hadn't had a break in her thoughts from the night before. The room in the morning light was every bit as inviting as it was in the night with the fire. As she was imagining her life with Ian she heard a light knock. "Come in," she called out. Bradana entered with food and wine and set it on the table next to the bed.

"Good mornin' my lady," said Bradana cheerfully, as she went to pull the tapestries back to let in the light. "It's a bonnie morning it is. Usually another maid would take care of you, but I wished tae do it myself. My daughter lives and with no scars because of you, thank you again my lady."

"Truly no thanks needed. I am a healer and I enjoy healing people, I'm especially fond of children, they get inside my wee heart. You understand?"

"Aye, I do indeed! My children are my world. There will be the boys tae bring you a tub for your bath. My lady thought you could use the extra rest, so I didn't rise you tae break your fast this morn. Please eat, the food is good. My lady has the best cook."

"It smells divine," she said as she breathed in the aroma. Suddenly she felt queasy and knew she was going to be ill. She threw back the furs and hurriedly went behind the screen where a pail sat, and wretched. She wretched again and lost the contents of her stomach from last evenings meal. She couldn't believe she was sick on top of everything else.

"My lady are you aright?" She heard Bradana call to her and her shuffling as she grabbed a cloth and wet it from the bowl from atop the table. The maid came around the screen and leaned over to wipe her forehead and mouth. Her stomach still rolled despite it being emptied. The maid pulled back her hair and gave her an assessing stare. When she felt in control she went back to the bed and laid down. "I must have eaten something awful," she said. "I hope no one else is sick."

"I doona think so." Laughed the maid. "I'm fae, and I've been takin' care of the McGregors for many, many years, my lady in particular. She knew early on when she got pregnant because she'd be sick almost instantly. I always told her it was because she had so many twins. Four sets she had. Ian and Eoghan were her first. Angus and Dougal her second set. Conall and Cameron her third, and Fiona and Catriona her fourth. The others were in between and of course Akira was the baby."

"Pregnant? How can that be? I haven't known Ian that long."

Bradana laughed. "I can tell you how that could be, but I think you ken. I think it's wonderful. Ian will be so happy. He's always wanted tae have a family. He may be tough, but family has always been important. Out of all those boys, he has the kindest heart."

"Pregnant." She couldn't stop her smile. She rubbed her hand over her belly. "Ian and me, a bairn. It's amazing. I hope he is happy about the news. You sure I haven't caught something?"

Bradana walked over and felt her head. "You aren't warm with fever. How do you feel now?"

"Weel quite normal actually," and she got up. "I

doona think I want tae eat, though."

"Eat the biscuits my lady. It always helped Moira. She could keep them down. It only lasts a few months and you'll be okay."

"A few months? I have tae be sick every day for months? Never mind that question, tae have a bairn with Ian, I could be sick the entire time." She laughed. A knock on the door startled her. Bradana went tae open it while she covered up. She just had on her night-rail. Two older boys brought in the tub and water. She could see the steam rise and thought a bath sounded lovely. The boys left.

Bradana helped her up. "I'll help you with your bath if you like."

"I think I'd like tae eat my biscuits and soak. You doona need tae help me, a quiet soak sounds good tae me."

Bradana smiled. "Weel, pull that red rope if you need me. I'll leave you tae your bath then." She could see the excitement of the maid's and knew that she couldn't wait to tell Moira the news.

She ate the biscuits dry and swallowed the bites with water. She waited between bites feeling queasy. She finally got two down and waited to see if she'd throw up again. When her stomach felt settled, she undressed, and stepped in the warm water.

She smiled at the size of the tub, remembering her bath with Ian. She sighed, leaned back and closed her eyes. She thought of Ian and the battle he was facing. "Mither, da, if you can hear me take care of Ian." She lay there thinking of Ian and their time together. She had absolutely no regrets and would do it again. And again. She giggled and dunked below the water.

When she went down the stairs Moira greeted her cheerfully and reached out to take her hands. "Come let's talk."

"Where are the girls?"

Moira laughed, "The same place they've been since you picked out the material for your weddin' gown, they are in the solarium sewing. They willna let you in. They said you couldn't see it until the day afore in case they need tae alter it. Now sit and you can tell me aboot you and Ian." Moira grinned from ear to ear.

"Bradana told you, didn't she?"

"Let me tell you aboot Bradana. If she kens anything, everyone kens it, but she has the kindest heart of anyone I ken. She does an excellent job, and ne'er means any harm tae anyone. We all love her. Do you want tae tell me?"

"Weel, all of a sudden I got sick this mornin'. Came on after I smelled the food. After I emptied my stomach, I felt better. I managed tae eat two biscuits though, then take my bath. Thank you, Moira. It's wonderful being here. I never had a family and always wanted one. My parents were killed when I was wee. Then I went tae the monastery where Mither Thomas raised me. She taught me aboot healing."

"You were ne'er taught tae run a household?"

"Nae."

"I can teach you. Follow me around you'll learn in no time. You speak our language weel, Elspeth."

"It was my first language. My mither and father are Scot's. When I went tae the church Mither Thomas would hit my mouth when I spoke my language. She said it was nae proper for a young English lady."

"She sounds harsh."

"Not really. She truly believed it. After Mither died she was all I had. She taught me a lot. She died two years ago, then my broth…" She choked up but couldn't help it, she broke down and cried. "My brother…Drakkor killed him. Ian heard the truth from his verra mouth." She sobbed and couldn't stop.

Moira moved to put her arm around her and held her. "You've been through a lot Elspeth. I'm here, just let it oot. You're my daughter now."

She drew in a shaky breath. "Call me Els, if you like. Ian calls me Els. I like it. I doona ken why I've been cryin' so much lately. I never cry, but it seems that's all I do."

"Els it is, then. Els, gettin' sick isn't the only thing that happens tae a pregnant woman. Nae, she cries a lot tae. Over nothing most of the time. But you have been through a lot. Tis only normal. Now I'll teach you aboot being pregnant and running a household if you like."

She sobbed harder. "I'd love it if you'd teach me. Bein' at the monastery, I never dealt with pregnant women, Mother Thomas never spoke of the ways. I want tae be the best wife tae Ian. I want tae make him happy!"

"Weel, my plans for today are tae go tae market if you feel well enough. Ian wants you tae have clothes and jewels. The girls have been asking me for a while now. Would you like that?"

"I'd love nothing better." Hearing laughter, she dried her eyes quickly with her hands. She couldn't cover up her red eyes though, and the girls were smart. Catching her embarrassment Moira moved away.

"Weel be going tae market today. Els said she'd like tae go," said Moira.

The girls squealed and ran to the table. Akira caught sight of her red eyes and said, "Why you cryin' Elspeth?"

Moira looked at her daughter, exasperated, "She's pregnant, Akira. I've told you what it is like."

The girls squealed again louder. Akira piped up. "That's wonderful. Does Ian ken? How long? When did you find oot? The weddin' mither. Shouldn't it be right away, you ken, rounded belly and everythin'…wouldn't want people tae talk aboot…"

"*Akira!*" Moira gave her a stern look.

"I mean we should be makin' the weddin' plans. I remember you said you cried all the time with Finn. Da, couldn't keep her from it. And sick. Mither said she was sick all the time, retching."

"*Akira!* Stop it now. Elspeth just found out. She was sick this morning. I think it'd be nice if we all acted like the family we are and take good care of her."

"I'm sorry Elspeth." Akira slumped. "My mouth gets the better of me. Mither always says it will get me in trouble."

She laughed. "I absolutely adore having the sisters I never had. No need tae apologize. I love the way you talk, but your mither is right, some may not like it. You can be yourself with me Akira, I find you refreshin'."

"See mither, I'm refreshin'!" she ran to hug her and so did the other girls. "Och we are going tae market today! We best get ready." And they all ran upstairs. Leaving Moira to shake her head.

"Those girls, especially Akira are going tae be the death of me." Moira laughed. "Come let me show you the kitchens and you can talk tae the cook while the girls get ready. I am tae go over the list of this week's menu with her. She's not very talkative, our cook, and strict, her kitchens are always clean, but she is the best cook I've ever kenned." Moira slipped her arm through hers and it gave her a warm feeling.

After a quick packing, they found themselves on the way. The sun was shining. They all rode beautiful horses. Moira brought two large guards, because it was not safe for a group of women to travel alone. Plus, they'd have to stay in a lodge for the night.

Moira said she and the girls had made the trip many times. The inn keepers were friends and they would stop there first to claim their largest room.

Moira mentioned they could mist to the market, but she thought better of it. She wasn't sure she was full vampire yet, so hadn't better try. She was early in her pregnancy. She didn't know how traveling that way would affect the baby. Ian would never forgive her if something happened. She thought about it and didn't know what being a vampire entailed. Ian hadn't had the time to explain things. She would have to ask Ian's mither later. The skies were clear and everyone was talking. She was enjoying herself immensely. They all were.

Catriona said, "I forgot how much fun riding a horse is."

She took a deep breath of the clean air, glad that her stomach was staying calm. "I always enjoyed it too. I'd ride whenever I could. There's just something aboot a horse given its head and running through fields. It's a feeling of unexplainable freedom."

"When I'm a warrior, I'm going tae have a black stallion, the biggest you have ever seen. His name will be Night and he'll prance. I'll have my own armor, and people will get oot of my way. I already ken how tae throw knives, and I practice with a wooden sword. Ian is goin' tae get me a real one someday. I can't wait. I want it now, but he said I have tae get better with the wooden one. He practices with me sometimes. I love it when he is home. Are you both going tae live here when ye marry? I doona want Ian tae move away. You should live with us."

"I'll live wherever Ian does. I hope tae make a home somewhere."

"Of course, she can live with us." Moira piped up. Where else would they live?"

She thought of Wesladus. Merlin would want him there with his troops. She loved it there, but she enjoyed the McGregor castle, loch, and certainly the cottage, as well. She didn't mention her thoughts because she was unsure what their future held.

After securing their room and leaving the horses at the stables they walked to the market. She had never seen anything so big or colorful. It was bustling with men and women calling out wares, people buying and laughing, food vendors with smoking fires and wonderfully delicious smells of food. At least she was feeling good, her stomach finally settled.

Brightly colored flags of all colors of the rainbow fluttered in the breeze. She'd eaten only the two biscuits and her stomach growled. She was hungry but was nervous about eating. The smells didn't bother her, but she wasn't going to take a chance on eating, at least not yet. She certainly didn't want to become ill at market. The girls grabbed her hands and pulled her toward a shop with gowns. The wide stone house held a weaving loom in the window and piles of dresses on a table outside. The beautiful day dresses caught her eye.

"Her really good gowns are inside," said Fiona. "She's the best dressmaker that ever lived. Come let's go inside." She followed Fiona, Catriona, and Moira inside while the others remained outside.

Fiona was right. The gowns were fit for a queen. Moira smiled at her. "Get whatever you fancy. Ian insists. We wouldn't want tae disappoint him." She didn't have to say it twice. "I think you should have at least twelve," said Moira, leaving her shocked at the thought of owning so many dresses.

She picked out seven of the most beautiful dresses she had ever seen. Two green, one light and one dark to match her eyes, a blue, a dark purple, a rust colored, a red, and a yellow.

She didn't think the red would go with her hair, but Moira insisted it enhanced her hair, and brought out the highlights. Moira picked out two for herself and the two girls got five each as well. Then they moved on to day dresses.

She and Moira looked at several. She settled on seven. Moira insisted she have at least that many. And even though she hated corsets, she liked the way they pushed her breasts high. So, she got those too.

There were satin slippers to match her gowns and several pairs of day slippers to choose from. She also purchased under shifts and several nightdresses. Eight sheer ones, as sheer as the ones Merlin had gifted her. She thought Ian would be pleased with those the most. She smiled thinking of wearing them for him but more at the thought of him taking them off.

After the girls and Moira finished purchasing their things they walked the market streets until they came to a jeweler's shop. Moira insisted she buy jewelry to match her dresses. She found necklaces of rubies for her red gown, and citrine for the yellow and green gowns, amethyst for the purple, and cobalt for her blue gown. She was happy with these.

Moira disappeared while she was looking at the pieces but soon returned to help her make the final decisions. The girls didn't get jewels, nor did Moira, she said they had more than enough.

The experience was so exciting she found herself rambling much as Akira did. They spent the rest of the day looking around. They stopped to purchase small fruit pies they ate along the way. Much to her surprise she didn't feel ill at all. She actually felt great.

By the time they returned to the inn they were all exhausted and requested dinner be sent to their room. She laid her gowns out on one of the beds and placed the necklaces over her gowns, switching back and forth, then stepping back to admire them.

"They're bonnie," said Moira, admiring her choices. "Like you. Ian will be thrilled."

"Speaking of him, I doona ken if they battled today, or if it's tomorrow, but I'm verra worried for him and his brothers."

"After hundreds of years you think you wouldn't be. But I am too. I always worry when they go tae battle, but I've been lucky for the most part. I did lose Lachlan and Eoghan. I miss them so much. Lachlan was and is the love of my life. We kenned when we first met, we belonged together. It's just the way of our kind.

"We wait, and wait, then one-day you look across a room and there he is. That was the way it was with

Lachlan." Moira leaned her head back and sighed. "I could never love another man. My boys are enough for now. I'll be with Lachlan again. I ken it.

"I too, got pregnant right away," she whispered. Causing them both to laugh.

"It was me. I couldn't keep my hands off him. I drove him nuts. I wore a very low-cut gown and a corset that made my breasts practically jump oot. The dress was tight and had a bow on my arse. He stared at me from the moment I entered the room. When I asked him to walk with me, he couldn't wait tae get outside. Needless tae say, he took me beneath a big oak tree on a full moon night." Moira laughed. "I had grass stains on my behind for days."

She joined in Moira's full out laugh at the image that created.

"I guess I'm just as bad. Ian and I were so dirty from the two days in the cave we took a bath together. He was being very gentlemanly washing my back and I wanted him so bad.

"So, I stood up and bent over in front of his face with the offer to wash his hair. He shouted at me that a mon could only take so much and carried me tae the bed drippin' wet."

This time Moira joined her in laughter. It felt so right talking to Moira. Sharing the things daughters shared with mothers and friends. It almost made her cry again, this time with happiness.

Back at the castle she waited for Ian. She didn't want to wear any of her new dresses until he was there to see them. Days went by and she became sicker every day. Now she threw up morning, noon, and night. She didn't think it'd ever quit. She could barely hold down anything, but worse she was becoming frantic with worry for Ian.

She sat on his bed lovingly holding the horse he had given her. Her only close tie to the last time they were together. She only hoped that in giving her his good luck piece he hadn't compromised his safety. A tear dropped on the piece of wood, turning the wood a shade darker. She closed her hand around it and lay back.

He'd promised to return right after the battle. That was at least five days ago. Moira didn't say anything, but Elspeth could tell she was worried too. When it got to be ten days with no word, Elspeth cried daily. When she wasn't retching she was crying. Moira tried to help.

Finally, she told Moira her suspicions. "He's hurt or dead Moira. I can feel it in my heart. It hurts so bad." Moira had told her she'd known when Lachlan and Eoghan died so she too feared the worst. They were sitting at the table talking when Akira came running in. "There's a green dragon in our yard! *Hurry!*"

They ran outside. Saphira was standing there. Elspeth broke out in tears. She screamed, "It's Ian isn't it! Saphira what's wrong?"

"He lives child, but he's hurt badly. He's not healing and he should be by now. I've come to bring you to him. Maybe you can heal him."

"Who's watching Kalon and Sorrilth?"

"Ator, he too was injured in battle. He's almost well, but it's difficult for him to fly. His wing is damaged but new bone and scales are growing. He'll be all right. It's Ian everyone is worried about. He won't talk. His brothers think he blames himself for the large number of deaths."

"Did we lose, Saphira?"

"No, they got all the Kearals and Asurads, his brothers think Ian feels responsible for not saving those fae and vampires as well."

"Nonsense, he did everything for all those men." She started to cry.

"What is it?" asked Moira. "What did she say?"

Elspeth repeated it quickly. "I must go Moira. Thank you so much for everything." She hugged Moira and apologized for her tears soaking her dress. "I'll get my things later, Moira."

"Of course, you must go. I'll see you get them. Please send word when you can."

Elspeth nodded, and Saphira took to the skies.

In a matter of minutes which seemed like years they were in Wesladus. She jumped down and without a word ran through the doors past Ian's brothers who stood right inside, up the stairs, and into their room.

What she saw stunned her. Her man lying there, his cheeks gray and hollow, eyes glazed and yellowed, staring at the ceiling. She didn't notice Angus in the dark corner until he spoke.

"We take turns watching him. Somethin's not right. He should have healed days ago, but his wound continues tae leak. We've tried giving him blood and he refuses it. We thought maybe you can heal him, talk tae him, reason with him. I've never in my life seen Ian like this afore, it's not like him. Not at all. I'm verra worried. The wound is on his right side, no others. He willna speak." After several moments of heavy silence, he continued, "Weel, I'll leave you two alone. Good luck, you need it."

She waited until Angus left and she leaned over Ian

243

and kissed his forehead. He just lay there, showing no recognition of her. She pulled back the furs and saw the clean bandages on his side. She gently started to remove them. Ian moved slightly. After she got them off she put her hands above the wound to heal it. Ian reached quickly and grabbed her hands. "Nae," he said. "Doona." He turned his head away.

"Ian, what's happened tae you?! Let me heal you. Please for the sake of the gods!"

Ian responded, "Damned be the gods."

"What is wrong with you, Ian? Damn you talk tae me! I'm tae be your wife!"

"I'm not fit tae be your husband, Elspeth. Find someone who is. Please leave and doona try tae heal me." He turned his face away.

"Nae, damn you! You talk tae me now!" and she pulled his face toward her. "I'm not leaving until you tell me why you are like this."

"If I tell you, will you leave?"

"If that's what you truly want, yes."

Ian barely looked at her, sighed deeply, and coughed. He wiped sweat from his head and leaned back. "I've made some horrible mistakes and it cost many men their lives."

"What do you mean?"

"First, I dinna save the ether bottles or at least remove the caps to free their souls. But my biggest mistake was thinking I kenned it all. I dinna ask for help from the werewolves and they ultimately saved us. My pride Elspeth. Those men are dead because of my pride. I doona deserve tae live."

"Ian you can feel bad, people make mistakes, it happens, you gave those men everything you had tae give. You cared for them, trained them, made decisions tae help them. You're fighting against evil. It's the evil tae blame nae you. You dinna change those vampires and fae. You dinna steal their ether. You fought against it the best you kenned how. Doona blame yourself. If you die, then they win. Is that what you want? Your men doona blame you, they love you. You are a good leader, a good mon. You are going tae be me husband. Someday we'll have children…"

"I'm not fit tae be a father, or husband, or leader. If you are finished, please go."

"Now you listen tae me, Ian McGregor! You are doin' nothing, but feelin' sorry for yourself. Let me heal you and get your arse from that bed. Show your men you willna lay down and die. If you doona they willna have confidence in themselves. You are not a quitter, doona let them think you are."

"Are you finished?"

"Nae, I'll never be finished with you. You saved me, you dinna leave my side, and I'll be damned if I leave yours. It willna happen, not now, not ever. You understand me Ian McGregor? Nae, Nae, I willna leave. Now let me heal you."

"Please leave." He turned away again.

Unsure what to do. She kept her word and she left. When she reached the bottom of the stairs, she was sobbing. The brothers stood there, concern etched on their faces.

"What happened, Elspeth?" asked Angus. "Did he talk?"

"Aye, he blames himself for all the deaths and not just those of his men, but for not saving the Kearals as well. He said he made a mistake by not goin' tae ask the werewolves for help. He said his poor decisions killed those men."

A stranger Elspeth never met before stepped forward. "I'm Larc, Alpha of the werewolves, the Ogourax. Yes, I would have helped, and when he called on the animals we came. I have men who want to join this army and fight against Athdar and Drakkor. Ian was wrong when he said to me he didn't think we'd want to help because it wasn't our fight.

"Maybe it wasn't then, but we've made it so. Our world is in danger as well. Ian is a good leader; any number of my men would follow him in battle. Hell, I would. He's lost men, casualties of war. He didn't kill them. He must figure that out for himself. If he wants to wallow in it for a while, it's his choice. He'll eventually come around."

****

Ian lay in bed, his head pounding. There was something he had to do. What was it. Els…Els was here. He loved Elspeth he knew he loved her. He had to save her. How, from what? He reached up and grabbed his head. A small voice came through to him. "Remember who you are." Who was he really. I'm not fit to live. I must die. No! I must live. I have to live. At that thought, a sharp pain surged through his skull. Something happened, what happened?

"Fight this!" he said aloud. "For Elspeth, fight this before it is too late. Must get to her." He rolled to the side of the bed and placed his feet on the floor. One foot in front of the other he told himself. Must…save Elspeth. He made it halfway down the stairs in time to hear Larc comment on how he should wallow in it.

"Els?" he said. "He's right. I am wallowing. It's

time tae stop. You're right. If I let myself die, they've won." Pain shot through his skull. "Musss…t fight this. Musst." He wobbled and almost fell from the stairs. "I love you, Els," he whispered. Then his eyes rolled to the back of his head, and he collapsed.

Angus and Connor moved with the speed of light and grabbed him before he injured himself further. Angus quickly picked Ian up and they headed upstairs. She ran behind them into the bedroom. She still felt nauseous, but she hadn't eaten, she didn't think she'd get ill, but she felt her stomach roll. Not now she thought and calmed herself. After they laid him down, Elspeth saw the blood, a lot of blood. He was so thin as if he'd been sucked dry. She turned to Angus, "Somethings not right about him. I have to heal him while he's out. Did he get hit on the head?"

"Nae, just the blade cut to his side," said Angus. "Unless he was hit and we didn't see where. But he needs blood, please heal him Elspeth, then I will give him that."

Elspeth raised her hands above the wound and chanted with all she had to give. Instantly a greenish white light surrounded her and flowed from her hands through Ian. Within seconds his wound stitched tight and the bleeding stopped.

She felt something in the healing light and her connection with him opened something that had a residual, black oily feel to it. The something not right was there in his mind, she felt it, then she heard it. Echo's, the echoes of what the voice had told him. Suddenly she understood it all. She chanted louder, deeper, and called on more gods. She knew what she had to do to heal him, and she did it. The gods heard her call and came en masse. Through the green light appeared a white ray that went in his head causing his face to glow. When she felt the heat dissipate she removed her hands. She turned to look at Angus and fainted.

Angus immediately grabbed her and lay her down next to Ian. "Get some water," he said.

Connor grabbed a glass from the table and handed it to Angus. Angus splashed some on Elspeth's face and she sputtered then opened her eyes. "What did you do that for?"

"You fainted, I was worried, that is what you do to people who faint," he said smiling.

Suddenly everything came back to her. "You need to give Ian blood. Wake him. We need to talk. I ken what happened." Angus and Connor were both stunned speechless. Angus finally spoke, "You are an amazin' woman Elspeth, it's no wonder our Ian loves you."

"Thank you," she said. "Now he needs blood."

Ian slowly awoke and looked at Elspeth. "I'm sorry, Els. Can you forgive me? I didn't mean tae hurt you. You were right. I was feelin' sorry for myself. I'll take that blood now Angus, Connor. If you want tae leave, Els…"

"Nae, I'm not leaving…you doona remember do you?"

"Remember what?" he asked.

"Let's get some blood in you, and we'll all talk. I ken what happened tae you, Ian," she said looking up at his brothers. She went to the edge of the bed and sat down beside him. Angus went to the other side of Ian and held out his arm. Ian's fangs came down and he latched on.

She watched in fascination as Ian took the nourishment he needed. Angus stopped him from taking too much, then Connor stepped up to give him more.

"He'll need more later today tae heal fully," said Angus. "It was a severe wound, and he refused nourishment or any help. We had tae wait for him tae pass oot before we could bandage him. He took them off for a while but became too weak to fight us. I'm glad you're here, sister. Thank you for talking some sense into him."

Connor bent down and kissed her cheek. The men stood to leave but Connor paused, "Welcome home brother. I'll leave and let Elspeth help you with a bath."

****

Later downstairs, Ian sat and listened intently to Elspeth sitting at the end of the long table holding his hand. The great meeting room was eerily quiet as all the brothers, Larc, and Lysanthir listened intently at what she was saying. When she finished, Ian cleared his throat.

"I doona remember," he said. "These kearals are more dangerous than I thought. We will have to be extra careful. We must tell all the men about this ability they have. I want to say thank you all for not giving up on me, thank you Els for healing me, even after I refused it. You must ken that was not me." Everyone around the table agreed and a few relieved sighs were heard.

"Well that explains a lot. How do you feel now?" asked Larc with a worried look.

"I actually feel great. Really great to be honest. If Elspeth could bottle whatever she shot me with, we could heal the entire planet of people."

"I had extra help," she said. "A few extra gods stepped up."

He wondered about that, but he felt revitalized, like a new man. It was time he acted like the man he knew he was. This wouldn't happen again, but neither would he take things for granted. If he needed help with something, he'd by god ask for it. His pride got shaved, and he supposed he had that coming. He wasn't going to lose Elspeth.

After his brothers left, and he and Elspeth were once again alone in the bedroom, he looked at Elspeth and wiggled his eyebrows. She in turn laughed. "I ken that look Ian, and no it willna happen. You aren't completely healed. I will help you get ready for bed, and then it is to sleep for you."

After he was undressed and he lay upon the bed, he pulled Elspeth down beside him where she sat. He was tired and he was still a little weak. "I suppose you are right, I haven't the energy tae make proper love tae you, but I can think aboot it. You make my blood run hot, and all I can think aboot is how I'd like tae take you down and make love tae you until the sun comes up. I've missed you Els, when I was gone, you are all I thought aboot. Come," he said, "and lay beside me. Let me hold you."

She smiled at him, crawled in beside him, and he pulled her close. He put his face in her hair, inhaled deeply and fell asleep.

****

The next day Elspeth waited as the brothers took turns giving Ian blood. She kept her morning sickness from him and after the nooning lunch she managed to break away once more when she became ill. It seemed the sickness was slacking off some and had hoped when she healed him it had healed her sickness, but it wasn't the case.

It seemed it only worked for the short time she was healing him. She sighed, she guessed some things were meant to be, she couldn't deny nature. It was evening and Ian was up and around feeling much better. When she went to check on him he was building a fire in the fireplace.

"Good you are here. I thought we might have dinner up here tonight, just the two of us."

"That sounds wonderful, I'll go…"

"Nae, let me. You've been takin' care of me. I'll go and get us dinner. I'll be back," he said as he opened the door, then turned to smile at her. "You make yourself comfortable."

After he left, she was glad he wanted to eat together, alone. It was the perfect time to tell him. She wanted to look nice for him, beautiful for him. She'd left one nightdress here and a day dress she could wear tomorrow. She was glad she had something to change in to because everything else was at the McGregor Keep. She retrieved the white night-rail she'd left behind. It wasn't her favorite blue one but it would do. Now she wished she had her new things. Soon, she thought. She put it on and the feel of the soft material brushing her breasts made them peak. She felt beautiful. She rushed to brush her hair then stood in front of the low fire so her silhouette showed through.

Ian came up with food and stumbled with the tray when he saw her. She smiled at him and she saw his control slip even more. "Damn woman! Now the only thing I want tae eat is you." He sat the food down and reached for her. Pulling her close to him, he ran his hands slowly over her, touching her through the fabric.

"You have tae wait a bit, Ian. I need tae eat, and we need tae talk." Ian instantly had a worried look on his face. She laughed. "Doona look so worried, it isn't bad."

"Okay…but you'll drive me wild wearing that. You are so bonnie, Els." They sat at the small table and ate.

She was so hungry and it smelled so good. She was ravenous. The days of being ill had left her hungry. Maybe since she was with Ian and no longer worried, it would abate. Between them they cleaned the trenchers of food. Then he got up and stoked the fire, throwing on some logs.

"Come luv, sit on my lap and we'll enjoy this mighty fire." She went and sat, putting her arms around his neck.

She kissed him softly. "There's somethin' I need tae tell you, Ian." Her stomach rolled. Gods not now. Too late. She shouldn't have eaten so much. She jumped up and ran behind the screen barely making it before she retched and lost the contents of her stomach into the pail. She gagged and retched again and again.

Ian jumped up. "What's wrong Els? Why are you sick?" He ran to the table where the bowl of water sat. He wet the cloth and ran to her. "What is it, sweetling?" he asked concerned. She couldn't talk as the waves of nausea rolled over her.

He leaned over and pulled her hair back. "What can I do? Please Els, your scaring me. Did you eat something bad, are you poisoned?" She tried to catch her breath. Her stomach heaved again.

"I canna tal…" her words were cut off as she threw up again. "Ian, I…I och, goddesses. I'm sick."

"I ken. I'm here. Did I make you sick, because I'm so sorry about earlier."

She laughed in between bouts of sickness. "Nae, not earlier, weel earlier, earlier…" She laughed then sobbed. She couldn't get anything right. She wanted to tell him while sitting on his lap in front of the fire. Not like this.

He held her and washed her face, and waited a bit to ask, "Better?"

"Aye, nae, och, I doona ken, Ian." He picked her up and carried her to the bed and gently laid her down. "Here drink this." He poured a glass of water from the pitcher and picked her head up so she could drink. After a few sips, she lay her head back down, silently crying, tears rolling from her eyes.

"I wanted it tae be a surprise. I was goin' to wait tae tell you, but for as sick as I am, all the time, you'd figure it oot, and I wanted tae tell you, but not like this."

He got up rinsed the cloth and came right back. "Tell me what?" he asked gently wiping the corners of her mouth. "Have you got a sickness? Should I call for a healer?" he kissed her forehead. "Look at me dearling. What is it?"

She just blurted out, "We're going tae have a bairn." She sobbed and…waited. "Och, Ian, say somethin'."

He stared at her, apparently at a loss for words. "Did you just say we're goin' tae have a bairn?" Tears filled his eyes. "You…and me?"

"No, me and a goat," she said grinning. "Of course,

you and me."

"We're tae have a bairn? Och, Els. That's the greatest gift a mon could have from the woman he loves. Are you certain?"

"Verra. Your Mither told me. I'm certain of it now. I got sick the first day at your Mither's. Bradana brought me breakfast and the smell made me sick. At first it was just mornings. Now it seems every time I eat, I get sick. Are you happy Ian?" She asked, scared of how he might feel.

"My bonnie, bonnie wife tae be. How could you ask? Aye, I could nae be happier." He teared up again and put his face on her belly. "I've always wanted a woman tae love, and her tae love me. I've always wanted bairns. Lots of them. A love like my Ma and Da's. Are you happy, Els?"

She sobbed. "Ian, I love you so. When I first got back here and saw you, you scared me. I felt my world crumble. I thought I lost you. My heart broke, Ian."

"I ken Els, regardless of what happened to me, I still didn't like the fact so many were lost. And with that mind meld thing that kearal did on me, I forgot who I was for a bit. It still doesn't change the fact that I'm tired of the bloodshed and the death of losing good men. Men with families. When my pride got in the way of asking for help from ones who are strong enough tae kill the Kearals, I felt responsible for those deaths, regardless of what the kearal did to me. That guilt I will always carry.

"But you were right about everythin' you said. I willna give up this fight, because if I do the consequences would be devastatin'. These men need a leader, so first light tomorrow, I'm goin' tae speak tae

Larc about he and his men joinin' us."

Chapter 27

Ugalhar Monastery, Atop Mount Zomm

Athdar was furious. "Do you know how long it took to get those men! We were just starting to increase our numbers! With Arthur and his men, we would have had enough to go to war! So close! Now we must find more fae and vampire to change and we still have to get Arthur and his army. We can't win this war without them!"

"Don't just blame me. I told you the McGregors were hard to kill, and it was your choice not to change Rulm and his army yet, all because of some damn promise about your sister!"

"She's not my sister! I owed King Rulm. He helped me kill Elspeth's parents and took me in so I'd have a good place to use my magic. He always wanted Elspeth and he was waiting until she was ripe for his games. I never cared what happened to the little healer.

"That is why I brought her back from the monastery. He wanted to keep her and play with her. I promised him, and I keep my word that he wouldn't be changed until it was time for war. I didn't think we'd need them right away. Our numbers were up.

"It's a small setback. We will get there again. But, make no mistake, I will kill Merlin, only after I've tortured and killed that damn Ian McGregor and my so called, *little sister,* while he watches. I will suck enough ether from Merlin so he won't be able to lift a finger, let alone use his magic. They will pay and I know just how we're going to do it."

He grabbed his book, *The Grimoire to the Dark,* and slammed it to the table. "Bring me wine Drakkor, we have work to do."

"Sir, excuse me we have a problem," interrupted Damon from the doorway.

"What is the meaning of this, Damon? Do not disturb me, *means do not disturb me!* Can't you see I'm busy? What the hell is it?!"

"There's unrest with the men, sir. There's talk of a revolt, after what happened. They are organizing and there is already a faction. One of them betrayed the others by coming to tell me."

His voice grew shaky showing nerves. "A…group left in the middle of the night. The group calls themselves the Curce. They have a leader, but I don't know who it is. They…"

"Bring me the man who told you this. Now!" he said, through gritted teeth. Enraged he pulled on his long dark blond hair, eyes blazing, trying to control his temper, but failing miserably. He grabbed his cup of wine and threw it against the wall, knocking off a painting of a group of angels overlooking children playing in a garden.

Red wine splattered the walls and ran down. He picked up a chair and busted it in pieces against the table, gripping a broken leg, sharp at one end, he pointed it at Damon, "*Now!*" then threw it, impaling the wall near his head.

"Right away, sir," said Damon in a wobbly voice,

and hurried from the room.

"I thought you had control of all these Kearals, Athdar. Didn't you say they were bespelled as well as changed?" asked Drakkor.

"Yes," he gritted. "I thought they were. I don't know what they're thinking of doing by themselves, but with so much evil in them, they must lack fear of me. Big mistake, as they will find out. I would use the dungeon at the castle, but our cover is blown.

"The big question is how many men Ian and his brothers have. I think when I'm done with this man, I'll pay Merlin another visit and question him. In the meantime, we'll find out how many men left, then organize a search party according to the number. They can't get far, it's cold and this mountain is steep. There's only one path they can follow. We'll get them."

A knock sounded at the door. "Enter," he shouted.

Damon walked in with a tall, thin, shaggy dark haired and bearded man, with a face that looked like it collided with charging elephant. The man had little eyes and reminded Athdar of a skinny little weasel. His first thought was to kill him. Maybe he would after he got the needed information. "Come in here, my good man, and give me your name," he said with a forced smile.

"My name is Der," he said in a thin voice.

"Explain to me, Der, who the instigator of this revolt is, and how many men left with him in the middle of the night."

"His name is Juppar Heiwynn. I'm not sure the number of men went with him exactly, but I would say near a hundred."

"How the hell could I not know about a hundred men leaving here!" he shouted. "What direction did they take? Why do you just come now to me? Speak up you damn troll, why?" he grabbed him around his throat.

Der tried to breathe and couldn't talk. Finally, he released him.

"Because." He coughed putting his hand instinctively around his sore throat. "When Juppar found out I wasn't going with them he put a spell on me and left me in the cave."

"A what on you? What cave? Make sense damn you!" He was beyond patience.

"When we all joined you, it was with the promise of wealth and taking over this veil and the two earths. We are all alike in your army. Except for Juppar. He thinks he can do a better job of things than you can. All who follow him have promises better than yours.

"He is different than all of us because he is a mage. You didn't know because he didn't want you to. He put a sleep spell on all the men before he left. When he saw that I hesitated in following, he put a spell on me. After that, I know nothing, but I do know he opened a portal. I've never seen it done before. Where it opened to I don't know, but the men went through it. He is a powerful mage."

"He's *nothing* compared to me!" He grabbed Der around the throat with one hand and choked him. He angrily said an incantation and Der turned red, his blood literally boiling, his eyes and ears bleeding until he died and turned to ash.

"We are going to the cave and I am going to see if I can do a locator spell. I'm not sure how, but we are going to find those men. I don't know what they have planned, but we are damn sure going to stop it. Then we are going to talk to our army.

"Drakkor, look in on Merlin make sure he still breathes. Come back and we'll leave by portal. I'm going to check a spell in the book. Make it quick!" Drakkor left and he opened the grimoire.

Chapter 28

Wesladus

Ian came down to break his fast in high spirits. He hadn't had much sleep the night before staying up with Elspeth, but that was okay. They talked, laughed, planned, made love, and had a wonderful time. He shook his head for being so stupid. Not going to happen again, he told himself.

He took his seat and noticed Larc was joining them. "So good of you tae be here," he told Larc. "We need tae talk." He looked at all his brothers sitting around the table. "I want tae tell you all, I'm sorry for the ordeal I've put ye through. It was a mistake tae behave that way, and I'm sorry. Now that I've said that, let's get down tae business. Where's Dougal?"

"He's workin' on the locator spell for Merlin, makin' sure he has all the ingredients. He's been at it day and night with Cameron on the grimoire."

"Any luck Cameron?"

"I think I found a way tae locate Athdar, but I'm not sure. Athdar was created oot of crushed bone and a bairn sacrifice, using the bairns blood. He was returned to Elspeth's parents tae be raised as their own. They ne'er ken. It's true that Athdar's bone was used, but it was the bairns blood, Elspeth's brother. It's a verra dark and demonic spell. It should have ne'er been used."

Cameron looked around, "Where's Elspeth? Is she coming down tae break her fast?"

He knew she was tired and that she got sick mornings, but he wasn't ready to tell everyone about the bairn yet. So, he answered with. "We were up late talking so she is still asleep." The brothers laughed but didn't say anything else. "I'll have somethin' sent up later."

"Good," Cameron continued. "Because what I have tae say I doona want tae say it in front of her. Since I believe her brother was sacrificed tae bring Seamus back tae life we may be able tae use some of her blood for the locator spell. It's only Athdar's soul in the body. The blood that runs through is still tied tae Elspeth and her parents. I'm not sure how tae ask her, so I'm leaving that up tae you, Ian."

He felt concerned. "How much blood do you need?" he asked.

"Not much. A small prick on the end of her finger should do it."

"Och, that shouldn't be a problem. When she wakes up I'll ask her. Larc," he said, as he changed the subject. "Thank you and your men for coming tae our aid in battle. If not for you and them, we would have lost. Arthur would've lost his army, his men, and we would have lost our earth's. We are in your debt.

"I'm going tae get right tae the point here. I made a big mistake in not going tae you a while back tae ask you for your help. If my pride hadn't been so big, I would've. Many men died because of it, and it is a regret I will always carry with me. Now that I've said that. We need your help. If we have any chance for survival, we need the werewolves with us. That was proved at the battle."

Larc smiled and tilted his head. "Thank you for that Ian. When Merlin told us what was happening, many of my men were ready to join your army. We were just waiting to be asked. Now that you have, we are more than happy to join forces. I of course want to be kept in the loop. I would ask to join with you and your brothers as one of you. My men are as important to me as yours are to you. I would ask to lead and train them alongside of you, make decisions alongside of you. If you can accept these terms we are ready to join forces."

"I see no problem with that. Do any of you object?" he asked, directing his question to his brothers. Naes came across the table.

"Let me know how many men we need to start. I'll make the arrangements and bring them here. We'll come by the fort's portal."

"That sounds great, Larc. When we finish eating I will show you around and you can meet the men, see the long houses, and show you a room you can have here in the castle. Of course, you will want tae have your first here as well."

"Yes, I also need to make arrangements for my brother to take over the pack while I'm gone."

With that part of the conversation over, two maids started bringing the food to the table. He motioned for one to come over. "Could you have some biscuits sent up for Elspeth along with fresh water, and help her with a bath?"

"Yes, my lord. Would she want that now or should we wait a bit?"

"Now would be fine. She's probably awake."

"Och," said Finn. "You starving the lady for some reason?"

"Weel, I guess now is as good as time as any to make my announcement." He paused with a big grin. "Elspeth and I are going tae have a bairn. She gets sick when she eats like mither did and biscuits are all she can keep down."

Finn was the first to congratulate Ian, but was soon drowned out by all the hooting, hollering, and jokes. Ian laughed with them and had a few of his own.

****

Elspeth was on her way down to join them and heard Ian's laughter. She stood out of sight and listened, very happy to hear them having fun. Even at her expense. She started to giggle and held her hand over her mouth thinking about how she joked with Moira. If only they would have heard *that* conversation. She silently turned around and went back up the stairs, smiling.

Chapter 29

Ian stood in the training yard looking at his remaining men. They'd lost thirty-two of their forty-eight men. More than half. Today new Crixior, Crimson Keepers, and Ocrul were coming to make up for the lost men. The werewolves were coming today as well.

It would be good to add the Ogourax to their army. The addition of the werewolves would add six men to each squadron raising each to eighteen. His small army would have a grand total of seventy-two soldiers, not including all the dragons.

He thought that was a good-sized army when you considered what the soldiers were. It wasn't the size, he figured, as much as what these men were capable of doing together as a group. He sadly watched the remaining men in the training yard. He'd hear a command or two from one of his brothers, but for the most part the only sounds were the clang and scrapes of the swords.

Morale was low, but to be expected after the battle they just waged. He was hoping that would change soon with the new recruits arriving this morning, and the werewolves later in the day.

Tomorrow the yard would be fuller than this army has ever seen it. He planned a speech in hopes to boost morale. The battle was over, but the war wasn't. Not until Athdar and Drakkor were dead, and he meant to see that happen, he *would* see that happen, he vowed.

He brushed his hands on his thighs and turned to walk inside the castle. He needed to speak to Elspeth about sharing her blood for the locator spell. There was no way around it, he'd have to bring the sore subject up again, that bairn never had a chance because of Athdar, and he hated talking about it. It always left her sad. Hadn't she been through enough already?

He sighed and went inside the castle, and up the stairs to where Conall, Dougal and Cameron sat discussing the magic they'd use to find Merlin.

"Yes," said Dougal, "you need tae add styrax tae the wymote and golden star root. Withoot it we canna break through the barrier."

"I dinna read that in the book," explained Cameron, getting exasperated. "It dinna mention that anywhere. It has tae be perfect tae work."

"It has tae work the first time," he interrupted, walking in, "because I'm only taking blood from Elspeth once."

They all looked up.

"Cameron doesn't seem tae remember what Merlin said about the book not being complete," said Dougal. "I ken my spells, and what goes together, and you canna leave styrax oot."

"Did you get the blood from Elspeth yet?" asked Conall.

"Nae, do you need her here? If not, one of you needs tae come with me because I doona ken how much you need. I doona want tae bleed her any more than I have tae. Besides to get it, I have tae bring up the whole subject again, I was hoping she could forget it. She doesn't understand the details, and I doona wish tae have tae give them tae her. I'll just tell her that her blood may help tae find Merlin. If she has questions, then I'll just have tae address them then."

Dougal frowned, "why doona you bring her here. With us she may not be so taken by the news. You can watch the spell and see if it works."

He sighed, "I will talk tae her alone, then bring her here for the blood. I may need tae help her process it. She may need tae cry aboot it, you ken being with bairn and all."

"We understand," said Cameron, "Take your time."

He left trying to form the words in his mind exactly what to say. In the end, he thought he'd just tell her the truth. She deserved that, no matter how bad it was.

When he went through the bedroom door to the adjoining solar, Elspeth sat at the window humming and sewing. She looked up and smiled. "What brings you here, Ian? I thought you were at the trainin' yard."

"What you sewin'?" he asked, avoiding the inevitable.

"I'm practicin'. I was never taught tae sew or how tae run a household. Your mither is going tae show me, and your sisters are teaching me tae sew. I want tae be able tae make nice things for the bairn and you."

"Els, I need tae tell you some things aboot your brother, and there's no easy way tae say it. We need a sample of your blood for the locator spell, for Merlin."

"But Merlin said my brother was killed, sacrificed. That means my brother is dead. I doona understand how my blood can help. Of course, I would gladly give my blood to help find Merlin, but I doona understand."

He sighed, he knew it would come to this. "Everything aboot Athdar, is your brother, the blood that runs through his veins, is your brother's. At the time of death, your brother's soul was released and Athdar took over the body. The body of your brother. There were ne'er two bodies, and that is where we were confused." He sighed. "We thought all of his blood was drained, it wasn't.

"It was true when King Rulm said he saw him die, he failed tae mention he was brought back tae life with a different soul. What he said was truth, but he didn't tell the whole story, and he lied when he said he made the man pay for his sins, so I think he was part of it.

"Since it was your brothers blood used tae create Athdar, my brothers think if they use yours they may find where Merlin is at with a locator spell. I thought you'd be verra sad aboot it."

Elspeth smiled, a sad smile. "You mean sob aboot it?" She answered herself, "Nae, I've done my crying over my brother's death, for now anyway. Afore I was with bairn, I never cried, now it seems I do a lot. I'm trying not tae. I just wish I could've kenned him. Weel, you need my blood. How do you want it?"

"Come with me, sweetling. We'll go tae the lab with Conall, Cameron and Dougal. They said we could watch the spell if we want." He took her hand and pulled her up for a short, sweet kiss, before leading her out the door.

"Sit here, Elspeth," said Dougal, "we need just a wee bit a blood. Your finger should do. I'm going tae nip it with the point of this knife and drop a few drops into this bowl with herbs and root. I've got my pendulum soakin' in it. After we add the blood, I'll say the incantation and hang it over the map in hopes it shows where Athdar has Merlin. Since he made the spell, your blood can maybe tell us where the cloaking spell is at, if we can break that, we will find Merlin.

"Are you ready?"

"Aye, I sure hope it works. I'm worried aboot Merlin," she said, as she took her seat in front of the table and held her hand over the bowl.

Dougal picked up the knife. "You can close your eyes if you like."

"Nae, doesn't bother me ever so much. I've seen blood afore."

Dougal made a very small slice and carefully pinched her finger to make the blood flow. He had a wet cloth with some herb on it to clean her finger. She sat back.

Dougal stood above the bowl with his hands over it and said an incantation. When he was finished, he pulled out his pendulum and it glowed. He held it over the map and waited as it turned in a large circle searching for what they hoped was Merlin.

It was supposed to shrink in to smaller and smaller circles before focusing on the point where Merlin was located. But, it didn't do that. The circle ever widened. After a few minutes Dougal dropped it. "It didn't work," he said, disappointed. "Back tae the book."

Cameron looked at Dougal. "There is nothing more on the subject. We've tried everythin', and that was our last hope. I doona ken where tae go from here."

He thought for a second, then said, "Are there any books listing monasteries? Maybe we can look at a list and find one in the cliffs."

"I can look in Merlin's library," said Conall. "Why doona I do that while you settle in the new recruits. We can meet at dinner. If I find something afore that, I'll let you ken. I'm sorry Elspeth, we were sure it'd work."

"That's okay, Conall, we all have tae do all we can think of tae find Merlin. We're just doing our best. I'll do anything I can tae help."

He took her hand and helped her up. "Do you want to go back tae the room tae sew?"

"Aye, I'd like that. Then I want tae go for a walk on the beach. Maybe find those shells I lost." She smiled, and Ian smiled back. She felt Ian's brother's eyes on them and smiled to herself at sharing a secret with Ian. If his brothers could only guess.

Chapter 30

Mystic Kingdom

Angus walked inside Mystic Kingdom's castle and straight to where the queen was. He didn't have time to fool around with guards, or anyone else who to tried to stop him, he simply threw them out of his way. Ian had sent him here to do a job, clean up the books, protect the queen. He'd found out this time of day, she was in the library talking with her aids. He was tired of being jerked around and he didn't care who heard him coming. He pushed a guard out of the way and slammed through the door.

Queen Edina looked up with surprise on her face, which quickly turned to anger. "I suppose you are the one who's been all over looking for me? Before you say anything, you can leave. I don't want or need your help."

The Queen's closest aid stood with a scowl. "I'll remove him my lady."

"You can try, but you willna get verra far," he said, with a low growl.

The Queen frowned, "Remove him Dedrick."

Dedrick jumped toward him to grab his throat. Angus stepped aside, flung his arm out, grabbed the back of Dedrick's shirt and in one smooth movement, sent him against the doorframe knocking him out.

He stayed where he was crossing one leg in front of the other and leaned against the door contemplating his fingernails. Without looking away, he said in a low deadly voice, "If you want that toad tae live, you may suggest tae him, to mind his manners."

The queens look of anger increased. "Sirrah, I could have you put in the dungeons for your despicable actions."

He looked at her then and a shock went through him. God's, she was gorgeous, especially spitting fire from those dark eyes. Though her anger did nothing to temper his.

"You and your army couldn't put me in your dungeons if my hands and feet were chained. Shut your geggie and listen tae what I have tae say!"

"Guards!" Three came through the door instantly. "Seize this man and take him to the dungeons."

He pulled his sword. The first went at him and he sidestepped, smacked him on his arse, and sent him flying against the corner of a table, knocking him out. The second had his sword out and ready, he knocked it from his hand, grabbed and twisted the guy around, kicked him in his arse, and shooting him up against the wall. The third came at him with his sword, he parried and punched him square in the nose and down he went. The three guards lay sprawled on the floor, all out cold. He stood and yawned as if bored.

"You need tae listen to what I have tae say and I'm not leaving 'til you do." He was so angry he flashed a bit of fang.

The Queen's eyes widened, but her look of annoyance grew. "I'll give you three minutes, then you leave."

"That's a fine thank you for someone who travelled such a long distance tae protect your sorry arse, and that of your kingdom. You need tae have better manners, Queen."

The Queen looked as if she had never been more insulted. "You, sirrah, are the one without manners! I don't know if it's because you aren't smart enough to know your manners, or you didn't have a mother to teach them to you. But I, nor my kingdom, needs the likes of you."

He felt fury. "You can talk all ye want tae about me, but you will not speak ill of my Mither." He tried to stop it, but his anger brought down his fangs and his fae part made him glow.

Edina looked at him with obvious amazement but not with the fear he expected to see. He knew she saw a huge man, dark shoulder length hair, glowing silver eyes, short cut beard almost a shadow, sculpted face, and fangs. She should be afraid, but she wasn't, she seemed…enthralled.

"You must be the devil himself," she said, "but you don't scare me. I was married to one, and my thanks to the one who killed him."

"Nae, not a devil, one trying tae save you from them. And that would be my brother you're thanking. He killed your husband trying tae violate his wife tae be. Only you wouldn't understand it, because you probably liked it, bein' as how you married him."

The queen stood up straight and walked up to him and slapped him as hard as she could across his face.

That shut him up, and he retracted his fangs and dimmed his glow to normal.

"You know nothing of me," she seethed, "or my

marriage. You will explain what you meant by the devils, then you will leave this castle, these grounds, and this kingdom never to return. Do I make myself clear?"

"Maybe I dinna make myself clear. I have a job tae do, and if you doona care aboot yourself, you should care aboot the people in your kingdom. I'm not from here, I come from a different place than your world. A different earth than this. Species you have never heard of live there. They have special gifts unlike humans.

"Merlin, I, and my brothers, have been protecting your sorry arse for hundreds of years, yes, we live that long and longer. There is an evil you can't comprehend tryin' tae take over your planet and ours. Your husband was helping him tae do it.

"Athdar? He is the evil and he's not from here, he's from our world, and he's changing our good men into evil, he's changing your kings and soldiers into evil. If you've ever kenned evil, you canna fathom the hell he'll be creatin' for you and your kingdom.

"You saw part of what I'm like, I'm half vampire, half fae, with many powers. I can make it rain so hard your gardens, houses, and castle would wash away, I could call the lightning tae strike you, the wind tae blow you away, get where I'm going with this?

"But instead I protect you, your kingdom, and this world from just such things. I'm here because Athdar is after your soldiers, if he turns them, you lose. Do you understand? A bairn was sacrificed to bring him back tae life and your husband helped."

The queen grew quiet and slowly returned to her chair. Her face confused as she took in his words and what they meant for her kingdom.

A groan came from Dedrick as he regained his feet. The aide immediately turned his attention toward Angus.

Quickly he said, "this man should be executed for what he's done." He looked around at the moaning guards. "Guards!" He shouted. "Kill this man!"

"Leave us Dedrick and take the guards with you."

"But, Edina…"

"Edina, is it?" He laughed. "You let your men call you by your given name?"

Edina didn't blush, but Dedrick did. He was furious and his hatred showed. His face was beet red and spittle left his mouth. "You let this man beat your men and speak to you like this?!"

"Leave Dedrick, before I have *you* taken to the dungeons."

He smiled, "I guess she told you!" He grinned.

The queen became exasperated. "If you two would kindly quit with your cock fight. We have matters to discuss. I won't say it again. Dedrick, you, the guards, out!"

The two guards pulled the remaining unconscious guard up and out the door. Dedrick brushed past him and growled through gritted teeth, "This isn't finished, you dirty Scott."

"Aye, I think you're verra finished, you slimy Sassenach."

Dedrick slammed the door.

****

"Let me make myself clear, Mr. Whatever your name is. I don't like you, I don't know who or what you are, but I do believe what you're saying. For the sake of my people, I will listen to you."

"Weel, the feelin' is mutual. I doona like you either, but make no mistake, I'm here tae do a job, and I weel do it, and no one weel stand in my way. Do I make that clear enough for you? My name is Angus McGregor and from here on oot, we go by my rules. Which, so you ken, I'll be takin' the King's quarters as my own, while I'm here. It will be the best way tae protect you."

She looked daggers at him. "You just stay out of my way, McGregor. After you've told me your plans, you will see me on a need to know basis only. Do I make myself clear?"

"I wouldn't have it any other way."

She didn't know why that comment made her feel rejected, when it should have made her happy, but it didn't. This overbearing, pig headed, insolent, despicable, and infuriatingly handsome man gave her so many mixed feelings that she literally wanted to scream in frustration, and she never screamed.

"While I'm here there will be changes. While I'm protecting this place, I'll be working for the people. Ian told me of the expenditures the king and you have indulged in. The gold armor and all other gold will be melted down and sold, the money given tae the people. I'll be going over the books. I've noticed the people here are poor and work hard. This extravagance comes tae an end. Now. You should be ashamed of yourself."

The queen had always felt bad about her people going without. She always tried to give to them. But that did it, she didn't need this man rubbing salt in a wound she'd carried herself for years. "I have never taken from my people, what I have came from my father, King Aaric Guhn, from the Gealea Kingdom, who arranged my marriage to King Rulm with the promise that he never touch me or he'd die!"

Why she raised her voice and shared that with this stranger, she didn't know but she was tired of his accusations. "That is why I don't know the specifics of his activities with women. I've only heard rumors. You can sell all his things and give it to the people, it was my intention anyway! And you, you overbearing, all assuming, pig hearted fool, know nothing about me!" She was shaking she was so upset, then she broke out in tears. "Leave! Just get out of here!" She turned away and caught a sob in her fist.

"Look here, Queen Edina. Maybe I was a wee bit harsh on you. Kenning your husband as I did, I thought you were like him." He walked to her and turned her around and grabbed her shoulders. Then he did the strangest thing, surprising himself. He reached down and kissed her.

She jerked away and backed up quickly putting her fingers to her lips.

"What do you think you're doing? If you think I'm one of your wenches, you are dead wrong! I could have you hung for that, sirrah!"

Angus laughed, "now, that's better." He turned around and walked out leaving her standing with her fingers still on her lips.

She picked up a cup and threw it hitting the back of the door. She heard him walk away, roaring in laughter. She stood there wondering what just happened to her self-control. She'd never acted that way in her life, and in anger she told this stranger more about herself than she'd ever told anyone.

****

277

Now Angus was curious. He walked up the stairs, went to the king's chambers, opened the door, and looked in. "Och!" He said loudly. "Opulent arse!" He shut the door and went quickly to the Queen's door. When he opened it, he was surprised.

It was done tastefully in greens and blues, paintings of people, simple yet elegant things. Perhaps she wasn't lying. He shook his head and went in search of the weasel Dedrick.

He found him in the ledger room with another man. They looked up at him.

Dedrick glared at him. "What the hell are you doing in here?"

"Oot!" yelled Angus. "I'm takin' control of the ledger room and its contents. You two weasels oot."

"You can't tell me what to do!" said Dedrick.

"I verra well can. You better go see your queen and ask her aboot it. Now run along boys, your nae tae come in here again. Your Mither's callin' you. Or do I need tae spank your arse again and remove you? Leave the books now!" He took a step forward. The other man figured it out right away and headed for the door. Dedrick didn't. "You dense man, or just wish tae die?"

"Oh, you'll pay, Scott," Dedrick said as he left.

He knew before he even sat down what the books were going to look like. He sighed. It only grew worse as he went over the numbers. He felt a headache coming on. He spent the rest of the day there.

When he left, he was hungry, and his head was pounding. So, he went in search of the kitchens. The cook was there preparing things for morning. She was a big lady, white hair pinned atop her head, tall and very round. She leaned back against the counter and looked at him. He gave her his brightest smile. "You got anything from this evenin's meal left, my bonnie lady?"

She grinned from ear to ear, and her face lit up. "Well what do we have here? A Scotsman! Well for you, I'm sure I could find something. She went to the fire where some stew was simmering and scooped him a trencher full, got another plate and put some fruit and cheese on it, then grabbed some small loaves of bread.

"You got some mead tae go with that?"

"Of course, I do. What room are you in, and I'll have it sent to you?"

"Weel thank ye, sweetling. I'll be up in the king's room."

The cook laughed, "You're serious."

"Aye. My name is Angus McGregor and I'm here tae set it right for the people and protect the queen. You will probably hear aboot me and probably not favorably. Especially from that walloper Dedrick. What a bawless lizard that piece of dirt is."

Cook laughed. "That he is. He's after the queen, has his eye on her, he does. He doesn't understand she'll never have any man."

"How aboot I eat right here at this fine table and you can me tell something aboot her."

"She was done poorly, I'm afraid her father sold her to that crazy man, king Rulm," she said as she sat and leaned her elbows on the table. "As far as I can tell the only thing nice he did for her was make sure the king never touched her. They were both bad men, her father and the king, but Rulm the worst, I'm afraid." She *tsked*. "There's stories of what he's done to ladies that would make your hair curl."

"I ken, it was my brother who killed him for trying

tae take advantage of his wife tae be. He left Elspeth beat up, he did."

"Our Elspeth? That poor dear. I knew she wasn't a traitor. She was our healer and a good woman, like our Queen."

"You sayin' the Queens good?"

"My yes, it wasn't her fault she had to marry that black-hearted bastard. She never wanted to, but like I say, the king bought her. She's always helping the people though. She sees to the sick, the old ones, and provides some tutoring for the children. She always said a smart kingdom is a happy kingdom. She needs a good man. Maybe someone like you."

He coughed. "Nae, not me. I'm not ready for a permanent woman." He wiggled his eyebrows. "Now if someone like you came along…"

She laughed. "My names Galena, Angus. I've probably said more than I should have. How's your meal?"

"Mostly gone. It tasted great, you're a damn fine cook Galena. A mon could get fat eatin' this kind of cookin'," he said. Then he leaned back and patted his belly.

"I think I'll take this pitcher and tankard with me and go up. I wish there was some way to shut down the sunshine in that room. Och, how could anybody live in the middle of that much gold?" he shook his head and stood, his head pounding. "Thank you, Galena. That was great," he said grabbing his head.

"You have a pain in your head?" she asked, concerned.

"All day. I went over the numbers in the ledger room. Seems the pilfering didn't stop with the king's death."

"Dedrick," she said, knowingly. She turned and grabbed a cup from the sideboard and put in some herbs, poured hot water on top, and handed it to him. "Drink this, tis for your head."

He sniffed it and cringed, the smell was terrible. He looked up at her and she tilted her head as if to say, "do it, or I will pour it down you myself."

"My Mither gets that same look," he said, drinking down the foul brew. Galena laughed. "Thank you, Galena. I'll be leavin' now, dinner was good."

"You're welcome in my kitchen any time, Scotsman. Don't you be a stranger."

"I willna. You couldn't keep me away. Goodnight." And he walked out and up to his new room.

When he got there, he stoked the fire, and heard sobbing coming from the other side of Edina's door. He walked over to it. "Edina, is that you? Are you okay?"

"I'm fine," she said, "go away."

"Weel, goodnight, then."

She didn't respond.

He lay in that huge bed staring up at the canopy, wondering about the Queen. There was a lot to do here, he thought. He wondered how long he'd have to be here. He fell asleep thinking about his brothers and Merlin. He hoped their luck was good.

Chapter 31

Wesladus Veil, Pendragon castle

The morning was bright and brisk but not cold, the yard dusty, and the sounds of swords clanged and scraped. Training was going well. Ian looked at the men and was happy at the addition of the werewolves.

Larc stood beside him and they laughed. They were fast becoming friends. They weren't so different. Life dealt Larc the same deal as Ian. They had similar stories, about their men, their lives, and things in general.

Larc hadn't mated yet and it seemed their pack had a problem with having children. He told Ian he thought it was because they mated within their own pack for so long. He was afraid they were going to have to look outward. Ian told him what it was like being half vampire and half fae.

Larc laughed when he found out how many children were born in his family. Larc told him his family had the litter, making him laugh. The weres were good for morale and great fighters. It seemed they were the piece missing from his army all along. They were teaching the others a thing or two.

Conall came tearing across the training yard, interrupting their laughter. His eyes were wide and his nostrils flared. He recognized the warning signs that

Conall had either just spoken to a ghost or saw something not of this world.

"What is it Conall, what did you see?"

Larc watched him curiously.

Conall pulled his hand through his hair, another habit while dealing with aberrations. "Merlin was just here. I was in the library looking for monasteries and he came tae me. He said tae ready the men, he would lead us tae him. He was weak and just a projection, it took a lot out of him tae come here.

"He said he'd be back tomorrow tae show us the way. We are tae meet at outer earth, at the portal opening, early in the morning, they are there in outer earth. He said he couldn't tell us where he's at, he can only lead us, because it's so well hidden and cloaked, we couldn't get there any other way. He said there's only one way in and that's up through a valley. It's on a cliff. He looks bad, Ian, we have to get tae him."

"Och, we will, Conall, my gods, Merlin. Larc ready your men for battle. Lysanthir!"

"Ian? What is it?"

"Merlin came tae Conall. He'll meet us at the outer earth portal. I think he's somewhere there. We'll take the stationary portal from here tae outer earth, damn good thing it's nae inner earth, we'd have to go tae Wattingham fort for that portal. We have tae be ready tomorrow.

"Baws, are we ever going tae get the time we need for training? I need you tae ready our men. Gather them all, I will talk tae them. I'll meet you in the yard in two hours. I need tae see Elspeth and my brothers at the castle. Tell them tae pack light, but warm. We're going up a mountain. We leave at day break. Tell Lauren,

Finn, and Taryn what I told you, tell Connor's men as weel, I need him at the castle."

"Connor! I need ye inside now!" Connor came jogging up. "Follow me." He walked off leaving Lysanthir and Larc shouting at their men.

"Connor, I doona ken how many we face, I doona ken the layout of the land where we're goin'. I need you tae think of all possible scenarios. We're goin' up a mountain, the only way is through a valley. A good place for them tae ambush us. We need a way tae get through there. Come up with somethin' tae do that. That's all I ken. I need tae see Elspeth. We'll need her here tae care for the wounded. Bullocks!"

He left to search for Elspeth and found her in the solarium sewing by the window, humming. He realized she enjoyed it. It warmed his heart. God's, she was beautiful. "Hi sweetling," he said smiling.

"She looked up and smiled. "Hi, yourself. Och, what now, Ian?"

"Merlin came tae Conner in a projection. It took a lot of his energy. Connor said he isn't well and looks bad but can lead us tae him. We leave at day break tae find Athdar's army and Merlin. I need you here, Els, for the wounded."

Elspeth stood, laying down her sewing, and with a concerned look, walked to Ian and put her arms around him. "Are the men ready?" She asked, looking into his eyes.

"They are all good soldiers tae begin with. They've had a few days tae integrate and get tae ken each other. We doona have a choice we have tae go. With the werewolves, we have a great chance. They're a great bunch of men. I worry aboot you."

"I'm fine Ian, I am here for you and the men, and I'm here for Merlin. Doona fash yourself, I'll be fine. I just hope the men will be. Do you ken where you're going?"

"Only, up some mountain. Doona ken where, on outer earth though." Ian knew her thoughts and worry weighed on her. "I'll be fine. I'm thinkin' when this is over I will retire for good. I have you and the bairn tae think aboot. I want tae raise my family and spend my days lovin' you. I have tae go talk tae Dougal and Cameron, then talk tae the men. I'll pack later. Then later…later…,"he said and wiggled his eyebrows.

Elspeth laughed and slapped his arm. "You better think of later…later," she smiled, pressed her bosom to his chest and kissed him.

"You do that, and there'll be nae later…later only now…now!" he kissed her back hard, and grabbed her behind and pulled her in, groaning.

"Later, later," she whispered, barely catching her breath.

After he talked with Dougal, Cameron, and Conall, who had returned to Merlin's library, he walked out to the yard.

He stood atop the podium and looked at all the men. His brothers, Lysanthir, and Larc below, standing beside him.

"Thanks for being here and for being part of this. Our last battle was hard, and I ken we lost a lot of good men, but now we ken better what we are dealin' with. I want to thank Larc and his men for joining with us in this common cause. We've all taken a soldier's oath tae protect both worlds and now that time has come."

He looked out over the men assembled and felt

proud of the hard work they had put forward. "Each one of you is a good soldier, and a good mon. Now I've explained what these kearals are capable of, and we all ken it's not good, but you've all agreed to continue on. To fight.

"I want you tae look at your brothers next tae you. Ken each one of you has each other's back. Today we are not just Ocrul, we are not just Crixior, we are not just Crimson Keepers, we are not just Ogourax. We are not segregated. Today we are soldiers, we are men, we are brothers.

"We are *all* fighting for the same thing. We are fighting for the weak, who canna. We are fightin' tae live in a peaceful world, where we can love, raise a family, and be safe. So you look at your brothers, because we are goin' to war as one. A rather different one..." and they all laughed, "but a war nevertheless. We will watch each other's backs and protect each other. I need tae reiterate, make sure you keep their hands from around your heads. That's a power they have that we have to avoid.

"I donna ken exactly where our destination is, Merlin will be leading us there. I ken we will be going up a mountain and through a valley tae get there. In that valley, they are likely tae ambush us. We ken now what we are up against. It's not goin' tae be easy, but I ken for a fact we can do it. Are you all with me, give me an Aye!"

"*Aye!*" again "*Aye!*"

"Good luck men. Eat good tonight, pack warm but light. We'll be treckin' up a mountain. We'll be taking our horses through the portal here in the morning. We leave at day break. Dismissed."

He climbed down and pulled his hand over his face. He tried not to think of the men they recently lost or the battle they had. He knew they were now sitting good with Larc and his men, he just didn't want to lose any more soldiers.

It was his responsibility to see to their safety. He hated going into unknown territory, but it had to be done. They had to face Athdar and his army. He wasn't so ignorant to think they could eradicate Athdar's army, but they could win this battle, hopefully along with killing Athdar and Drakkor.

He knew Merlin and he knew Merlin would die before he would lead them all to their death. He had to trust his judgement. He knew Merlin had studied his surroundings, carefully planning his moves. He must have spent all the time he could listening to Athdar, projecting when he could, and getting a feeling for Athdar's movements and daily habits.

At least that is what he himself would do. He and Merlin were a lot alike. Merlin wouldn't be coming to them unless he was ready. So, like it or not, they too, had to be ready. At least Elspeth would be here, safe. He wanted to see what strategies Connor would come up with. Lysanthir had good strategies as well. Together they'd figure things out.

He walked around the other side of the castle and down the hill. He called Ator and within minutes he was there. "Ator we found Merlin, sort of. In the morning at day break we leave for outer earth. Merlin will meet us at the portal there and lead us to Athdar and Drakkor. I need you and your dragons with us. Can you ready them?"

"We'll be ready. We can fly on ahead and up and

meet you there if you like."

"No, it's cloaked, you better follow us. We are in uncharted territory. I want tae make sure you get through with the rest of us. I doona ken what the process of breaking through a cloaking spell entails, but I am sure it isn't pleasant. We need tae follow Merlin, because we aren't sure of our path. Meet us at the portal at daybreak."

"We'll be there." And Ator flew off.

He walked through the doors of Pendragon and into the meeting hall where his brothers were discussing ideas. Larc and Lysanthir just joining them.

"What have you got, Connor?"

"I think our grouping should be larger this time and not so spread out. By the time we all rejoined the group the first wave was tired out. I know it was because of the layout and we really couldn't do much else, but we need a tighter grouping. Ian have you contacted Ator yet?"

"Yes, he is meeting us at daybreak at the portal with his dragons. Conall go over everythin' you saw and heard with Merlin again, even if you think it not important. I doona want tae miss anythin'."

He looked up and saw Elspeth enter the room. "Hi dearling, care tae join us? We are goin' over Merlin's visit with Conall and trying tae plan for what little we ken. Maybe your fresh outlook could help us oot."

"Weel, I doona ken how much help I could be, but I weel join you. I just hope we can get Merlin back safely. I hope I can heal him, although I'm not sure of all that is wrong with him, or if I'm capable." Elspeth took a seat at the table.

Conall brushed his hand over his face. "Like I said,

I was in Merlin's library looking for references tae monasteries and their locations. I looked up and he was there, but not. I could see through him and had trouble at times understandin' him. I doona ken if it's because he's ill or weak or if it was because he was a projection of himself, but he does not look good at all.

"He's thin and older looking. His face was gray and much more wrinkled. He had trouble with keeping his eyes open and his speech was off. I just hope he's strong enough to go through with it. He started tae fade a couple of times, but when I called his name he became brighter.

"I couldn't tell where he was because he floated here, away from his surroundings, so it was unlike Lauren and his dreams. He said he'd lead us tae his location. Our danger will be in the valley when we cross.

"In the afternoon Athdar trains, he hopes tae have us there then, it will be easier tae get in the monastery. He knows they're cloaked, obviously. He says, mornin's Athdar and Drakkor are gone and at night Athdar comes and drains a little of his ether.

"He's not sure aboot scouts, but he believes they have men on watch, and that they scout daily. There is a large building on a hill close by, from there, Merlin said, he could hear men's voices. He sees it when he travels oot. He has tae be careful Athdar doesn't see him. He's the only one who could tell what Merlin was doing.

"He thought it may be a building for animals because he could hear and see horses outside. He thinks the soldiers stay there and that's where they train. That is aboot all he said. That and he will be there in the mornin' at the portal while Athdar and Drakkor are gone. He said he couldn't leave while they were there for fear Athdar would know what he was up tae. That is all I ken."

He looked around the table. "Anyone have anythin' tae say?"

"I canna think of what tae do," said Connor. "I doona have a map, I doona ken the layout of the land, I have nothin' tae go by. I doona ken where we are goin', nor even how many men we are up against. The best I can say is we should stick together as much as we can."

The room was quiet with everyone deep in thought. Most worried about Merlin.

"Weel, I guess there isn't anthin' we can do other than follow Merlin," he said. "We should eat, pack, and get tae bed early. Finn, I know you want tae go, but I'm goin' tae ask ye tae stay here and watch over Elspeth. Even though Cameron and Dougal will be here, they will be busy with the books and spells. I need someone who can keep an eye on her. Do you mind?"

"I'm fine, Ian, you men need tae go," said Elspeth. "I doona need watchin'. Seriously, I'm safe here in Wesladus. I doona want anyone tae watch me. The staff is here, that's all I need."

"She's right," said Finn. "The only trouble will be wherever Athdar is. I think she'll be fine."

"Elspeth, I'd feel better if one of my brothers stayed."

"Dougal and I will be here," said Cameron. "I want tae read more of Merlin's book, but if something should come up, I'm sure I can handle it. I want tae anyway, I'm in the middle of reading the grimoire. I have it half memorized, and soon I should have the whole thing in my head. You wouldn't mind keeping me company, would you Els?"

"I suppose," he said not giving Elspeth a chance to answer. "You and Dougal are just busy with readin' and I thought we should have someone nae as tied up."

"I said I'd watch over her, Ian," said Cameron. "I can do both."

"Weel, I guess that would be fine. Now I feel better. It's time we eat. *Morag!*"

Morag came from the kitchens with tankards and mead. "I'll be right back with water, for you Elspeth. Dinner is ready and will be right out." The tiny maid rushed out.

A few seconds later, two women carried in civet of hare, loin of veal, stuffed chicken, and a quarter of stag. The usual frumenty. Breads with different jellies were scattered about, and gilt sugar plums and pomegranate seeds adorned the middle and each end of the table. There were hard boiled eggs covered with saffron and flavored with cloves, plums stewed in rose-water, various wines, and large pies.

He looked around the table at those gathered there. "A bountiful feast to say the least. Eat up, I doona ken when our next hot meal will be."

After everyone ate, they all talked for an hour, when Ian announced that he was going to pack, Elspeth offered her help, and they got up to leave. After "good nights" were exchanged, everyone left the table to get ready for the morning.

"You need tae take this warm cloak, Ian," Elspeth said as she packed things for him."

"Nae my tartan will keep me warm. I doona need anything warmer but thank you." He looked at her and smiled. "I think I have all I need. Now all I need is you."

Elspeth stopped and smiled. "Then I think, it's later later." She moved everything from the bed. "Come here," she said, and held her arms out.

"You doona have tae tell me twice," he said, as he moved and sat down beside her. He took her hands and looked at her. "I want you tae know somethin,' Els. This battle willna be like the last. I was not myself last time. That was the first time I ever felt the way I did. I want you tae ken, it willna happen again."

"I ken, Ian. I understand you more than you ken. You forget, I was in your head. I ken what happened. I'm not worried aboot you. Everything will be fine. Now kiss me you big bloke. I need you."

And so, he did. They made love slowly and he ended by tasting her sweet blood on his lips. He drank deep, not only for the purposes of the feeling it invoked, but because he wanted to take a little of her and the bairn with him. He pulled her against him, his hand curled protectively on her stomach and fell asleep with a smile on his face.

Morning came way too early for him, he lay there thinking about the lost men. He couldn't get it out of his head. Finally, he shook himself and gave himself a stern lecture. His remaining men needed his consideration. He had no room for mistakes.

He kissed Elspeth on the forehead and silently removed himself from the bed.

"You canna leave me, Ian McGregor, without a kiss and farewell." Elspeth turned toward him with a yawn. "Are you sure it's even mornin' yet?"

"I'm sure. I was going tae leave you sleep and see

you after we were ready tae go. I'll be back," he said, and kissed her anyway.

"Mmmmmm. I wish you were in this bed with me."

"Me as weel, sweetling. After this is over you are all mine."

"I'm all yours anyway." She smiled.

He put his hand on her belly. "You just take care of yourself and our bairn. I doona want anything tae happen tae her."

"You mean him," she said, and grinned.

"She's a fire-red haired girl, with emerald eyes, and as bonnie as her Mither."

"He's a dark-haired boy, with silver eyes, and so handsome all the girls swoon."

They both chuckled. He kissed her again and left.

In the yard men were talking. Spirits were upbeat and he joined in. For as chaotic as it sounded, things were moving along nicely. It was a gray sky and soon it would be turning red. He hurried the men on.

Horses were packed, men mounted and ready to go as the first red streaks reached the horizon. Elspeth met him in the yard and they held each other for a second before reluctantly parting.

He gave the call and they went to the stationary portal that led to outer earth. Ator and his dragons flew up. Ian looked around at his misbegotten army and smiled, now they were complete.

He was happy with Larc and his men, they boosted the rest of the men, the dragons were a site to behold, yes, he felt good about this. They were able to enter two at a time on horseback. The dragons followed them through. Their transition went smoothly. Soon they were all gathered on the other side of the portal.

"Do you see Merlin yet, Conall?" asked Ian?

"Nae, I doona see him, not yet."

"Weel, we wait."

****

Mount Zomm, in the cave

Athdar looked at Drakkor. "Did you get the bone from Elspeth's mother and father?"

"It was easy, I remembered where I buried them. How does this work, Athdar? What is the bone used for?"

"Well Elspeth is a healer. My plan is to use Merlin to bring her to us. I will use the bone dust to send Merlin to her. She will by her very nature want to heal. Because of my ether connection to Merlin, I will know the minute she touches him, and when she does I'll immediately pull them back here.

"She will become our prisoner." He laughed. "It will be such fun killing her in front of Merlin and Ian. I can't wait to see their faces. When it sinks in and I've had my fun, I will then kill Ian, my brother's favorite McGregor. Then I will kill my brother, the same way he killed me, only slower. With this."

He took the knife off the stone alter that lay in the huge cavern. "It's the magical knife that killed me. Using his blood, and its power, each slice will bring fire to his veins, but instead of killing him quickly as he did me, I'm going to kill him slowly." He relished the thought of making his brother suffer. How ironic, he thought. His laughter echoed off the walls.

"What if someone else touches Merlin when you go to bring them back here? Will they also transport here?"

"Yes, but the more the merrier. If I can get more McGregors all the better and the less I have to get later."

"How are you going to get Ian here?"

"If he isn't with her, once he finds her gone, he'll come looking for her. After I have her, I'll drop the cloak so he can find me. Only this time I'll be ready for him. I'll have my army set up to ambush them in the valley, with the stipulation Ian is to be brought to me alive."

He mixed roots and herbs in a large bowl as he spoke. He and Drakkor collected different ones every morning. Sometimes taking a portal to distant lands in search of the rarer ones. Now his collection was complete. He had everything he needed.

"Once I've finished with grinding the roots, I'll grind the bone and add it to this. It will all be ready, when I say my incantation, I only need to add my blood. Of course, Merlin will be here. I have a small spell that will cut off his voice, so he can't warn Elspeth, and voila! We'll have her, and anyone else who wants to tag along for the ride. It's a perfect plan."

Drakkor laughed. "I can't wait to see the end of the McGregors. They have always had their nose in everything I do. Once they're gone there will be no one stopping us, Athdar, no one. We can complete our goals without interference. You will be the strongest wizard alive and I'll be demon king. Things we both deserve, and we'll be unstoppable." Drakkor grinned. "Speaking of which did you find Juppar Heiwynn? Are we going get the men back?"

"I have an idea where he is. I'm not worried about them yet. I have plans in mind for Juppar Heiwynn. I will take care of them when we finish with Elspeth, Merlin, and McGregor. Here help me with the rest of this. You grind up the mother's bone. We don't need much, just enough in the bottom of your hand should do it."

They each stood at the alter with mortar and pestle. They both had about an inch of bone that they crumbled and were now grinding. Both laughing and talking as they worked, about the things they wanted to have and do.

****

The portal at outer earth

The men waited only seconds before Merlin showed. Conall yelled, "there," and pointed. Conall was the only one who could see him. Ian followed him as he walked his horse toward where his brother saw the wizard.

Conall was quiet a moment and then relayed Merlin's words. "He said he can get us tae the edge of the mountain this morning, but he has tae return tae the monastery afore Athdar. He will tell us the path tae take, then return when Athdar goes tae training.

"He said about half of Athdar's men haven't returned tae train. He doesn't ken what's happened to them, but he hopes they're gone. That means less you have to worry about."

"How many men does he figure that Athdar has?"

"Aboot a hundred tae a hundred and fifty men." Conall suddenly looked worried. "Merlin! Merlin! Hey you with me? He looks bad Ian. We need tae go."

Conall took off fast. "He's headed this way. Keep up!" The men responded to his shout and took off in a gallop.

After quite a distance of running the horses, they finally slowed then stopped. They were at a river. Ian held up his hand for silence and looked around. He could hear him talking to Merlin. Finally, after arm waving, and pointing to various spots, Conall stopped. He rode to meet him.

"Merlin said tae rest the horses here, water and feed them, and for us tae eat as weel. After our rest, it will be a non-stop trek up. He had tae leave, but he'll find us on our path this afternoon, and lead us through the valley. He said tae take that path there and follow it. It looks like it stops up ahead, but that's because of the cloaking. The farther we go, the more path we'll see.

"He said once we get close to the cloaking edge we will start to feel fearful and be compelled to flee. The horses might spook, but we must keep going straight. Once the barrier is breeched we will be fine."

He turned toward the rest of the group. "I will tell them what you told me." Some of the men led their horses to the water to cool them down and allow them to drink. Others were stooped over washing the dust from their faces and hands.

He looked toward the direction they were headed. The path appeared to end, but then again looks could be deceiving. Athdar could make it look different, he supposed, but in the end, they'd still be going up that mountain. Most of it was covered in fog, the work of Athdar no doubt. It looked and felt menacing. He wondered if the horses would have to be left behind at some point.

After they ate the dried meat, bread, and cheese they were ready to follow Conall along a path they couldn't really see. But they knew Merlin and no one dare question what he had to say. So as a group they crossed the river then fell in line as they began on their path upward.

It wasn't straight up as he'd thought, in fact it wound around. When they hit the shroud barrier, it was as Merlin said, the closer they got, the more unease the men and the horses felt. There was some chaos as the men tried to control the horses, until finally they all broke through.

The dragons went through easier, just behind the men. The path became clearer and the fog cleared somewhat. So far, the journey wasn't as tough as he'd expected.

They continued for a few hours when Merlin showed back up. Conall called out to Ian that he was with them. As if on cue they came to a place where the road split off, and Merlin showed them the correct path.

When he looked back from where'd they come, the fog shrouded where they'd been. It must work both ways, he thought. He turned and concentrated on Conall. "What's Merlin got tae say?" he asked him.

"We aren't far from the valley. We best get the men ready for an ambush.

****

Mount Zomm, training yard

Athdar and Drakkor stood in the yard watching the men, when a scout came galloping up. Pulling his horse to a rearing halt just beside Athdar, he shouted, "men coming to the valley! About a hundred!"

Athdar looked up at him surprised. "Men? Damn, I wasn't ready for this. How the hell did they get through the cloak? Men to the valley! If Ian McGregor is there, bring him to me alive. Do you hear me? Kill the rest!

Drakkor come, we are implementing our plan now. We need to get Merlin and get to the cave."

When they got to Merlin's room, he tried to wake him and found he couldn't. Then it dawned on him. "He's projecting! That's how the men got through the cloak! I didn't think he'd have the energy for it. You sneaky bastard!" He slapped him hard.

Instantly Merlin was back and awake. He saw fear on the old man's face as he opened his eyes and realized his plan had been discovered. He threw him over his shoulder and called for Drakkor to follow.

When they got to the cave he dropped Merlin on the floor. His hands and legs still tied. He knew Merlin had no energy to fight anyway. It probably took most of what he had left to project. It didn't matter to Athdar anyway, he was implementing his plan now.

"Athdar, you can't use the spells in the Grimoire. You face certain death if you do, and me as well. You know the Gods warned us against using those spells. Do not use the dark book, you know the consequences."

He laughed. "I broke that rule the minute Drakkor brought me back to life. And the minute I took your ether and all the others. No Merlin, I won't be stopped this time, but you're right you will die, but not because of using spells from the Grimoire, no because of me. Now shut up!"

He waved his arm and said a few words, and his brother could no longer speak. He stood above the bowl he'd prepared and began chanting. He could tell Merlin recognized the spell by his look of fear. "Do not!" his thoughts loud and clear to Athdar.

He laughed, then sliced his hand and let the blood drip into the bowl. Then he poured in some black wax which caused the contents to flame up. After the flame receded, he took the bowl over to Merlin. He dipped his fingers in the paste, and wiped it across Merlin's forehead, still chanting. When he finished, he said, "be gone!" and Merlin vanished.

****

Pendragon castle in Wesladus

Elspeth sat in Merlin's library talking to Ian's brother. She was bored and wished to have someone to talk to so she sought out Cameron. He was telling her stories about battles, and about Ian, she was really enjoying herself. She loved hearing about the crazy things Ian did before she met him.

He was a ladies' man, but she'd figured that out anyway, and even though Cameron didn't go in to detail about the women, she could read between the lines. Those days were over for him. She'd make sure of it she thought with a laugh.

It was in the middle of one of those stories Merlin appeared. Suddenly, he was there laying on the floor at her feet. She screamed "Merlin!" She jumped up with Cameron right behind her.

When she realized what bad shape he was in, she bent over to check him. Cameron at his other side. "Hurry," she said. "We need to see if he's injured so I can heal him." They both began to search him.

Merlin opened his eyes, he tried to tell them something but nothing came out. He shook his head, no, but she couldn't understand his meaning. They worked to remove his clothing when suddenly the air around them blurred. She looked up and around. "Where are we?" They appeared to be in a cave, in the same positions they had been in the castle.

Cameron looked around. "This isn't good."

Athdar and Drakkor stepped from behind the alter. Drakkor spoke, "Well, well, Cameron McGregor, this is an added surprise. Athdar threw out his hand and in a deep voice said an incantation. She watched as Cameron's demeanor changed. He seemed suddenly tired and dropped to the floor.

She screamed, "What did you do to him? You pig! You God forsaken, pig!"

Athdar smiled. "God forsaken, yes. Drakkor, tie her up. Then we must go meet Ian." He laughed. "We'll leave her on the alter. And this is Cameron McGregor you say, Drakkor?" Drakkor nodded. "Well, well this day just keeps getting better, tie up Cameron McGregor. He'll be down, but I don't want to take any chances."

Athdar grabbed the ropes and handed them to Drakkor. Then he leaned over and grabbed her. She struggled but was no match for him.

"Ian will be here for you and your men. You willna get away with this."

"Oh, but I will," he said then grinned wide. "He will be here, make no mistake, but he'll watch me kill you, then Merlin will watch you both die, and for the grand finale, I will end Merlin's miserable life." He laughed.

She felt a blast of worry go through her when she looked into Athdar's evil glare. He no doubt believed every word and she wasn't so sure she didn't either. Stay strong, she told herself. Think of the bairn.

Athdar and Drakkor left after she was tied atop the alter. She thought about the monastery and the monks, she thought about where she was raised, and thought about Mother Thomas. She hadn't really prayed since she left the convent. Now would be a good time. "Listen tae me," she said beginning. "Maybe I haven't done things the right way, but there's a reason I met Ian. There's a reason I'm goin' tae have his bairn. Please doona let it end like this.

"I have believed in you all my life. I have given my life tae protectin' the ill and injured and have asked for nothing in return. I have believed in prevailing good, always, and you ken that. Please help us." And she began to sob. "Please," she said, "doona turn away this time. We need you." She continued to pray.

****

Athdar was in a rush. "They will come to the monastery looking for us, and we need to be ready. If some of his soldiers make it here, I want them trapped outside. I want McGregor in and them out. I'll open a portal from inside and take Ian to the cave. You be prepared to grab him when he comes through. I'll freeze him, you tie him. I want him awake and alert to watch what I'm going to do to Elspeth. I'll revive Merlin enough to watch, but not all the way. He got the best of me once. He won't do it again."

****

Ian and his men fought. They made it to the valley at the same time as Athdar's men did. There wasn't time for contemplation or planning, the battle was on. There was all manner of magic and mayhem, the black clouds rolled across the heavens in rumbling anger, lightning struck, the ground shook and then cracked open, and large hordes of black nasty insects were born. The swarm yielding a *clacking* sound that was almost deafening.

Ator and his dragons dodged lightning and battled through gale winds, tracing fire lines down on those they could. They fried the insects before they could fly toward the crowd of men fighting with swords. They backed up Ian and his men wherever they could.

The werewolves were true to form. They were the size of ponies with two rows of sharp gnashing teeth, claws the length of daggers, growling, attacking, biting, and ripping out throats. The vampires were biting as well, ripping at throats and leaving gushing streams of blood shooting from necks. The fae held fire in their hands and when they threw it onto their opponent's chest, explosions of sparks left the men screaming. It would have been mass hysteria to anyone looking on, but in this battle very few of his men fell.

They made quick work of Athdar's army and when there were but five enemy soldiers left, they bolted. He screamed, "follow them! They'll lead us to Athdar."

Athdar's remaining men reached the monastery first, running up the steps and through the doors. Athdar and Drakkor were there to greet them. Athdar yelled over the chaos. "McGregors! Ian! If you want to see Elspeth McLellan alive you will stop your men."

He held his hand up to halt the men. "Ye doona know where she is." He kept his voice confident while his stomach sunk. He hoped Athdar was bluffing, but knew he was telling the truth. This was one time he wasn't sure knowing someone spoke the truth was a good thing. He felt sick.

"Make no mistake I have her, in fact I'll show you. You and all McGregors shall enter. No one else is to even try or she's dead. Do you understand?"

Ator sent a silent message. *"We can burn the*

monastery and force them out."

He thought back, *"Nae, I canna take the chance that Elspeth will die. We'll go in, I doona have a choice.* Athdar! We'll come in!" He called for his brothers and ordered all else to stand down. "We're coming in Athdar. If it's a trick, my dragons will burn you alive."

The door slowly opened. As soon as he and his brothers came through, the door slammed shut. Athdar was on the other side of the room. He instantly froze the McGregors. "Drakkor, guards, tie them up. I'll open a portal and we'll bring them through. I've put a spell so none can enter. We haven't much time." Athdar opened the portal. After the men were tied. Athdar released the freeze.

"Anyone try anything and Elspeth dies. We are going through the portal to where she is. I reiterate, don't try anything stupid."

"You heard him. I willna take a chance on her life."

As soon as they went through he saw Elspeth on the alter. His heart sank. "You okay?" he asked.

"I'm okay Ian, but he plans on killing me in…"

"Shut up, Elspeth! I will tell them what I am going to do!" Athdar shrieked. "She's right, Guards hold the McGregors! He flew his hand through the air and they all became weak. His brothers dropped to the floor unable to stand.

He watched, his anger so bad, he didn't comprehend the weakness that befell him. He looked around and saw Merlin and Cameron on the ground. "Are they alive?"

Athdar turned toward him with anticipation in his

eyes. "Oh yes. Your brothers will watch the show, then they die, but first I have an order in which I will do things. I am going to kill Elspeth first so you and Merlin can watch, and then I'll kill your brothers, and just before Merlin, I'm going to kill you. My brother, last but not least, will see you all killed, and then I will enjoy killing him slowly. You see there's nothing you can do." He laughed and walked over to the alter.

He thought to Ator, *"Ator, we're in a cave somewhere. We went through a portal, so I doona ken where. Find us. Athdar plans on killing us all. We're weak, some spell. Can you hear me?"*

"Yes, I'll look for you. Not sure where, but I'll spread the dragons out. Hang on Ian."

Athdar flung his arm around the room removing the weakness from the McGregors but not Merlin. Another wave and the McGregors became frozen again. The only thing they could move was their eyes.

He watched as he walked to Merlin and pulled him in to a sitting position. He raised his hand and sent a jolt into Merlin, half reviving him. "I want you to see the show, Merlin, and the boys too."

Athdar walked to where Elspeth lay and picked up the spelled knife that Merlin originally used to kill Seamus. He ran the tip down Elspeth's chest. "I've waited a long time for this. I plan to enjoy it. You see this knife is a special knife. My brother made it. Specially forged to kill any species. It's quite magical, kills vampires, fae, most anything, and is very painful. Ironic isn't it, that I should use a knife that my brother made to kill all that he holds dear? Except for Ian, I owe him a stake to the heart. You see he took an old friend from me with a stake, and well…neither here nor there, his death will be by stake, yours by Merlin's knife," he spoke as if caught up in another world.

He looked at Elspeth curiously. "I see you've mated. Ian, I suppose." She didn't answer and Ian saw she was frozen in fear. He knew Athdar was completely mad. Athdar drew the knife across her chest. Her breathing became fast and shallow. He traveled across one breast and down to her belly. Ian pushed against the freeze spell enraged at not being able to move, anger eating at his insides. He was ready to explode.

Athdar looked farther, and after a frown he smiled. "Well it looks like I won't be killing only McGregor brothers. It appears to me you have some little McGregors."

He was stunned. McGregors? More than one?

"Ah, you didn't know did you. There's two little heartbeats in her belly." He laughed. "I'll cut them out and show you Ian."

Elspeth finally reacted. "Nae!" she screamed. "Nae!"

He looked toward Merlin. He looked a bit better than he had when they arrived in the cave. Maybe he would be able to help them.

He struggled harder, screaming in his head, but was unable to move a muscle. He was frantic and terrified of being unable to save Elspeth and the bairns. Damn it if only Merlin could break the spell.

Athdar held the knife in one hand and picked up something else. "See this? It's the stake that is going to kill you Ian. It's been blessed in holy water, so don't get your hopes up that you'll live through it, I guarantee you won't."

He glanced around the room at his brother's frozen

forms. Merlin caught his gaze and gave a slight nod of his head. As Athdar picked up the blade and held it over Elspeth's belly, Merlin gave a jerk of his arm. He felt the spell fall away. He could move.

He turned but before he could reach Athdar, the bastard drove the knife in her chest. He felt his heart sink and his blood boil, letting out a blood curdling scream he lunged for Athdar. He wasn't quick enough. Athdar grabbed the stake and sunk it in his chest, hitting his heart. Everything went black as he hit the floor.

Athdar laughed insanely as the rest of the McGregors and Merlin fell silent. He knew there was nothing they could do.

****

Ian jumped up. Beside him lay his body. Instantly he was pulled through a swirl of flashing bright lights. He heard a cacophony of men's voices and realized they were all him. In an instant, he went through every life he ever lived. In each one he was a warrior. Different times, different places, but he remembered them all. Suddenly his purpose was clear.

When he began as a spark, it was as a soldier for good. He started as a thought, then energy, then life. As but a spark he broke away from the One Great God with the intent purpose of fighting for good. Some of his lives were short and some long. He looked different in each one.

In many of those lives he had a wife, a different one each time. No not different, just different vessels just like him. It was Elspeth, always Elspeth. He remembered her and screamed for the God of Light. "Come you bastard! Now!"

Suddenly he was back in the room. He quickly looked around. No one moved. Time had stopped.

"Ian? Son?"

He looked toward the voice. "Da? Eoghan? What are you two doing here. Why has time stopped?"

"I doona ken, son. But it's good to see you. Though not under these circumstances. I'm sorry son. We've been watching over you and the family since we've been gone. I miss Moira. Is she happy?"

"Not without you, da, or Eoghan. She thinks of you always. What's going tae happen tae Elspeth and the bairns?"

"We'll leave that up to you," came a booming voice. Suddenly the room filled with light and a red glow. The God of Light and the God of Dark appeared in the room.

"What do you mean by that?"

"Think Ian and remember. Your many lives, your existence, how many times you've fallen in battle. Tell me what you're fighting for."

"I'm fighting for the rights of others, for the ones who canna do it for themselves, for myself and my family. In all my lives, I've battled evil, not once has my family and I lived tae an age of peace, tae watch the ones I love tae grow, I'm tired of the fight.

"I want tae live in peace and be able tae love my family without thinking we're all going tae die every time I turn around. I understand why I am and I have worked hard tae make sure people and places were safe, now I just want tae live my life with my family. I want tae feel love, and joy, peace, and know what it is like tae just live. I want my Da and my brother back.

"Is it so much tae ask? I want tae see my bairns

born, and have many of them, a large family, full of love. Look what's happened, it always does, I want a different life, one with no worry."

"You will find there's always worry, Ian. You will understand there is no pleasure without first knowing pain. You can't know peace without war. There is no happiness until you've known sadness, you can't understand life, until you've understood death.

"Think about that. If there was un-ending peace what questions would you have. Would you understand it as peace? Balance. Understanding. In your heart, you know. You have worked very hard Ian, this is true, and you certainly deserve the happiness you seek.

"If this is your true wish, I will grant it. Eoghan will return with you. It wasn't his time to leave yet, anyway. Lachlan I'm sorry, you cannot go back.

"You will have your peace Ian but think on it and think hard. The choices are yours. You won't remember your other lives when you go back or who you truly are, and only a minimal amount of our conversation, but you will have to remember at some point. When you do, I'll come again and we'll re-evaluate your circumstances.

"You'll remember dying and Eoghan going back, your life will be at peace, but your brother's lives, remain the same. You will go back to McGregor castle and be lord there and live your life in happiness, your brothers will return to Wesladus at Pendragon and continue their work there."

"What will happen with Athdar? What of Drakkor? Is Elspeth and our bairns alive?"

"Athdar will not be killed. You know the balance of good and evil, as it stands, a necessity. Of everything, including in each one of your souls. Athdar will be taken by the Dark Lord. He will be imprisoned in the bowels of hell for a very lengthy time. You won't have to worry about him coming after you.

"Drakkor is now dead, Kahn took his life immediately for his transgressions against the rules, his spirit resides in turmoil in demon hell. He cannot rise again. This last fiasco Kahn could not ignore, he had to take action, or answer to the One Great God. As far as Elspeth goes, she's in bad shape. Speaking of bad shape, *Merlin!* Wake up." The God of Light turned to Merlin.

"Am I dead?"

"No Merlin, you know the world can't get along without you." The God of Light laughed. "You're looking a little under the weather and old too. I'll fix that. He waved his hands and before his eyes Merlin became healthy and young.

"Your brother beat death and is young once again. You know how I like things equal. You have a job to do Merlin. You know what that is."

"Yes, I do." Merlin smiled. "Thank you."

"Will you heal Elspeth, please." He knew he begged, but felt he had no choice.

"No, Ian, I will not, but behold the beauty and fight of life." The God of light swept his arm in front of him and disappeared. He was once again in his body. The stake was gone and he jumped up to fight Athdar and Drakkor. They too were gone.

He ran to Elspeth and grabbed her hand. Everyone was released from their frozen states and Eoghan was there.

His brothers were hugging and talking, but he

could only see Elspeth. He pulled the knife from her chest. "Wake up dearling, please." She didn't move. He watched in slow motion as the blood seeped from her chest and drop by drop slid slowly down her side and off the table to hit the floor, each drop a splash he could swear resounded through his body. The whole slow-motion scene surreal. The ripples from each drop flowing through him, killing him as surely as someone slowly pushing a knife in his heart and twisting. He watched her life blood leaving.

Then in a sudden moment of clarity he pressed his hand to her wound to try and stop the bleeding. He fell to his knees and lay his head to her chest and listened to her heart beat slow.

In his anguish, he raised his head and gave a grief ridden howl that bellowed from deep in his soul, echoed loudly through the cave walls, shaking all around. All his brothers stopped and gathered around concern etching their worried faces.

Silence hung in the air as he buried his face in her neck and sobbed. She lay dying, still, silent, and pale. Ian held her limp hand and squeezed, with his other he gently placed it to her stomach, unknowingly, gently rubbing over his dying babes.

All his training as a soldier and leader seemed pointless. He was losing his woman, the only one he wanted for his wife, his only love, and his whole world. His children he'd never meet, never see their first steps, hear their first words, or watch them grow up. The tender heart that Elspeth single handedly nourished in him until it bloomed, shattered.

His grief was beyond words, he held her, feeling her slip away and knowing there was nothing he could do to stop it. "Why couldn't you save her?" He yelled to the God of Light. He gave up then, he no longer cared to live or die. He wanted to go with her, he wished he could have stayed dead. He knelt there in a stupor, until Merlin nudged him. He brushed his hand from his shoulder.

"Ian, look," said Merlin. He raised his tear stained face.

"Leave me, Merlin. All of you!" he shouted. "Oot! Get the hell oot!"

"Damn it, Ian, look," said Merlin, shaking him. He forced him to turn his head. There within Elspeth's stomach, dimly but sure, came a green light that traveled from its starting point to the wound in her chest. Dumbfounded, he watched in amazement as the wound slowly began to heal.

Little by little the bleeding stopped, and the wound began to knit before his eyes. When it was done, the light went out and she halfway opened her eyes. "Ian," she whispered hoarsely. "I thought you dead. I saw Athdar stake you. You're alive!"

An anguished moan slipped from his lips. With a quiver to his voice, he said, "Elspeth, my Elspeth, so are you. How? You were dying, so close to death. You are amazing Elspeth you healed yourself while you were oot."

She looked confused. "I canna do that, Ian, tis not possible."

"Then how did you heal, if the God of Light dinna do it, then who?"

She suddenly seemed to understand. She put her hand on her belly. "I think we are goin' tae have some lil' healers on our hands, it was the bairns. They healed me." She rubbed her belly softly.

He had tears in his eyes and he thought about what the God of Light said about the beauty and fight for life. His was indeed a beautiful life.

He looked at Elspeth. "Everything is goin' to be all right from here oot. I promise. Athdar and Drakkor are gone. They were taken to hell. Athdar pretty much for good, caged there. Drakkor is dead, Kahn killed him, and he's suffering in demon hell.

"As long as he isn't here, that's all I care aboot. I love you Elspeth," he said as he kissed her. "I'm officially retired. We'll live at McGregor castle where I'll be laird and you lady, alongside Mither of course. We'll raise our family and be happy."

Suddenly he felt a twinge, something niggling the back of his brain. A small voice flowed through him. "Remember who you are." He'd heard that voice before when he lay in bed after the kearal did something to his mind, he let it go, shuddered, and shook it off.

"I love you too Ian. Can we get oot of here?"

He laughed. Over joyed, he grabbed up Elspeth in his arms, kissed her soundly until Merlin grabbed his forearm. Merlin stood beside him. "My gods you look young and handsome!"

Merlin laughed. "I think everything turned out all right this battle. Let's get your men and dragons, and go home, shall we?"

Home he thought, hmmm. He shook his head. "Come Els, I need tae thank the men and tell them a job well done. There is usually a celebration after a battle is won. I'll have the men spend the rest of today getting their wives, ladies, whoever they want.

"Tomorrow we'll have a daylong party in

celebration in Wesladus. Then I'll tell them I'm retiring and have someone fill my place." He grabbed her hand and pulled her up.

Merlin looked at all the boys. "I think it's time you all went home for a while and enjoy yourselves. Stay until the wedding and the party afterward. With Athdar deep in hell with no way out, we should be sitting good for a while.

"There's still the issue of the ether and unaccounted men. But none of your concern Ian. Now is the time for joy, and celebration, Eoghan is home! We have so much to be thankful for. I will get the portal ready and we can go to where the dragons and men wait.

"I will take care of Pendragon while everyone's away. I have some reading to catch up on. I will be there for the wedding though."

He watched Merlin ready the portal. "I doona think I'll ever get used to seeing Merlin young. Has anyone here ever seen a young Merlin?" Everyone agreed with him that it was a sight to behold.

"He's been old as long as I can remember." He went to Eoghan. "I'm so glad you're back brother!" He hugged him. "We have to talk aboot what happened. I doona remember much. Blasted God of Light wiped some of my memory."

"I doona remember much either, only that when I died it was not my time. I could come back, but da couldn't. Why, I wonder…"

"Come on, the portal is open," said Merlin. "Let's go."

When they walked through the portal, outside the monastery, everyone cheered. He loved these men.

He'd miss them. "Remember who you are…" came the whisper once again from the back of his mind. "Who said that?" He asked and looked around. No one else seemed to notice, so he let it go.

He smiled at the men then held up his hand for silence. It took a bit, but they finally settled down. Elspeth stood beside him holding his hand, smiling along beside him.

"Men," he said. "First off. Job weel done! We beat the Kearals! Dragons bless you for being here! Thank you. We couldn't have done it withoot you! You guys kicked them all back tae hell!" Cheers went up, and he held his hand up again. "I couldn't be prouder of my men or you dragons. You should be proud of yourselves! We had a job tae do and we did it.

"The rest of today you go and get your wives, lady friends, or friends because tomorrow we celebrate. Be back tonight, because tomorrow is an all-day affair! Dancing, drinkin', and making bairns You can take leave now and find your friends here in outer earth, then use the stationary portal back tae Wesladus."

"See ye all there, and congratulations on a job well done. Dismissed."

Everyone roared and talked at once.

Ator caught his attention. *"Ian, I know what happened to you and Elspeth. I'm sorry you went through it. You really need to reconsider your retirement. These men need you. You are a great leader."* Ator had a look, and he felt he knew more than he was saying.

"You ken something doona ye, Ator. You ken everything that happened when I died, you were there in my mind. What did you see, what did the God of

315

Light make me forget?"

"I cannot tell you things, I am not at liberty to talk about, Ian. Don't ask. I will just say this, there are some things you have to decide for yourself. Now leave it at that for I will not say any more."

"A damn good friend you are," he said, frowning, without thinking and not really meaning it.

"That I am, Ian, and one of these days you will understand that."

"I'm sorry, Ator. I didn't mean it, you ken that. I ken the God of Light, it has tae be hard on you. Thank you for bein' here with us, fighting with us."

"I know Ian. You just went through a great deal, I understand, truly. I'm glad to oblige. Please, though, think about your men they do need you."

"With Athdar gone, the men can train. I'll make sure one of my brothers replace me, and that the men will be in good hands. We'll still be close. I willna forget you."

"I know Ian, but your brothers, they aren't you, Ian. You have leadership talent. Please think about it. I'll miss you."

"Elspeth and I will visit often," he said, knowing full well his friend was going to miss him. He felt Ator didn't want him to leave his men, because he didn't want to lose him. He wouldn't let that happen. "While all the family is at the McGregor Keep, why doona ye and Saphira stay above the loch. It would be nice tae have you there. Besides there's a little girl, weel not so little anymore, who wants tae ride a dragon."

"I'll ask Saphira, we'll have to move the little ones again, but I think she'll want to. She is very close to Elspeth. Well, I'll leave you now and get my dragons

back."

"Hey Ator…"

Ator turned around, "*yes*?"

"Thank you, you and all of your dragons, but especially you. You've been a true friend through everything, and I just want you tae ken…"

"*I know*," said Ator. *"I feel the same."* He smiled a wide dragon smile and then left.

Elspeth was talking to Eoghan and he walked up and took her hand. He caught part of something about the bairns. She laughed and looked at him with longing. He felt it inside as well. He was happy. "Ready?" he asked.

"Aye."

Back at Wesladus in Pendragon, Elspeth was upset. "Your Mither was goin' tae teach me how tae run a household. I ken nothing of having a party. I wish she were here."

"Eoghan! Can you come here for a bit?"

"Sure, what do you need?" he walked over.

"I think it would be nice if you went today and saw Mither, spend some time with her. Bring her and the girls back here for the party. But, not tae late. Elspeth would like her here tae help arrange things. Would you do that?"

"Sure, I'll leave right away."

"Problem solved." He grinned. "My Mither will be here tae help."

Elspeth kissed him. "My new dresses! I forgot, I can wear one tomorrow. Och, Ian, a party. It'll be such fun!" and she kissed him again. "Later, later," she whispered.

He looked in her eyes. "Yes, most definitely, later,

later." He grabbed her and kissed her hard.

"Better yet, now, now, and he picked her up and started up the stairs." Leaving the men all laughing downstairs. He didn't care. He loved Elspeth, they were both alive, and he intended on celebrating the fact.

He threw her on the bed and she laughed. He tore at her clothes and she did the same to his. They couldn't get naked quick enough. He kissed her deep and passionate. His erection bounced to life. It seemed because of what happened everything was heightened. He could feel her every breath, every touch left sensations across his skin. Her dress was half torn off, his shirt the same. She laughed, "get me oot of this!" she said as she tugged her dress. He had that and his pants off in an instant.

He was back beside her licking her neck, she shivered and clawed at his shoulders. He didn't have time to slow down. Not this time. He reached down and felt her damp and ready. He didn't waste time and in one smooth stroke he entered and buried himself inside her and had the intense feeling of coming home.

She sunk her nails scratching across his back. She was so hot, and sheathed inside her wet tightness, his breath caught and he groaned. He stilled waiting for the throbbing to ebb. When it did, he withdrew and buried himself again. God's, she felt good. He didn't think he'd last long.

She grabbed him around the neck, "Please Ian, hard and fast. I need it now." He did. They slammed against each other, staring in each other's eyes, and when she was about to shatter he sank his fangs into her neck.

She screamed his name and came apart in his arms.

He screamed hers and stiffened while his seed emptied. When he let go she latched on and sent them both to the place of another earth-shattering orgasm. They were breathing hard and she was gulping. They laughed and held each other. Worn out from earlier, they fell asleep holding each other.

When they awoke a couple of hours later, they decided they should make an appearance downstairs and headed to the meeting hall. Merlin came through a portal with Moira, the girls and Eoghan. Just in time he thought, he could tell she'd been crying, her eyes were red.

He supposed it was happiness for Eoghan, but sadness for Lachlan. Whatever the case, she was clinging to Eoghan like she might lose him again if she let go, but she finally did. She went and hugged Elspeth. "A party, hu? It weel be such fun. Do you know which dress you'll be wearing? I brought all your things."

"Thank you, I was hoping you'd help me pick it oot… Moira? I doona know how tae throw a party, will you help me?"

"Of course, child. Stick by me and you'll ken how by the end of the day." Moira laughed, and he loved it.

He looked around at his family. He thought about his Da. He whispered, "I wish you were here, Da." He smiled. He knew Lachlan was watching. He could feel him in the room. Elspeth and Moira went to the kitchens laughing.

The girls wanted to go to the ocean and find shells. Merlin looked around. He still couldn't get over a young Merlin. He laughed. He wondered how long he'd stay young. He watched as everyone laughed, he too felt good. He thought he'd go outside and greet the soldiers coming in. He snickered at his brothers, then turned and left the castle.

****

Ator stood with Saphira, exasperated. *"Saphira, I was there, you know how the connection works. I heard everything that the God of Light told Ian. Ian's whole purpose is, has been, and always will be a protector of the weak. He can't retire, and I can't tell him. The God of Light wiped his memory. I have to help him remember, if he wastes his life, and remembers when he is old, he will hate himself."*

"You know you cannot go against anything the God of Light says or does. You cannot tell him the truth about anything that the God of Light has wiped from his memory. No Ator, you stay here, leave Ian be, I'm sure there is a reason for it. You aren't to interfere."

He paced and thought, snorted smoke, and thought some more. Saphira laughed, and he quickly turned. *"What?"*

"You are a good friend, Ator. You care deeply for Ian, that is obvious, but there are some things he must figure out on his own. Have some faith in your friend."

"Perhaps you are right." He snorted again. *"I shall go hunt and get this energy off my chest."* He went to the edge and dove off.

He landed outside Pendragon as Ian was walking outside, good, he thought, he didn't need to call him. Ian looked up and smiled. "Weel, I see you made it back. What brings you here, are you going tae stay above the loch for the weddin'?"

"Oh yes, but I've come to tell you something else you may want to know. I wasn't going to mention it,

because you want to retire so bad, but I'm going to tell you anyway in hopes you'll reconsider your position.

"When we flew down the mountain, I'm sure I saw Athdar's remaining men, but that's not all, I think there is someone else that may be close to Athdar in skill. It was someone I'd never seen before, tall man, dark hair and eyes, could be anyone, I know, but he opened a portal, and they went through. It seemed this person was leading them."

"Hmmm," said Ian. "I will tell Merlin, perhaps he knows. He and my brothers will take care of it, I'm sure."

He looked at Ian, exasperated, but he knew what he had just gone through. Time, he thought, perhaps in time he'd change his mind. He had to quit pushing him, but he just couldn't help it. He just had to try. He had a bad feeling about the man he saw, and he felt the only one smart enough to figure things out, was his friend and leader of the Myraid Army.

If he could just pull a thread of his memory out, well maybe then he could remember everything. He had hoped, oh well… He'd leave it go for a while. Knowing tonight was going to get him nowhere, he changed the subject.

"I will leave you to the men. Saphira and I are going to have our own celebration, if you know what I mean." He snorted.

"Yes, I do, in fact, Elspeth and I have started ours already." Ian laughed. "We're lucky tae have such fine women, are we not?"

"Indeed, we are. I shall see you tomorrow, we'll all fly around and dip in to say hi. Sort of join the party."

"Do dragons dance?" Ian asked and laughed.

"Actually, we do, we have a mating dance we perform when we select a mate. But it only happens once. Have you ever seen a fat dragon try to dance? Not a pretty sight, believe me.

"I don't know whether the females find it funny, or attractive, but it's been done throughout history. I should ask Saphira. Now I'm curious." They both laughed. He put his snout near Ian and Ian reached up to brush the side of his face. *"I'm glad you're alive Ian, I would have sorely missed you had anything happened."*

"I know," said Ian. "I never knew a dragon and a mon could form a bond, but it's pretty thick, isn't it?"

"Yes, as Saphira is with Elspeth. Which speaking about, I'm out hunting berries and worogild. I'm not here, right?" he snorted.

"Right. I never saw you, and you dinna tell me anythin'."

****

Ian turned and watched the men coming in. Most laughing and hanging on to a female. He thought the party a great idea. It would be good for the men to bond over something besides battle.

He hoped some good friends would be made and not limited to their own species. He hoped those boundaries would fall during this party. How was he going to leave these men? He scratched his head, the voice again floated through his mind. He ignored it, shook his head, and took off toward the keep.

His brothers were already hitting the mead, their deep boisterous voices floated out to meet Ian. He was happy and anxious to get in his cups and join them. He grabbed a tankard and poured himself a full cup, drank half, and slammed it to the table. In seconds, he was caught up in conversation about the battle.

Elspeth and Moira went floating by, Elspeth dropped a kiss on his head, he went to grab her and put her on his lap, but she avoided him, laughing. "Your Mither and I are headed up tae our room. She's going tae help me pick oot a dress."

"Weel, I willna stop you then. I canna wait tae see you tomorrow Els. Your bonnie anyway, but tae see you all done up in a fine dress, weel thinkin' aboot it makes my mouth water," he whispered, and grinned.

****

Moira and Elspeth laughed the entire time. They had all the dresses spread atop the bed. Elspeth held up a necklace. "I was trying tae think if I have a favorite necklace, but I love them all. Which dress should I wear Moira?"

"Weel since Ian didn't see you yet in any of the fancy gowns, let's dazzle him tomorrow. My favorite dress is the dark green one," she said as she lifted it from the bed. "It really brings oot the color of your eyes. They are so bonnie, Elspeth, they sparkle, especially when you are looking at my Ian. You really love him doona you?"

She stopped and looked at Moira. "So much, that sometimes I feel I may explode with what I feel. You ken, I can feel him when he's comin' tae me, when he's close I can hear his thoughts, and he mine. I've never experienced such a feeling afore."

Moira laughed. "Och, my Lachlan could make me feel the same, and if he was upset or mad, I could always get him laughin'. I think lovin' someone fully is like that. We just ken what tae say tae each other, we ken what each other is feelin'.

"I wish he could have come home with Eoghan. I miss him so much that there are days I feel I canna go on. If I dinna have my children, I doona think I'd be here now. He's the first thing I think of when I wake, and the last thing I think of when I fall asleep. I'm happy for you Els, you have Ian and he's retiring for you and the bairns. You willna lose him like I did Lachlan."

"You will be with him again, Moira, I ken it in my heart. Someday."

"Aye, someday, but it doesn't keep me warm today. That sounds selfish of me, doesn't it?"

"That's okay, Moira. When it comes tae love, I think we need tae be selfish, sure you have the children tae think aboot, but love for Lachlan is what made those children. Withoot him and you together first, there'd have been no bairns. Almost losin' Ian made me see some things clearly.

"Withoot him, I doona think I would want tae live. He's changed my life in such a way I never kenned existed. I feel whole now, like all my life half of me was missing, and it was. It was Ian, he's filled so many holes in my life, that I could never go back tae the way I was. Ne'er."

Moira squeezed her hand in understanding. "Weel, what do you think? The dark green? I think it is lovely. Plus, with a corset, Ian's eyes may pop from his head. You are going tae fill the dress oot fabulously. I canna wait tae see you in it either. What shoes do you have? Did you get the satin slippers tae match?"

"Aye! I almost forgot aboot them." She rushed to

the wardrobe where her dresses hung. She bent over and shuffled around coming up with them. The dark green satin was definitely beautiful, she thought. She brought them over and placed them on the dress along with citrine necklace. She leaned back turning her head side to side. "What do you think, Moira?"

"Perfect," she said. "You will be the bonniest of them all."

Elspeth put the dresses away and turned to Moira. "Thanks Moira, you've been such a great help tae me. I learned so much today aboot having a party. It's quite fun tae prepare for one. Choosing food, and finding music, I can hardly wait." She yawned. "Och, what a day it's been. Did Eoghan tell you my bairns healed me?"

"Yes, he did. Tell me Elspeth how do you feel aboot Ian's retirement?"

"I willna try and persuade him one way or another, but personally I think he is making a mistake. He's an excellent leader, he loves his men, and it is just who Ian is. Tae take that away from him, is taking part of who he is, and that is part of what I love aboot him.

"He is verra strong willed, he feels he is doin' right by us, but he doesn't understand, I'm a healer, my bairns are healers, at least one of them is. If they are tae follow their destiny, what do I teach them? Tae be a healer a person has tae have true convictions tae it, or it willna work. Tae be a healer you are around wounded soldiers more than any other, I doona want tae hide them from what they are, I doona think I can. I doona want Ian tae hide from who he is, but I canna tell him. He has tae see it. What do you think, Moira? Am I wrong?"

"Nae, my dear, you are right. If Ian wants tae protect you and your bairns, he has tae to do that. Doona forget he lost his father tae a fight. He kens how that made him feel. He came close, verra close, tae losing you just today. He couldn't live with himself if he lost you. I ken my son, it would destroy him.

"Give him time tae figure things oot. In the end, he'll make the right decision, and if it is tae leave the battles and the wars behind, you need tae ken if you can live with that. You can teach your children tae heal the sick and old, they may not want any more than that. And that is something you willna ken until they learn aboot themselves.

"Right now, nothing has tae be done or decided. We have a wedding tae plan, bairns tae be born, a life filled with pleasure. There is no one tae fear at this time, so I say we enjoy ourselves." Moira smiled. "Ian chose wisely, I'm happy you are part of the family."

"Thank you, Moira, for everything. I feel at ease speaking my true feelin's to you. I've never had that afore." She hugged Moira who returned the hug with affection.

"Shall we see aboot dinner? I think my boys are probably in their cups by now. We should probably feed them."

They walked arm in arm down the wide staircase. Moira commented on the ornate surroundings and was lighthearted. She felt the same way.

After dinner Ian jumped up and grabbed her. She giggled and said, "put me down! Your family is watching."

"I doona care if the whole damn world watches. I'm taken the woman I love tae bed!"

"Ian, the mead has clogged your brain."

He took her up two steps at a time. She squealed all the way.

After they made love twice, they fell asleep in each other's arms. She felt safe, and she felt the same for their bairns. Maybe Ian was right. Maybe they could have a peaceful life together.

****

Moira was at the table when she and Ian walked down the next morning. The boys came dragging themselves down and were quiet as they ate breakfast. They were all deep in their cups the night before, and this morning it was apparent they were feeling it.

Elspeth wondered what they'd be like tomorrow. She smiled. Everything was pretty much set for the party. They had a few hours yet before it'd start. Merlin had the music coming, so she didn't need to worry about that.

Food would be brought out all day and set on the sideboards, that way people could eat when they wanted. She had watched Moira get the cook and maids in order, and she felt things would run smoothly. She was going to have Moira do her hair.

After she broke her fast, she returned to her room to take a bath. She had her gown, slippers, and necklace on the bed, ready to be put on. She thought about being here at Wesladus. It felt like home to her, and she was going to miss it. She liked McGregor Keep and especially the people in it, but this place held a special place in her heart.

She'd miss hearing the shouting and sounds of training in the morning. She'd miss this room, she'd especially miss the dragons, Ator, Saphira, Sorrilth, and

Kalon. She wished Ian would realize what he was doing. She couldn't help but think he'd miss these things too. She'd let it go though, she loved Ian that much, if this is what he wanted, then she too wanted it.

She sighed, leaned back and closed her eyes. As she did, a soft knock came and Moira and the giggling girls burst in the room. She was pleasantly surprised. Moira had on a red velvet gown and with her long black hair, looked stunning. "You're so bonnie, Moira, red suits you favorably, especially with your long black hair. You girls bonnie as weel, you all look like a field of fine bloomin' flowers."

"Thank you, Elspeth," said Moira. "I'm going tae put my hair up like I'll do yours. We came tae help you get dressed and do your hair."

"I'd love that, thank you."

They laughed, giggled, dressed, and did their hair. She felt that they looked striking when they headed down the stairs, the girls following behind.

****

The music was going, people laughing and talking, the party was in full swing.

Ian was in a corner talking to Larc, Conall, Eoghan, and Finn. When he looked up and saw his Mither and Elspeth walking down the stairs arm in arm, he stopped mid-sentence.

He didn't think Elspeth could be more beautiful. Her hair was done up and red stray ringlets brushed against her long white neck. Ian's incisors started to come down and he had to hurriedly take control.

The green gown matched her sparkling eyes, her bosom bounced with each step, her creamy white cleavage begging to be touched. The tight waist showed off her voluptuous hips, and his mouth watered.

Each pleat of the full skirt shown like silky waves as the light hit it. This was definitely his favorite gown for her to wear. Green was his new favorite color, but she was definitely his favorite woman.

Moira and Elspeth seemed to float to them. His Mither was a good influence on her. They were both smiling and happy.

"Enjoying yourself?" Elspeth asked.

"Aye, immensely," he said staring at her. "Especially now, my bonnie lady."

She blushed. The music sped up and Ian grabbed her to dance across the floor.

Moira watched and smiled. Larc looked at Moira, "Would you like to dance, my lady?" Moira smiled a wistful smile and let Larc lead her out.

After lots of dancing a portal opened and Merlin appeared with Angus and a dark-haired stranger. He watched his brother argue with the beautiful woman.

Elspeth whispered in his ear, "That's my queen, Edina. But why are they arguing?"

They moved across the floor to meet the newcomers.

"I didn't want to come! I didn't need to come! I don't need to be here," said the queen.

"I am supposed tae protect you!" said Angus. "I told you I would do my job, and I will. Now shut your geggie and try tae have some fun. These soldiers saved your sorry arse and they deserve some respect."

Edina frowned and then donned a smile that was clearly forced.

"Look at it this way Edina, now that the threat tae you and your people are taken care of, and as soon as the books are set straight, and your people in a better place, I can leave. That shouldn't take much longer. 'Til then I weel be protecting you. That should make you happy."

"That will make me very happy," she said tentatively.

He moved with Elspeth by his side to greet Edina. His mother, Larc and his brothers were right behind him.

Edina seemed pleasant and remembered Elspeth immediately. "Elspeth, what a pleasant surprise. I am glad to see you happy and well. I am sorry for what happened. I didn't know…"

"Doona fash yourself. You aren't like him. I ken. I felt bad for you."

The party ended with a few brawls which was normal. It was a great success and almost everyone left in their cups stumbling about. When the evening died down and Angus left with the queen, Elspeth turned to him and asked. "What did you think of the queen and Angus?"

"I think they hate each other."

Elspeth laughed. "I think quite the opposite. Dinna you see him watchin' her all night? I think he doesn't ken it yet, but he is struck by her."

He laughed, "Angus? No way. Now, let's go up and let me take you oot of that dress like I've been wanting tae all night."

Elspeth put her arm through his and they walked up the stairs.

Chapter 32

Juppar Heiwynn, Wardhurst Castle

Juppar turned and glared at the God of Darkness. "You have no right to tell me how I must do things."

"I have every right. You are my son. I made you. Only the One Great God could create souls before, but I have a secret. You, my son, are the first of your kind. Made from me. Not quite like the One Great God's souls, but close, and I won't lose you. The God of Light thinks everything is tied up equally, yet he's used Merlin for a millennium in his cause for good. No more!" He roared.

"You will do things the way I see fit. You are not to attack yet, they are too strong, and you haven't enough Kearals. Did you get the grimoire?"

He moved to the side of the room. Placing a candle beside the bookcase, he pulled a lever behind some books and the book case slid forward. "Follow me."

The God of Dark followed him inside a large chamber. Dark gray and black cobwebs hung from tall dark rafters, the two's presence making them sway and flutter in the light breeze of their passing. Skins of animals hung about, along with shelves full of bones and jars of different liquids. The smell of decaying flesh hung in the air like a thick cloud.

One shelf held jars of ether. There were dark oily

veins of water seeping around rock, meandering down the western wall giving the air a moldy smell. The room was cold and no fireplace to warm it.

He didn't feel the cold. The elements never affected him. The old castle did well for him. It was huge with very large, cold, dark rooms. It was here he made his magic. He retrieved the grimoire from his work table and held it up. "I have the book. I also know what it contains. I will make my army bigger, but I have no fear of the McGregors. I can take them all out now."

"Juppar, The God of Light does not yet know of you. He destroyed my plan for Athdar and so as not to draw suspicion to my hand in bringing him back, I had to imprison him. I did not appreciate that one bit. But I have you. If you don't want the same fate then pay attention to what I tell you. You are truly my son and have god like powers. Use them wisely. If we want to succeed, he cannot learn of you. We do things my way. Do you understand?" His glowing red eyes telling him in an instant what his words did not. His continued existence was at stake, for now.

"I understand. However, it's not necessary. I could take care of it without him finding out."

"Do as I say!"

"As you say." His own eyes glowing red with flames.

"With Athdar encaged in hell, you are the only one left to carry on. I won't have you destroyed as well."

"I will grow the Kearals. I will do as you say."

"Fine, then we are done." Then just as quickly as the God of Darkness came, he was gone.

****

McGregor Keep

Saphira flew in low and landed with a squealing Akira on her back. Laughing hysterically Akira tried to get her words through her lips. "Again?" She managed to ask, the one-word question being the only one she could manage.

"Saphira said she has to get back to the babies, she will give you another ride sometime soon," said Elspeth smiling. "Come, your Mither and I have lunch waiting and we're discussin' the weddin'."

"Och," said Akira. "Isn't Saphira just the best? I wish I could understand her like you can. Do you think she'll be back tomorrow? I sure want tae ride her again. That was so much fun. Do you miss being at Wesladus? Do you think you will go back? I hope you doona. I want you tae stay here. I want the dragons tae stay here."

She laughed. "My goodness you can say a lot in one breath. It's as if you talk like someone might steal your words away. What do you say we go eat?" She took Akira's hand in hers pulling her toward the keep.

They had been here just over a week, and Elspeth, leaving Akira's question unanswered, did miss Wesladus. As they were going in through the large double doors, Ian was coming out.

"Why such a hurry?" he asked grabbing her around the middle and hugging her close. Akira giggled and he let go of her, looking at his sister.

"I was riding Saphira, did you see me, Ian? She took me up tae the clouds and we dove toward the loch, she flew close to the tops of the biggest trees, then swept me into the sky. It was the best thing tae ever happen tae me. I wish I had my own dragon I could talk tae. Doona you love owning your own dragon?"

Ian looked at her quizzically, "You canna own a dragon, Akira. They are our friends and equals, not our pets. We work together, if you want tae think pets, it'd be the other way around. They are stronger than us in almost every way. Do you like being called a pet?"

"Weel, if you put it that way, nae, I suppose not. I dinna think, Ian." She turned with a frown and lowered her head. "My mouth talks withoot me kenning it."

She and Ian laughed, with their arms around each other they walked in with Akira slowly bringing up the rear, deep in thought.

****

Weeks went by and the wedding was coming soon. Things were quiet in Wesladus, Merlin visited often and was happy to report the peace there. It was good to have the family together, and Moira enjoyed it.

Moira thought about the decision she'd made and decided to wait until after the wedding to announce what her intentions were. She just hoped the family would understand. She stood looking out the window with her arms crossed, tears threatening her eyes.

It was time, she decided, Elspeth and Ian could take over running the castle, and the family, she couldn't live without Lachlan any longer. She had fought the undeniable pull toward Lachlan, ignored it to the point of spiritual pain, pushed herself beyond measure, to stay with her children.

They were old enough now. If she continued to live her spirit and mind would disintegrate to the point she'd become insane. She was surprised she lasted this long. In their species, and with a true mate, it was known that if one died, the other followed.

It wasn't a choice, but a fact. She didn't know how she lasted as long as she did, she was thankful for the time she had with her children. She pushed a strand of hair behind her ear and looked toward the sky. "Soon, dear Lachlan, soon," she mumbled and turned toward the kitchens.

****

The days rolled by. Ian spent his time carving the two cradles he was making for the bairns and Elspeth. He'd forgotten how he loved working with the wood. His dusty hands lovingly brushed one of the legs he was working on.

He had plans for other projects after he was finished with these. He enjoyed going to the woods and felling trees to use in his work. It was quiet and peaceful. He was enjoying himself for the first time, in a long time.

If he wasn't working with wood, he was fishing or hunting. He liked bringing home food for his family.

He enjoyed going out early with all his brothers in a hunting party, he was glad they were all here for the wedding. Soon they would be back at Wesladus and it would just be him, the only man of the family left here to take care of the women. He thought about he and his brothers hunting with their father. He thought Lachlan a lot lately and couldn't understand why he couldn't return with Eoghan.

Surely his mother deserved that, especially after all their family did to keep peace. He'd never understand the gods. Shaking his head, he went back to work on the cradle. He had almost finished both of them.

He wanted to give them to Elspeth on their marriage day. He was also secretly working on a nursery attached to their room. It had been a small solarium he kept locked, so Elspeth wouldn't see it yet.

He planned on having it all finished to surprise her on their wedding night. He also planned the fae mating ritual. Their spirits would join and it would be immensely pleasurable, unlike his vampire side which had required the painful change.

She had to become vampire to mate with him, but fae could not be created. You had to be born fae. He grinned thinking about his wedding night, he was excited, he was happy. Sighing he laid his tools down. It was getting late and it was close to time to eat. He wanted to see Elspeth.

****

The day before the wedding Elspeth stood in the solarium in the dress the girls had made. The light green silk material was so soft and the darker green satin beneath flowed over her skin like water.

The girls had embroidered flowers along the open edges of the silk over coat from neckline down. The thread color matched the darker satin. At the bottom of one edge a small dragons head adorned a corner. Akira's idea. It looked almost like the flowers unless you looked closely.

The low bust line, in a v shape, had a bit of lace, but her ample breasts puckered up through the top nicely. Ian would approve. She stood as they hemmed the bottom of the full satin skirt. Her waist was tight, any tighter and she didn't think she'd be able to wear it. She was showing, but not overly.

At her waist, she wore the McGregor colors. A thick band like Ian's tartan created a belt and she would wear the same color ribbons in her hair. She felt beautiful and absolutely loved the dress. She blocked out the girls giggling and chattering as she thought about the wedding. A pounding on the door brought her back to the present.

A guard rushed in, "Elspeth, you need to come right away. King Arthur is here and he's brought a small army with him. Everyone is outside and he's demanding to see you now. Ian is holding him back, but you must come now."

She knew Arthur wanted her, the brothers had filled her in, but he couldn't want her for treason. Surely, he knew she was innocent. Merlin should have told him. She couldn't possibly understand why he wanted her. With her nerves skittering beneath her skin she shuddered.

She quickly changed and the girls became silent. Once dressed they all hurried down the steps and out the door. As she stood at the top of the stairs in front of the doors she quelled her shaking and looked at the man atop the horse in the forefront.

****

A huge handsome man, the king, his wavy red hair shown bright in the sunlight like fire. Ian watched as his blue eyes connected with Elspeth's, the place silent, he stared. Arthur didn't look menacing or angry, maybe a bit confused, but finally he broke the silence. "Elspeth McLellan, I need to speak with you. In private with only you and the McGregors."

He stepped up. "You will not take her! You will not hurt her. We marry tomorrow. You hurt her and I will kill you!" His jealousy came sparking to the forefront. Friend or not, King Arthur would not have his Elspeth for any reason.

337

"I'm not here to hurt her. Why would you think such a thing?"

Connor stepped up. "You were so angry with her when we were there at your castle. She did not commit treason."

"I know that," laughed Arthur. "I was angry at king Rulm not her. I was worried for her, not angry at her. I will not tell anyone why I am here until I have first told her. I need to speak with you lady Elspeth. Please, it's important."

"I will hear what you have tae say, King Arthur," she said a bit breathlessly, and bit her bottom lip.

Moira piped up. "Please come in Arthur. We'll have drinks and you can tell us why you are here. Will you please stay for the weddin'?"

"If you'll have me, yes." He nodded.

"First we need tae ken why you are here." Ian crossed his arms and spread his legs in defiance. King or not, he wasn't going to give him any quarter.

"Of course. May we please go inside and have those drinks? I have something of import to show Elspeth." Arthur climbed off his horse and walked toward the steps. He let him pass and followed close behind as he went up the stairs to Elspeth.

When Arthur got beside Elspeth he felt the strangest feeling go through him. Arthur and Elspeth's eyes locked on each other and Arthur grinned. He held his arm out for Elspeth to take. It took her a second to understand what he was doing, and when she did she blushed, and put her arm through his.

His jealousy doubled and flowed through his veins to the point he saw red. This had better be damn good, he thought, stomping up the remaining stairs behind them.

Once inside Moira asked for mead and wine to be brought to the table. Bradana hurried to the kitchens to get the drinks. Suddenly a blue light appeared and Merlin stepped through a portal.

"Have I missed anything?" Merlin asked with a wide grin.

He looked at Merlin. "You ken what he was aboot dinna you?" he glared at Merlin.

"It wasn't for me to tell. Now let the boy have his words. I think you'll find this fascinating." Merlin smiled. "I know I can hardly wait." Merlin grabbed a tankard and filled it full of mead, drank half down, and slammed his cup to the table. Sitting down he got comfortable. "Come now. This is all *good.* If I thought Elspeth was in danger Arthur wouldn't be here. Everyone grab a drink, take a breath, and relax. Let the King have the stage."

Arthur grabbed a tankard and filled it but remained standing. Moira handed Elspeth a cup of elderberry juice. She drank it down as if it were wine, and found some courage, standing as well. "Please, King Arthur, what can I do for you?"

"I think the better question is, what can we do for each other?" he put a shaking hand inside his jacket pocket and pulled out a worn parchment. "I think you should read it." He leaned past Ian and handed it to her.

Elspeth took the parchment with equally shaking hands and read what it had to say. On her second reading tears filled her eyes and tumbled down her cheeks. She looked at Arthur and whispered. "Is this real?" Her tears flowing freely.

"What does it say?" asked Ian. "Please read it."

Elspeth looked at all the quiet faces. She looked at Arthur. He smiled and tilted his head. "Go ahead and read it aloud," he said.

"Och, okay," she said taking a deep breath fighting her tears. In a wobbly voice, she read.

"*My dearest son, I ken this was the worst thing for a human being tae do, but I couldn't let Drakkor and King Rulm take you. I doona ken what he plans on doing with you, but I ken it canna end well. I have taken a child from a woman who died from complications while birthing.*

You are two days apart. In her dying breath she asked me to care for him. My heart breaks at what I am tae do, but I feel I have no choice.

I am giving you tae one of the castle maids in hopes she will find a good home for you. She is a true friend. This other child I will give to King Rulm in your stead, he will think he's you.

I write in tears as I will not see you grow up, I will not ken who has you, or if you are weel cared for, but you will be alive. For that I am grateful. Please ken that a mother's love kens no bounds, I protect what is mine, and so I hope you can go forth and have a prosperous and happy life. I will love and think of you always.

With my deepest sadness and love, your mother forever and always, Lainie McLellan."

Elspeth dropped the parchment to the table crying freely. She looked at Arthur and he too was crying.

Arthur cleared his throat. "My whole life I thought the King was my father. On his death bed but a year ago, he told me the truth. He said he saw me at market and that my head full of red hair beckoned him. When he saw me, he fell instantly in love. He took me from the maid that our mother had given me to.

"He didn't know about the note at first, it was in a pocket beneath my carrier. He found it when they changed the nursery back in to a sitting room. I was two and a half then. He had me declared his legal son and he loved me through my life. He and my mother. I have had the best life.

"You can understand my shock. They never had other children, I was an only child…until I found out about you. I've searched you out day and night. I couldn't tell anyone about this until I first told you. I was worried sick when I found out what King Rulm's plans were. I was never angry at you, Elspeth, my fury lies with Rulm. I want you to understand that. I just didn't want you to find out from anyone but me, and I wasn't sure how you would take the news.

"The men out there? They aren't solders they are family. McLellan's and our mother's family the Anndrasdans. Our parents were shunned when she refused a man her father picked for her and she ran away with our father to Mystic Kingdom. These people outside are cousins and distant cousins and we are here for the wedding…if you'll have us."

He watched Elspeth sob and run to her brother's arms. Moira sighed with tears freely falling, "I do love very large weddings!"

He now knew why he had the strange feeling on the steps. He looked at the two sobbing and their hair matched in redness. He mistook brotherly love for lust. If he would have quelled his McGregor temper he would have seen the resemblance. He shook his head, berating himself. They looked a lot alike, as he looked around at his brothers, he knew they were seeing the same thing. The place was quiet, full of people...family, all clearing their throats, and not a dry eye in sight.

Merlin raised his newly filled tankard. "A toast to the brother and sister reunited." Everyone started talking at once.

He shouted. "Here's to Elspeth and Arthur!" Shouts of Here! Here! went up and laughter filled the place. Elspeth walked over to Ian and he put his arm around her. He watched Moira push the tears off her face and then give up and sob. He put his hand to his mother's shoulder with a smile and shed some tears. "Who'd have thought," said Ian. "Arthur is finally becoming part of our family for real." Moira smiled at her son's comment and downed her wine. What a fine day it turned out to be.

****

The sun shone bright the next day. There was a faint breeze and upon it the smell of the water and flowers. Rose petals dusted the walkway Elspeth and Arthur would take to meet him. They fluttered in the light breeze making them look alive. People gathered and their excited talk filled the air. It was warm and perfect.

The crowd was large and Ian couldn't see all the people. Most of them family coming from all over. Ian stood in front of the priest waiting patiently outside near the loch under a trellis adorned with large white flowers. He was decked out in his finest kilt and tartan, his shiny midnight hair falling freely and lightly across his chin in the light breeze. He stood patiently waiting.

****

Moira was upstairs and she looked at Elspeth in the

green gown that her daughters had lovingly sewed for her. She held a wooden box in her hand. Elspeth looked up at her while Bradana put the finishing touches to her hair. She felt elegant and beautiful.

"Your neck is bare Elspeth. I have a little something for it." She opened up the box. "My gift to you on your weddin' day."

She looked inside. It was a large, beautiful, simple, one stone, tear drop, emerald necklace. She didn't know what to say. It was perfect and out of all her jewels this was going to be her favorite. "Moira, it's lovely. I've never seen anything like it. I doona ken what tae say, except thank you."

Moira hugged her. "I got it at market the day we went shopping. I was hoping you dinna notice me gone at the shop. I had another mon show me this in a back room. I kenned it would match your eyes and dress."

She took it out and put it around Elspeth's neck, completing the perfect wedding ensemble. She touched it lightly with her fingers as Moira held a mirror up. She almost didn't recognize the beautiful woman in the mirror. She had finally and fully grown in to a woman and was excited at the prospect of her new life with Ian.

"Come," said Moira. "It's time you marry my son." She took her hand. At the bottom of the stairs stood a most handsome King Arthur, her brother, in his full regalia. His smile was wide as she descended, and he held up his arm for her to take. "Are you ready for this kitten?" he asked. "You are absolutely stunning, sister mine."

She took his arm and nodded. "Thank you," she whispered shedding a single tear of happiness. "I'm so happy you found me. I kenned you were alive, I always felt you. Now my life is complete," she said smiling sweetly at him.

"Likewise," he responded. "I too have always felt something, something incomplete, now I know." He smiled back warmly. "We must get you to Ian before he decides to take a piece of me."

****

Ian heard the crowd grow quiet and watched as Arthur led her to him. She was stunning and he had to clear his throat. She was gorgeous in the green gown. The satin shimmered in the sunlight.

He was proud to see his colors about her waist and he stood straighter. Her hair glistened like fire and was high about her head in curls, green ribbons flowing down and fluttering in the breeze. She was beaming, despite the fact no one got much sleep the night before.

Between getting everyone settled from family members travelling in, to King Arthur and his men, and staying up late listening to Arthur and Elspeth chattering about family, and her telling Arthur about their mother and father, it was wee hours of the morning before anyone got to sleep.

It was good though, no one seemed tired. Elspeth reached him and Arthur placed her hand in his. Her face was flush and she looked radiant. He felt smitten all right and was damn sure happy about it. He beamed. He didn't know how he managed to repeat the words he was supposed to recite, but he did.

He couldn't take his eyes off Elspeth and when it came time to kiss her, time stood still. It was short and sweet, but to him it lasted a life time. He picked her up as she squealed and shouted to everyone, "Meet my wife! Elspeth McGregor!" The crowd cheered. He carried her up the hill and through the castle where everyone followed.

At the party, eating, drinking and dancing was boisterous and riotous. No one fought which was unlike most parties, but loud and joyous. Everyone had a grand time and then came the announcement from Moira that it was time for the women to take Elspeth to the bedroom and prepare her for him.

****

Elspeth heard tell of the custom but until this point she never really understood it. They went up the stairs in giggles and laughter. Moira at the head of the crowd. Moira once again held a gift to her. A pale green silk nightdress. After helping her put it on, she asked in a nervous voice. "How do I look?" Elspeth glanced to the giggling women and back to Moira.

The night dress hugged her curves and dropped to the floor just past her feet. Simple yet elegant. See through and sheer. It felt so soft against her skin. Before Moira could answer she heard the boisterous sounds of the brothers bringing Ian.

Laughter and pounding hit the doors. The women squealed and opened the door. Throwing Ian inside they waited at the doorway. Ian shouted. "Oot! You all oot! Now!" He pushed the men outside. "Women tae!" He growled.

****

He looked at Moira and smiled. "Thank you, Mither." He grinned and kissed her cheek. "Now oot." He led the giggling women to the door and lightly shoved them out, closing and locking it. He heard the laughter of men and woman descending the stairs. The party would go on most of the night. He wondered how many bairns would be made tonight.

He shook his head and stared at Elspeth standing in front of the fire. With the light behind her he could see her voluptuous curves through the barely there, nightdress. He was instantly hard, though truthfully, he had been since he got his first glimpse of Elspeth walking toward him on Arthur's arm.

He licked his lips and told himself to take it slow. He poured wine from the pitcher that was sitting on the table near the bed. He walked slowly to her. Two cups in hand, he held one out to her. He could see she was a little nervous seeking out his silver gaze. He knew she wanted everything perfect. He was glad she hadn't been sick in a while so he didn't worry about that any longer. She reached for the cup. He slid his fingers over hers and she shuddered.

"My bonnie wife," he said huskily. "I could drink you in all night, gaze at your beauty until I go blind, and never, never get enough of you." He pulled her in for a slow intimate kiss. Breaking away he said, "I have something for you and the bairns I want tae show you. Come." He took her hand. He unlocked the door that connected to the adjacent chamber, took a torch, and put it on the wall inside the smaller sitting room.

In it were the two cradles he had made for the bairns, dark wood and waxed to a high shine. The room was decked out with furs on the floor, wooden toys on shelves and strewn about. Paintings of puppies and horses and children playing. It held a warm and comfortable feeling. He glanced at her waiting for her response.

"Och, Ian it's gorgeous." She walked to the cradles where various sized rattles lay inside them. She picked one up. "This is what you've been doing during the days. I dinna ken. These are wonderful. She gazed wide eyed at everything. He beamed and was pleased at her reaction.

"My gift tae you and the bairns," he said proudly.

"But, I have nothing for you, Ian. I dinna ken."

"Hush my bonnie wife. You give me the greatest gift. Your love, and—" he placed his hand warmly on her stomach. "—the bairns." He turned her for a kiss and she squeezed the tears from her eyes as she closed them and met his delicate kiss.

When he broke away he said, "Come, tonight we bond in the way of the fae. Are you ready?"

"Yes," she whispered. "More than." And he led her back to the room.

"Come by the fire, we will do it here. Her pulled her night dress off her slowly and removed his clothing.

"Stand in front of me and put your hands tae mine." He raised his hands up in front of him, palms out. "Look into me eyes." He stared into her eyes and their bodies touched slightly, tingling.

****

A greenish light slowly surrounded him and that glow grew to encompass her. She felt the heat travel her body and her loins grew heavy. Never breaking eye contact, she felt herself melt into him in a way that engulfed her very being, and before she knew it an orgasm overtook them both sending them in space of a thousand million stars, together they traveled the path and soared, and it felt endless.

She never knew such a thing as wonderful as this could exist. When she didn't think the pleasure could get any better, they exploded together again, and traveled yet higher. A third orgasm took them, and then another, each time more intense than the one before. It continued until they were two flames floating in the darkness.

They merged together and became one, in an explosion of colors dancing as one large flame, and then they melted in each other's arms and the light about them faded. When she moaned, Ian brushed the hair from her face.

"It can only happen once for a fae. When they choose their mate. I heard it was extraordinary, but I never realized myself, how so, until tonight. Are you aright?"

"Mmmm," she purred against his neck. "That was the pinnacle of making love, can we do that again?"

"Nae my bonnie bride, now we spend the rest of our life duplicating it the old-fashioned way." He gave a deep throaty laugh. "We can start now."

"I adore that idea, and you. I doona think I can take more withoot you inside me anyway. I would desperately miss that."

"Our souls united tonight. That is what this is aboot. We have given each other ourselves. I am completely yours, and you mine, and I want what's mine," he huskily replied kissing her hard, lifting her off her feet and carrying her to the bed.

Laying her there he climbed over her. She pulled her legs up widening them, showing herself fully to him. He lay atop her between her legs and nestled himself at her core without entering. He leaned down and licked the side of her neck where her vein increased in beats.

Her blood heated up and pooled in her mid-section

and she wiggled against him trying for access to his overly large hard erection, and she whimpered. "Not yet, luv. I want tae savor ye." He licked down her neck to her nipples where he pulled one deep in his mouth, sucking gently, while he used his hand playfully on her other one.

He jerked against her, which in turn made her insides quiver. She tugged at his shoulders, silently begging him to enter her. Instead he kneeled between her legs and pulled her up to his mouth. She gasped. Mating as fae was definitely great, but this was truly her world of pleasure. The feel of his mouth, the feel when he first enters, filling her. The feeling at the pinnacle of release. She moaned. "Please, Ian, inside now."

Ian chuckled against her, then looked up. "My you are a wee bit in a hurry. I'll please you lass, of that you can be sure." Then he dipped his head and continued his ministrations.

Ian was cooling down, at least that is what he told himself. But the taste, the noises she was making, the perfume, and the silkiness of her skin, did nothing to abate his roaring desire to take her. Finally, he moved up and looked at her flush face, and her half-mast eyes. "Aboot time," she whispered, panting.

That's all it took, he climbed on top of her, with himself at the precipice of her core, his manhood bounced against her with a mind of its own. If he wasn't careful it would spill his seed with a mind of its own. Knowing he wouldn't, couldn't last, he entered her. They pumped toward each other never breaking eye contact and when they came together this time it was carried with the joining they felt earlier. Ian knew it was yet again different even now, even better that he had joined her in the fae way of bonding. He gently rolled over and pulled her to him, spooning they fell into a blissful deep sleep.

****

The next morning the noise of horses and people talking and laughing, and getting ready to leave, woke the couple. Ian looked at his sleepy wife and she snuggled closer. A knock came to the door and Bradana brought in breakfast. "How are you happily married couple doin' this fine morn?" she asked setting down the food beside them. "I willna stay long, doona worry. I'm goin' tae stoke the fire and leave." It was customary that the newlyweds stay in the room three days and Ian had absolutely no problem with that. "Do you wish a bath, Ian for you and Elspeth?"

He glanced at Bradana, "Yes, that would be great." He pulled the covers more fully over Elspeth, and she snuggled deeper. "That sounds wonderful," she mumbled closing her eyes again.

****

Most of the people left that day, though some of the family stayed on to visit for a couple longer. The castle was much quieter. Moira would make her announcement when all the people left. For now, she was enjoying herself, and her family, and children. It was tough to go through the wedding without Lachlan.

Her mind and heart returned to the memories of their marriage day. It was one of her happiest memories, but she wouldn't spoil this yet with her announcement, she'd wait until the right time. Until then she would enjoy what she could.

****

It was a few weeks later while at dinner she decided to finally speak. No easy way she thought, but she'd made her decision. Tomorrow most of her sons were leaving for Pendragon in the Wesladus Veil to begin training their men again. It had to be tonight.

She listened at the laughter of her family and knew she would miss them, but she couldn't go on any longer without Lachlan. She had to decide now while her mind was still intact. She'd somehow bought time, more than anyone else she'd ever known. She was on borrowed time now. She cleared her throat.

"I have an announcement to make." She waited for the chatter to quiet. When it did she cleared her throat again. "I ken that Ian and Elspeth have agreed to take over control of the McGregor Keep, for which I'm thankful, and ken they will do great here. Och, there's not an easy way tae say this. I canna live withoot Lachlan any longer. I feel my mind a goin'. I have decided to quit takin' the blood."

The group let out a rush of breath in shock. Elspeth leaned toward Ian and whispered. "Doesn't that mean…?"

"Yes," replied Ian. "She will grow old within a year and die. Mither, have you thought this through? We all still need you. I doona understand."

"You of all my family should understand now that you have Elspeth, but nae, you wouldn't unless you lost her, you want me Ian, none need me as much as I need Lachlan, and he needs me. I ken you doona understand, but you all ken, that when one loses their mate the other dies within days. I have managed a little longer than a year, somehow with my mind intact, and now my time has come. It's unavoidable."

The children all talked at once, all in naes and doona, except Ian.

"She has every right," said Ian. "We've all been selfish with Mither. It's time she had her happiness, she had her mate, our father, we ken what we felt losing him, think how she felt, she wants, no needs, tae be with him. We canna deny her that. You ken it's the way of our kind."

"I agree," said Elspeth. "Kenning what I ken now, I couldn't live withoot Ian. When I became united with him, I can't imagine life withoot him. I wouldn't want someone tae keep me from him. The pull is life itself."

"Thank you, Ian and Elspeth," said Moira with tears in her eyes. "I need you tae all understand, and hopefully give me your blessings. I need Lachlan and I feel he needs me. I've stayed this long because my love for you all is so great. I feel my mind leaving me and I canna live with that. If I go on, and my mind completely leaves me, you are left with a shell tae care for, and I willna have it.

"Most would have left months ago. I thank the Gods for the extra time I have had with all of you. I need you tae understand. Ian and Elspeth will do great here, and I have no doubt their ability tae care for all of you. I will nae do this withoot your blessings, but ken this is my wish."

Taryn the logical one spoke first. "I ken not what it is like tae have a mate and go through the binding rituals, but you have always spoken how once done, one canna live withoot the other for long. You have gone to great lengths Mither, for us all. I for one support your decision to be with Da."

"Thank you, Taryn. I appreciate that." She wiped at

a tear. "It was a hard decision, because of my love for all of you." She waited to hear what the rest of her family had to say.

Her daughters broke down and cried, but it was Akira who spoke up. "I ken ye love Da. I love Da and miss him too. Even though I will terribly miss you, I support your decision."

"Being the baby, Akira, that means a lot coming from you."

The rest of the family said their piece and ultimately gave their consent, save Angus.

"I canna see how love would make someone wish tae die. I canna understand it. Nae. If only for yourself, you should want tae live. I canna support death."

"Angus, I will nae die, I'm only going to where Lachlan is now. I doona want, nae canna, be apart from him any longer. I ken ye doona understand, but please try. When you find your true mate, you will understand."

"I will nae give you my blessing, but I will support your decision, even if I doona understand it. You are my Mither, and smart, I ken you have givin us all you can. I will support you, but I doona have tae like it."

"That's all I can ask for, Angus, and I thank you for that much. Now I think I will retire. You all have desert. Bradana, please bring it in."

Bradana was in the shadow of the doorway listening, like she often did, and she knew it. That is why she'd asked for the desert. She rose and left everyone at the table to think about her decision. It was finally out in the open. She only hoped her children could understand.

Making it to the main bedroom she made it inside,

closed the door, then slumped down in front of it. She was weakening, she was surprised she hadn't way before this. Most died within days of their mate's death. It was unavoidable. She had somehow managed to live this long. Her and Lachlan were so tied together, the web so tight, her mind was with him more and more. She tried to stop it, gods how she tried. She knew she was now losing the battle. She leaned her head back and looked up and whispered. "I'm sorry Lachlan, I held oot as long as I could for the children.

"My mind is goin' I can feel it. I canna tell them how far it's progressed. Somehow, I've managed to keep what's happening to me hidden from the children, but I ken I'm losing what little control I had. I canna hide these things any longer, they are going to find out. One minute I'm in the solarium, the next minute I'm in an orchard and I doona ken how I got there. I've gone to the kitchen several times to eat something, and cook looks at me strange and says I was just there eating. Two days ago, I woke up standing in the loch, and it was so cold. I doona ken why? I canna have them takin' care of me. So, I told them, Lachlan, tonight. I have tae go."

She felt the rush of air pass through her, as she often did when she felt Lachlan's presence. Then she sat and sobbed. She wanted to be with her children, she wanted to be with her grandchildren, and she wanted Lachlan back with them too.

She knew he would if he could. She felt his anguish and wherever he was, she knew he was proud of her. "Just a little longer, please?" she asked out loud. "Just give me a little more time." She was always asking for a little more time. But she knew she had made the decision. No, it was coming, she knew it, it was time. Then she sobbed at the loss she felt.

Chapter 33

Pendragon Castle, Wesladus Veil

Cameron was deep in the Grimoire in Merlin's library. He was thinking about how peaceful things had been these past few months since Angus took over leadership and didn't need to guard the queen any longer.

Ian was restless of late and his brothers worried about his quiet countenance. But he was also anticipating the birth of his two bairns. The first was always the most worrisome, his mother had said. He was worried about her too. She was aging and becoming forgetful. He didn't like to see it, but he understood it.

He was reading about how to make magical swords when a portal opened and Merlin came through. "We have major problems," Merlin said breathlessly. "You need to get your brothers and meet me here."

Cameron looked up. "Merlin, what now? I knew peace was too much of a good thing."

"Get your brothers. You think Athdar was bad, you haven't seen bad. Now go get them."

"Right away, I'll be right back."

The men came through the door while Merlin sat looking at what Cameron was reading, waiting. "Sit boys, we have a big problem. First and foremost, the

Grimoire to the Dark is missing, good news is I know who has it. When I did a spell, a certain person was holding it, and I saw him. Juppar Heiwynn. But that's not the half of it. He is the one who stole the Kearals from Athdar, about a hundred of them. He's making more as we speak. The thing is, he isn't like my brother…"

"That's good then, isn't it?" interrupted Dougal.

"No, I'm afraid it's worse. I saw his eyes and they weren't just red like a demon's. They had flames in them."

"What does that mean?" asked Flynn.

"Nothing good. He's the God of Dark's son. He was created by him. It means Juppar Heiwynn has god-like powers. We must stop him. I'm not even sure the God of Light knows about him yet. This is bad, very bad," said Merlin.

"It's funny you should mention that," said Cameron. He pushed the book aside and looked up. "I was just reading about swords, and the only way to kill a god is with *Godslayer, The Longsword.*"

He continued. "It explains how to make it minus one ingredient, blood from a specific individual, *The Peacekeeper.* It doesn't say who that is. Of course, the answer to that is in the other Grimoire. We canna make it, Merlin. It calls for a metal I ne'er heard of afore, called Dharan metal, it comes from the Dharan ruins, from the extinct Dhara race. Do you know where these ruins are?

"They were the only ones to mine it and made many technical gadgets from it. It's the strongest metal ever made, rare, and holds magical properties. When properly forged it has a golden glow to it. It also calls for fairy dust. The fae don't have fairy dust. It's a myth. The fae come from the ancient Fairies, but they don't match the stories in the myths."

"Yes, they do," said Merlin. "You don't know it, but there are different species of Fairies. Not in the sense of what we know fae to be. Don't ever call a true fairy a fae, they see it as an insult. These Fairies live in a land cut off from everyone. Their powers have evolved tremendously and are unlike what we know or expect of our fae. Your part comes from the ancients, Tuatha De Danann, these fairies are completely different from you.

"They are Aos Si. Evolved from centuries of change. You are nothing alike. You have the basic power, they have incredible power and magic. I'll see about the fairy dust. Now what does it say about the blood?"

"The blood needed to complete the final step can only come from this one man who always exists. It says he incarnates over and over bringing peace to the worlds. The man's soul is titled the *Peacekeeper* and he was started from a spark, from the One Great God Himself.

"The Grimoire doesn't tell us who that person is or how to get the Peacekeeper's blood to put on the sword, yet he is the only one who can wield it and its magic. We can make it, if we can find the metal, but how do we find the Peacekeeper? How do we get fairy dust? Where do we get the metal for the sword?"

Merlin frowned. "I can ask the angels, maybe Junius would have some answers. You boys get what ingredients you can to make this sword and I will scour around and ask questions." Merlin opened his portal and turned to the boys. "Don't dally, this one is dangerous."

The boys looked at each other after Merlin left. "How do we stop a dark god?" asked Finn.

"Even a better question, how do we find the Peacekeeper?" asked Taryn.

"We better make the sword," said Conall. "What all do we need?"

Cameron looked back at the book, "Several herbs to burn in with the Dharan metal. The metal canna be held by human hands. Only the Dharans have used it. I'll have tae research more. I doona ken what it is, or even where it is. Most all the other ingredients we've got. Hmmm, there's another one I've never heard of afore. Some weird weed. I must ask Merlin about it. The dreaded fairy dust. Blood from fae, vampire, werewolf, gargoyles, dragons, and from a virgin for purity."

"I know where I can get the virgin blood," said Angus. "If she lets me anywhere near her," he mumbled. "I'll leave now and get it. I need to check on her anyway."

"Nae, you should wait, Angus, until we have all the herbs. We will need fresh blood."

"The Queen?" asked Lauren. "Are you sure she's a virgin?"

"No one can be as cold as that woman, and not be. Besides, King Rulm bought her, and the only way her father gave her up was with the express purpose that he would never touch her or he would die."

"Sounds a little crazy to me," said Cameron. "What father wouldn't want their child to know the joys of lovemaking?"

"Moreover," said Angus, "What kind of father would sell their daughter to King Rulm in the first place. What price did Rulm pay to have her and why?" Angus scratched at his beard with a frown.

"Och, shite," said Cameron. "How the hell do we get fairy dust. Ancient fae? Different types of fairies? I can't wrap my head around that piece of information."

"If Merlin canna get the fairy dust, we're in trouble," said Lauren grabbing the book. "Wait here's information about the fairy realm. Wow. It says there are no portals to *Lanenia, Land of the Fairy* and Merlin can't open one. One would have to travel over the Scarlet Sea and through Vision Valley to get there. If the Scarlet sea doesn't eat ye alive, visions from Vision Valley would turn you mad. We have tae speak aboot this tae Merlin. I think fairy dust is oot of the question."

****

Merlin at the Light Angel's Court

"I cannot answer you, Merlin. I know not who the Peacekeeper is, only the God of Light knows, and the One Great God. I don't think either is going to say," stated Junius.

"Doesn't the God of Light know about Juppar Heiwynn?" asked Merlin.

"He does know," came a bellowing voice as the God of Light appeared. "I've known since his conception, he exists."

Junius bowed his head to the floor. "My God, what brings you?"

"I've come in answer to Merlin's plea, but I will not tell you who the Peacekeeper is. In due time, all will be known, if the future is as I predict."

"What if it is not?" asked Merlin. "Future can

change. If Juppar wins, it could be devastating for the worlds. Are you willing to take that risk?"

"For the Peacekeeper, yes."

"How can we find him?"

"He will find you," said the God of Light. "For the Dhara metal, see Tepu." The God of Light disappeared.

"Well that was certainly helpful," Merlin said sarcastically.

"I'm just sorry I couldn't help," replied Junius with a frown.

"I guess it's back to the drawing board then." Merlin opened his portal and stepped through.

****

McGregor Keep

Ian couldn't concentrate on fishing, lately he had trouble concentrating on anything. He thought constantly about the men in training, and his brothers. He knew he should be happy with the new-found peace and it was great for a while, but now he kept thinking about Wesladus and Pendragon, and the men…his men.

But he couldn't change his mind, he promised his wife peace, for her and the bairns. He also promised his Mither he would control McGregor Keep, and Ian never went back on his word. Ever. He sat in his boat and let the waves move him about when Bradana came running out.

"My Lord! The bairns are coming. Moira and Elspeth need you, hurry."

That brought him out of his reverie and he quickly rowed to shore. Throwing the small boat on the bank he went running through the castle and up the stairs. He ran through the door to their room and knelt at her side.

Moira smiled. "It will be awhile yet, Ian. It always

is the first time, but her water came, and the pains are coming on time. She asked for you."

"I'm here, dearling. Do you need anythin'?"

"Just you." She smiled. "I thought you should ken you are goin' tae be a father today."

He kissed her hand then her forehead. "I will be right here with you, Els. We'll do this together. Mither what do we need?"

"Bradana is bringin' hot water and cloths. She'll need tae have her brow and face wiped often. Can you handle that job, Ian?" Moira smiled at the two lovebirds. "I remember the day you and Eoghan were born. Lachlan was in worse shape than me. I thought he'd pass oot and I'd have tae take care of him. You are not going tae pass oot are you?"

"I doona think so," he replied chagrined.

Bradana entered all smiles, placing the water and cloths on the table near the bed. "Isn't this wonderful! Bairns today. It's been years since this place has heard the cries of bairns."

"Yes," said Moira. "It's very excitin'. You may want tae keep it down a little so Els can concentrate. Remember what it was like for you?"

"Goddesses yes, I thought the pains would never cease."

"Bradana! I think you need tae check on things for dinner."

"Och, aye, I see. I just...need tae...check on things for dinner," she said hurriedly. "You ken where tae find me." She sauntered out the door.

Elspeth let out a yelp and grabbed her sides. "I need tae move."

"Ian," said Moira. "I think she needs tae walk a bit.

If you can squat it will help the bairns tae come quicker. Help her, son, tae walk some."

****

Bradana stood at the foot of the stairs listening to Elspeth's screams. She sent up a silent prayer that the bairns would come soon. It had been all day, and night was quickly coming. She took up food, but no one ate. Ian was sweating as much as Elspeth. Bradana wanted to wipe his head. She smiled and went to turn away when she heard the first cry. She ran up the stairs and up to Ian holding his first born, a son with very dark black hair, and lots of it. The bairn was wailing and Moira was encouraging Elspeth to push.

Elspeth let out another loud scream and bore down. A red-headed bairn showed its head then come flying out, landing in Moira's hands. "It's a girl!" she shouted. I thought for sure it would be a boy after the first one. Bradana take her and clean her up while I work with the after birth.

****

Elspeth watched Ian with their son as he walked over to peer at their daughter. "She's beautiful Els," he said in his husky voice. He walked over and handed Elspeth their son to nurse. He latched right on and Ian bent to kiss them both.

"We did good dinna we Ian?" Elspeth asked her glowing husband.

"Yes, we certainly did." A feeling of protection for his children surged through him. He heard a voice, "Remember who you are." He recalled hearing the same voice at the cave and again at the wedding. He pushed a hand through his hair as if that would help. "I must be goin' crazy," he said out loud not meaning to.

"What?" asked Elspeth then she cried out. The after birth came out and she fell back suddenly, exhausted after the long birth. Moira picked up their son and Bradana gave Elspeth their daughter to nurse.

"Have ye picked their names?" asked Moira.

"Yes," he said. "Our son's name is Domnall, it means ruler of the world. Our daughter's name means the same, Donella. We thought it fitting for such young ones who saved their mother's life at such a young age."

"Hmm," said Moira. "Donella and Domnall. I like their names, yes very fitting. I'm so happy for you!" she said. With tears, she hugged him.

She then took the quiet Donella from her sleeping mother and Ian took his son and they walked together down the long staircase. When they reached the bottom, a portal opened and out walked Merlin and all his brothers. The girls came screeching down the stairs and he stood proud.

He held up his son. "Domnall our son!" and everyone clapped.

"Let us see your other son!" said Conall.

Moira held up their daughter and shouted, "Donella their daughter!"

Everyone cheered. "May I hold her, Mither, please?" asked Akira.

Donella cried out and her face got red. Domnall was quiet now after eating. Moira pointed to a chair. "Be careful her tiny head."

Akira beamed as she sat and cooed to the tiny one. He hung onto his son as the men came close to see him, while the girls gathered around Donella.

Moira looked at her family, "I wish your father

could be here." He smiled at her but his attention quickly returned to his children. He heard his mother excuse herself and thought that she was tiring more easily now.

Bradana came to help with the bairns. Finally, he thanked everyone for coming but insisted he return to Elspeth. Merlin left with his reluctant brothers and his sisters headed to bed. Bradana helped him take the babies back upstairs, where they found Elspeth awake and waiting.

He put their daughter to breast because she was fussy and he laid his son in the cradle for the first time as he slept. He covered him and made sure the fire in the room was warm, leaving the door open so they could listen in. When he could, he lay with his wife during the night, but couldn't sleep.

Something in the back of his mind nagged him and he couldn't relax. He spent most of the night carrying bairns to Elspeth or returning them to their cradles.

Bradana showed them how to change diapers and he did most of that as Elspeth was worn out. At one point both bairns lay asleep in their cradles and he took turns watching them sleep.

He finally lay down next to Elspeth early in the morning and dozed off, when Bradana came in cheerfully with breakfast. He quickly covered his head and groaned, then both bairns awoke with a wail.

Elspeth got up and moved slowly to the nursery. Bradana followed. Each carrying a baby, Elspeth settled back in bed and learned the fine art of how to hold two crying bairns to nurse them at the same time. One cradled in each arm she leaned back and watched them with an amazed look. He watched her and smiled.

"I love you, my bonnie wife," he said.

"I love you, my handsome husband, Ian McGregor."

Chapter 34

Mystic Mountain

Merlin stood at the edge of Mystic Mountain, waiting for Tepu and Hermaditt to come down to him. As soon as he touched the edge of the mountain from the valley, he knew they would come awake, noticing his presence. He looked up, "ah here they come now," he said as he watched them flying down toward him.

"Merlin," said Tepu in greeting. "What brings you to our mountain?"

"The God of Light said to see you about a metal we need to make the Godslayer Sword."

Tepu looked at Hermaditt with a shocked look on his face, then back to Merlin quickly. "Sorry, can't help you."

"What do you mean, can't help me, or won't?" asked Merlin.

"Either one, take your pick," answered Tepu. "We are busy, we must leave."

"Doing what?" asked Merlin. "From what I could tell you were doing nothing but standing there in stone. You didn't look busy to me."

"We think a lot," answered Hermaditt.

"That's the damn, dumbest answer, I have ever heard," he said, exasperated. "Look, the God of Dark now has a son. We got rid of Athdar and Drakkor, but this Juppar Heiwynn, this son of the God of Dark, has taken over. Now the only way to fight this madman, God, or whatever you want to call this flame-eyed creature, is by using the Godslayer sword. The only way to make the sword is with the strongest metal ever created, Dhara metal. The only one who can wield it is the Peacekeeper. Without the metal there is no sword, the God of Light said see you, and I'm not leaving here without it. If you don't want me to turn you both into toads I suggest you help. Gods I do not have time for this! Do I make myself clear?"

Tepu narrowed his eyes, put his arms around his chest, and said, "I'm not afraid of you Merlin. The Dhara ruins I'm scared shitless of. Turn me into a toad. I'd rather that than face those ruins."

"Why are you scared of the ruins?"

"They are cursed. We guard them here on Mystic Mountain, but we never go near them. Some have ventured close never to return. There are spells about the place, howls from tortured souls sound from its depths. It's downright scary. How do you think you can get any of their metal?

"Besides the ruins are far beneath the earth, and I only know of one way in. It's one of the many secrets kept by the mountain. The civilization is the oldest known civilization to man. It's supposed to be a secret, if people find out, this place will be overrun. Even with the threat of being turned to stone. We can barely keep the secret of the berries. Now you want to go digging around in the Dhara ruins? No."

"Maybe you should understand something, Tepu. If Juppar Heiwynn takes control of both earths no one will have to worry what the ruins might do. He will do much worse and he will do it to everyone. Now, the God of Light said see you. He wouldn't say that if he didn't expect you to help us. Do you get my drift? Me turning you into toads is nothing compared to what he might do to you. Are you willing to take that chance?"

Tepu put his hand on his chin and rubbed, contemplating what he'd said. "Hummm," he said. He looked at Hermaditt. "What do you think?"

"I think we should help him."

"You what?"

"You heard me. He's right. If the God of Darks son is on the loose it can't be good. If the God of Light wants our help how can we refuse?"

Tepu looked at Hermaditt for a second, then slowly nodded his head. "Well," he said. "I guess we take a hike to the Dhara ruins." He shuddered. "Gods help us all."

"Precisely," said Merlin. "I'm ready, if you are."

"Never," said Tepu, "but let's go."

He followed the low flying gargoyles up the mountain. They trekked through the forest, down a river, through a cave, and to a spot where a large cavern surrounded the way down deep inside the mountain. He stood at the edge looking into the dark abyss below, then up at Tepu.

"I don't know how you're going to get down, but we'll fly," said Tepu. "Do we need to go with you?"

Merlin squinted at him and he quickly got the point.

"Looks like we'll meet you at the bottom?" asked Tepu.

"Yes, I can disappear and reappear at the bottom. I'll create a light when we get in. Just then a screeching howl came from the cavern mouth. "Is that what you thought was screaming?" he asked Tepu.

"Yes, did you hear that? They are screaming!"

"That's wind," he said, laughing.

Tepu's face turned red. "You sure?"

"I'm sure. Meet you at the bottom. Tepu and Hermaditt flew down inside the mouth of the cavern, Tepu screeching the whole way.

He disappeared and appeared again at the bottom. When his feet touched down, a dim light appeared all around him. He looked around and his mouth fell open. Crazy machinery and gadgets everywhere.

They stood in a round tub full of holes drainage for rain from the opening he figured. He had no idea what anything was or what it was for. There were nobs, buttons, levers and funny shaped glass caps on metal bodies. Funny designs that looked like some kind of Sanskrit writings.

He walked over and touched one, causing buttons to light up and whirring sounds to come from it. From the ceiling protruded some sort of metal tubes. The metal had a golden glow to it.

At the opening of the tubes were crystals that fit in perfectly. He was fascinated. This had to be the type of metal they were looking for. He leaned against a lever, while still looking overhead, and when it moved light came from the tubes. It glowed like sunshine. He instantly squinted and had to look away. Only a few lit up, and he wondered why the others hadn't. He soon found out, when he moved another lever.

That lever caused another whirring sound, and doors surrounding the room, opened and the other lights came on shining in through the doorways. He was fascinated by the technology, he had never seen anything like it. Sure, the future had unexplainable stuff, but this was now, and this from a species that was extinct? He had some rethinking to do.

Tepu and Hermaditt stood shaking with their mouths open. *Whooshing* sounds surrounded them as the several doors opened around them. "Don't touch anything," he said.

"No need to worry there," said Tepu.

He walked toward one of the doors motioning for the gargoyles to follow. They entered a large room with wood all around it and with more tubes and light. "Sure saves on candles," he mumbled.

He looked around in awe, "Amazing. But I need to stay focused. We must find the metal. Spread out, look in every room you see. Tepu and Hermaditt took off and he gave one last glance at the room with a very nice wooden long table, a fire pit with a hole above to let the smoke out. Cabinets, chairs, and another funny machine. Gathering himself he quickly left. When he got out the door, he heard a screech from Hermaditt. The gargoyle quickly called out, "I'm okay. I just scared myself."

Merlin chuckled and went to the next room. "Found something!" shouted Tepu. He immediately started in the direction of the shout. He followed the sound to the mouth of a large tunnel heading deeper inside the earth.

They proceeded down the tunnel turning right, then left, then straight, only to turn again. They finally came to a large cavern that held glowing white metal. He went to touch it, and felt the energy come from it. "This has to be it."

He said an incantation and his hands began to glow. He reached down and picked up a large bar of the glowing metal. The strong energy level that came from the bar made him almost lose his grasp. It felt alive, but surely it wasn't.

He turned to Tepu. "See Tepu, this place isn't…just then a glowing net dropped from the ceiling and landed on the three of them. He immediately repeated the same incantation he'd used to protect his hands and spread it out until all three of them were surrounded by it.

"I can't hold this spell for long, we have to get out of here. Quickly, take my hands." He placed the large bar inside his coat. It was heavy, but he thought he could do it. He began his incantation and as he spoke the last words they were transported outside the first cavern. He collapsed from exertion.

"Help me," said Tepu. "We'll take him to the cave near the river." Together they carried Merlin down the side of the mountain toward the cave. They placed him inside. Looking around he found a broken bowl that would still hold some water. He ran quickly to the river and returned to splash Merlin in the face. He awoke sputtering.

"What the hell did you do that for?"

"You're welcome."

He patted his coat and felt for the metal bar that was between his coat and his shirt. Although it wasn't touching skin or burning him, it was very warm. "I must get back. I told you the place wasn't cursed. It just had things protecting it. Nothing more. Thank you for taking me. I'd like to come back and study it further when all is over."

"I'll let you, Merlin. But only you. Thanks for showing us that there is nothing to fear from the place. We can help you down the mountain if you like."

"No, I can disappear," he said standing, dripping water from his face and hair. He laughed. "You two have such a way."

"As if you don't," said Tepu, laughing.

He shook their hands, and then disappeared.

Chapter 35

Two and a half months later

Angus shook his head. It had been hell looking for The Peacekeeper. They still had no idea of who he could be. His brothers were back at Wesladus getting ready to make the sword anyway. They had the metal Merlin retrieved, from where he wouldn't say. It lay glowing in the corner where Merlin dropped it. Merlin had given them protective gloves that he swore would protect them, but no one had been brave enough to touch it. The glow and the heat that radiated from it had them all a little on edge. They'd never seen a metal like it before. They all glanced at the strange Dhara metal often. The time was coming that they wouldn't have a choice, it needed to be forged.

It had taken two and a half months to find a plant they needed. Cameron didn't recognize it and Merlin finally found it on top of a mountain in Asia, but only after seeking help from Junius. Now that they had the final plant ingredient, he was in Mystic Kingdom seeking out the Queen.

He walked to where he knew he'd find her. Walking in unannounced as the guards were used to him by now, he found her sitting alone staring out a window. She turned to look at him. Instead of yelling at him, like she usually did, she simply stared at him. "I have come tae ask you a favor," he said, finally.

"That's unusual, coming from you."

"The God of Dark has made a son and he is walking in Athdar's footsteps. The only way tae stop him is by making *The Godslayer longsword.* The only way it can be made is by using herbs and certain species blood in the makin' of it, but we also need the blood of a virgin, and…"

"Okay," interrupted the queen. "I'll give my blood."

"Just like that? You'll give your blood? No yelling, sarcastic remarks, jabs?"

"If there's one thing I've learned about you McGregors is that when you have something in your mind you don't stop until you get what you want. It's for a good cause, so, yes, I'll agree to it. Simple as that." She flashed her brown eyes at him.

Damn but she was beautiful. He wished there was some way to melt her icy interior. He felt a throbbing hard on hit him and he moved to reposition himself. The queen looked back out the window. He didn't know how to handle this version of her. Who stole the ice queen and replaced her?

"What do I need to do?"

"I have a vial that we can put some…" Suddenly there was a crash and he looked toward the door. He pulled his sword. "Get under the desk!" he shouted. Dedrick burst through the door wearing a wicked smile and leading six Kearals in his wake. "I told you I'd make you pay."

"You just made the biggest mistake of your life, Dedrick."

"Turn over the queen and she won't get hurt."

"I doona think so," he said, his voice low and deadly. His eyes spit fire and his incisors dropped as the green fae glow surrounded him. Dedrick reared back with a horrified look on his face. "What the hell are you?" he asked in a shaky voice.

"I'm the man who is goin' tae kill you for what you have just done."

He attacked like a bull gone mad. He didn't have time for a pissin match, not with kearals heading toward the desk, he was long gone, done, with Dedrick. He'd had enough. He quickly grabbed Dedrick, and without giving any quarter, he ripped the flesh from his screaming neck. Spit it to the floor, dropped him, then he turned to the kearals. He beheaded the first, ripped out the second's throat, fought the third with his sword, and when the last three came at him he blasted them with wind.

Surprise gone, he knew he couldn't take the last three by himself. He ran behind the desk where Edina huddled. "Merlin! Now would be a good time!" he shouted.

He grabbed the Queen's hand. "You're coming with me it's not safe here." He pulled her to her feet and at the same time sending more wind at the Kearals and pushing them away.

"Merlin, get your arse here!" He yelled.

A portal opened and before Merlin could come through he jumped through pulling her with him. They landed in a heap in Merlin's library. "Great," he said, "saves me the trip back."

The queen pushed against him. "Get off me!" she screeched.

"I see your back tae your old self and you're

welcome," Angus said standing, holding out his hand to help her up. Lauren, Conall, Cameron, and Dougal looked up from the grimoire at the scene in front of them. Merlin jumped up and exclaimed, "What happened?"

"Six Kearals just tried kidnapping the Queen. I think they were new and didn't expect me to be there or be who and what I am. Why would they want you Queen?"

"I…l…honestly don't know. I'm nobody special."

He was still angry. "Come on, King Rulm buys you from your father, spending gods ken what to get you, marries you, doesn't touch you when he's kenned to violate and kill women, what am I supposed to think?" he asked, flustered.

"I'm telling you I don't know!" she cried and then began to sob.

He grabbed her and held her while she broke down. "Come and sit down. Maybe we can figure this oot."

"Thank you, Angus, for saving me. I haven't been easy to get along with, I know, but you haven't either. It doesn't excuse my behavior, but you do have a habit of bringing out the worst in me."

"Perhaps you're right. What we need to concern ourselves with right now is why they want you."

"I will see what I can find out," said Merlin. "But until we figure this out you are to stay here in Wesladus. No arguments. I will see to Mystic Kingdom and make sure it is safe and taken care of temporarily, until you can return." With that Merlin opened a portal and left.

Edina looked at the brothers. "How can I help? You need my blood, take as much as you need." She sighed.

"Come," said Cameron. "We need just a small amount. Enough to fill this small vial. If you sit here, I will make a small slice in your finger and that should do it."

After he finished he marked the vial and put it in a cold locker. "That's all we need. The rest will be easy. We should have the sword finished soon. Ator will be bringing a gargoyle in the morning and the rest of the items on the list are here.

"Merlin will be getting the fairy dust. We have all the rest of the species needed on site. We can't use our blood because it's mixed and we don't want to take the chance of it contaminating the sword. The only thing now is finding *The Peacekeeper*.

"I wish you all luck," said Edina.

"Are you hungry?" he asked. "Let's find you somethin' tae eat, shall we?" He reached his hand out and grasped hers, and they walked out together.

Conall looked at his brothers. "Are you all thinkin' what I'm thinkin'?"

"Aye," they said in unison and then broke out in laughter.

"Angus just may be following in Ian's footsteps," said Lauren. "He...just doesn't ken it yet." They all laughed again.

****

McGregor Keep

Ian and Elspeth were playing with the babies. The two bairns were awake and happy at the same time. Ian laughed at his son cooing and blowing bubbles. Elspeth was nursing their daughter. Akira came running in out of breath and shouted. "There's four dragons in the yard. Saphira and Ator and two smaller ones. Hurry come see!"

"They must be here to see the bairns. Come Els."

"I bet Sorrilth and Kalon are with them."

When they reached them, Elspeth noticed how big Sorrilth and Kalon had grown. They were a bit bigger than half their parents size. They were beautiful.

"*We have brought you a gift for the babies*," Ator said. "*It's unusual but considering what you have done for us and what you have done for all, this will be the best gift we can give you.*"

"A gift from a dragon?" laughed Ian. "I can only guess what it could be. But, whatever it is, I'm sure it is wonderful. Come my friend, any gift from you is appreciated. This is my son Domnall," he said, holding him up for Ator to see.

Ator leaned down and nuzzled the top of the boy's head and Domnall squealed. "*Come Kalon and see Domnall*," said Ator.

Kalon waddled up and sniffed the child and smiled a dragon smile. "*You saved me, Ian McGregor, as Darlath was sure to kill me. Now I will do for you.*" He leaned back and blew fire of blue directly at Domnall. Leaving his dragon mark on Domnall's small chest, the child giggled. "*He will always have my protection. You saved us as babies, only fair we protect yours.*"

She and Ian stood speechless.

Saphira waddled up to Donella. She nudged her forehead and smiled her dragon smile. "*She's beautiful, Elspeth. Come Sorrilth, meet Donella.*"

Sorrilth came up and sniffed Donella, repeating her brother's actions, leaving the replica of herself on Donella's chest. "*She will be like a sister to me and a friend. I shall watch over her forever.*" Sorrilth smiled.

"I doona ken what to say, Ator," said Ian. That is the most wonderful gift a father could ever ask for."

After handing Donella to Ian, she ran and hugged Sorrilth, then Kalon wrapping her arms around their necks. "You are all my family," she said with tears. "I doona ken how tae thank you, but I do."

They stayed together for most of the morning. Saphira gave Akira another ride. Ator, Kalon, and Sorrilth gave Brenna, Fiona, and Catriona their first ride, being careful and gentle with them. Moira laughed and watched her daughters with delight. Ator and Saphira nuzzled the babies whenever they could. She and Ian laughed at them and with them. The visit was wonderful and so was their gift.

****

The next morning Moira was very tired and ached over her entire body. She felt drained. Domnall and Donella were her greatest joy. She noticed Ian was strangely quiet of late and worried about him.

She tried talking to him and whenever she did, he would make an excuse to either leave the room or the castle altogether. She was walking down the stairs and listening to the cries of one of the babies, when darkness closed in on her vision.

She made a grab for the wall but it was too late she tumbled most of the way down the stone stairs and dropped in front of a screaming Catriona.

Ian came running to the stairs, Bradana and Elspeth following each with a bairn in their arms. Ian leaned over to pick up his unconscious mother. He carefully raised her in his arms. "I have to get her into bed. Merlin! We need you!" he shouted, and a portal opened.

"What is it, Ian?" he asked.

"It's Mither, she fell down the stairs. I need you to check her. I doona think she's healing and she's growing old very quickly. See if she has any broken bones. Follow me." He ascended the stairs carefully carrying his mother.

****

After Ian laid her on the bed, Merlin looked over Moira and then left his body to enter hers. It was something he didn't normally do, invade another, because to do so he'd tap their minds as well and to him that was an invasion, but this was Moira.

He had to make sure she was all right and not suffering. He tried to avoid the rush of her memories, but they were instantaneous. He felt what she felt for Lachlan, her children, and him. He knew the pain and lengths she went to remain alive for her family. He truly admired her strength and courage.

"Oh Moira," he inwardly sighed, "I know your pain." He carefully searched her bones, arteries, and blood vessels. Finding everything intact, he retreated to himself and a waiting Ian. The rest stood outside the door waiting.

"How is she, Merlin?" Ian asked, worry etching his face.

"Well." Merlin sighed deeply, "her bones and vessels are intact. That is the good news. The bad news is her aging rate is intensified, but not surprising knowing she lasted as long as she did. She isn't going to last much longer. She's in a sleep that she won't wake up from, Ian. You need to know. We need to have the boys come home.

"In a few days, it is the fall equinox, the time the fairies celebrate. I must go that day to acquire some dust for a project we are working on in Wesladus. When I get back I'll bring them here. I think Moira will last at least a week, maybe two."

"Two weeks? Doesn't seem possible, och, mither," he said gently raising her hand to his.

"I will leave you with your mother, Ian. If you need me call." He opened his portal and left.

****

Hearing about a project at Wesladus made Ian cringe. He wanted to know more. He missed his men and his life. There was no way around it, but he wouldn't go back on his word, not against his family who meant everything to him. He lovingly looked at his mother and sighed inwardly.

After a while of sitting with Moira, he stood to go and relate the news to those waiting outside. He paced a bit in his grief and pulled his hand through his hair and over his face. He knew there would be a lot of crying from the girls, Bradana and even Elspeth, he hated tears from those he loved, it was hard for him to see, but it had to be done.

Even though everyone supported Moira's decision, he knew the devastation it would cause them, especially the girls. He opened the door to face them with the news.

****

Wesladus

Merlin stood in his library with all the McGregor boys, save Angus. He was with the Queen. Of course, Ian was also absent. When Merlin finished telling them about Moira, they sat in silence.

382

Finally, Cameron spoke up. "Do we abort making the sword?"

"No, your mother will last a couple of weeks. In three days' time is the equinox, only twice a year this happens. This day makes the fairy dust the strongest and it is the day I will go and retrieve some."

Lauren spoke up. "That's a suicide mission, Merlin. No one is kenned tae have crossed the Scarlet Sea and through Vision Valley and live. I've read about Lanenia. The fairies are well guarded in so many crazy ways. You also want tae go when their magic is strongest? Why is this day so special tae them?"

"It's only one of two times a fairy can choose a mate. I've heard it takes but a kiss from both fairies to initiate the bond then mate for life, but both must feel it, if only one does then the bond doesn't take, kiss or not.

"It's a full day party and the fall equinox is one of two longest days of the year with the planets aligned. Their magic is at its maximum capacity then. I must go. We need the dust and it is the only way."

"Merlin, you could die. We canna have that. Too many people depend on you. Let me go in your stead," said Dougal. "I ken magic and you can tell me what I need tae do."

"No, you couldn't survive Vision Valley. I have some tricks up my sleeve. I'll go and I'll have Ator fly me. That will help."

"You will not go!" bellowed the God of Light's voice as He appeared before them surrounded by an almost blinding brilliant light. You will not survive the trip. Besides you won't have to, if the future plays out as I see it."

"If I don't and it doesn't play out as you see it, we

383

cannot make the sword," said Merlin.

"If it does not play out, as you say, I will take you there myself before dark. But I usually know when something will be as it should, and so far, it is. You will not attempt to travel there, Merlin, unless I take you. Am I clear?"

"Yes, you are clear. I will not go without you." Merlin snarled, "You know we need the Godslayer Longsword, speaking of which are you ready to tell us about *The Peacekeeper*?"

"I told you, in due time he will come to you. Now back to work." The God of Light disappeared.

"Ken what I like aboot that guy?" asked Finn, not expecting an answer. "He's a man of soooo many words, always beating around the bush, and never saying anythin' straight forward, you ken hangin' around and liking tae drink the mead and party." They all laughed at his sarcastic comments.

****

Three days later

It was the morning of the equinox and Edina felt restless. She always did during the equinox. It always had a strange pull on her. She was grouchy and didn't feel like being led around today by Angus. Why did that man crawl under her skin so? She wasn't attracted to him, we'll maybe just a little, all right she admitted to herself, maybe a lot. His eyes always drew her in, his body sculpted better than any statue she'd seen, and she'd seen many.

Perfection, the man was perfection, and when he was close? She shuddered. He could make her feel things no one else ever had. But he also brought out her worst. No, you bring out your worst, she chided herself, he makes you feel, and it scares the heck out of you. She rubbed her arms and continued her walk along the beach.

"Mornin'!" came a shout and she looked up to see him walking toward her. Her heartbeat raced, gods he was gorgeous. He was in his kilt, chest bare, bronzed by the sun, his muscles glistened, and his black hair free in the wind blew across his square jaw. "Angus," she said.

"It's a bonnie day, is it not?" he asked, strolling toward her. She was at a loss for words. Was he bewitching her? She certainly had feelings she never knew existed coursing through her veins, and it immediately scared her. "What are you doing out and about, Angus McGregor. Can't a person walk quietly on the beach anymore?"

Angus laughed. It seemed every time she tried to cut him down, or stop him, or really try and stop her feelings for him, he laughed at her. "What do you find so funny?" she asked.

"You, you are a very funny woman, you hide your feelin's behind your armor better than any soldier I ken. But nae, you doona fool me. I can see how you look at me. I can feel the intense emotions coming from you," he said coming closer. She instantly felt her mouth go dry. She gulped as she saw his sparkling gaze sweep her body. She shuddered at the scorching look he gave her and suddenly felt completely naked in front of him.

For the life of her she couldn't put two words together, sarcastic or otherwise. When he got so close she could feel the heat of his body, she lifted her eyes and gazed into his. He put his hands on her shoulders and pulled her closer. She lost the ability to breathe. Her body instantly betrayed her mind. Her blood suddenly ran hot and pooled in her midsection, without thinking, she wanted this man, this infuriating, boisterous, self-assured, handsome man. She leaned in for the kiss wanting it more than she had ever wanted anything.

Their lips touched and a trembling Angus groaned, he teased her lips to open with his tongue, when she sighed he entered her mouth. At first, she was dumbstruck by the action, but she liked it, so she teased his tongue with hers. Warmth invaded them, then became something altogether different, explosive. She had never felt such a thing in her life.

Suddenly rainbow colors surrounded them, and they were lifted up in the air and slowly spun, colors swirling around them, she heard voices around them, somehow joining them. Light shot from within her into him and from him into her. She suddenly knew his entire life and he hers. Breaking away they landed in a pile of sparkling dust. She opened her eyes to him and he to her.

"You sparkle!" They said in unison.

"Of course, you sparkle!" came the loud voice of the God of Light standing next to them. "Now you've gone and done it Angus McGregor."

"Done what!?" he said confused. "Kissed a beautiful woman?"

"Yes, you two have bonded you are now mates. You, Angus, just kissed a fairy on the equinox, and not just any fairy, but the queen of fairies, and she kissed you back, making you king. The voices you heard, are the voices of your people recognizing you've taken a mate, and that you are indeed alive."

"You are now mated for life and you Angus have

made a change by bonding with the queen. You are now fae, vampire, and fairy.

"Edina, you were sold at birth by a nefarious fairy to the one whom you've called your father, but was not your true father, then he later sold you to King Rulm so he could use you on this very day for your powers. After meeting Athdar, they joined forces. They were both going to use you. Which thankfully they did not accomplish. Today in your kingdom you would come of age and fully gain your powers and if all was as it should be you would have also chosen your mate.

"You have done that unbeknownst to you. You accepted Angus. You will be mated for life. Now you will give your fairy dust to your brothers for the sword and then go to Lanenia, Land of the Fairies where you will rule together and learn your powers.

You will fight the fairy who killed your parents and sold you. Lanenia has needed you for a very long time, there's a lot of strife and a lot of work to be done. Your bonding and your light shone bright in fairyland. They now know you exist and that hope will bring them here if you do not return.

"I will take you two there and I'll make a stationary portal from Pendragon, Angus, because you will need the help of your brothers in this…"

"Now wait a god's minute!' shouted Angus. Are you saying I doona have a say in this? Over a kiss?"

"You made your decision, Angus, and you did it with the Queen of the Fairies. So, no, you don't and can't change your mind. Search your heart, you'll find your answer. Now we go to your brothers, they need the dust for the sword. Oh, and the portal to Lanenia, even though it will be invisible to all fairies save you and

Edina, be careful. If they find it, it could be trouble.

Edina, your true name is Eladrin, the mortal world could not use it, because to use it would also call upon the Fairies. Get used to that name, it is the first of many names you will carry, and things you will find out when you get there. Now let's go." The God of Light touched them and they were transported to Merlin's library.

"I've brought your fairy dust!" bellowed the God of Light.

The men all stopped and looked up. "You're glittering, Angus," said Finn trying to hide a smirk. "You too, Edina. You two downright sparkle, just like a fairy."

Angus groaned. "Shut up, and doona ask."

"I will tell them," the God of Light said, with humor, and he did. When finished all the men laughed. Finn snorted. "All is as it should be," said the God of Light. "Now they must go." And they disappeared leaving a pile of fairy dust behind.

Chapter 36
McGregor Castle

It was near the end for Moira. All the boys were home, Merlin even went through the new portal to Lanenia to retrieve Angus. Now they all stood by Moira's bedside. The girls crying in the corner.

The twin bairns asleep in their cradles, with Bradana watching over them in their room. Merlin had told Ian everything going on in Wesladus. He could barely refrain anymore from going back.

He was a mess, no sleep, barely eating, he couldn't think straight. Standing here now looking at his dying mother he did some soul searching. He should have protected his father and brother. Damn, it was his responsibility. His responsibility? "Remember who you are," came the voice stronger than before.

"Who am I really?" he asked himself. "Do you really want to know?" came the voice from within. "It will interrupt your peace." "Please," begged Ian. "I need to, I can no longer live like this. I need to know who I am." He glanced at his mother again, and at the ones he loved sobbing, even Merlin had tears. "Please," he thought. "I need tae make this right somehow, it's just all wrong. It shouldn't be this way."

Suddenly the God of light appeared. Ian stood up from kneeling at his mother's bedside. "You heard my thoughts."

"Yes, Ian I did. You have made a decision to know, what you do with it will be up to you. I will grant you your memories, all of them, then you choose."

The God of Light touched him. Suddenly his lives came back to him. In each one he was a warrior. In each one he had a family. He had Elspeth and he was happy, but most of all he had purpose and he knew what that purpose was.

Maybe he didn't always live in peace, but he tried hard to keep the peace. He protected his family, he didn't sit back and wait for someone else to do it. He relived those lives and knew he had been genuinely happy.

Then he saw the beginning, where he first broke off from the One Great God. He was called *The Peacekeeper* by his Father and was sent forth to protect those he could. He understood who he was. He had to maintain peace, he had to go back. He had to be himself. The light died away.

"Do you understand now Ian? What is your choice, *Peacekeeper*?"

"Peacekeeper?" asked Merlin.

A hush went around the room. The brothers in shock all asked, *"Peacekeeper*, Ian?"

"Och!" said Cameron. "Our brother...is *The Peacekeeper*? The one we have been looking for? *Theee Peacekeeper*? The one to wield the *Godslayer*?"

"Yes," said The God of Light. "The only *Peacekeeper*. Now you understand why I could not tell you. Ian wanted peace for his family and he deserved to have what he wanted. It was granted. He just forgot he was the one providing it for them. Now he remembers and he's made the right decision."

"I have made a promise tae my Mither and wife, but I canna do what I have promised them. I am a warrior. It's who I am. I have tae go back to being the leader of my troops. I have tae fight Juppar Heiwynn. I canna let evil go free, but my promise, my word tae my family?"

Elspeth ran into his arms surprising him. "I'm so happy we are going back. Finally, Ian, I've watched you mope for months. I ken you needed tae go, but you needed tae ken it too. I can also be the healer I ken I am. Life has no guarantees but together we can fight tae keep our family safe. I love you Ian. The man I ken you tae be. I'm so happy."

"My promise tae Mither. Who will take care of the castle, and the girls?"

"We knew this time would come Ian, your mother and father don't remember, but before their life they set up this sacrifice so you would remember when the time came. Their suffering was to complete this one goal. Everyone in your family, before this life, knew they would all make this sacrifice for you."

"What? I doona deserve that. Why them. This should have never happened."

"You were getting tired of the fight, Ian. Even before this fight. You were forgetting who you are. They all banded together to help you in this life, return you to the roots of who you are. So, for your parents? I think something can be arranged," said the God of Light. He pointed toward the wall where a bright light appeared and an opening from a beautiful place came in to view. Then Lachlan appeared. "Come ahead Lachlan," said the God of Light. "You couldn't come with Eoghan because this needed to happen for Ian to find himself. He needed to remember his way. Now you may return." Lachlan stepped through and everyone shouted and ran to hug him.

He looked to the God of Light. "Mither?"

The God of Light looked lovingly at Moira. "She suffered the most." He touched her forehead, and Moira was once again young. She opened her eyes and looked around, when she saw Lachlan she screamed his name and they embraced. Then she embraced all her children, sobbing tears of happiness.

He looked at the God of Light. "Thank you," he said.

The God of Light shrugged his shoulders. "Someone has to take care of these girls. Moira couldn't bear leaving them and she fought the law of death between mates, when one dies, the other shall go. A remarkable woman, your mother. All is as it should be." And he disappeared.

He didn't have time to register all the God of Light told him about his family, when Bradana came running in. "The bairns!" she screamed. "They're gone! The devil took them. I couldn't stop him. He froze me. Ian, the bairns!"

His heart dropped. "What do you mean, Bradana, the bairns?"

"They're gone! A man with flames in his eyes. He froze me. I couldn't move. I watched him grab the bairns and he didn't even use a portal. He just disappeared with them."

"To Wesladus!" shouted Merlin. "Ian grab the bairns clothes. I'll do a locator spell. Boys we must go. Ian, you need the sword. First your blood. Let's let the love birds reunite, and the girls see their mother and father. Come we have a job to do. Bullocks!"

****

Wesladus, Pendragon Castle

"My bairns!" shouted Ian, pacing with his hands on his head. "I'll kill him with my bare hands!"

"Stop, Ian I have to concentrate on the locator spell," said Merlin.

The room became quiet and they waited.

Finally, Merlin stopped. "I can't locate them. He has them hidden and hidden well. I could breach a cloaking spell, but this is something more. I think…"

A light appeared in the room and they all startled. A holographic image of Juppar Heiwynn appeared. He immediately attacked it, falling through, Juppar laughed. *"Peacekeeper!* I have your babies. They are cute, but when they started crying, well I had to put a sleep spell on them. Had to shut the rats up."

He saw red. "If you've harmed them, I'll tear oot your intestines and feed them tae you. Let me see them! Awake."

"As you wish." The vision melded to the two infants. Juppar snapped his fingers and they awoke, crying. He snapped his fingers again, and they went back to sleep.

"You bastard! You will not live when I get my hands on you!"

"You, Ian McGregor, *Peacekeeper,* will come to me. Alone. This is between us and will be handled by us alone. No men. You will come to Wardhurst Castle in the Stygian Mountains. The faster you come the more alive the infants will be. Tally and they will fade, until dead." The vision faded.

He was breathing hard, his eyes wild, he smashed

his fist through the wall. "Where is this place? Merlin, can you open a portal?"

Merlin frowned, "This isn't good. It's located in the Cimmerian Veil."

"I've read about it," said Cameron. "It's Hell's Veil. You'll die going through that veil, Ian. It's treacherous, dangerous, and all sorts of hell's demons live there."

Elspeth sat sobbing, then cried out. "Ian, I can't lose you, or the bairns. You must take your army! Merlin, go with him! Please for goddesses' sake, help him! Bring back our bairns!"

He went and put his arms around her. "It's me he wants. I willna take a chance with our bairns life. I will take the Godslayer with me."

With unabashed determination, he picked up the lightly glowing forged sword, not thinking about holding it with bare hands. He merely picked it up like any sword and sliced his hand open, putting his blood to the blade. It instantly drank in his blood then the sword melted like a flowing frosting up and over his hand and traveled up his arm, infusing itself with him, when it spread over his body as far as it could go, causing him to radiate a white glow, it then retracted back to a sword, then left his hands and rose up in the air, hovering in front of him glowing white.

It spun in front of him, emitted a cloud of sparks, spun again, then stopped in midair, the white glow dissipating, it landed at his feet emitting a pure golden glow. He picked it up and felt a warm tingle travel from it through his body. It changed, reshaping itself and weight to fit his hand.

He stood with a light glow about him, leaned over

and picked up his scabbard and attached it around himself and sheathed the sword. Then he heard Ator's voice, as the glow dissipated.

"I'm taking you, Ian. No arguments. I heard all and I came as quick as I could. I'm outside Pendragon waiting for you. Come now, we must hurry."

"You canna, Ator, I willna let you. You could die. I have tae go alone."

"I will follow you. I will not take no for an answer. He did not say no dragons, just men. I'm taking you. That's final."

He thought about it. "Okay, Ator. Merlin, can you get us inside Wardhurst Castle?"

"No, too well warded. I can get you through Cimmerian Veil and possibly on the Stygian Mountains, but that's as close as I can get. It will take an invocation. There are no portals for obvious reasons. We must get started. I'll meet you down with Ator."

He held the sobbing Elspeth, stroking her hair. "I'll get them back, if it's the last thing I do. I will kill the bastard. I promise. Brothers, please take care of my wife while I'm gone. Take her tae Mither."

"Nae Ian!" she said, hysterically. "I'm waiting right here until I hear from you. I will not leave. Just bring our bairns home alive."

He looked at his brothers, and with silent understanding they all nodded. They would watch over Elspeth. Then he turned back to her, "I will, Els. Now I must go."

He met Ator at the meadow behind the castle. "Ator are you sure about this?"

"More than. We can do this Ian."

"Yes, you can," said Merlin, walking up to them.

"Ator and Ian, I need some blood to make this work. You will feel a tremendous pulling sensation while you traverse through the veil. It will cease after a few seconds of reaching your destination.

"You will feel disoriented, get used to that as it won't go away. It's hot there, a lot of fire and lava, be careful the tubes. The demons there are devils. You will have to fight. Ator try and keep him in the air. You will get winded, so you must land at intervals to rest, the heat can hurt even a dragon."

"It sounds like you've been there, Merlin."

"Unfortunately, a few times. You will become acclimated, but it will take willpower. Hallucinations can happen, be strong and realize what they are. You ready?"

"Yes, get on with it." He settled on Ator's back, and they waited while Merlin said the incantation. Then a cloud surrounded them and they were pulled through the void.

He felt as if his face was being pulled off and Ator was flung dizzily around in circles. When they landed, it was on the mountain, on a path. The air was hot and heavy and everything had a red tinge to it. Ian fell off Ator and threw up.

He retched for several seconds. Ator shook his head and neck as if trying to get his bearings. Several large creatures flew overhead screeching loudly. Devil demons rushed them. The one in front tall, lithe, with crazy lizard yellow eyes. "Ahhh, fressshhh meeeat." It drawled, its long pointy tongue flickering in and out. It lunged for Ian.

"Not today." He drew his sword. The creature and its followers laughed.

His sword warmed in his hand and sent tingles through his body. He raised the glowing white sword in his hands and started for them.

The one in front backed away. Fear etched the creatures faces. "The *Goooodslaaaaayer*," said the one in front. "Run!"

Ator shook his head again. *"I don't think they liked that sword of yours."*

He stared at the sword and smiled. "I think this is a very handy tool."

"Come, mount up we must go."

Once in the air a fire tornado headed straight for them. "Is this a hallucination?" he asked Ator.

"I don't think so," and the dragon quickly ascended over the top of it.

Creatures with red dragon like bodies, pointed tails, and dinosaur jaws came toward them. He lifted the sword to strike and it once again glowed. The creatures screeched and turned around.

"I like this sword. It seems tae have a mind of its own. I hope it does that to Juppar. We should hurry. Head to the top of the mountain."

As Ator flew up, he saw all his dead dragon friends heading for them, distorted faces, and snarls.

His bond allowed him to see the same vision, he quickly reminded him, "Ator, it's a hallucination. Fly through them. He was suddenly assaulted with the faces of the people he had killed came in to view flashing in front of him, large, with iniquitous laughter.

"Go, Ator, keep going up!" He closed his eyes and when he opened them the aberrations were gone. They landed not far from the top for a brief respite, as Merlin had warned them to do.

As they stared toward the top, he could see the castle, appearing very small. They had a way to go yet. He leaned back closing his eyes for a moment, sweat pouring off him. The ground started to shake and rumble beneath them. "*Hurry,*" said Ator, "*lava tubes!*"

Ator soared up as the lava tubes erupted a hundred feet in the air. They continued to climb high in the air until they reached the top. They landed near the castle. After letting him down, the dragon said, *"I can go in from here, but not without breaking down the walls, and I don't know where the babies are located. I'll wait right here for you. If you need anything let me know."*

"Thanks, Ator, now I'm goin' tae kill the bastard." He went through the big double doors and shouted, "Juppar Heiwynn! You have my bairns. Show them tae me, now!" He continued searching until he came to what appeared to be a library. There he found the bairns tucked against a corner on the floor. He picked his still son up and kissed him then did the same to his daughter. Then he heard the clapping.

"How touching. Now I have you where I want you. You can watch the infants die, then I'm going to kill you. You will no longer be the *Peacekeeper.* I'm going to send you back to the one who made you."

"I think not, Juppar," he said as he pulled his sword. He expected the same warmth and light he'd been accustomed to with the sword, but it didn't appear. He didn't have the time to wonder why. No matter, he would wield it just the same.

He charged Juppar. Juppar flung out his hand and a force threw him backward against a wall and he crumbled, sliding down the wall. Shaking his head, he jumped up and charged him again. This time Juppar threw out his hand and froze him, then laughed.

"I tire of your games, you can't win. Now watch as I eat these infants for lunch. You know their blood is very sweet at this age."

He was enraged. His anger was so intense he began to glow green. Frozen to the spot in mid step, sword held up, he tried to move, and couldn't. He called to the power of the sword.

He felt the sword trying to show him something. Something important that he needed to know or do. As Juppar walked toward his children he tried to calm his mind. He pictured himself and the sword as one.

He felt the energy travel from the sword to his hand and up his arm.

Slowly the sword heated all of him, he felt as if he were melting, when in reality, he was becoming unfrozen. He understood then, the sword had secrets, special secrets. It seemed to have a mind of its own, showing him things in increments. He knew this time it was using more power, sending more energy through him. It didn't happen at first because too much energy could have killed him. It was feeding him and he was learning to take more. He felt the energy in his blood, he felt invincible, truly alive, more than ever before in his life. He was ready, he was filled, he had power, deadly power, power enough to kill a Devil God. He spoke in a dead calm. "Now you die."

Juppar looked around at him. "Ah you think the *Godslayer* will stop me? Yes, I know about it. I didn't know you had it, but no bother, by the time you reach me one of your infants will be dead. Now let's see which one first? The girl or the boy?"

Ian started for him. "You will kill neither. You

never threaten this mon, you never threaten my wife, you never threaten peace, but most of all you never threaten a mon's bairns!"

He wasn't sure what he was doing, but instinct took over and he threw the sword in the air with one command. "Heart!" In an instantaneous blur, the sword shot across the room and in through the back of Juppar as he reached for the sleeping infant. It pierced his heart dead on. He said, "return," and it flew back to his hand. He sheathed it and ran toward the twins. Juppar's body went up in flames. He picked up his sleeping children, not knowing how he was going to wake them.

"Excellent!" came a booming voice as the God of Light appeared next to Ian. "I hate coming here. The God of Dark will know. We don't normally visit each other's realms. It'll make him angry and he will just create another son. You won't see the last of things like this. But for now, the infants need to wake and you all need to go back to Wesladus, Ator included. I will send you back. Come Ator awaits."

"Why dinna you just stop this afore Juppar took the bairns? Why do you wait for someone less strong than you tae do the dirty work?"

"I'm already in trouble from the One True God. I could get demoted. He says I interfere too much in the great dance of life, especially after bringing your father and brother back to life. Besides this was for you. You had to see it, feel it, know it. You had to become you again.

"I don't know what will happen to me for all of my interference, but the balance was too far in the dark sides favor, I felt the need to help, and to warn you of more to come. You may not see me for a while, but I help when I can. I push when I can. Now let's get you all out of here."

****

Wesladus at Pendragon Castle

In front of the fireplace in the sitting area off the great room at Pendragon Castle all the McGregors gathered. They had finished one of the best dinners Ian had ever eaten. Conversation and laughter arose all around. Merlin and Arthur argued over who was going to hold Domnall. Merlin being the winner, was bouncing him up and down, while Arthur leaned over him making faces. Lachlan and Moira laughed over Donella's antics. He chuckled watching his family, while his arm hung loosely around his wife.

He was home, where he needed to be. He was happy and he knew Elspeth was too. His life wasn't so bad, in fact it was quite wonderful. He'd face the coming evil head on with his sword blazing. When it reared its ugly head, he would have no compunction about dealing with it all. He and Elspeth had moved back into Pendragon in the Wesladus Veil, and he picked up where he left off. It was as if he'd never left.

****

The God of Light hung in the air above them, invisibly. He smiled to himself, watching the happy family. The whole happy family. He did love a good ending. Well to this part anyway. The McGregors weren't finished by a long shot. He had faith in them, and he'd watch over them. He'd help when necessary. He sighed. "Everything is as it should be," then disappeared.

Elspeth smiled up at Ian and whispered in his ear, "Do you think we can trust these people tae watch the bairns?"

"Why, what are you thinkin', Elspeth?"

"I think it's later, later," she huskily whispered, grinning.

He looked in her eyes and grinned wide. "I ken it's later, later," he said picking her off her feet. He carried the squealing Elspeth through the great room and up the stairs and didn't let go until he dropped her on their bed, where he showed her just how happy he was with his life, with her, with his family, and to finally, be home.

A word from the author…

I was born and raised in a small mill town in the Midwest where the river, lakes, woods, and nature were my playground, and my horse my best friend. My father spent winter months turning out lights and lighting the fireplace, where we cuddled around in blankets to listen to stories. I continued the tradition.

I grew up as an artist, as a photographer my specialty was taking black and white photos of old ghost towns and hand tinting them. I lived in Santa Fe, New Mexico, for fourteen years indulging in my artwork.

I've always enjoyed storytelling and now I write. Certainly, a dream come true. I currently reside in Indiana.

Thank you for purchasing
this publication of The Wild Rose Press, Inc.

If you enjoyed the story, we would appreciate your
letting others know by leaving a review.

For other wonderful stories,
please visit our on-line bookstore at
www.thewildrosepress.com.

For questions or more information
contact us at
info@thewildrosepress.com.

The Wild Rose Press, Inc.
www.thewildrosepress.com

Stay current with The Wild Rose Press, Inc.

Like us on Facebook

https://www.facebook.com/TheWildRosePress

And Follow us on Twitter
https://twitter.com/WildRosePress